"Your gift is responding to me."

Keiko shook her head and jerked at his coat. "What gift? It doesn't do anything except let ghosts…hurt me." Her gaze dropped to his coat, and she frowned. The coat seemed to be darkening right under her hands and becoming…black with red trim, and the buttons looked more gold than silver.

He pulled his palm from her belly to catch her chin, drawing her gaze to his. "You have the power to make the dead live and feel again. For a short time, anyway." He released her chin, and set his palm back on her belly. "And it lives here. This is what those…creatures were after." He looked into her eyes. "They wanted to feel alive.

Keiko frowned in confusion. "By biting me?"

He scowled. "They terrified you to make the gift spill into your blood. They bit you so they could drink your power straight from your veins."

Clutching his coat, she shivered hard. "Like vampires?"

He snorted. "Without doubt. Vampires are supposed to be blood-drinking ghosts."

She looked up into his eyes. "Is that what you want from me? To drink my power?"

His smile vanished, and an aching hunger filled his midnight gaze. He licked his lips. "Yes."

This book is a work of fiction. Names, characters, places and incidents either are products of the author's imagination or are used fictitiously. Any resemblance to actual events or locales or persons, living or dead, is entirely coincidental.

Hungry Spirits - A Hentai Fantasy
Copyright © 2006 Morgan Hawke
ISBN: 1-55410-662-1
Cover art by Eiris Key
Cover design by Martine Jardin

All rights reserved. Except for use in any review, the reproduction or utilization of this work in whole or in part in any form by any electronic, mechanical or other means, now known or hereafter invented, is forbidden without the written permission of the publisher.

Published by eXtasy Books, a division of Zumaya Publications, 2006
Look for us online at:
www.zumayapublications.com
www.extasybooks.com

Library and Archives Canada Cataloguing in Publication

Hawke, Morgan, 1963-
  Hungry spirits / Morgan Hawke ; cover artist: Eiris Key.

Also available in electronic format.
ISBN 1-55410-662-1

  I. Title.

PS3608.A83H85 2006   813'.6   C2006-900625-3

Hungry Spirits

By

Morgan Hawke

A very special thank you to:

Virginia E. — For being there when I needed you.

Jaynie, Jaynie, Jaynie — For keeping me on the mostly straight, and fairly narrow.

An extra special thank you to:

Erin S. — For helping me out of a jam.

Brent N. — Without you, this book would not have been nearly so much fun to write.

To Stef — for the Miracles you have wrought.

Book One

~Chrysanthemums & Lightning~

~One~

"This historical mansion is supposed to be haunted. Isn't that cool?"

Thunder boomed, rattling the rattan frames of the long, rice paper sliding walls on the left.

"What?" The rubber soles of Keiko's pink house slippers caught on the antique red and gold carpet, making her trip. She barely kept from pitching into the student directly in front of her. With the entire class crammed in the narrow hallway, there was barely enough walking room, never mind room to fall. She turned to her left, and frowned at her classmate. "Tika, did you say the house is *haunted*?"

"Yep." Tika smiled, showing the boy-grabbing dimple in the heart of her cheek. The light shining through the warm cream of the rice paper wall on their left gave her oval face a warm glow. "The ghost of an old samurai is supposed to be watching over the family."

Keiko winced. "Great." Her class *would* arrange a *haunted* house tour during an autumn storm. She wiped her damp palms down the black jacket emblazoned with the university's logo over her left pocket. Her hooded slicker had saved her hair and blazer from getting soaked, but the hem of her plain black skirt and her stockings were still damp.

Suddenly, the rest of Tika's comment sank in. Keiko turned to frown at her. "The ghost is watching over the family? Are you saying they're in residence? They still live here?"

"Yep." Tika put on a grim expression, and lifted her finger in imitation of their instructor. "This is a private tour granted to the university by the highly esteemed house owner; a very respectable alumni." She leaned close to Keiko's ear. "And I hear that the son, and heir to the family company, is currently attending, and..." She winked. "He's supposed to be really cute, too!"

Keiko frowned in confusion. "Where'd you hear all this?"

Tika rolled her eyes and shook her head, her sleek black hair falling into a perfectly trimmed wedge at her chin. "It was in the documentation passed out in class. Didn't you read it?"

"Yes, I read...some." Keiko's cheeks heated. Actually, she hadn't read any. "I was working on my essay." She fiddled with the plain black ribbon tie around the collar of her white blouse. "I missed the bit about the ghost." She glanced around, but saw nothing unusual about the rattan-framed sliding walls on her left, or in the paintings hanging on the polished cedar wall on her right. "How big is this house?" *How long is this tour?*

"Really freaking huge; I bet we'll be walking all day." Tika sighed and reached out to stroke the rice-paper wall they were passing with her fingertips. "On top of that, with all the sliding walls in this place, it's more of a maze than a mansion. Someone is bound to get lost."

"Not me." Keiko had absolutely no desire to wander away from her fellow students; not in a haunted house. She peered over the shoulders of the students ahead of her.

A tall man in a gray, military-style uniform leaned casually against the polished cedar wall on the right, as though he was some kind of guard. His arms were folded, defining muscle normally hidden under long sleeves. His sleek black hair was tucked behind his ears and a little overlong, falling just past his nicely broad shoulders. The tailored cut of his gray coat showed a flat stomach and narrow hips.

Keiko sucked in a breath. *Damn...* Whoever he was, he was seriously fine.

He lifted his chin and scanned up the line of students.

Keiko turned her head so he wouldn't notice her impolite staring, and peeked from the corner of her eye. His uniform looked familiar, but she couldn't quite place where she'd seen it before.

The line stopped, only two students away from the man against the wall. No one looked at him; not even a glance.

Keiko frowned.

Tika sighed and started cataloguing just how handsome her latest boyfriend was. Her favorite subject.

Keiko smiled, then turned slightly away, rolling her eyes. Tika would probably be chatting non-stop for the next hour. Her gaze drifted to the man in gray against the wall. Not one student looked his way, as though they just didn't notice him standing there.

Weird. Curling a finger around the end of her long black ponytail, Keiko looked over at her schoolmate.

Tika was deep into describing the perfection of her boyfriend's butt, grinning and gesturing enthusiastically with her hands.

Keiko's brows lifted. Tika wasn't noticing the guy against the wall either, and that was really strange. He was blindingly handsome. There was no way she would have been able to resist flirting with him. What was going on? She turned back to look at him.

His face was…perfect, not too angular, not too oval, and he had a mouth to die for—but there was not one drop of color in his face, or in anything he wore. He looked as though he had stepped from an old black and white film.

Keiko suddenly realized where she'd seen that uniform. Although it was gray, rather than black, she was clearly looking at a military uniform from over a hundred years ago. She felt a far too familiar humming inside the back of her head, and the hairs at the back of her neck lifted.

She was staring at a ghost.

He turned and looked straight at her. His midnight eyes under straight black brows danced with flickers of unearthly blue fox-fire. He unfolded his arms and straightened, his eyes narrowing. "You see me." His voice caressed the inside of her head with the warmth of late summer, and the perfume of faded chrysanthemums.

Keiko jerked her gaze away and grabbed onto Tika's arm.

Tika yipped, then grinned. "What? Did you see the ghost?"

Keiko dug her fingers into Tika's arm. "No."

A summery chuckle echoed across her thoughts. "Yes…"

Keiko cringed, and peeked from the corner of her eye.

He was gone.

"Take it easy with the death-grip, will you?" Tika shrugged out of Keiko's hold, then smiled. "If you're that scared, I'm sure I can find a guy to hold your hand?"

Keiko clasped her hands behind her. "No, thanks, I was just startled." Guys were even more trouble than ghosts.

Tika raised a perfectly manicured brow. "If you're sure…?"

"I'm fine, really." Keiko gave her a big fake smile and jaunty wave.

The professor, at the very head of the double line of students, lifted his arms to signal that the tour was turning down a hallway on the right. He began droning on about the esteemed house's artworks. The students directly ahead moved forward.

Tika tugged on Keiko's sleeve. "Go, go, go!"

Keiko rolled her eyes. "I'm going! I'm going!" Her slippers slapping on the carpet and her long black ponytail swinging against her back, she trudged after the student before her. She was very careful to look away from where the ghost had been standing.

Thunder crashed overhead, rattling the paper walls.

Keiko looked up toward the ceiling. The dangling Victorian era light fixture swayed slightly overhead.

Tika gasped, tripped and fell hard against Keiko's left side.

Keiko toppled over toward the cedar wall on her right, and threw out her hands, falling… She landed on her shoulder and sprawled on the floor. Groaning, she sat up, rubbing her aching shoulder. "Thanks a lot, Tika." She froze. Right in front of her, where Tika and the rest of her class should have been, was a cedar wall—and no door.

She gasped, and looked up. The shadowed ceiling was very far away and artfully draped in magnificent sheets of scarlet and gold silk. She twisted around on her butt and discovered that she was sitting on the floor at the far end of a long and deeply shadowed audience chamber. The walls were lined with gigantic wall screens embroidered in brilliant rainbow hues and illuminated from behind.

"What...?" She scrambled to her feet. "How did I get here?" The hair on her neck lifted and the back of her head shimmered with awareness.

"You fell through the door." The voice came from right behind her.

Her breath caught and her hands turned to ice. She whirled.

The gray man, the ghost, was directly behind her less than a foot away, leaning against the cedar wall with his arms crossed. He smiled, and blue flames blazed in the midnight depths of his eyes. "I am Ryudo. Welcome to my home."

Keiko sucked in a deep breath, turned on her heel and bolted. Her slippers slapped loudly on the woven *tatami* mats fitted across the floor. She skidded to a stop near the wall screen at the opposite end of the huge empty room. There had to be a door somewhere.

Near the left wall a seam of light spilled across the shadowed floor from between two screens. A sliding door.

She lunged for it.

The screens slammed together.

Keiko jerked to a halt, her heart slamming in her chest. A shimmer of awareness tingled at the back of her skull. *Ghost...* She backed away from the door. Her back came in contact with the opposite screen. It slid under her hands. She turned and pulled on the bamboo frame. The wall parted, revealing a window.

She stuck her head out onto a dark cross-hallway. No lights were lit and no one was in sight. Windows lined the entire opposite wall. Beyond the glass, rain fell on a magnificent walled-in, outdoor garden, complete with shrines and fountains. The storm's wind tossed the branches of the carefully pruned trees, and blown leaves stuck to the wet glass. Thunder rumbled.

A sigh came from behind her, and the scent of faded flowers.

Keiko charged into the hallway. Something caught the collar of her coat, trapping her in the doorway.

"Going somewhere?"

Keiko gasped, barely stopping her scream. She tugged, but her coat was caught fast. She wriggled out of it, and plunged into the hallway. Her slippers skidded on the slippery, waxed wood floor, and she nearly crashed into the window across the hall. She turned around. The door she had just emerged from was gone, and her coat with it. She faced one long wall of identical bamboo-framed panels.

She stepped out into the middle of the hall with no clue which way she should go, left or right. Both ways led to a blind corner. There was not a sound but wind and rain. She was lost—in a haunted house.

She turned to her right and took a hesitant step.

Thunder rumbled, then lightning flashed beyond the windows. Shadows from the tossing branches moved in the hallway around her. Six long paces ahead of her, in the center of the hallway, something shimmered in the air. The shimmer coalesced into Ryudo.

Keiko's breath stopped. She backed away. "Why are you chasing me?" Stupid question, she knew good and well why ghosts chased her.

Ryudo's black brows lifted. "Why are you running away?"

Keiko kept backing up. "You're a ghost."

Ryudo scowled. "I assure you, my...status of being was not my choice." He stepped toward her.

Keiko whirled and bolted. Her slippers flew off her feet. She let them go and kept running in her stocking feet. Sliding across the waxed floor, she grabbed the corner and hurled herself around the right-hand turn. She skidded into a long gallery filled with standing glass cases crammed with vases, brass statuary and funeral urns. The hall was dark but for the lights within the cases.

Keiko hurried along the slippery floor past the displays, trying not to slide into any of the cases while searching for a door. There had to be a door. The end of the hall was a left hand turn, and then another long gallery of cedar walls lined with silk paintings. This hall was even darker than the last, but light shown at the left turn at far end.

She scooted into the hall.

Thunder rumbled, and the scent of chrysanthemums whispered in the air.

"Don't go. Stay."

Something pulled at the tie in her hair. She didn't think, she shook her head and lunged into the dark hallway. Her long black hair loosened from the tie, tumbling free down her back to her waist.

"Ah… Very nice."

Keiko turned the corner, gasping for breath, and found another cedar-walled hallway. This one was very narrow, and lined with antique silk robes under glass. The light came from the cases. Her legs shaking, she walked as fast as she could. All this running was seriously beginning to tire her out.

A shimmer appeared at the end of the hall.

Keiko stopped dead, then backed away.

Ryudo coalesced with his hands behind his back. His booted feet were clearly not touching the floor. "Are you ready to stop running?"

Keiko scowled, and kept backing away. This game of his was getting on her nerves. "Are you ready to stop chasing me?"

"My pursuit will end when you stop running." He tilted his head, and pursed his full, colorless lips. "Though I will admit, I haven't been this entertained in quite a while."

Keiko stopped, her hands fisting at her sides. "You think this is *fun?*"

Ryudo's brows lifted. "Pursuing the attentions of a pretty girl?" He gave her a breathtaking smile. "Absolutely." He raised his hand, and gestured.

The black ribbon tie around Keiko's collar fell out of its snug bow. She stared down at her loosened tie. "What…?"

"The only thing I find more entertaining…" Ryudo made a snatching motion with his hand. "Is undressing one."

The ribbon slithered off her neck in a whisper of silk and sailed across the room to his hand. Keiko gasped in shock. "My tie!"

Ryudo tilted his head. "Aren't you a little warm, all buttoned up like that?" He gestured again.

The top button at the throat of Keiko's white blouse popped open. "Hey!" Keiko grabbed for her shirt. "Stop that! You…pervert!"

He blinked. "Pervert?" A completely masculine smile lifted his lips, and pale blue fox-fire gleamed in the heart of his black eyes. "I can show you perversion, if you like." He lifted both of his hands.

Oh, shit! Keiko turned and bolted back down the hall. She spotted an inch-wide crack in a seam in the left wall, between two *kimono* displays, and grabbed for it. The wall slid open to the left. She didn't look, she just squeezed through.

Keiko found herself in another dark gallery, this one with murals embroidered in silk hanging along the right wall, with rice-paper walls lining the left. She groaned. Tika had been right. The house was a freaking maze.

Rain could be heard pattering against the roof tiles.

Keiko looked up. She had to be close to the outside.

The hint of summer heat and flowers washed across her thoughts. "Wait, I was just starting to get to know you."

"Yeah, right." Keiko glared at the ceiling, and marched up the hall with determination. "By taking off my clothes?"

"I was merely curious." Soft laughter echoed. "Would you like to know what's under mine?"

Keiko's imagination suddenly filled with an image of a strong masculine chest, silky black hair falling across broad shoulders, and a stomach defined by sleek muscle. She shook her head. *What am I thinking? He's a ghost!* But he did have nice-looking hands, and a mouth to die for… *No.* She would not even consider…what his butt really looked like. She ground her teeth, and forcibly slammed a lid on her wayward imagination. "No, thank you!"

Warm, summery chuckles followed her down the hallway.

~ Two ~

Keiko turned a corner and padded down a long—and very empty—hall with absolutely nothing in it, just polished cedar walls, and deep shadows. Silence reigned but for the soft falls of her feet on the smooth wood floors.

She groaned and rubbed at the back of her neck. She was tired, thirsty and more than a little annoyed. She knew her entire senior class was somewhere in the house, but she had yet to run across them, or anyone that lived there. She strongly suspected that Ryudo had something to do with that.

A seam of light spilled across the floor.

Keiko stared at it. Another door. She rushed forward, found the crack in seams of the wall and peeked through it. The crack revealed that she was at the end of a very long and well-lit cedar-walled chamber filled with medieval weapons in glass cases.

There was another door, standing wide open, at the far end.

Keiko licked her lips. Finally, a real exit, and no ghost in sight. That didn't mean he wasn't there, but she didn't sense anything, or smell any flowers. She shoved the wall panel to the side, and cautiously stepped through.

With hurried steps, she passed by the gleaming weapon cases with a real sense of disappointment. She loved weapons, which was why she'd taken the history course that had brought her here, and this looked like one of the best collections she'd seen yet. Unfortunately, she just couldn't afford to indulge herself, not with a ghost chasing her.

A case filled with ornate *tantos* from various eras caught her attention. She could not resist a quick look.

Though the handgrips of the daggers were wound with brilliant silk thread in various elegant patterns, the squared blades were all of the same efficient design. Sleek, graceful and deadly... Antique *tsubas,* elaborate circular cross guards of brass, silver, and jade, were placed flat on a bed of gold silk, displaying their intricate filigrees of trees and beasts.

She bit down on her lip and continued on. *Stupid ghost...*

She passed an open doorway on her right, and looked in. Within a small alcove room, against the right wall, was a seated suit of samurai armor, lacquered in scarlet and black and threaded with gold silk roping. The stag-antlered, flared helmet had a snarling gold mask. Two swords, a long *katana,* and a shorter *wakizashi,* were posted on a traditional lacquered wooden *daisho* frame at the armor's booted feet. Unlike the rest of the exhibits, this one was not under glass. The whole display gleamed in a patch of sunlight cast by a row of small windows close to the ceiling.

Intrigued by the antique armor, Keiko bit her lip and stepped through the door to get a better look. She'd never seen one that wasn't within a glass case.

The room was very small, and unusually warm. The scent of sun-warmed lacquered rattan, rich silk, and oiled leather filled the small room. She leaned close, but didn't try to touch. The intricacy of the armor was spectacularly beautiful, and very real. Her heart burned, and tears welled with joy at seeing something truly rare from the distant past, and with the pain of what was lost. *Bushido,* the way of the warrior...

Keiko stepped back and bowed. The carefully preserved silk and rattan armor represented the blood and spirits of those that had fought and died in defense of their people, and in service to their emperor. *Samurai,* to serve...

Her tears dampened the simple rice mat at her feet, and she was glad to leave something of herself behind.

"Tears. A worthy gift." The voice was a whisper from summers past.

Keiko jerked upright, hastily wiping her cheeks, and looked about. No one was there, but the doorway on the right, the one she had entered, was gone.

Huh? She walked over to where the door had been, but it was a solid, unmoving wall. She stepped back and looked around. A seam had opened on the opposite wall, right next to a big clunky wooden door-handle. A line of bright light blazed across the floor from the seam. It looked like sunlight. One door was gone, and another had appeared.

She'd been tricked.

Keiko looked up at the ceiling, and stomped her foot. "You pain in my ass!"

There was a whisper of summer flowers in the air, but nothing beyond that.

Keiko groaned and faced the other door, and its large handle. She could stay in the tiny room, or she could take the rather blatant invitation being offered. She rolled her eyes, and crossed her arms. *Great, some choice.* Her gaze moved to the door. It couldn't hurt to at least see where it led.

She heaved a sigh, and walked over. Grasping the handle with both hands, she slid the door open, and found a small perfectly contained outdoor garden surrounded by smooth white walls. The sky was a faded blue and the sunlight seemed…golden. Insects buzzed in the humid warmth.

Under cleverly pruned trees, a pebble walk wound through the grass around a trio of tall decorative stones that were practically engulfed by late summer flowers. The walk ended at a stone, moss-covered small shrine that occupied the garden's far corner. Beside it, a small bubbling fountain trickled into a tiny pond holding a single broad lily pad and a single perfect bloom.

In the very center of the garden was a very old and well-groomed cherry tree. Under the tree's twisted, but neatly trimmed, leafy branches squatted a low circular table of polished golden wood with two thick, black silk sitting pillows.

The garden was filled with late summer—but she knew for a fact that it was late autumn. There should be no flowers, and the trees should have been bare of leaves. It had been raining just minutes ago, and yet the grass was dry.

The hair on Keiko's neck lifted and the back of her head shimmered with awareness. A warm breeze, carrying the scent of chrysanthemums, caressed her cheeks.

"Good afternoon."

Keiko's breath caught and her heart slammed in her chest. Her hands turned to ice. She whirled.

The eerily colorless Ryudo stood directly behind her, less than a foot away, blocking the door. He smiled, and blue flames blazed in the midnight depths of his eyes. "Would you do me the honor of joining me in the garden?" He stepped toward her.

Keiko stepped back in a hurry, moving off the slate step, her stocking-clad heels crunching onto the pebble walk of the impossible garden. She winced.

He stepped out, following her with booted feet that didn't quite touch the ground. Behind him, the door slid closed with a snap. "Thank you." He nodded, and his smile broadened.

Fear chilled her spine, and anger followed in its wake. Her hands fisted at her sides. "Why are you doing this?"

Ryudo lifted his brow. "I thought you might be ready for a rest, and a cup of tea." He lifted his chin and stared past her shoulder.

Keiko blinked. *Huh?* She turned back to look at the low table under the cherry tree. A small, square wooden tray occupied the table's center, holding a rectangular terra-cotta teapot with a bamboo handle. The pot was richly glazed in several shades of aqua. Steam curled from the pot's square spout, and two small angular cups sat beside it.

Keiko's anger dissipated under a wash of confusion. He brought her *tea?* She glanced back toward the handsome and bewildering ghost.

Ryudo stepped toward her.

She backed away to avoid him, stepping off the pebble path and onto the neatly mown grass.

The ghost strode across the grass to the low table, and stepped around it to the far side. He tugged the skirts of his coat back and knelt on the cushion facing the door, clearly leaving the cushion facing the cherry tree, for her. He looked at her expectantly.

Keiko lunged for the door, grabbed the wooden handle and tugged. The door refused to slide sideways and open. She put her full weight into it. *Open, damn you!* Her stocking feet slipped on the slate step. The door didn't budge. She turned to face the ghost, fear chilling her heart while anger heated her temper. "Let me out."

Ryudo set his elbows on the table and folded his fingers together. "Don't you want a cup of tea?"

"With you?" Keiko set her free hand on her hip. "No, thank you."

Ryudo scowled. "Why not?"

"Why *not?*" Keiko set both hands on her hips. "Maybe because you just spent the past hour or so chasing me through the house?"

He frowned. "I wasn't chasing you, you were running from me."

Keiko's mouth fell open. "Of course I was running from you, you're a ghost!"

"Yes. I am." He looked away. "I am a spirit, in a house full of people that cannot see me, or hear me." He clasped his hand together. "I just want a bit of conversation with someone that knows I exist." He looked up at her. "Is that so very terrible?"

Keiko tightened her hand on the door handle. She knew, quite painfully, what it was like to always be on the outside looking in. But, her odd sensitivity to ghosts went further than seeing and speaking to them. She had the very physical scars to prove it. "I need to get back to my class. They'll miss me."

"Of course." Ryudo held out his hand, indicating the pillow next to him. "After you have a cup of tea."

"You're not letting me go?" Keiko's hands fisted at her sides.

"This is kidnapping!"

Ryudo's brows rose. "It's an invitation to tea."

Keiko scowled. "That I refused!"

"You refuse your host's invitation?" Ryudo dropped his chin and lowered his brows. "How terribly impolite."

Keiko's mouth fell open. *She* was being rude? "You're not the owner, you're just a ghost!"

"Just a ghost?" Ryudo set his hands flat on the table, and his eyes narrowed. "This entire house is under my personal guardianship, and *my* domain, therefore you are *my* guest!"

Keiko backed against the door, and swallowed hard. She was not only trapped by the house's guardian spirit, she'd just succeeded in pissing it off. But damn it, he was being rude, too. One did not force one's guests to...have tea.

She released a breath. *Forced* to have *tea*...Merciful Lady, that sounded silly. "Do you regularly lock your guests in when they won't have tea?"

Ryudo's brows shot up, then he glanced away with a small shrug. "Only occasionally."

Keiko snorted and crossed her arms. "No wonder you don't have very many guests."

His brows dropped low over his eyes and he glared at her. "What is so terrible about having tea with me?"

Keiko sighed. "It's not the tea, it's the fact that you just spent half the day scaring me to death, and now you expect me to keep you company?"

He sighed, and looked down at his hands. "It was not my intent to frighten you."

"Is that so? Then why did you take my coat, and my tie?" She tugged at a lock of her hair. "And my hair-bow?"

He winced. "I was perhaps a bit overly enthusiastic."

"A bit?" Keiko set her hand on her hip. "You threatened to undress me!"

He rolled his eyes. "It's not as if I can do anything to you. I *am* a ghost."

Keiko shivered suddenly. But he could. Apparently, he *didn't* know about her…oddness. She had no idea how he'd missed it, when so many others had not, but at that moment, she was truly grateful. "I would really like to leave. Now, please."

"Of course." He rose to his feet, standing with his head bowed, and his hands stiffly correct at his sides. "Please, forgive me." His voice was barely a whisper. "One should not treat one's guest in such a shameful manner."

Keiko froze, confused. The ghost was presenting her a formal apology?

Ryudo's hands tightened at his sides. "As you truly wish to leave…"

The door abruptly slid partway open under her hands.

He's letting me go? Keiko pushed at the door, and it slid easily, all the way open.

"It's just that I haven't had the pleasure of…a young lady's company, in a very long time."

With one foot on the flagstone threshold, Keiko hesitated. If Ryudo's uniform was any measure of his age, he had been a ghost for over a century. She couldn't imagine existing that long in a house full of people that didn't even know he was there. And the one person he *could* speak to—wanted nothing to do with him.

Not even…tea.

She closed her eyes, and shame brought heat to her cheeks. Yes, he was a ghost, but clearly, he was acting out of desperate loneliness. He hadn't actually done anything truly awful, just embarrassing. Merciful Lady, he'd given her a formal apology. That was not the action of a night terror, a monster out to cut her to ribbons, but of a man who had done something he was ashamed of.

What could it hurt to have tea?

Keiko turned around to face him. "I accept your apology, honored Ryudo." She set her hands on her plain skirt and gave him a deep bow, her long hair falling beside her cheeks. "I am Keiko, and I would be honored to have tea with you."

His head lifted his eyes wide. His lips parted. "You will?" He straightened and shook his head. "I mean, by all means, please do!" He held out his hand, indicating the other cushion, and a truly breathtaking smile bloomed.

Keiko nearly reeled from the effect. Ryudo might be a ghost, but Merciful Lady, he was a gorgeous ghost. She swept her hands across her skirt, smiled and strode to the table.

Ryudo tugged the tails of his coat out of the way and knelt, a host awaiting his guest.

Keiko smoothed her skirt down over her knees, and knelt on the offered pillow. A refreshingly cool breeze caressed her through the white cotton blouse. The blazer would have been uncomfortably warm.

Ryudo set his chin on his palm and gave her that wonderful smile. "Lovely."

She rolled her eyes. "Oh, please…" She reached for the teapot. It was surprisingly warm, and very full.

Ryudo tilted his head. "You don't like compliments?"

"I don't mind them." Keiko gave him a tight smile. "It just doesn't happen very often, not to me." Carefully, she poured green tea into the two square cups.

His brows lifted. "I find that hard to believe."

Keiko did not want to talk about her lack of…appeal. She set the pot on the square tray and lifted her cup. "Out of curiosity, how did you…?" She lifted her free hand, indicating the garden. "Arrange this?"

"Ah, so you noticed." Ryudo smiled sourly.

Keiko snorted. "Kind of hard to miss when it's really raining outside."

"Oh, yes, well…" He winced. "It's an illusion."

An *illusion*? She froze with the cup halfway to her mouth. "Then, where am I, really?"

Ryudo smiled tightly. "We're really within a rather empty room."

He raised his hand indicating the tree, and the sky, overhead. "Once upon a time, this garden really existed, right here, just as you see it." He peered down at his hands, and lifted his shoulder in a half-shrug. "They expanded the house, and it was…lost."

Keiko knocked on the table. "Wow, this is an amazingly solid illusion."

Ryudo chuckled. "The table is not an illusion; nor is the cushions, or the teapot."

Keiko peered hard at the cherry tree on the other side of the table, but it looked perfectly solid. "Incredible." She sipped at the tea. It was wonderful. "So, how are you doing it, the illusion?"

Ryudo looked away. "I would rather not say."

Keiko eyed her phantom host. It would have been horrifically rude to insist on an explanation. "All right." She looked at the tea she had set before him. He hadn't touched it. Probably because as a ghost, he *couldn't* touch it. She glanced away. "So how did you come to be in this house?" She flinched. Obviously he had died to become the house guardian. Perhaps that wasn't a polite thing to ask. "You don't have to answer, if you'd rather speak of something else…?"

Ryudo smiled sourly. "It was…asked of me, and I agreed." He looked down at his hands. "It is not a bad existence. I can do a number of things I could not as a living man."

Keiko nodded. "Like the illusions."

He gave her a brief smile. "Yes, and the moving of objects without actually touching them." He stared at the teapot and gestured with his fingers.

The pot obediently lifted and floated toward Keiko.

Her heart in her mouth, Keiko locked her hands in her lap. *I will not freak out.*

The teapot tipped steaming tea into her cup, then returned to the tray.

Keiko released her breath very slowly and pasted a smile on her lips. "Well, that must be entertaining."

Ryudo set his elbow on the table and propped his chin on his hand. "Oh, yes, all the screaming and running away from floating objects, can be quite entertaining." He rolled his eyes and sighed. "But never leaving the house, and having no one to talk to, can get a little dull."

Wanting to comfort him, Keiko set her palm over Ryudo's hand. She froze. She could feel his long cool fingers under her palm, as solid as her own.

Ryudo stared at her hand over his. "I can feel...your *hand*."

~ Three ~

Merciful Lady, why had she done something so stupid? Keiko jerked her hand back.

Ryudo caught her wrist in his fist. "I can *feel* your hand." His gaze narrowed at her and blue flame leaped in their depths. "You have the gift."

Keiko pulled at her wrist. "It's not a gift—it's a curse!"

Mouth tight, Ryudo rose from the table and pulled her up with him. "Why didn't you tell me?"

Keiko glared at him. "Why should I? The last ghost that found out sent me to the hospital!"

Ryudo's mouth opened. "What? But, why?"

Keiko curled her lip. "Because it bit me, but no one could see the blood but me. They brought me to the hospital because I passed out. I woke up a week later with a machine pumping air into my lungs and a brand new scar."

Ryudo stepped away from the table, pulling her closer. "Why did the ghost bite you?"

Keiko dug in her heels, but Ryudo's grip was too strong to break. "Because it was a monster."

"A monster?" Ryudo's brows lifted. "It didn't look human?"

"No." She tried twisting her wrist, but couldn't budge it in his grip. "None of them did."

"Them? How many of them were there?"

"You're the first I've met that actually looks like a man." Keiko grabbed his wrist with her other hand and tried to peel it off her. "Let go."

Ryudo caught her other wrist, holding them both. "Stop fighting me, you'll only hurt yourself."

Keiko glared up at him. "Let go!"

Ryudo stared down at her. "Answer the question. How many ghosts have attacked you?"

She jerked back in his hold. "I told you, *all* of them." She couldn't twist free.

"Keiko." He trapped both her wrists in one hand, and caught her chin, forcing her gaze to his. "Give me a number."

She glared up at him. "Twelve attacks, I think. Some of them had more than one ghost"

"Twelve attacks?" He released her chin and looked away. His brows dropped and he scowled, his expression clearly puzzled. "They all bit you?"

She turned away. "Some of them...cut me."

"Show me."

She looked at him, startled. "What?"

His jaw was tight and his eyes narrowed. "Show me the marks."

She scowled at him. "I am not taking my clothes off."

His gaze narrowed and blue fire blazed in their depths. "You will show me where they hurt you, or I will unclothe you myself and search."

Keiko jerked back. "You wouldn't..."

"Wouldn't I?" His gaze dropped to the buttons of her blouse. "I will see what was done to you."

The top button at her throat was already open from before. Keiko abruptly felt the second button release. And then the third, right over her heart. Panic struck. "Stop!"

"You will show me?"

She glared at him. "You're going to have to let me go, so I can unbutton my sleeves."

"All right." He stared past her shoulder.

The door from the garden, leading into the house, slid closed with a hard slam.

Keiko jumped and looked over at the door. Her heart beat in her mouth. She was locked in. Again.

"You are not leaving, until I see what was done to you." He released her wrists.

"Fine." Keiko stepped back, turned away and tugged the buttons at her wrist. Once he saw her scars, he'd let her go. Her ugliness chased everyone away. "Why?" She unfastened both wrists. She looked over at him. "Why do you want to see my..." She swallowed. "Scars?"

His face was a mask of anger. "To see what has attacked you!"

"I told you! They were monsters!" She glared at him, and jerked at the rest of her blouse buttons. "Monsters, Ryudo, with big teeth and claws!"

He flinched back. "How long has this been happening to you?"

She unbuttoned her blouse to the waist. "I was just a kid, still in grade school, when the first one bit me."

His eyes widened. "Grade school?" He looked away, and folded his arms. "That's not supposed to happen." He shook his head. "You're not supposed to come into your gift until you reach sixteen, or older."

"Yeah, well, apparently I got it early." She turned her back to him, and tugged the white cotton from her shoulders, revealing the back of her plain white bra, then jerked the blouse off her arms, leaving it hanging from her skirt's waistband. She scooped her hair from her back and draped it over her shoulder. "There." She closed her eyes. Her back was a complete mess of jagged rips from claws, and teeth...and other things. "Look all you like."

Summer insects, buzzed in the silence.

"God...! Your back!" His voice was tight, angry, and very close. He was standing right behind her. Cool fingers stroked the ridges along her back. "Are there more?"

She flinched away from his touch. "More, what?"

He set his hand on her shoulder, holding her still, for his

exploring fingers. "Did they damage more than your back?"

She folded her arms across her breasts, and shivered under his light touch. "Just my back, but the scars go down to my knees."

"Keiko, these are demon marks; bites from creatures made with hate. What are you doing to attract that kind of ghost?"

"I told you, I'm cursed!" She turned to glare at him from over her shoulder. "I attracted you, too, remember?"

Ryudo's brows lifted and his lips parted, then he scowled. "Keiko, I am nothing like those."

Keiko smiled grimly. "Oh, no?" She pointed at the door. "Show me the difference, Ryudo. Let me go."

He took a breath, his chest seemingly expanding with air. He released it in a sigh. "I...can't."

Keiko closed her eyes and felt the betrayal burn in her heart. He had been so wonderful, a handsome man flirting over tea, not a...a monster. Then, he had discovered what made her truly different. She could feel the dead, as though they were real, not the phantoms everyone else barely knew were there.

"Keiko, I need you."

Wearing only her bra, her blouse hanging from the waistband of her skirt, she refused to look at him. "For what?"

"I need...Keiko, look at me."

Keiko hunched her shoulders, and looked over at the closed door. "Just bite me, or cut me, or however you intend to make me bleed and get it over with, so I can go home."

"Keiko! Damn it, I don't want to *hurt* you!"

"Then what *do* you want?" Keiko looked over her shoulder at him. "Just say it!"

Ryudo's mouth was tight and his expression grim. "Turn around."

She shook her head. "There's nothing to see. They only got my back."

"Keiko." He took hold of both her shoulders. "Show me."

"You don't need to see any more." She leaned away from him. "They only got my back."

"Keiko." His fingers tightened on her shoulders. "Just turn around for me."

She closed her eyes in frustration. He wanted to see and he wasn't going to let it go until he saw, so… "Fine." She turned around under his hands and stared defiantly at him.

His gaze slid down her unmarred throat to her crossed arms, then down her smooth belly. He frowned. "Put your arms down."

She jerked her arms down, letting him see her plain white bra.

Ryudo's frown deepened. "Nothing."

She rolled her eyes and gave him a sour smile. "I told you so. Happy now?"

His gaze roved over her, and he seemed to take in a breath. "God, you're beautiful…"

The air slammed out of Keiko's lungs. "What…?" Her voice came out in a tiny airless squeak. Even though he was a ghost, he was still a very fine looking man, and his clearly admiring words sent a spear of warmth straight through her. Heat filled her cheeks.

Ryudo looked up into her eyes. "Keiko those…things scarred your back because they were trying to frighten you, not kill you."

Keiko scowled. "They sure acted like they were going to kill me!"

"They were *trying* to make you afraid." Ryudo shook his head "If they had wanted you dead, they would have gone straight for your stomach, where your spirit sits." He dropped a hand from her shoulder, and pressed his cool and very solid palm flat against the soft skin of her belly.

The contact was so unexpected, her breath caught. Sweat formed at the base of her spine and soaked into her blouse, but she couldn't tell if it was from fear, or the fact that his touch felt so…right. She caught hold of his coat. Gripping the heavy wool with both hands, she was amazed. "I can actually feel your coat." She pressed her hand to the buttons over his heart, and felt his body beneath it. "I can feel…you."

He nodded and pressed his fingers into her belly. "As I feel you, but no one else."

Erotic heat flared under his palm and spread. An exciting rush poured into her veins, tingled up her spine, and spilled into the back of her skull. A small moan escaped. Her knees weakened, and gave out, folding under her.

"Ah!" Ryudo caught her around the waist before she could fall. "I have you." He pulled her against him, keeping her upright, with his palm against her bare belly. He smiled, and color seemed to bloom in his cheeks and full lips. "Your gift is responding to me."

Keiko shook her head and jerked at his coat. "What gift? It doesn't do anything except let ghosts...hurt me." Her gaze dropped to his coat, and she frowned. The coat seemed to be darkening right under her hands and becoming...black with red trim, and the buttons looked more gold than silver.

He pulled his palm from her belly to catch her chin, drawing her gaze to his. "You have the power to make the dead live and feel again. For a short time, anyway." He released her chin, and set his palm back on her belly. "And it lives here. This is what those...creatures were after." He looked into her eyes. "They wanted to feel alive."

Keiko frowned in confusion. "By biting me?"

He scowled. "They terrified you to make the gift spill into your blood. They bit you so they could drink your power straight from your veins."

Clutching his coat, she shivered hard. "Like vampires?"

He snorted. "Without doubt. Vampires are supposed to be blood-drinking ghosts."

She looked up into his eyes. "Is that what you want from me? To drink my power?"

His smile vanished, and an aching hunger filled his midnight gaze. He licked his lips. "Yes."

She ducked her head while her hands turned cold. Another bite, another scar...

"Keiko, I don't want to hurt you. There is another way, a better way."

She looked up at the handsome ghost, and trembled, teetering between desire and terror. "What way?"

Ryudo's arms closed around her, and the pale blue fox-fire in his dark gaze trapped hers. "Fear is only one way to bring your gift to potency." He tightened his hold, pressing her breasts into his chest, and pulling her hips against his. "The other is passion." His hand slid down her bare back, and shivers followed, then awakening heat. He lowered his head, his black hair sweeping against her cheek, his lips a breath away. "Kiss me."

She focused on his lush mouth, and hesitated. She licked her lips. He was a truly handsome man, and it was only a kiss. What could it hurt? She lifted her chin, and brushed her lips against his.

The cool, velvety softness of his lips parted, delivering unexpected warmth and breath. "Yes…" His damp tongue slid across her bottom lip, then darted in to stroke the tip of her tongue.

She met his foray and lightly swept her tongue against his. He tasted like fresh, clean water and shadows. He tasted exciting. She sought more, and her eyes drifted closed.

He swept his hands up her back, and cupped her head, angling her mouth to fit his. Drawing her tongue into his mouth, he captured it and suckled.

A small moan escaped her throat. She released his lapels and skimmed her hands around to his back, feeling the firmness of his body beneath his coat. Vibrancy and darkness pulsed in a delicious, yet shivery combination under her palms.

He moaned softly against her lips. "Yes, more…"

She slid her hands around his waist, pulling him tight to her. The simmering dark within him brushed against her heart. Carnal hunger bloomed. Her nipples tightened to aching points under her bra. Urgency coiled tight, and moisture seeped into her panties. She gasped and trembled.

"Yes, that's it." He lapped, then sucked on her tongue, moaning in greedy delight. His erection swelled and lengthened against her belly. The hint of aroused male perfumed the air.

Simply unable to resist, she rolled her belly against his growing firmness.

He skimmed one hand down her back to cup her butt, holding her snug to him, and groaned into her mouth. The fingertips of his other hand brushed the nape of her neck, drawing tiny shivers. He sucked the plump fullness of her lip into his mouth, and very gently bit down, holding her mouth to his.

His tender bite surprised her, and she sought to repay the caress with one of her own.

He chuckled, and engaged her questing tongue while skimming his hands across her back. He touched her bra strap and stilled, his fingers resting on the catch. He tugged. The bra parted, and opened.

Startled, she pulled from his kiss.

He locked her in his embrace, and took her mouth. He subdued her alarm with gentle, yet determined incursions of his skilled tongue.

She sighed, giving in to the hot drugging spiral of excitement building urgently within her.

He pressed his warm palms to her back, and explored her contours, slowly drifting downward, to the waistband of her skirt. He tugged on the skirt's zipper, and drew it down.

She pulled back. "Wait, what are you doing?"

He locked his arm around her waist, holding her firmly to his chest, and smiled. "Undressing you."

~ *four* ~

He was *undressing* her? Alarmed, Keiko pushed at the ghost's all too solid chest. "Ryudo, I thought you weren't…?"

"Keiko." Ryudo caught the back of her skirt, bunching it in his fist. "I can't seduce you with your clothes on." He tugged. The black skirt slid down from her hips and fell to the grass, revealing the white lace garter-belt holding her stockings, and the white lace panties over them. His brow lifted. "Lace and stockings? Very nice." He ducked down and set his arm under her knees. "Modern pantyhose is annoying." He rose, scooping her up into his arms.

Lifted into the air, Keiko gasped softly, and threw her arms around his neck. "Ryudo, wait!"

Ryudo turned slowly, with her in his arms. "Keiko, I have already waited a hundred and fifteen years." The world around them began to darken and fade. "My waiting is done."

Keiko looked around in alarm. The trees and flowers became shadows that changed shape and dimension. The sounds of summer drifted away, replaced by the sound of thunder rumbling somewhere, far away. She turned to look into Ryudo's shadow-filled eyes. "You're going to…you mean to have sex with me?"

"Is there another meaning for seduction?" Ryudo gave her tight smile. "Terror spills your power into your blood, but it does not release it from the body." He strode forward, carrying her into a darkness filled with the sound of late autumn rain on a tile roof. "To taste your power, they have to break the skin, and drink it from your blood."

Lightning flashed, briefly illuminating a bamboo framed folding screen of plain rice paper standing before a broad window.

His voice whispered intimately against her ear. "When I bring you to erotic climax, orgasm, I can take all I need in a single kiss."

Thunder rumbled again, louder and closer. Another lightning flash revealed a thick *futon* bedroll upon the floor, angled outward from a shadowed corner by the window. Two low pillows rested side by side. The bed's coverlet was scarlet silk.

A warm golden glow bloomed against the back wall, opposite the window. The glow coalesced into an antique Victorian oil lamp, with a scrolled oil font resting upon the head of kneeling girl of brass. Flame brightened in a slender glass chimney, revealing that the lamp rested in the very center of a low table of golden oak, pushed up against a cedar wall. On the table, less than a hand-span from the oil lamp, a rectangular aqua teapot rested on a square lacquered tray, accompanied by two square cups. Two black pillows rested on the polished wood floor.

A delicate, bamboo-framed banner of white silk, the room's only decoration, hung on the wall opposite the window, directly behind the table. The silk was finely embroidered with a magnificent spreading cherry tree.

There was no door.

Ryudo released her legs, setting Keiko down on the smooth wood floor. He cupped her shoulders and smiled down at her. No longer was he a gray image, but a man fully realized, wearing a neatly pressed, black wool uniform, decorated in scarlet and gold braid, with glossy black boots.

Keiko looked up at Ryudo's face. "This...seduction is the only way?"

His features seemed carved from ivory, though his full lips were a rich dark red. His hand closed on her shoulders, and his fingers, no longer cool but warm, caught in her bra straps. "Yes." He drew the white elastic straps down her arms. "I prefer drinking from the fount of desire." He tugged the bra from her arms and let it fall to the floor.

His eyes narrowed, and his smile turned feral. "Pleasure serves no finer banquet."

She shivered under his gaze, but left her hands at her sides.

His gaze lifted, and his dark eyes caught hers. "Exquisite."

Keiko licked her lips. There was no escape. She was not leaving until the ghost had taken what he would of her. Her belly clenched in sudden and ravenous anticipation.

He smiled and dropped to one knee. He shook back his silky black hair, and thumbed it behind his ears. Trapping her gaze, blue-flames flickering within the hearts of his eyes, he eased forward, opened his mouth and captured the pink tip of her nipple, sucking it hard into his mouth.

Carnal fire speared straight down into her core, and focused on the tiny point of her clit. Her belly clenched in dark hunger. She gasped and her knees weakened. She grabbed onto his shoulders, nearly falling atop him.

His hands cupped the fullness of her buttocks, and his fingers closed on her lace panties. He suckled on her nipple, making loud wet sounds of masculine enjoyment.

Bolts of rapture, stirred by his lips and tongue, stabbed straight down to her clit. Her belly tightened with a voracious greed that ruthlessly demanded more. Soft, needy sounds slipped from her throat.

He clamped his teeth down, in a tender bite, then flicked his tongue hard against the sensitive flesh.

The inflamed point of her clit echoed the throb in her nipple, jolting her with exquisite agony. She choked, and her body went rigid with violent anticipation. Her breath stilled.

He jerked on the lace with both hands, and tugged her panties down.

She took a single breath.

He closed one hand on her bare ass cheek, and slid the other hand up, between her legs. His palm cupped her feminine core. He pulled back from her breast, and captured her gaze. "Open for me."

She gripped the shoulders of his coat and gasped for breath. Her heart's shock warred with her body's fierce tormenting hunger. Hunger won, and her legs parted, all by themselves.

He smiled. "Ah...good." Two of his strong fingers delved into the soft hair and past, between the plump lips, then deeper still, among the sensitive and wet folds of her secret flesh. "You're very close." His fingers curled and found her swollen clit.

She gasped and came up on her toes, bucking against his palm. She dropped to her heels, trembling.

He licked his lips. "Almost there." He brought his hand up from her butt to grab her hair at the base of her neck. His dampened fingers flicked against her clit.

A bolt of erotic lightning struck, and her body eagerly tightened. She lunged up on her toes in anticipation of a glorious fall... Her mouth opened in shocked delight, and a small cry escaped her throat.

"There." He pulled his hands from her.

She slid back from the brink and cried out, collapsing over his shoulder, panting and shuddering in acute disappointment.

His smile broadened. "You're ready to be taken." He lifted her from the floor, cradling her in his arms, and carried her from the lamp's light into the shadows.

Keiko's heart slammed in her chest, but she couldn't tell if it was from fear, or wicked eagerness.

Ryudo knelt on the broad futon and sat her on her knees in the center. His lips brushed hers. He sat back on his heels and pulled a red length of silk from within his sleeve. He stretched it between his hands, then leaned close.

Keiko started. "What...?" She reached up to touch the red silk.

"For your eyes." Ryudo brushed her hands away. "You are not yet ready to see."

"Why not?" She froze and fear washed cold down her spine. Was he monstrous after all?

"Do not be afraid." He pressed the cloth across her eyes. "I will bring you only pleasure. This I swear." He pulled her forward, against his chest and knotted the cloth behind her head.

She shivered in his embrace. He wasn't a man, he was a ghost, and he had her trapped in a room with no exit. She was completely at his mercy.

He caught her shoulders and pressed her back until she lay against the mattress. "Be at ease." He straddled her with his knees, and his hands closed around her wrists, pulling them above her head. "Only pleasure." His lips brushed hers in a gentle kiss, but he did not release her wrists.

A hot sultry breeze swept across her skin, carrying the scents of late summer. The sound of rain on the tiles was loud, and thunder rumbled far away.

He rose above her, with the sensation of hot shadowy flesh, as though his clothes had evaporated. His voice whispered from the darkness. "I will give you pleasure unlike anything a mortal man can give you." His mouth closed on her breast, and his tongue made wet circles around her tender nipple.

Carnal hunger quickened and clenched in her belly, a banked fire leaping to furious life. She arched and moaned.

Hot, moist breath whispered across her other nipple, and then a tongue, and yet his mouth still lapped at her other breast.

She gasped in confusion, even as arousal stormed through her, instigated by her deliciously tormented nipples.

Hands cupped her breasts, and yet his hands were still on her wrists. Fingers came from nowhere to caress her hips, even as other hands slid under and down, to cup her butt and squeeze.

She arched her back under a sea of gently stroking palms and exploring fingers. A moan escaped her throat.

A mouth opened on her belly and a tongue investigated her navel. Teeth gently scored her hips, her belly and her inner thighs, nibbling, then gently lapping the sting away.

Hands lifted her knees and parted her thighs. Hot breath washed against her intimate flesh, and then a tongue stroked her with wicked purpose. The tongue swirled across her folds, then flicked across her clit, delivering delicious bolts of brutally salacious delight. Yet still, tongues circled and flicked at both her nipples.

Her legs were lifted higher, and another hot, wet tongue circled the tight rose of her anus with forbidden intent.

She cried out, overwhelmed by the sensual assault of tongues, lips and gentle bites, writhing in voluptuous and voracious passion.

The tongue at her core slid into her, and lapped, then lengthened into a finger that stroked and flicked against something truly delightful.

She moaned and bucked against the hands that held her, striving for more of that riveting sensation.

The finger within her thickened, becoming rigid and deliciously knobby. It thrust inward deeply, striking that delicious spot.

She arched back with an impassioned cry.

"Yes, oh, yes," he whispered. "Give me your pleasure. Give me your rapture. Give me…everything."

The rigid length pulled back, and thrust, then again, and again…

She bucked against him, her body welcoming the delicious invasion. Sweat ran from her skin, and the musky scent of exertion, and lust, became a thick perfume permeated by the scent of chrysanthemums.

The mouths on her nipples clamped down in brutally tender bites that seared her with ferocious delight. Tongues lapped at her skin. Fingers and hands caressed her ass, her thighs, and squeezed her breasts for the mouths that plundered them.

Climax rushed upward and crested. She trembled hard, teetering, balancing on the razor's edge of the abyss, wanting the fall into pleasure, but afraid of what would happen once she did.

"Yes!" His summer hot breath caressed her lips. "Give it to me!"

Something small and damp, a tongue, lapped at her clit, delivering an unexpected spark.

Her breath stopped. Climax exploded, slamming her down into a pounding spiral of agonizing rapture that ripped screams from her throat.

His mouth covered her lips, stealing her cries, stealing her breath, filling her mouth, and possessing her.

He released her mouth from his devouring kiss. "Your essence is as potent as plum wine, and just as sweet." His many hands and lips traveled across her skin, delivering light caresses and soft kisses. "Oh, yes, a worthy keeper, and protector, of my heart."

Keiko trembled in his hold and gasped for breath. "I don't understand."

"You will." His lips brushed hers. "I want to love you again." Teeth bit down on her breasts in gentle enticing nips and nails scored her flesh, leaving trails of shivering delight. The shaft within her pulsed gently, in time with her heart. A tongue swept across her lips. "I have so much to give you."

She moaned. "How much more?"

"No more than your heart can bear." A mouth sucked hard on her nipple.

The bolts of pleasure wracked her with tiny shudders. "I can't take...I can't take much more."

"You can. You will. You were made to receive my love. You were made for me."

Restrained by invisible hands, twisting among limbs she couldn't see, mounted and taken while wreathed in wet tongues and wetter mouths. The pulsing shaft fucked her cunt, relentless and tireless, like the mouths that tasted her flesh. She writhed in a mindless abyss of physical sensation that shredded all thought but her body's joyous rapture.

And through it all, Ryudo's voice echoed in her mind with the searing heat of late summer, and the aroma of flowers. "Give me your passion. Feed me your ecstasy. Love me, Keiko. Love me...forever."

~*five*~

She awoke to the sound of rain, and opened her eyes to an opaque rice paper folding screen obscuring a broad window in a cedar-walled room. She shifted and found that a heavy silk kimono of deep scarlet covered her naked body. She groaned and sat up on the thick futon, clutching the heavy kimono to her breasts. She was still wearing her stockings and garter belt.

"Are you all right?"

She yelped and turned.

Ryudo was gone. Instead, seated on a pillow at the table, by the cherry tree banner on the opposite wall, was a very human young man, not much older than she. Dressed in dark pleated pants and a white dress shirt, his tie was loose and his cropped black hair just a little mussed, as though he'd scrubbed his hands through it. In the light of the oil lamp, his face was sculptured perfection, with a mouth made for sin.

"I'm…" She clutched the kimono tighter and looked for her clothes. "I'm okay."

He smiled. "Good. I didn't think he'd hurt you, but he doesn't always understand our limits."

"Hurt me?" Keiko turned to look at the beautiful youth. "Who?"

The young man folded his arms, looked firmly at the wall and scowled. "Ryudo."

Her mouth fell open. "You know about him?"

The young man rolled his eyes and smiled sourly. "I should. He's my house guardian. I'm Kentoku."

His house guardian? Then this was...*his* house? And she was an uninvited guest. "I'm terribly sorry...!" Clutching the robe to cover her nudity, Keiko lunged off the futon, and tripped on the robe's hem.

Kentoku launched off the pillow, hands out. "Are you all right?"

She backed away and bobbed a small bow. "I'm Keiko. I was part of the tour. Please excuse me, I didn't mean to stay..."

"Relax!" He held up his hands. "I know, Ryudo told me."

She stilled. "You can talk to him?"

Kentoku shrugged. "I'm the only one in the family that knows he's there."

Keiko shook her head. "My class, my instructors... They must have hunted all over the house for me!"

Kentoku hunched his shoulders and stared at the floor. "Uh, no, they didn't."

She jerked back a step. "But I was gone so long, they must have missed me...?"

Kentoku turned away. "Ryudo contacted me before...before anyone knew you were gone. He didn't want you missed." He turned to look at the silk hanging of the cherry tree. "I told your instructor that you weren't feeling well, and left in a taxi." He released a breath. "It was the only thing I could think of at the time."

Keiko's shoulders slumped. "Oh. Thank you." She frowned. Ryudo had told him that he had her? Her chin lifted. "Then you knew all along?"

Kentoku scowled at the floor. "I knew Ryudo had you in the house somewhere."

Keiko stepped back. "And you let him...do this?"

"I didn't *let* him!" He turned to face her, his hands fisted at his sides. "Before I said one word to your teachers, I tried to find you first. He locked all the doors on me, and moved the walls around." He turned away and hunched his shoulders. "I couldn't get to you. I couldn't...stop him."

Keiko looked away. He had tried to rescue her. "Oh..." She closed her eyes. "I'm...sorry."

Kentoku sighed. "*I'm* sorry. He's *my* house guardian, but he's really powerful, and no one knows he's there. No one knows these apartments even exist but me." He turned away and scowled. "No one wants to know."

Keiko rolled her eyes and sighed. "No matter how often you tell them, they won't believe, because they don't want to believe."

"Exactly." He looked up and smiled.

Keiko smiled in return. It was so amazingly wonderful to meet someone else who knew, and understood.

Abruptly, he averted his gaze. "Oh, yes, and I'm to…" He swallowed. "Arrange for your accommodations."

"Arrange for my, what?" She shook her head. "I don't understand."

Kentoku turned to the side, shoved his hands in his pockets and studied his stocking toes. "As Ryudo's formal consort, you're entitled to living quarters—"

She gasped. "As his *what…*?" She put up one finger, and shook her head. "Oh, no, I am no one's mistress!"

Kentoku frowned at her. "But I thought you just, uh…" He swallowed and blushed furiously. "I meant, that he…and you…you both, just finished…" He threw out his hands helplessly and gestured vaguely toward the futon in the corner.

She scowled. "Had sex?"

He winced. "Yeah, that."

"We did." Her hands fisted in the scarlet silk she held. "But that doesn't make me his mistress."

Kentoku lifted a hand and scrubbed at the back of his cropped hair, wincing in obvious confusion. "But he said you…?"

Keiko stomped her foot and turned her back. "I don't care what he *said.* I'm not!" She looked up at the dark ceiling and released her breath. She was being rude to someone who did not deserve it.

Kentoku gasped. "Your back…"

Keiko flinched. Her scars. She was holding her robe in front of her, and he could see her entire naked back side.

"What happened to you?"

Keiko slowly turned back around and kept her gaze down. "Ghosts. That's what they do to me, when they catch me."

"Ryudo didn't...?"

"No. He didn't, but others have."

"My God. I'm...sorry."

She peeked at his expression. He didn't look disgusted, only concerned. She took a deep breath. Better not to think about it. "I'd like to go home now. Do you know where my clothes are?"

He smiled suddenly, and brilliantly. "Sure. I'll even give you a ride home." He strode for the gleaming table.

Keiko tilted her head and her brows lifted. "You're going to let me leave?"

Kentoku picked up a neatly folded bundle from the pillow under the table. "Are you kidding? I've been beating my skull trying to find a way to explain you to my father." He walked over to her and presented her clothes. He rolled his eyes. "Father does not believe in ghosts."

Keiko took her clothes and smiled wryly. "So a ghost's mistress...?"

Kentoku snorted. "Oh, yeah, that would go over real well." He carefully turned his back to her. "Though Ryudo is going to go ballistic when he finds out I let you leave."

Keiko padded over to the futon and set the kimono down. So what if he looked? He'd already seen the worst, her back. "What will he do?" She pulled out her bra, but didn't see her panties.

"Who? Ryudo? He'll knock things over, and torment me in the night..."

Keiko winced and shrugged into her blouse. "I'm...sorry."

Kentoku sighed. "It's okay. Ryudo is much easier to deal with than Father. All I have to do is spend a few nights at a friend's house until his temper cools. He can't follow me out the house, or disown me." He jingled the change in his pockets. "Though I suspect that this tantrum is going to be a whopper." He scraped his heel on the wood floor. "He says he can...feel you, like a real person. That's why he can actually, um...be with you."

Keiko rolled her eyes while tucking her blouse into her skirt. "You mean, have sex?"

Kentoku shrugged. "Yeah."

Keiko knotted her tie around her collar. "So, we had sex. People do it all the time." Okay, so with Ryudo, it was really weird sex. "Don't you have a girlfriend?"

He scowled. "Of course, it's just that we don't...do that."

"Why not?" She shrugged into her jacket and folded the scarlet robe neatly on the bed.

Kentoku winced. "I'm supposed to wait 'til we're married."

Keiko froze. He was a virgin? The giggle just slipped out.

Kentoku turned and glared at her. "It's not funny!"

Keiko shoved her hands behind her, and bit down on her lip. "Oh, no, of course not." She took a deep calming breath, but the smile crept onto her face.

Kentoku rolled his eyes. "Come on, I'll take you home." He walked to the left wall and slid open a door.

Keiko frowned. That door hadn't been there until he opened it.

On stocking feet, she followed the young master of the house through a number of narrow halls.

He tugged open a door and signaled her to wait. He dashed out. In only a few minutes, he dashed back and held up a pair of plain black loafers and a bright blue, hooded rain slicker. "These yours?"

Keiko nodded and took them gratefully.

He closed the door, and led her into another set of even smaller hallways. He turned and whispered. "Servant's access halls." His quick stride led her through sudden turns and sharp cornered halls. They stopped at a door that led into a garage. Sitting on the garage steps, they slipped on their shoes. He hurried past several expensive cars parked in a neat row on the left and stopped at a silver Subaru parked right by the wide door.

Ensconced in the passenger side, and pulling out onto the rain,

Keiko suddenly realized that her house slippers were somewhere in Ryudo's room. She scowled. He was welcome to them.

The ride through the city was rainy and quiet, but for the sound of windshield wipers.

Keiko looked down at her hands. "Kentoku, I'm sorry you had to…find me, like that."

Kentoku slumped in his seat. "I just wish I could have gotten to you before…anything happened."

"Does he do this regularly?"

"No." Kentoku's hands tightened on the steering wheel. "There are a few stories about his…mistresses, but I just thought they were stories. Supposedly, the last woman he had was, oh…back during the last Imperial war. The story goes that she broke into the house, so he kept her."

The *last* mistress was during the last Imperial war? Keiko frowned. "How old is he?"

Kentoku pursed his lips. "I'm not sure, Ryudo won't say, but the house records say that he's been there since the house was built during the early feudal era."

That meant Ryudo was…*hundreds* of years old? Keiko's mouth fell open. "If he's that old, why is he wearing a late imperial uniform?"

Kentoku shrugged. "He does that. It's in the records that he modernizes his appearance every century or so."

Keiko frowned at the passing traffic. It sounded like Ryudo modernized his appearance with every new… She swallowed. Mistress.

Kentoku frowned up at a traffic light. "Look, I'm sorry for Ryudo's behavior. He's not normally like that."

Keiko smiled sourly. "But according to your house records, he *is* like that."

Kentoku winced. "Seriously, I thought it was just a pack of stories. I've never seen him do that before, lock someone in the house and try to keep them." He smiled. "Though I can see why he would want to keep you."

Was that a compliment? Keiko firmly decided that she didn't want to know.

He looked over at her. "This sounds really awful, but if you want to stay free, don't come back."

Keiko's brows lifted. "You got me out that time…"

Kentoku shook his head. "Only because he didn't know I was going to help you leave. He's not like a normal ghost. I've seen him make illusions that you can't walk through." He glanced at her. "If he had been paying attention, I would not have been able to get you out because the door would not have been there."

"And you live like this, all the time?"

"You get used to it after a while. He moves walls and doors around, and throws random objects, but he can't actually touch me. " He sucked on his bottom lip. "Not the way he can physically touch you."

Keiko stared out her window.

"I've heard about people like you." Kentoku looked at her briefly. "It's said that the reason ghosts can touch you is because you bridge this world and the next."

That was news. Keiko turned to face him. "Is that it? Really?"

"I did some reading on this." Kentoku nodded. "It's like you're halfway in both worlds, at the same time." He frowned. "It also means that you don't have the basic defense against the dead that most people have." He held up his palm. "Life itself."

Keiko frowned. "But I'm alive…"

Kentoku shook his head. "Physically you are, but spiritually you aren't. That's why they can touch you." He winced. "And hurt you. From what I understand, the only defense against the dead is something really and truly alive." He looked at her. "If I were you, I'd take a martial arts class and find something you can use as a weapon against them."

She shook her head. "I can see the martial arts class, but a living weapon?" She frowned. "Wait, a *bo*, a quarterstaff, is made of wood..."

"That's right!" Kentoku sat up straight. "A rattan staff that's still green ought to work."

"And no one will think twice if I carry a bo around. I can just say I'm taking it to class!" Keiko smiled. "Thank you, Kentoku, that's brilliant!"

Kentoku blushed. "Please, my friends call me Toku." He stopped the car in front of her apartment building. "Well, here you are." He turned to look at her. "Look, I'm sorry about...Ryudo."

Keiko opened her door. "It's all right, really." She turned and smiled at him. "Because of him, I met you and you gave me the secret to protecting myself. As far as I'm concerned, it was well worth it."

Toku turned to catch her eye. "Keiko, I wish..." He swallowed hard. "I wish I'd met you first."

Keiko froze. She lunged across the seat and pressed a quick kiss to his cheek. "Goodbye." She slipped out of the car and closed the door.

Toku waved and pulled away.

Keiko watched his car disappear into traffic. Martial arts classes and a *living* weapon... Could it be so simple? She turned and walked into her building. Her jaw clenched. She would not be victimized by a ghost again. Not even a loving one.

Book Two

~Cherry Blossoms & Shadows~

~ Six ~

Six Months Later

Shido stood directly across the sparring mat from Keiko, and curled his lip. "Must you use a *bo* that's still green?" His heavy canvas karate *gi* was blindingly white. Both the cross-folded top and the loose pants were neatly pressed with strong creases. The perfectly knotted chocolate-brown belt, sporting the two white stripes of his rank, had been ironed, too. He held his six-foot dark teak staff carelessly upright. It gleamed with polish.

Keiko tightened her hands on her cloth-reinforced, five-foot long, dark green, rattan staff. It was as thick as her wrist, and sported two small slender leaves sprouting from the joint, about a hand-span from the very end. She held it upright in the proper position, by her right shoulder—right hand up, fingers inward, left hand down, and across her middle. Her feet were spaced shoulder-width apart, and her knees slightly bent. "I have my reasons."

Her *gi* was second hand, not quite so bright a white, and the creases came from folding, not an iron. The cut was about ten years out of date, too, but the fabric was as soft as a kiss. Her slightly worn belt was as green as her staff.

Shido rolled his eyes. "But the thing still has leaves!" His lips curved into a blatant sneer. "What? Did you cut it right before class?"

Snickering escaped from some of the other students in the karate dojo.

Keiko smiled only slightly. Rattan lived longer if you left a leaf or two on them, and yes, she had cut it right before class. Her last *bo* had finally died at a ripe old age of four weeks. Their opinions on her choice of weapons didn't matter. To them, the class was entertainment, a sport. To her, the lessons meant the difference between life and death.

"I can see why you have it wrapped." He moved his stance very slightly, and lifted his *bo* into a more aggressive position. "That thing must wobble like it's made out of rubber."

Keiko was too busy watching the slight shift in Shido's footing and the tension showing in his shoulders to bother with his words. He was preparing for an attack. The senior student was a full foot taller than she, and much broader in the shoulders. He had the advantage in experience, strength and reach. Her only advantage was speed, close observation and knowledge of how her weapon actually worked.

"Shido." The instructor's voice was soft, but commanding.

Shido froze, and his gaze flicked to the left. His mouth closed tight. He bobbed his head toward the instructor in a small bow of respect. One absolutely, positively, did not question the Shihan—not in this class. Shihan firmly believed in rigorous physical discipline.

Shihan nodded, acknowledging the bow of apology. "Begin!"

Shido launched a slashing attack toward Keiko, swinging his staff overhand.

Keiko caught his attack on her staff, turning it just enough to clear her shoulder, then closed in. Twirling the end of her staff around his, she used the flexible greenness of her staff to smack his hand while she was at it.

He hissed, but he didn't let go. His jaw tightened, and his eyes narrowed, clearly annoyed rather than hurt.

She pressed the advantage by flipping her *bo*, end over end, into an overhand strike.

He threw up an overhead block, but didn't lift his staff near high enough, and kept it too far forward. Her green staff rapped hard against his rigid *bo*, and flexed over it, rapping him smartly on the skull.

He gasped.

She repeated her overhand attack.

He repeated his block.

Her *bo* rapped against his staff, then flexed right past his over head block, to rap him in the skull yet again.

He howled in fury and swung, viciously fast, left to right.

She ducked down and under his swing, replying with a sideways swing of her own—that caught him cleanly in the ribs, right above his kidneys, and bent around him. She used the strength of the staff's recoil to propel her to the side.

His overhead downward spear-thrust missed, slamming into the mat. He swung at her, hand over hand, then back and forth, hard and fast.

She blocked and replied, her *bo* flexing right past his shallow side blocks to whack him in the ribs time and again. She could not believe that he was not adjusting his technique to take the flexibility of her staff into account by extending his blocks further from his body. It was as though he refused to admit that her *bo* wasn't like his.

The students shouted in astonishment, then laughed uproariously.

Completely focused on Shido's furious attacks, she barely heard them. The scent of the sandalwood incense, burning on the *kamidana* to the spirit of war, Hachiman hanging on the wall at the front of the dojo, was barely detectable.

"Halt!" Shihan's voice cut through the shouting.

In the middle of her swing, Keiko pulled back hard, stopping her springy staff from striking Shido's head, but only barely.

Shido froze, and glared at her.

They both set their staffs at their shoulders, backed away to the ends of the sparring mat, and then bowed respectfully toward each other.

Shido's jaw was tight and his eyes narrowed. He was clearly less than satisfied with the results of their bout.

Shihan called on another pair of students to take the mat.

Alone in the white-walled and spare changing room, Keiko pulled off her chilly, sweat-soaked *gi* top and dropped it on the bench against the wall. Groaning, she peeled off the equally soaked, sleeveless white muscle-shirt she wore beneath it. Her tight exercise bra was soaked too. She skimmed out of her white *gi* pants and panties, turned to her plain green gym bag and set out her street clothes. Damp, sticky and naked, she shivered. She was dying to get under the hot water just to warm up from waiting in her damp *gi*.

There was only one dressing room in the dojo, and she was the only female, so she was forced to wait until all the other students were finished. Senior students had priority and Shido out-ranked her, so she was forced to wait until he and all the other male students finished with the showers. This time, they had taken extra long in the dressing room, and she knew damned well it had been deliberate.

A chill shivered across her limbs, making her teeth chatter. "Pains in my freaking butt…" She reached up and pulled her clip from her hair, freeing her long black braid to tumble down her back. Her entire back and both arms protested the movement. She groaned.

This last session had been particularly grueling. Shihan had turned over the class to his two highest ranking students, and spent most of the two-hour class drilling her. He'd had her go through each and every exercise and *kata* form she'd learned over the past six months, checking her positioning and stance with hard swift smacks to the offending limb. She released a long, tired breath. The shower would warm her and rinse off the sweat, but she was going to need a long soak in her tub at home to ease her muscles, not to mention her bruises.

The test of her skills had gone well, all things considered, but she hated the fact that he'd done her testing right in front of the others again. The other students didn't understand Shihan's focus on her, and it was obviously grating on their nerves. They didn't know that Shihan had made her fight-training a personal mission. She was in class six days a week, compared to their three; and she had no intention of telling them. They were making enough problems for her.

Naked and sweaty, she pulled out her towel and carried it over to the tiny shower stall. Shido in particular was becoming a problem. She was gaining in rank far too fast for his personal comfort. What a crying shame, too. She entered the tiny shower stall and twisted the knob, setting the water to hot. Shido was incredibly cute, and had been so nice in the beginning. For a while there she had thought he might even be interested in her. Not anymore. She sighed and shoved her head under the hot water. *Bliss...*

The shower door opened.

Keiko gasped, dashed the water from her eyes and looked over her shoulder.

Shido stood in the shower stall's doorway, dressed in a black muscle shirt and tight black jeans. His mouth was slack, and his eyes wide, his gaze fixed on her naked back. "Holy shit..."

Keiko clenched her jaw. He was looking at her scars. "Did you come here to stare?"

Shido looked up to meet her gaze, and his eyes narrowed. "I could care less what your back looks like; I want to know why you're working so hard to make me look bad in front of the class."

Keiko glanced away. "I'm not trying to make you look bad..."

Shido's lip curled. "Oh, really? Using a rubbery green rattan staff against my teakwood *bo*? It sure looked like it to me. And while we're at it, why is Shihan so concerned with *your* training? He barely notices the rest of us anymore; he's always focused on you. What makes you so damned special?"

Keiko winced. She'd been afraid of something like this. "Shido, I..."

Shido leaned into the shower. "I just want to know, are you sucking Shihan's dick after class?"

Keiko's hands fisted at her side. "Get out."

He smiled coldly. "Because if you're in the mood to suck dick, I'll teach you anything you want to know..."

"I said, get out!" She lashed out in a side kick and slammed the heel of her foot into his chest.

He went flying back, and slammed into the wall. The plaster crunched behind him, leaving a dent in the wall. He slid to the floor and sprawled, choking, the wind knocked out of him.

Keiko blinked in surprise. *Damn...* She hadn't realized that she was going to kick him until her foot was already planted in his chest.

Shido sucked in a deep breath and scowled. "What's the matter, my company not good enough for you?"

Keiko's temper chilled to ice. She stepped out of the shower, the water spilling down her body. She eased back into a fighting stance, too coldly furious to consider that she was naked. "Get out, now." She could barely get the words past her clenched teeth.

"Fine, I'm leaving." Shido rose slowly to his feet, wiping his hand across his mouth. His jaw clenched. "But this isn't over."

Keiko kept her mouth shut, and didn't relax her fighting stance until the door to the changing room closed behind him. Her breath exploded out of her. "Bastard!" She stomped back into the bathroom to finish her shower.

Keiko stepped out of the shower, still fuming mad. She toweled off, then braided her wet hair with quiet ferocity. She couldn't believe Shido had walked in on her like that. *What a pervert!*

She tugged on fresh underwear, then stepped into her faded jeans, moaning with her body's discomfort. She must have strained every muscle in her legs when she kicked Shido across the bathroom. It had been one hell of a kick. She tucked in her plain white T-shirt, and frowned. Her body had reacted without conscious thought. She hadn't realized she was going to kick him until her foot was already out. It had happened that fast.

She sighed and tugged on her gray, zip-up hooded, sweat jacket. Justifiable cause or not, Shido was not going to let her get away with it. His pride wouldn't allow for it. She winced and shrugged into her sleeveless denim jacket. If she was lucky she'd merely go home with a few new bruises after their next sparring match, but she wouldn't put it past him to wait for her in the dojo parking lot. She shook her head. How had everything gotten so complicated?

Relatively presentable, Keiko left the dressing room, carrying her green *bo* in its cloth case over her left shoulder, along with her green gym bag.

Standing in the doorway to the deserted dojo, Keiko faced Hachiman's tiny house-shaped *kamidana* hanging on the front wall and bowed respectfully. Late afternoon sunlight spilled from the row of windows that lined the whole left wall, marching from Shihan's office door all the way down to the student's entrance on the back wall. Just beyond the window glass, the cherry trees were scattering pale pink petals in the spring wind.

She padded around the edges of the glossy oak floor toward Shihan's office in the front left corner of the dojo. She needed to pay her respects before leaving. Her plain white socks made no sound on the floor.

Shihan's door was open.

The older man was still in his black instructor's robes, seated facing the door at his plain wooden desk. His office was barely large enough to contain it. His mouth turned down in concentration, he wrote in a ledger book with a swift hand. Behind him, on the dark cream wall, hung a long plaque with red tassels, stating the school's full lineage of instructors. Completely windowless, a small desk lamp cast the only light.

Keiko set her bag and her encased staff by the window just outside his door, and knocked on the doorframe.

Shihan concluded his writing, and closed his book. He opened a desk drawer, pulled out a rather worn earth brown cloth belt and set it on the desk. He smiled. "Please, join me, Keiko."

Keiko bowed, and entered. There was no place to sit, so she stood before his desk with her hands at her sides.

"You have been studying very hard." He turned to the left where a tiny table held his brown glazed earthenware teapot perched on a small hot plate. He picked up the teapot and poured fragrant and steaming jasmine tea into two small brown cups that sat on his desk.

She stared down at his desk. "I want to thank you for teaching me." She looked up at him. "For believing me."

"You are welcome." He nodded and held out a teacup in both hands. "Have you been approached by...spirits, since your training began?"

Keiko took the warm cup and held it in her palms. "Not yet, Shihan."

"This is a good thing, yes?" His gaze flicked briefly to hers.

Keiko smiled tightly. "I'd like to think so, Shihan."

"Ah, good." Shihan lifted his cup and sipped.

Keiko raised her cup and sipped. The jasmine tea was tart and fragrant on the tongue. For several long moments there was only the sound of tea being sipped in comfortable silence.

Shihan set his empty cup down. "I believed you because I have a friend, a holy man, who knows of others like yourself." He folded his hands on the desk.

Keiko's hands tightened on her cup. "Others?"

Shihan nodded and smiled. "He is in town, and has expressed a desire to meet you." He sighed and looked away. "I believe he can help you, as I can not."

Keiko froze. He wasn't sending her away, was he? "Shihan, you've helped! You've helped me more than anyone...!"

Shihan held up his hand.

Keiko stopped cold.

"I can only teach you to defend your body." Shihan folded his hands on his desk. "My friend is a monk from the Temple of the Black Lotus, an Avatar. He can teach you to defend your soul." He held her gaze with his old black eyes. "His companion is a bound spirit."

A bound *spirit?* Keiko felt a chill that resonated at the back of her skull. She squashed it hard. She knew how to defend herself from ghosts. She would not give in to fear. "If you feel that he can help, I will meet with...your friend, Shihan."

"Excellent! Avatar Tsuke and his companion, Ryujin, are most anxious to speak with you." Shihan lifted the brown belt with both hands, and stood. "I truly believe that they can guide to your purpose, and destiny."

Purpose and destiny? That sounded forbidding. Keiko bowed deeply. "Honored teacher, please don't ask me to leave class."

Shihan laughed, the sound of a soft wind among leaves. "You gain a rank, and think you have mastered it all? Your classes will not end any time soon, Keiko." He held out the belt. "Now, take this, and please, return my green belt."

"Oh, of course." She took the folded belt in both her hands, as though accepting a sheathed sword, and bowed. "Thank you, Shihan, for everything." She grinned, and ducked out the door with her new rank in hand.

Shido slouched against the back wall, by the student's door with his arms folded across his chest. His black and red leather racing jacket accentuated his broad shoulders, and his snug black jeans outlined the strong musculature of his thighs.

Keiko froze. *Shit.* He was waiting for her?

Shido's gaze dropped to what she held, and his mouth turned down in a scowl.

Keiko's hand tightened on her brown belt. First she'd kicked him in the chest, then this, a kick to his ego. Well, he would have found out anyway, when he came to class. She turned away, and crouched to put the belt in her bag. He'd deserved the kick in the bathroom and she'd earned her new rank. If he couldn't deal with it, then that was his problem, not hers. She pulled out the folded green belt and looked back toward the student door. Shido was gone. Hopefully he'd stay gone. She turned to walk back into Shihan's office.

Keiko held the green belt out to Shihan. "Thank you for the loan of your belt, Shihan." And the old uniforms, and the extra classes.

Shihan took the belt from her hands, and sighed. "If only my other students had your devotion to training."

"Your other students don't have my…problems to deal with, sir." Keiko winced. Truthful or not, implying that the other students didn't have a reason to study hard wasn't the most politic of things to say about her fellow students.

Shihan smiled sourly and raised his brow. "They may not have spirits actively hunting them, but those that do not wish to be surpassed should study harder, not seek to dissuade the dedicated student."

Keiko blinked. So, Shihan *was* aware of her growing problem with Shido. "And what should the dedicated student do about the…" Merciful Lady, how did one put this? She tilted her head. "Problems caused by the…less than studious?"

Shihan snorted. "Refuse to be dissuaded by another's need for a superiority they do not deserve."

Keiko blinked. Oh, so, if Shido tried to beat her up after class, out of petty jealousy, she should just…beat him up instead. She sighed. *Terrific.* Just when you think you've made it out of the playground…

Shihan picked up a sheet of folded paper and scanned the contents. "I have arranged for you to meet Avatar Tsuke and his companion tomorrow."

Keiko stiffened. *Tomorrow?* So quickly?

Shihan set the paper down and smiled at her. "Come to the dojo at sunset, and I will drive you. They are staying at the Crimson Pavilion guesthouse, so dress for a walk through the park."

They were leaving at sunset? That meant she was going to deal with this Avatar, and his companion spirit, at night. The absolute worst time to deal with ghosts. Under any other circumstances, she would have found an excuse to avoid the meeting, but with Shihan having made the arrangements, there was no way out of it, not without shaming her instructor.

Keiko bowed. "I will be here, Shihan."

~ Seven ~

Keiko stepped out of the student's entrance of the dojo. Wincing in the late afternoon sunlight, she scanned the city street just beyond the parking lot's chain link fence. Neither Shido, nor his bright yellow and blue Kawasaki motorcycle, were anywhere in sight.

Good. No playground fights today.

She clomped down the wooden steps, turned to the left and strode along the white-washed cinderblock wall to the bicycle hitch bolted to it. Her silver ten-speed was the only bicycle left. She crouched and unlocked her bike, wrapping the chain around the frame. She was going to face a ghost tomorrow night, for the first time since…the incident in the mansion.

She froze. *Tomorrow* night—when Tika was having her party.

Keiko threw up her head and groaned. Tika was going to kill her. She fished her cell phone from her green gym bag, then stood up to punch in the phone number.

Tika answered on the first ring. "You got me, so talk!"

"Hey, it's Keiko."

"Oh, hi, Keiko, I just came back from shopping!" She promptly launched into a cheerful dissertation on the outfits she'd purchased, and how cute they were.

Keiko sighed heavily and leaned back against the wall of the school to wait for Tika to take a breath, so she could get a word in edgewise. She watched a swirl of pale pink cherry petals whisk across the parking lot.

Tika took a breath.

Keiko lunged into the gap. "Look, something important came up. I won't be able to make it to your party tomorrow night."

There was a hideous shriek.

Keiko yanked the phone away from her ear, wincing.

"What do you mean, you can't make it to my party?" Tika's voice suddenly switched to dramatic sniveling. "But I wanted you to meet my new boyfriend!"

"Look, I'm sorry, it wasn't my idea! Shihan sprang it on me all of a sudden." She hated disappointing her friend, but truthfully, she'd been hunting for a good excuse to skip the party. Tika's parties were too loud, too crowded and too full of young men that were too full of themselves.

"So this is a karate thing?"

Keiko bit her lip, and folded one arm across her chest. "Yes, and no, he wants me to meet a friend of his from out of town."

"Is it a cute friend?"

Keiko rolled her eyes. "Shihan is in his sixties. I seriously doubt his friend is any younger."

"Oh… Well, damn. Keiko, what am I going to do about you?"

Huh? Keiko's brows shot up. "Me?"

"Every time I think you're doing something that might get you a boyfriend, you blow it! I mean, you're cute enough, and you do attract the guys, but, then…nothing!"

Keiko shook her head in bewilderment. "What?" Merciful Lady, what was she talking about?

"I've tried everything! Everything I could think of! And still nothing. I've even tried giving you a couple of my exes, and my exes are always cute, but you didn't want them!"

Oh… Tika was in matchmaking mode again. Keiko closed her eyes and prayed for strength.

"You need a boyfriend! What are you doing for sex? Masturbating?"

Ah-ha! A question! "Yes, Tika, that's exactly what I'm doing." Actually, that's all she was doing. If only she could stop thinking of...a certain ghost, while she was doing it.

"You had a boyfriend, what happened to him?"

Keiko cringed. "Nothing." That was the absolute truth. He'd had a good time, every time, but she'd gotten nothing out of it, every time. "We broke up."

"Why? What's wrong with you?"

Keiko groaned. "I wish I knew!" After her...incident with Ryudo, sex had become unsatisfactory. No matter what she did, she couldn't seem to get to orgasm. She could do it just fine by herself, but when she was with another, something was always...missing. She sighed. "Look, Tika, I'm really sorry I'm going to miss your party..."

"Could you at least pop in before you go? Just for a few minutes?"

"I can't. Shihan is driving me out there to meet him. We're leaving the dojo at sunset."

"Oh, no!" Tika wailed dramatically, underscored by the sounds of paper ripping somewhere in the background. "I was so looking forward to the look on your face when you met my new boyfriend!"

Keiko rolled her eyes. "Why, is he a movie star?"

Tika's overblown pout suddenly stopped. "No...but it *is* someone you know!" She giggled.

An image of Kentoku suddenly came to mind, and it hurt, for no apparent reason what so ever. Keiko winced. If Tika was dating Toku, she was doubly glad she wasn't going to the party.

"I suppose, since you're not going to be there, I might as well tell you who it is."

Keiko cringed. If it was Toku, she *didn't* want to know. "You don't have to tell me, if you don't want to..."

"It's Shido."

Keiko's thoughts stilled. It wasn't Toku. The relief was so profound, her knees wobbled and she fell back against the wall. She smiled. "Oh, that's nice." Then the name sank in. "Wait, did you say Shido?"

"Yeah, tall, built, and in your karate class. Really, Keiko, how could you let such a gorgeous hunk of man go unmolested?"

Keiko jerked upright against the wall. "Uh, Tika, does he know I'm your friend, and that I'm supposed to be at your party?"

"Ahem, your *best* friend!"

Keiko rolled her eyes. "Yes, of course, my best friend." Her only friend, since grade school.

"Of course! I told him I was going to make sure you came when I started planning this party last week."

Keiko turned around and pressed her brow against the wall. "That's right. You told me you started dating this new guy a week ago." Which translated to: Shido had been plotting to corner her at the party for the past week. *The sneaky bastard!* She turned back over, and faced the parking lot, profoundly glad she was not going.

"Your teacher spoiled my surprise!" Tika groaned dramatically. "That's so unfair!"

Keiko made a mental note to be sure to put some incense out in the garden shrine to thank *Kannon Bosatsu*, the goddess of mercy, for spoiling Tika's—and no doubt, Shido's—surprise. She released a long breath. "You can tell me all about your party when I get back." As if she could avoid the graphic details. "In the meantime, could you do me a huge favor?"

"Sure, what?"

"Don't tell Shido *why* I can't go to your party." He didn't need to know that she was spending personal time with Shihan—when he wasn't.

"Huh? Why not?"

"He's already mad at me, for other stuff, I don't want to make it worse." What he didn't know wouldn't kick him in the pride—again.

"Oops."

Keiko's hands chilled. "Oops?"

"Keiko, he's, um, sitting right here. Shido? Where are you going?"

Oh, shit! She gasped. "Oh, ah, got to go! Bye!" She punched disconnect, and then the 'off' button on the phone. She groaned.

Could this get any worse?

Yes, it could. She had to get out of there, and fast.

Keiko shoved her sunglasses over her eyes, jammed her bicycle helmet on her head and threw herself onto her bike.

Pedaling hard alongside the late afternoon city traffic, she sped down the street on her ten-speed, her braid flying out behind her. Painfully alert, she dodged buses, trucks, and cars, none of whom paid all that much attention to traffic signals.

Traffic came to a standstill behind two massive double-decker busses loading commuter passengers. The loud howling roar of a motorcycle gunning its engine cut though the sounds of annoyed motorists.

Keiko looked across traffic to see a frighteningly familiar blue and yellow Kawasaki crawling between the cars, going the other way—toward the dojo. Though the rider wore a full-face helmet, she knew that red and black leather jacket anywhere. It was clearly Shido.

Oh, shit! He *was* coming to get her! Keiko ducked down to get out of sight, then squeezed into the narrow space between some halted trucks and the sidewalk. She had to get off the road, and stay off the road. Even if Shido went all the way to the dojo and came back, there was no way in hell she could outdistance him on a bicycle. She would have to cut through the park.

She hated the park. Things dwelled there, in dark corners. She still had nightmares about the playground.

Slipping past the trucks, she took a sharp left at the four-way intersection, moving between the stopped traffic. She crossed the street, dodging the cars that were moving, and bumped up onto the sidewalk. She zipped past a couple of pedestrians, their long raincoats flapping open over their business suits, and took a hard right, into the Center City park.

Pedaling for all she was worth, Keiko sped down the paved walk that meandered between the blooming trees. Sun-yellow daffodils and scarlet tulips lined the path's edge. Pink cherry petals and white plum petals floated on the light breeze, under a sky of crystalline blue. The larger trees were already showing the pale green of new leaves.

A pair of joggers lunged out of the trees on her left—and directly into her path.

Keiko slammed on her brakes and pulled up hard, skidding on her back tire. With the scent of burning rubber in her nose, she came to a complete halt within hand's reach of the joggers.

The joggers stared at her, wide-eyed, and frozen. They smiled, just a little, then jogged off at a slightly quicker pace.

Keiko slumped over her handlebars and panted. She needed to slow down before she hit someone. She was acting like a maniac, letting her fear drive her actions. She reached over her shoulder to touch her green staff, and took a deep, calming breath. She could handle anything that came her way. She would be okay. She rolled forward and proceeded to pedal down the walk at a far saner pace.

Keiko eased around a grove of flowering plum trees and saw a man and a woman standing under a massive cherry tree encircled by ironwork park benches. Dressed in long dark coats over darker business attire, they faced each other, but their heads were down, and their hands behind them. The wind had shifted, and the tree's petals fell away from them.

Keiko stopped, dismounted and pushed her bike off the walk, to go around them through the trees. What ever was happening was private. She did not want to embarrass them by walking into the middle of it. She eased through the trees and their voices reached her.

"You could have told me that you didn't want to wait." The woman turned her face away and folded her arms. "I would have…allowed it."

"You would have *allowed* it." The young man chuckled without humor. "You would have given me your virginity if I asked for it, after hoarding it all this time?"

Keiko froze behind a tree. That voice… It sounded like Toku. She peeked out to look.

The woman turned away. "I would have had to, eventually."

"You would have *had* to." He turned his face away from his companion, and toward Keiko.

Keiko sucked in a sharp breath. It *was* Toku. There was no mistaking his features. What was going on?

The woman took a step toward him, with her hands balled into fists. "I'm not some little tramp you play with whenever you get the itch!"

"No, you're a business woman angling for a prime position in my father's company, soon to be my company. Marriage is just good business to you, isn't it?"

She leaned back on her heels. "Is there something wrong with a marriage that benefits the company?"

Toku shook his head. "You just don't get it, do you?"

"I get that you had that woman up against a wall, and you were fucking her, Kentoku! You saw me, and you didn't even stop—in fact, you smiled at me!" She threw up her hands. "You smiled and *kept* fucking her!"

Keiko reeled back in shock. Kentoku had sex? In public?

Toku jammed his hands into his pockets. "It wasn't something I planned. It just… happened."

"It just happened." She shook her head. "It just happened, while I just happened to be in the next room? And then, when I found you, it just kept happening?" She lifted her chin. "Right."

Toku looked away from her, his mouth tight. "I don't know what else to tell you."

The woman stepped closer, trembling. "You can tell me why you didn't come to me first."

Toku crossed his arms, and turned to face her, lifting his chin. "Would you have let me lift your skirt and fuck you against the wall?"

She jerked back. "No! Of course not!"

Toku smiled sourly. "There's your answer."

The woman threw up her hands. "Damn it, Toku! Why use a wall when you could have simply used a bed? I wouldn't have minded a bed!"

His smile evaporated and his shoulders dropped. "I told you, it wasn't planned. It was very sudden."

The woman turned away to stare toward the trees across the walkway. "So, all of a sudden you just had to have sex, for no apparent reason?"

He looked away from her, toward the massive cherry tree they stood under. "Yes."

The woman stepped back. "Well, then, this can be sudden, too." She tugged at her hand and threw something to the ground. "Personally, I'm glad I found out what kind of man you really were, before I did something…regrettable." She turned on her expensive heels, and marched off.

Keiko's brows lifted. What the hell…?

Toku collapsed on the bench under the tree. "Fuck!" His shout echoed loud and strong. He rocked forward, setting his elbows on his knees, and scrubbed his hands through his slightly overlong hair. "Son of a fucking bitch."

Keiko inched toward Toku's bench, her ten-speed ticking softly at her side. "Are you okay?"

"Shit!" Toku jumped as though scalded. He grabbed the back of the bench and turned sharply to look at her. "Who…?" His eyes opened wide. "Keiko?"

"Hi." Keiko pulled off her bicycling helmet and gave him a slight smile. "A little jumpy?"

Toku slumped on the bench, letting his head roll back. "I have had the shittiest past six months you could imagine."

Keiko winced. "I'm afraid to ask."

Toku groaned. "That damned ghost has succeeded in making my life holy living hell, in every way possible."

"What's going on?" Keiko stepped forward, and her toe landed on something. She looked down, and saw a gold ring. It must have been what that woman threw. She reached down to pick it up. It was an engagement ring set with a good-sized diamond. The woman must have been Toku's fiancé. She looked up.

Toku was watching her.

She held the ring out to him. "On second thought, I'm not sure I want to know."

He took the ring from her palm, and pocketed it. "She caught me...fucking someone."

Keiko winced.

He looked over at her. "It wasn't me. It was Ryudo."

Keiko's eyes widened. "Ryudo?" She shook her head. But Ryudo wasn't physical enough to fuck anybody. She bit down on her lip. Except her. "Was it an illusion?"

"No. It wasn't an illusion." He patted the bench. "Have a seat."

Keiko leaned the bike against the far end of the bench's armrest and perched on the edge of the seat. "So, what really happened?"

He shook his head. "Okay, so it *was* me, but I wasn't in control at the time."

Keiko frowned. "That doesn't make sense."

Toku crossed his arms and looked away. "Ryudo...possessed my body."

~ Eight ~

"Ryudo possessed you?" Keiko sucked in a breath. "He can...do that?"

"That little scene..." He waved his hand in the direction the woman had left. "Or rather, the scene that caused it was only his latest stunt."

Keiko's hand balled into fists. "What has he been doing to you?"

Toku lifted one shoulder. "Ryudo told me that if I didn't find a way to get you back, he'd punish me." He faced her and held her gaze. "I told him to go fuck himself. Kidnapping was wrong."

Keiko cringed, just a little. "I'm guessing he didn't take that well?"

"You could say that." Toku chuckled dryly. "I left the house and stayed with some friends for about two weeks. Then my father called. I had to go back."

Keiko sucked in a breath. "Uh, oh..."

"Ryudo got...into me that night, and stayed for two days." Toku stared at the ground. "Apparently, he can leave the house as long as he's in my body." He snorted. "Guess how I found out?"

Keiko hunched her shoulders. "Do I want to know?"

"Probably not." Toku pursed his lips and tilted his head to the side. "Let's just say that by the time I went back to school the following week, I wasn't a virgin anymore." The smile that appeared was sharp and cold. "In any way, shape, or form."

Keiko's blood turned to ice. "Merciful Lady... Did he hurt you?"

"No, he didn't hurt me." Toku rolled his eyes. "But he was really, really thorough about my..." He glanced away. "Sexual education."

He jammed his hands into his coat pockets. "I had no idea you could do sex in so many ways, and in so many places."

Keiko smiled tightly. "It doesn't sound like it was too bad of an experience."

He slumped in his seat and refused to look at her. "No, not really, but some of the stuff he had me doing was…" He winced. "Embarrassing as hell."

Keiko grinned. "In that case, you can skip the details."

"Don't mind if I do." Toku chuckled. "Ryudo is a hell of a lot kinkier than I imagined."

Keiko covered her mouth to hide her sudden giggle.

"It wasn't all that bad, really. It was hiding it that got on my nerves." Toku pulled the ring from his pocket, gazed at it briefly, then shoved it back in. "The excuses, and the lying to my fiancé…" He looked over at Keiko. "You want to know the worst part?"

Keiko crossed her legs and leaned back on the bench. "What?"

"I'm actually relived she's gone." He hunched down on the bench. "Damn, that sounds awful, but I'm beginning to think Ryudo did me a favor by getting rid of her."

"You didn't love her?"

He shook his head slowly. "She was a nice girl, and all, but…no." A small tired chuckle bubbled up. "Once I started having sex, thanks to Ryudo, I couldn't stand to be around her." He folded his arms tight across his chest. "She was so…uptight. I simply couldn't imagine going to bed with her for the rest of my life."

Keiko stared down at the ground. "I'm sorry. It's all my fault…"

Toku glared at her. "Don't you dare blame yourself! You didn't *ask* Ryudo to kidnap you!"

Keiko leaned forward and crossed her arms. "But he's taking his temper out on you for helping me."

"So?" Toku reached out to touch her arm. "It happened in my house. It's my responsibility to keep track of what goes on inside it." He smiled briefly. "That includes rescuing cute girls kidnapped by my guardian spirit."

Keiko smiled tiredly. He thought she was cute. That was so sweet. "You know, Ryudo said almost the same thing."

Toku blinked. "What? About rescuing cute girls?"

Keiko smile widened. "No, about being responsible for what went on inside the house." Her smile faded. "I'm sorry you lost your fiancé."

"No big loss there." Toku waved his hand in his exiting fiancé's general direction. "I *didn't* love her. I'll get over it." He turned to Keiko and raised a brow. "But, I have never seen Ryudo like this. He's normally as calm and stable as you can get. His temper is short, but he's over it just as fast." He frowned. "But since you left, he's been…insane." He rolled his eyes. "And he never lets up. Every day he has to mention you at least once." Toku frowned up at the tree arching over their heads. "I'm really beginning to think he's in love with you."

Keiko jerked back. "Who? Ryudo?" She shook her head. "But that's crazy! He's only seen me once…"

Toku pursed his lips and raised his brows. "Love at first sight?"

Keiko leaned back and snorted. "That doesn't happen."

"Ah, but it does." Toku raised his finger and smiled. "Happened to my parents."

Keiko scowled. "Ryudo is a ghost…"

Toku shrugged. "So? He still has feelings."

Keiko lifted her brow and crossed her arms. "Ryudo has feelings?"

Toku groaned and leaned his head back. "Trust me, he has them. I can feel everything when he's in me. Ghost or not, I know rage and grief when I feel it."

Rage and *grief?* Keiko leaned away from him. "Are you saying that I broke his heart; that I should go back?"

Toku laughed. "Oh, hell no! You go back, and that bastard will make damned sure you never see the light of day again!" He looked at her, and his smile disappeared. "What I'm saying is that I don't think he's going to get over his feelings for you for a while. A long while."

"Oh." Keiko felt a sudden twinge of guilt. She'd never broken anyone's heart before.

Toku slapped his knees, and smiled at her. "So, now that you know my sordid little tale, what have you been doing?"

Keiko started. "Oh, me? I took your advice and took karate."

"Wonderful!" He turned toward her. "Did you find a weapon?"

She nodded, and inched closer along the bench. "I carry a rattan staff that's green. It even has leaves." She smiled.

He set his elbow on the back of the bench, and grinned. "So, no more ghost problems?'

She shrugged. "I haven't run across one since Ryudo, so I haven't actually tested your theory yet."

"You'll have to let me know once you do…" His smile faded. "On second thought, seeing me again might not be a good idea." He looked down and frowned.

Keiko frowned. "Why not?"

"If I see you, and Ryudo is driving…" He glanced at her, and tapped his temple. "Heaven only knows what he'll try."

"Oh." Keiko looked down at her knees. "Good point." With Ryudo possessing him, she really couldn't afford to see him again. A sharp pang hit in the region of her heart. "I'm sorry, Toku."

Toku snorted and gave her a lopsided smile. "I can handle it. He's just being a pain in my butt…" He rolled his eyes. "In more ways than one." He slouched in the bench. "The real pisser is that now that I don't have a fiancé, I still can't ask you out."

Keiko stilled, then looked over at him. "Ask me out?"

Toku shrugged, and set his arm across the back of the bench, right behind her. "Yeah, like to dinner, or the movies, or something." He leaned back and looked up at the blooming cherry tree overhead. He smiled. "Ryudo would have a freaking meltdown." A few pink petals drifted down from the tree and landed on his coat.

Keiko held out her hand and a petal drifted down to land in her palm. Toku wanted to take her out on a date? She felt something warm wrap around her heart, then squeeze tight. She closed her hand around the pink petal. "I would have liked that."

Toku turned to look at her, and smiled. "Ryudo's meltdown?"

Keiko smiled, and gripped the petal tight. "The date, silly."

Toku's gaze dropped to her mouth and his lips parted. "Oh…" He leaned toward her.

Keiko stilled. He was going to kiss her. Heat flushed her body, and gripped her heart. She wanted that kiss. She leaned toward him, and their lips met, gently, shyly. Her eyes closed.

He sighed, his breath warm and clean. His tongue swept across her bottom lip, a soft, damp question.

She replied with a flick of her own, and brushed against the warm wet velvet of his tongue. He tasted slightly of unsweetened tea, and aroused male—and something else. Something that shimmered on the edge of her perceptions; something exciting and… shadowed.

He groaned, and opened his mouth against hers, taking her invitation to taste, and explore. His hands closed around her arms, tugging her closer, knee to knee.

She reached up to grip the edges of his open coat in her fists. *Damn, the boy could kiss!* She turned to fit her mouth to his, exploring eagerly.

His tongue lashed hungrily against hers, and his hands moved from her arms to sweep across her back then down, to the hem of her jacket. He slipped under and skimmed up, his fingers exploring the curve of her spine through her thin T-shirt. He trapped and suckled on her tongue.

A shiver raced through her, and the need to touch him became overwhelming. She slid her hands under his overcoat, and then under his suit jacket to press her palms to his dress shirt, and chest. His warmth near scorched her though the fine cotton. Under her fingers, his nipples arose to tight points.

He moaned very softly, into her mouth. His hands swept upward, and outward, skimming along her ribs. His thumbs brushed against the bottom curves of her breasts.

Keiko stilled. His exploring thumbs were asking a question. Did she want him to go further? Her nipples tightened, and ached. Her belly clenched with anticipation. *Yes.* Yes, she did… She leaned closer, closing her arms around him, and embracing him, pressing her breasts against his broad chest to ease the tender ache in her nipples.

The grumbling howl of a motorcycle echoed in the park.

Keiko froze, and her blood ran cold. She broke the kiss to look.

Pedestrians scattered before a yellow and blue Kawasaki roaring down the walk, heading straight for her.

"Shit!" She lunged off the bench, slipping from Toku's hands.

"Keiko, what is it?" Toku snatched for her arm.

Keiko dodged his hand, grabbing her helmet and bicycle. "Sorry! Gotta go!"

"Keiko?" Toku stood up. "Keiko, what's wrong?"

"Bye, Toku!" Keiko shoved her bike into the bushes beyond the tree, and kept going. She tore through the low brush under the slender trees, in a hurry to get as far away from the paved walk as possible. In a matter of minutes, she reached the fairly steep embankment that signaled the beginning of the woods.

She turned to look back, and heard the motorcycle off in the distance, well behind her. It didn't sound like he'd followed her into the trees. Hopefully he hadn't actually spotted her. However, to keep from being spotted, she would have to avoid all the public walkways, and cut directly across the wooded park.

Not as easy as it sounded. The park was huge, heavily wooded and not flat, with fairly steep, rocky sections. It normally took well over an hour to cross, when one used the paved footpaths. Heaven only knew how long it was going to take to cross it off the paths. Unfortunately, she didn't have much of a choice.

She sighed, and looked up through the new leaves, checking the sun's location. Her apartment complex was due west, right across the street from the park. She jammed her helmet on her head, hopped on her bike and pedaled.

Her bike bumped across rocks, grass, and exposed roots. She hunched over her handlebars to avoid the larger tree branches. Small branches still caught on her staff, sticking up over her shoulder, and low brush whipped against her jeans. She smiled grimly. Good thing she wasn't doing this in her school clothes.

The sun dropped below the trees.

And she pedaled.

Keiko crossed a few of the paved pathways, but ducked back into the trees.

And she pedaled some more.

Keiko came out of the trees, and halted at one of the steeper embankments. She wiped at the sweat dripping down her brow, watching joggers trotting along the paved path, a full story below. It might as well have been a mountain ravine. It was too steep to go down and come back up without breaking something. She didn't have a choice. She had to find the bridge.

She followed the edge in a vaguely westerly direction, and discovered the footbridge.

And Shido, bent over a water fountain, with his back turned to her. He and his bike were about four car-lengths beyond the footbridge.

Shit. Keiko had no idea if Shido had known where she'd come out, or if it was dumb luck on his part, but she had to cross that bridge. Her heart pounding in her chest, she lunged out of the trees, pedaling hard, and slammed on her brakes to make the turn onto the footbridge.

Shido's head came up. His eyes opened. "Keiko?"

Keiko skidded onto the bridge, and kept going, pedaling for all she was worth. *Go! Go! Go!*

Shido shouted something behind her, and a motorcycle engine started.

Keiko crossed the bridge, hopped off her bike, then shoved her bike up a small embankment to her right and lunged into the trees.

The motorcycle faded into the distance.

She stopped, and looked back, panting. "Ha! Missed me!" Grinning, she pushed her bike through the brush, and kept going.

The sun dipped lower behind the trees, and shadows pooled in low places.

Keiko jouncing off-road ride took her to the deep and swift running stream that meandered through the park. It was a good sign, she was close to home. A stroll along the edge brought her to a stone slab footbridge. She carried her bike across the stream and continued on.

The shadows under the trees deepened.

The sound of street traffic and a distant train caught Keiko's attention. *Yes!* She was nearly there. She pedaled clear of the trees, then slammed on her brakes.

Immediately before her were swings and seesaws, with a maze of tunnel tubes on her right, and a towering arched jungle gym on her left. Beyond it lay the grassy field, and beyond that, the exit to the street.

Keiko's heart stuttered in her chest. She'd found the children's playground. The very last place she wanted to be.

The playground was completely deserted. Not one person was in sight, not even walking along the street. No surprise, everyone knew it was haunted. Keiko had the scars to prove it—since grade school.

And she had to cross it to get home.

The sun disappeared behind the high rises directly beyond, smearing the glass windows with the colors of flame and blood.

~ *Nine* ~

Shadows fell from the towering buildings and stretched, spilling across the playground, delivering twilight. The playground's overhead lights had never worked.

The breeze picked up, whispering among the new leaves. The swings drifted forward and back, just a little, creaking on their chains. A seesaw eased up, changing its tilt to the other direction.

Sudden chill washed across Keiko, and her breath steamed out. Awareness shivered in the back of her mind, and lifted the hair on her neck. She was no longer alone.

Something foul oozed across her thoughts, with the taint of cold wet earth. *Play?*

Fear froze her, then propelled her forward, pedaling at top speed past the swings and across the dragging sand, headed for the grassy playing field.

Distorted giggling and chill whispers pursued her. "Play! Play with us!"

Keiko didn't look. She did not want to look.

Something reached up out of the sand, wrapped a bitterly cold limb around her ankle and yanked hard.

Keiko shouted and grabbed onto her handlebars. Her bike rocked up on its back wheel, rolling out from under her, and ripping out of her hands. The silver ten-speed went flying, spinning through the air, and crunched to the ground, yards away.

Keiko hit the sand and automatically rolled over her shoulder and back onto her feet into a fighting stance. She blinked in surprise at her upraised hands. Her karate training had worked. "Well, damn!"

"Play…" Dozens of blobs of darkness oozed out of the sand, all the way around her. "Play with us…"

Oh, shit… She grabbed the green *bo* jutting from behind her shoulder, and pulled it free, leaving the cloth case slung across her back. She stepped back into a 'ready' stance with her *bo* positioned in an upraised spear hold.

The sand literally crawled with black, globular nastiness. They oozed toward her, and the giggling drifted into high-pitched chittering.

She did not remember there being this many of the little horrors. She frowned. She didn't remember them being this small, either. The shapeless black things were all about the size of a fat toddler.

Something dark and cold spilled across her foot.

Keiko's icy fear was washed away by a thick rush of hot anger. She yanked her foot back and slammed the heel of her staff down on it. "Don't touch me!"

It burst, like a mud-bubble, and a sharp squeal erupted. It became a white mist that drifted apart in the breeze.

Keiko's brow lifted. She'd destroyed it. It had worked. The green and living staff had worked!

A howling wind rose, and the temperature dropped dramatically. The grass visibly frosted at the edges of the sand.

Her breath steamed out. She had angered them. She smiled. Good. She looked over at the slow moving things crawling around her in the sand. "So, you want to play, do you?" She bared her teeth in a vicious smile, and spun her staff for the sheer joy of it. "Fine, you little shits, let's play!"

Viscous darkness slithered for her, breathtakingly fast, while others rose on stumpy legs to wobble toward her.

She stabbed her rattan staff down at the nearest blob. It squealed, burst and turned into a puff of mist. She swung at a pair of standing blobs, and cut them in half. More squeals, wet nasty bursts and more smoke.

Something cold touched her leg.

She back-kicked in pure reflex, and sent a blob skidding across the sand. She whirled, her braid flying out behind her, and swung her staff in side-to-side sweeps that wrapped all the way around her. Darkness splattered and squealed in her wake, surrounding her in soft bursts of fog.

And still, they came.

She dodged, swung and kicked, with her *bo* whirling about her, striking out at the moving, fetid darkness around her. Calmness stole over her. Her body moved faster, her *bo* swinging in a deadly dance that felt…euphoric. Swing, twist, kick, slash, stab…

And then, there was silence.

Keiko jolted, as though awakening from a dream. She swung her *bo* up, and gripped it with both hands in a spear hold, looking for moving shadows along the sand. The air warmed around her until she couldn't see her breath. There was no movement anywhere. They were gone.

Keiko's mouth fell open. She'd done it. She'd chased them off. She threw back her head and shouted at the top of her lungs. "Take that, you little shits!" She howled in joy and twirled, swinging her *bo* around her. The park rang with her laughter.

She stopped and gasped for breath. It was over.

Exhaustion crushed down on her, and she staggered on trembling legs. Muscle aches began clamoring for attention, and her ankle, the one the ghost had grabbed, stung like hell. She leaned on her staff, and it curved under her weight. She snorted at the sight of her wobbly weapon, and its two waving green leaves. It really did seem like it was made of rubber. The snort became a chuckle, and then soft pained laughter. "Mercy, I need a hot soak."

"What the hell was all that?" The voice was annoyingly familiar.

Keiko turned to look behind her.

Shido, tall, dark, and menacing in his black motorcycle leathers stood just beyond her fallen bike. He swung out a hand, indicating the night-dark playground. "What were those…things?"

Keiko groaned. *Great.* Just what she needed. Leaning on her bowing staff, she limped toward her bicycle, and Shido. If he tried anything, she'd whack him. She was too damned tired to salve his ego. "They were ghosts."

"Ghosts?" Shido stepped back from her, his hands clenched at his sides. "Ghost stories are for children and grannies!"

Keiko lifted her bicycle from the grass and examined it. The bike didn't look damaged. "Shido, you saw them, what else could they be?" She engaged the kickstand.

"I don't know what the hell I saw." Shido stepped into her line of sight, frowning. "What were you doing with…those things?"

Keiko focused on him. "Destroying them." She pulled the sheath for her staff from over her head.

"With that?" He waved at her green staff.

"Yep." She lifted the green staff, and peered down its length, looking for damage. She didn't see anything, but it was fairly dark. "They are dead, the rattan is alive." She slid the case over her *bo.* "The living rattan destroys them. Everything else passes right through them as though it's not even there."

Shido shook his head. "There's no such thing as ghosts!"

Keiko sighed, and tied the strings on the staff's cloth case. *Stubborn idiot.* Why was she even bothering to talk to him?

"They didn't come near me, they were all around you." Shido crossed his arms. "What did they want with you?"

"Trust me, you really don't want to know." She lifted the case and shoved her arm, and head, through the long strap, settling the *bo* across her back. "Don't worry, it's not something you'll ever have to deal with."

"Why?" He stepped back. "What's wrong with you?"

Keiko grabbed her bicycle's handlebars and toed her kickstand back up. "Let's just say ghosts are a personal problem of mine."

Shido clenched his hands into fists. "Ghosts don't exist!"

"Suit yourself." Keiko rolled her eyes. "But if you'll excuse me, I want to go home and have a soak, after destroying a playground full of things that don't exist." She pushed her bicycle past him, and kept walking.

Shido followed a few yards behind, a silent and seething shadow.

Keiko walked through the park gate, passing Shido's yellow and blue Kawasaki to her left. It was parked on the sidewalk, right by the fence.

Alert to traffic, she trotted her softly ticking bike across the night dark road and bumped up onto the deserted sidewalk. She turned to the left, along the balcony side of her apartment building, heading for the entrance stairs at the front.

Behind her, the Kawasaki roared to life. Tires squealed, and the engine's roar faded into the distance.

Keiko sighed. Shido had clearly been unnerved by what he had seen, but it wouldn't last. She knew from experience that he'd eventually convince himself that he hadn't seen anything at all, and be his old arrogant self again. She didn't really blame him. She hadn't wanted to remember seeing anything either, but her scars were ever-present reminders.

But Toku's theory had worked, and she had a new memory. One without a reminder. She smiled. The long nightmare, begun in that very park when she was a child, was over. She wasn't helpless anymore.

The tears came out of nowhere.

Leaning against the apartment building in the quiet street, she let the tears streak down her cheeks until her soul had emptied. She scrubbed her cheeks dry and continued on.

Unlike the side street in front of the park, the street in front of the apartment complex was busy with nighttime pedestrians fresh from the train station. Pairs of grim businessmen with briefcases, knots of laughing women with shopping totes and packs of school kids lugging school bags, all intent on heading home.

Keiko trudged past them, her bicycle softly ticking at her side. Merciful Lady, she was tired. She turned to the staircase and looked up. The entire front of the building was one huge maze of branching staircases rising above her. It was ten stories high, and her tiny apartment was on the eighth. She had to carry her bike all the way up.

She leaned down and lifted her bike.

"Keiko."

She stilled. She knew that voice. She leaned away from the stairs to look past them, her long black braid sliding over her shoulder. *Toku?*

"There you are." With a slight smile, Toku straightened from the small tree he was leaning against and tossed a lit cigarette away. He jammed one hand in the pocket of his dark dress slacks and walked toward her, his long coat lifting in the night breeze.

Keiko frowned. His suit jacket and tie were gone, but he still wore his white dress shirt and dark dress trousers. He must have been waiting here since she'd left him at the park. She set her bike down and leaned it against the stair railing. "Toku, what are you doing here?"

He dropped his gaze to the ground. "I wanted to…see you." His gaze darted across her and he frowned slightly. "Are you all right?"

"Huh?" Keiko looked down at herself. She was filthy from her journey across the park. "I must look a mess. I just finished a fight."

He stiffened. "A fight? A fight with who?"

Keiko grinned. "Toku! It worked! Your theory worked!"

"What?" Toku lifted his chin, dodging her gaze. "My theory?"

Keiko threw out her arms. "Yes, the green rattan works!" She darted a look at the passing pedestrians, and dropped her voice. "It works against ghosts!"

Toku frowned, glancing at her from the corner of his eye. "Are you saying you were attacked by ghosts, just now?"

"Yes, in the park!" She looked back toward her bike. The last thing she needed was someone walking off with it.

"Keiko!"

She turned to face him. "Yeah?"

His jaw tightened and his brows dropped low. "Were you hurt?"

"No! Not at all" Keiko practically hopped in place. "The green rattan worked amazingly well. They popped like balloons!"

He eyed the people walking past them. "We can't talk about this here. My car is parked on the side of your building. Walk with me?"

"Sure, let me lock up my bike." Keiko turned back to the stairs, dodging homeward bound pedestrians. Toku had wanted to see her, how sweet! He didn't seem angry about her leaving him the park so abruptly, earlier this afternoon, but he didn't seem quite his usual self either. He seemed a little…tense.

Toku leaned over her, and tugged at her sheathed *bo*. "Here, let me hold that for you."

"Oh, sure." Keiko handed her *bo* over, and knelt to unwind her bike chain.

"Keiko, what were you doing going after ghosts in the first place? They're dangerous to you."

"I didn't go after them." Keiko looped the bike chain through the stair railing. "I came out on the playground by accident, and they came after me." She stood and locked down her gym bag. "Trust me, I don't need to go looking for ghosts." She turned around to face him. "Okay."

"My car is only a short walk away." Toku set her *bo* over his right shoulder, and held out his left elbow, clearly waiting for her to loop her arm through his. He looked around and dropped his voice. "They were in the playground?"

"Yep." Keiko took his old-fashioned invitation and laced her right arm through his.

Toku tightened his arm holding her to his side. "Did you know they were there?" He began to walk.

Keiko matched her stride to his. "Oh, yeah, I knew." She felt a little awkward, walking arm in arm, but Toku was apparently in the mood to be gallant, and she didn't want to disappoint him again. "I normally avoid the park altogether because my first attacked happened there."

He frowned, watching the people around them. "Your first attack happened in that playground?"

"Yeah, Mom and I lived in this apartment building when I was in grade school. I moved back here because the landlord remembered my mom, so the rent was cheap, and the university is only two train stops away."

Toku turned to the right, leading her into the narrow and deeply shadowed alley between her building and the department store, next door. Cars were parked alongside both buildings, leaving little room for more than one car to pass at a time. He tightened his hold on her arm. "Keiko, I don't like you fighting with ghosts."

Keiko rolled her eyes. "It's not as if I can avoid them, and my training has helped a lot."

Toku's brows lifted. "Training?"

Keiko grinned. "The martial arts class, remember?" She shook her head. "I still can't believe how well all the fight-training took. It was like my body was on auto-drive, or something."

Toku looked down and caught her gaze. "You could have come to me, for training. I have many years experience in combat." Shadows and blue fire moved in the back of his eyes. "I spent a great many years on the battlefield."

The hair on Keiko's neck rose, and the shimmer at the back of her mind finally registered. *Ghost...* Alarmed, she jerked away.

Toku trapped her wrist against his arm, stopping her. Darkness glimmered within his palm. "Keiko, where are you going?" His eyes narrowed, and he smiled tightly. The expression did not belong on Toku's face, but she recognized it.

Keiko's heart slammed in her chest. "Ryudo?"

His brows lowered over his glimmering gaze. "You shouldn't have left."

Ryudo was in possession of Toku's body. She could practically feel Ryudo's hand within Toku's. And he was carrying her staff.

~ Ten ~

Toku's eyes danced with pale blue fox-fire, and Ryudo scowled with Toku's mouth. "If you had remained with me, you would not need to protect yourself. I would protect you." His fingers tightened on her arm. "No spirit would dare cross into my domain."

Keiko's temper flared, and she jerked him to a halt. "I don't need your protection." She balled a fist and pulled her free arm back. "Let go, Ryudo."

Ryudo lifted his brows. "Are you sure you want to punch Toku? This wasn't his idea, I assure you."

Keiko flinched. No, she didn't want to hit Toku. She put her fist down.

"Good." Ryudo nodded and tugged her onward. "I thought of you, often."

Keiko tried to wriggle out of his hold, but his grip on her arm, and wrist, was like a vise. "Funny, I didn't think of you at all." Her cheeks heated. Other than in her masturbation fantasies.

He smiled. "Is that so?"

Keiko dodged his knowing gaze. "So, how did you get…here?"

"I caught Toku when he was in the shower. He was too distracted by what he was doing to even notice I was there." Ryudo tilted Toku's head. "He had a rather interesting memory of you."

Keiko swallowed hard. The kiss on the park bench…

"I hadn't realized he knew where you live, and all this time. He kept that rather well hidden." He glanced about and stopped. "Ah, here we are." He turned to face her and caught both her upper arms.

"Be a good girl, Keiko, and don't hurt Toku." He pushed her backwards, between the back bumper of a sleek, silver Subaru and the front bumper of a battered, red Toyota parked by the side of her building.

Keiko dug in her heels, and twisted to break free, but Toku was head and shoulders taller and Ryudo was a powerful seething presence, right under the surface. "Ryudo, what are you doing?"

He continued to urge her backwards. "Giving Toku what he wants."

"What?" Keiko twisted in his hold, but was driven steadily backwards. "What does he want?"

Ryudo pressed her back against the brick wall, right under a steel fire escape. He pulled her arms above her head, then tugged her *bo* from his shoulder, and tossed it on the ground. It landed along the base the wall. He pressed Toku's warm body against hers. "You, Keiko. He wants you."

Keiko gasped. She could feel Ryudo's woolen uniform—and the hard muscle beneath it—right under Toku's body, one within the other.

His lips brushed against her ear. "Do you feel that?" He shifted his hips, and the length of a firm erection pressed into her stomach. "That's not me, Keiko. That's Toku."

Keiko stilled. The hot length against her belly stirred an answering heat within. Her core clenched, and her nipples tightened to aching points. She bit down on her lip to hide an unbidden hungry moan. She had to forcibly stop herself from rubbing against him. It had a long time since she had felt her body respond this strongly to anyone. Six months, in fact. If you didn't count the kiss in the park.

Ryudo held her wrists in one hand. With the other, he pulled a long length of red silk from his pocket.

Toku closed his eyes and shook his head. "Ryudo, I don't want..."

Ryudo's tight expression flooded across Toku's face, and his words slipped from Toku's lips. "Oh, but you do want. Very badly, in fact." He wrapped the silk cloth around Keiko's wrists, then looped it between her hands, binding them together.

Keiko tugged at her bound wrists. It wasn't uncomfortable, or even tight, but it was very secure. "Ryudo, what are you doing?"

"I already told you." Ryudo stepped back, tugged her hands up, and looped the silk scarf over a bar of the fire escape directly above her. "Letting Toku have what he desires."

Anger flitted across his face. Toku's voice and expression emerged. "Ryudo, I did not ask for this!" But his hands tied the scarf into a big bow, just out of Keiko's reach.

His expression shifted and Ryudo smiled with Toku's mouth. "Oh, no?" His distinct voice whispered in the back of her mind, and the scent of chrysanthemums washed over her. "Do you want to know what held him so rapt in the shower that he missed my presence entirely?"

Toku's body trembled against hers, and his expression shifted to wide-eyed alarm. "Ryudo, don't…!"

Ryudo's smug expression took over Toku's face. "Oh, but I think Keiko should know." He licked his lips and focused on Keiko. "I found Toku in the shower, with the most arresting image of you occupying his thoughts, masturbating."

Keiko sucked in a sharp breath, her mind flooded with an image of Toku under the shower. His head down and his eyes closed, with his body arched. The water slid down his strong back and his braced thighs. One hand was pressed to the tile wall, and the other gripped his shaft, pumping it hard and fast, his expression brutally intent.

It was painfully exciting.

Ryudo leaned close, his breath caressing her throat. "Can you imagine what his very entertaining little fantasy featured?" His hands closed on the scarf that bound her wrists. "You, bound for his pleasure."

Keiko jolted. Toku had imagined her tied up? It was wickedly shocking. Her nipples tingled, and tightened.

His gaze dropped below her chin. Positioned with her hands over her head, her breasts were thrust upward. Her semi-erect nipples were plainly visible under her T-shirt. "I admit to being a little surprised by the rather forceful tone to his desires." His hands slid down her upraised arms. "But it lacked realism. So, I decided to give him a taste of what I experienced while buried in your hot, wet cunt."

Visceral memory slammed into her; of scandalous hands, lascivious mouths and fervent thrusting. The ardent memory became an image of Toku, eyes closed and gasping while pumping his cock, his entire body rigid under the pounding water...

Heat flashed, and hunger tightened into fierce aching need.

Ryudo's voice, summer hot, and scented with the musk of masculine lust, echoed across her mind. "He came very, very hard, Keiko."

Keiko trembled against him. Inflamed by the images washing across her thoughts, her core clenched, aching with shameless hunger. She barely felt his fingers working the belt on her jeans open, then freeing the button.

"He wants you as badly as I." He lowered her fly, and his lips brushed her cheek. "And I want you very badly, indeed." He jerked her T-shirt free of her jeans. "I hunger for you." His warm palm pressed against her bare belly.

Cool shimmering darkness pulsed against her, and beat in time with her heart. Her nipples tightened to fierce hot points, and moisture dampened her panties. She tried to hold back her moan.

"Ah, so, you did miss me." His eyes danced with bright blue flames. He embraced her, chest to breast. "I missed the feel of you." With his other hand, he cupped her butt to hold her snug against his rigid heat. "I missed the taste of you." His hips moved, grinding his cock against her. "I missed fucking you."

She had tried to fill the aching void within her, but nothing, and no one could satisfy her desire for something more, something shadowed. A small whimper escaped, and she pushed her hips into his, unable to resist rubbing against the inticing length of his cock. It had too long since she had tasted true ecstasy.

"Damn, Keiko…" Toku groaned in his own voice, and pressed urgently against her. His lips hovered over her mouth.

Ryudo's summer-hot voice brushed across her thoughts. "Kiss me, kiss us."

Barely able to think past the carnal heat surging in her blood, Keiko closed her eyes and parted her lips against his, surrendering to the ravenous hunger within her.

Toku's hot, wet tongue surged in to lap strongly at hers, his kiss flavored with tea and midnight. He groaned.

Keiko gripped the scarf that bound her wrists over her head, pulling at it in an effort to seal her lips to Toku, and taste the shimmering night beneath his kiss.

Toku's hands slid up her waist and beneath her T-shirt. His warm fingers brushed the bra that defined the bottom of her breasts.

They both stilled.

Toku pulled back and licked his lips. Holding her gaze, he reached behind her to find the clasp to her bra. He tugged and the bra parted.

Keiko trembled. She shouldn't be letting this happen, but every fiber of her being was screaming to let him take her, let him satisfy the hungers stirring in her body, and in her soul.

His hands slid forward to cup her breasts in his warm palms. His thumbs brushed the swollen tips. Ryudo's midnight voice washed across her. "Such tight nipples." He smiled, and squeezed.

She threw her head back, moaning, and shamelessly pushed into his hands.

"Yes…" He dropped to one knee, and shoved her shirt and bra up, exposing her breasts. He focused on her nipples with avid hunger. His gaze lifted and locked on hers. He leaned close and sucked her nipple in, then lashed her with his hot, wet tongue.

Fire speared straight down to her core, and detonated with an impact so close to true orgasm, Keiko came up on her toes, gasping.

He sucked hard and enthusiastically, his eyes gleaming with blue fox-fire, and masculine triumph.

Overwhelmed, she pressed her breast into his mouth, and moaned. She was so close…

His hands slid down her jean-covered legs. He grasped her pants cuff near the ankle, lifted her foot and tugged off her sneaker.

Keiko felt her shoe leave her foot. "What…?"

Toku released her foot, wearing only her sock. He pulled his head back, but he wore Ryudo's expression. "You already know what I'm doing." He leaned close and claimed her other nipple.

The fire burning in her nipple, echoed in clit, and pushed her deliciously close to fulfillment. She moaned.

His hand slid down her other leg, lifted her foot and removed her other sneaker. He pulled back, his gaze drifting from one exposed wet nipple to the other. He looked up at her and curled his fingers into the waistband of her jeans.

Keiko couldn't look away.

He dragged her pants and panties downward over her ass, exposing the trimmed hair of her mound. He leaned close, and his warm breath caressed her naked flesh. He took a deep breath, and closing his eyes, he smiled. "The perfume of heaven." He pulled her jeans down her thighs, and gazed up at her. "Your panties are wet." He tugged them off.

Her panties were very wet. Shocked, thrilled and impatient, all at the same time, Keiko shuddered.

He rose, and unfastened his pants. Licking his lips, he let the pleated wool trousers and his boxers, fall to his ankles, freeing his cock. From a nest of closely trimmed curls, the rigid veined length curved upward, the purple head emerging from its sheath. He curled his hand around it, and stroked, encouraging the head to extend further from the sheath, and weep.

Keiko felt an answering trickle of moisture slick her thighs.

He leaned close, and took her mouth in a ferocious kiss, pushing her back against the cold brick. His hands curled under her thighs and lifted her until the hot tip of his cock head nudged at the wet opening to her body.

Belly to belly, she could feel the pulsing shadow of Ryudo pressing against her heart. Urgency became a howling craving to be filled. She wrapped her legs around his hips and writhed, desperate to bury him in her hungry flesh.

He let her down enough to press the head into her, and held her there. He smiled from barely a breath away. "Impatient?"

She glared at him. "Shut up and fuck me."

He grinned. "With pleasure." He let her drop down, and surged up into her, sheathing himself to the balls.

The abrupt fullness stretched her welcoming flesh, and struck that delicious spot deep and high in the back. She gasped with surprise, then moaned in utter satisfaction. His unyielding heat felt so right within her.

Toku's groan burned down her spine. "Oh, shit…" He gripped her tightly, trembling within her. "You're not…like the others."

Ryudo's summer hot sigh overlapped Toku's voice. "No, she's not." He shifted within her, just a little. "She was made for me—for us." His hands tightened under her ass cheeks and he lifted, sliding slowly from her until only the head remained in her flesh.

Keiko moaned and squeezed to keep him.

He drove back into her, shoving her back against the wall, and it wasn't gentle.

She bucked to meet him, and she wasn't gentle, either. Her need was too great for sweet lovemaking. She wanted to fuck.

He lifted her and dropped her, slamming her back onto his cock, driving a grunt from his throat.

She took him completely, and the stunning hammer-blow of delight forced a soft cry from her lips. She gasped. "More, damn it… More!" She squeezed her thighs, and pulled on the silk binding her wrists, lifting herself in a greedy rush.

Ryudo chuckled and tightened his grip on her butt, slowing her hurried lift. "Patience, have patience."

Toku's voice lashed out. "Fuck patience!" He shoved her up, and brought her down again with ruthless precision.

They both cried out.

Toku lifted Keiko halfway off his cock, and proceeded to thrust up into her in exquisitely ferocious and steady strokes.

Keiko shoved her shoulders back against the wall, bucking in violent counter-strokes. Frenzied by the rapacious fire building and coiling tight within her, she writhed and cried out in delirious and eager abandon, reveling in the agonizingly incredible pleasure that assaulted her with each of his powerful thrusts. "Yes…Toku, yes!"

The scent of raw lust, and acrid sweat filled the over-warm air between them, and beneath it, the more subtle scent of chrysanthemums.

"I'm…almost there." Toku panted, scowling with ferocious concentration and savage need. "Come with me. Keiko, come with me!" He tilted his head and bit down on her jutting nipple.

Exquisite torment radiated from her nipple and scorched a path down to her clit. Keiko cried out, and felt her climax crest in a burning wave. "I'm there… Don't stop!"

Toku shoved her tight to the wall, reached up and caught her by the hair. He opened his mouth and took her lips in a brutal kiss. And thrust, and thrust, and thrust…

Keiko felt her body tense, and her breath stopped. She teetered on the glittering edge.

Toku's entire body tensed. He moaned into her mouth and shook violently. He thrust hard and deep, clutching her tight while his cock pulsed within her. He thrust again, and then once more. The scent of liquid, masculine musk thickened the hot moist air.

Keiko's climax ignited. She fell into a brilliantly searing spiral of release that tore her soul apart, shaking her in a firestorm of rapture. She screamed her ecstasy into Toku's mouth.

"Yes!" Ryudo's triumph scorched the night. A summer hot wind of pure darkness exploded around them, embraced them, and swallowed them whole. *"Mine!"*

The breath was ripped from her lungs, and pain seared the small of her back. She broke the kiss, shouting and bucking in reaction.

Toku threw up his head, hissing. "What the fuck…?"

Keiko dropped her head on Toku's shoulder, exhausted and sated.

Toku leaned against Keiko, panting. "Are you okay?"

She sighed and felt a smile tug at her lips. "I'm fine."

"Did I…hurt you?"

"No, not at all." Keiko rubbed her cheek against his shoulder. "Did I hurt you?"

"No." Toku leaned back, his expression serious. "Are you sure you're okay?"

"I'm fine, really." Keiko smiled tiredly. "Can I get down now?"

"Oh, yeah, sure." Holding Keiko with one arm under her, Toku reached up to tug the silk binding her to the fire escape.

A shimmer appeared to Keiko's right. The shimmer solidified into a man leaning with one shoulder against the wall, facing them. Ryudo's face coalesced, and then the rest of him. He had changed. His hair spilled in a long, lustrous fall down his shoulders to the center of his back. Instead of a military uniform, he wore a snug, sleeveless black shirt that bared his heavily muscled and tattooed arms folded across his chest. Snug black jeans lovingly defined his muscular thighs, and were tucked into calf-hugging buckled motorcycle boots.

Frowning at Ryudo's form, Toku freed the scarf from the fire escape. "You've changed."

Ryudo nodded. "I can do so, when I have enough power."

Keiko released her thighs from around Toku's hips and felt the wet slide of his flesh leaving hers. She slid down his body and stood on shaky legs. She could feel Ryudo as a radiating ball of heat that literally vibrated all down her spine. He had been powerful before, but this was like nothing she'd ever felt. She pulled at the scarf that bound her wrists, trying to get her fingers around the knot.

Toku grabbed for the fallen trousers around his ankles. "I don't feel you in me."

Ryudo reached out and unknotted the scarf from Keiko's wrists.

"Because I am not."

Toku stilled, his brows drawn together, then fastened his pants. "You're...not?"

Keiko frowned at Ryudo's fingers unknotting her scarf. "I thought you couldn't leave the house without...being in Toku?"

"I fed from both of you. I now have enough power to do a number of things I normally can not do." He held up the red silk, passed it to Toku, and smiled.

Toku took the silk, crumpling it in his palm, and frowned.

Keiko stared at the cloth in Toku's hand, then turned away and hunched down to get her jeans. It had looked as though Ryudo had actually held the scarf—physically. Just how powerful was he? She stepped into her panties and looked up the alley.

Someone was standing there, at the very edge, partially concealed by the corner. A car passed and headlights washed against the exposed shoulder of a red and black leather motorcycle jacket.

Keiko sucked in a sharp breath. *Shido...*

~ Eleven ~

Keiko hurried into her jeans. How long had Shido been there, watching them? How much had he seen? She had to get out of there. She snatched for her sneakers, turned and leaned back against the wall to tuck her T-shirt in.

Ryudo was watching her with his customary smug smile.

Toku shoved the shirttail into his pants, and gasped. "Ow, shit!" He pulled his shirt back out, and pressed his fingers to the small of his back. "What the hell is that?"

Ryudo lifted his chin. "My mark."

Toku froze, and turned his head to look at him. "What do you mean, your mark?"

Ryudo lifted his brows. "It's my signature, or brand, I guess you could say."

Toku choked. "You've put a…brand on me?"

Ryudo nodded toward Keiko. "And Keiko."

Huh? In the process of refastening her bra, Keiko felt ice spill into her veins. She slid her hand into her jeans and investigated the small of her back. Something small and painful had raised the skin. Fury burned up the back of her skull. *That bastard!* She hooked her bra together and stomped into her sneakers.

Toku jammed his shirt in, and fastened his pants. "Why in hell did you do that?"

Ryudo held his gaze. "You've been touched by me, and that alone will draw others. It's a sign that you are under my protection."

Keiko straightened her jackets and stalked over to Ryudo. "I don't need your protection. I can protect myself. Take it off."

Ryudo pursed his lips. "It's not spiritual. It's a physical branding mark. It doesn't come off."

"You...asshole!" Keiko's fist lashed out so fast, her shoulder nearly wrenched from the socket. She connected to Ryudo's chin perfectly. The impact vibrated all the way to her heels.

Ryudo's head snapped up with the force of her punch. Eyes wide, he gasped, and fell backwards. And dissipated.

Toku blinked. "He's gone."

"That bastard!" Keiko stomped her feet and shouted out her frustration. "How dare he leave? I wanted to kick his ass!" She spotted her sheathed *bo* and crouched to retrieve it from the ground.

"I think you can consider his ass kicked." Toku snorted and covered his mouth, but the mirth as clear in his gaze.

Keiko straightened, curled her lip and gripped her staff in both hands. "It's not funny!"

Toku shook his head, and held up one hand, backing away from her. "No, of course not." But the smallest of sniggers slipped past his palm. He stumbled to the side of the silver Subaru. "On second thought, oh, yes, it was!" He leaned back against the car's door and exploded into laugher.

Keiko shoved her head and arm through the shoulder band of the *bo*, settling it across her back, and stalked after him. "Toku!'

Toku curled back from her and raised both his hands, laughing even harder. "Oh, damn, you *punched* him!" He gasped between fits of laughter. "I swear... The look of total surprise on his face!" He drew in a deep breath, and grinned. "The arrogant bastard never even saw it coming."

Keiko felt her cheeks warm and glanced away. "Truthfully? I didn't know I was even going to do it, until it happened." She shoved her hands into her pockets.

Toku straightened, and the laughter left his expression. "Keiko." He held out his hand.

Keiko looked at his hand suspiciously, but felt no trace of Ryudo.

She walked shyly over to him. "Yeah?"

He kept his hand out, lifted his brows and waited.

Fine, whatever... Keiko sighed, and set her hand in his.

He enclosed her hand, and tugged her closer. Holding her gaze, he raised her hand to his lips, and lightly kissed her knuckles. "I want you to know that what we did tonight wasn't just...sex. It was..." He sucked on his bottom lip and stared down at her hand. "It was special to me." He looked at her and his expression became stark. He pressed her palm to his chest. "It was something I will hold in my heart forever."

Keiko set her other palm on his chest and leaned closer. Lifting her chin, she pressed her mouth to his and kissed him, very softly.

His lips parted under hers, and his tongue flirted with her bottom lip.

She replied with a soft moan, and opened to receive him. Pressing closer, she slid her tongue along his, tasting the aftermath of the passion he'd given her.

He answered with sweeping wet velvet caresses, and slid his arms around her. He gently sucked her tongue into his mouth, and suckled.

She moaned, and pushed away, breaking the kiss.

He let her go. "Keiko, he wants you. I mean, really bad. I have the feeling that he meant to take you with us tonight."

Keiko nodded and bit down on her bottom lip. "I guessed as much."

Toku looked down at his shoes. "Would you consider staying with us?"

Keiko winced. "Ryudo would never let me leave the house again."

Toku shook his head, and smiled sadly. "Probably not."

Keiko looked up at him. "I can't live that way, Toku. I can't end my life before it's begun, and live in a cage, no matter how big, or pretty, or..." She took a deep breath. "Or, who's in it with me."

"I understand." Toku turned away, and opened the Subaru's door. Light from the car spilled onto the street. "If you see me again, assume it's Ryudo, and don't..." He took a deep breath. "Don't come near me." He looked toward the fire escape, then up at her building. "You may want to consider moving, too."

Keiko turned away, to face up the alley. "That might not be a bad idea."

"I'll...miss you."

Keiko had to take a deep breath. "I'll miss you too."

"Goodbye, Keiko."

"Goodbye, Toku." A fist of pain closed around her heart. She had to close her eyes just for a moment.

The slam of a car door echoed in the alley. An engine rumbled to life, and red light spilled around her, from taillights.

She started walking. It had certainly been a winner of a night. She had learned that she could defend herself against ghosts, and had found someone she could love, and could love her in return. Pretty much all she'd ever wanted. She could even have it, if she was willing to write off the rest of her entire life.

The car pulled away and the lights disappeared.

She shook her head and kept walking while her cheeks burned with tears.

After her eight-story climb, Keiko locked the door behind her and finally set her bicycle down in her tiny tiled entryway. She flipped on the lights and leaned against the wall, panting. "My next apartment will have an elevator." She toed out of her sneakers and shoved her feet into her worn house slippers. "Shower...I need a shower, and a soak."

She scuffed up the low step, and stared into the oval mirror hanging on the wall above the narrow battered table. She looked like hell. Her hair was every which way, her T-shirt was smudged with heaven only knew what, and her lips were very red and a little swollen. She touched them with a fingertip.

Toku's last kiss flashed through her thoughts. "Would you

consider staying with us?"

Keiko shook her head. Tempting as it was, she just...couldn't. She turned to the right and pulled open the folding door to the closet. She was not going to think about Toku, or Ryudo. She jerked off her coats, shoved them on a hanger and closed the door. She was going to take a quick shower, a long soak, and then go to sleep.

She turned into short hall on the left, and put out her left hand to shove open her bedroom door. She stared straight ahead at the bathroom door. She'd emptied the soaking tub last night. It would take time to fill. She sighed and headed up the short hall to her bathroom. If it wasn't one thing, it was another...

She flipped on the bathroom light, strode to the hip-high tub that took up the entire back wall, and started the water. In the West, her bath would have been referred to as a hot tub. One did not wash in a bath, one soaked after scrubbing thoroughly in the shower. Sitting in dirty, or even soapy water was unhealthy. She trudged back down the hall to her bedroom.

Facing the window, with her back to the mirror over the dresser, she undressed. The scent of Toku's skin and spent lust drifted from her clothes. Heat flashed through her, and visceral memory.

Toku had groaned into her mouth while his body spilled into hers, and Ryudo's shadow had pulsed within him.

She closed her eyes. *No.* She would *not* think of either of them. She turned to her left, took two long steps, and yanked open her closet. She shoved her jeans, T-shirt, and underwear in the bottom of her hamper, and closed the door firmly.

She opened the other closet and pulled out her thick futon. She unrolled it, laying it out in the middle of her floor, and looked at the thick blankets with deep longing. The clock on her dresser showed that it was barely eight at night.

Screw it, she was dead tired. Bath, and then bed. With no classes tomorrow, at either the university or the dojo, there was no need for her to set the alarm. She could sleep all day if she wanted to. Her only appointment was at sunset, with Shihan, and his friend...and his friend's ghost.

She shook her head. She'd worry about the ghost tomorrow.

Naked and aching, she padded to the bathroom and turned on the shower. She grabbed for her sponge, and the heavily perfumed sandalwood soap. She wanted the smell of sex off of her. She scrubbed her skin ruthlessly, watching the lather swirl down the drain. She scrubbed until half the apartment smelled of sandalwood, but she could still smell Toku, and chrysanthemums.

She turned off the shower and stepped over to the tub. She plunged her hand into the steaming water. The water was near to scalding, exactly the way she liked it. She turned off the spigot. The tub's cover, leaning against the wall by the door, would keep the water relatively hot so she wouldn't have to refill it for a day or two.

She stepped in and hunched down to sit. The small of her back burned in one tiny spot. She flinched and stood up to investigate the spot with her fingers. The skin was raised, and tender. *What the...?*

Ryudo's mark.

She climbed back out of the bath, and closed the door to look in the full length mirror on the back. She turned around. Her back was a maze of long, jagged scars. At the very top of her butt, two fingers above the seam, was a brand new scar.

She frowned. It didn't look like a cut. It looked like a burn. It looked like a...symbol. It *was* a symbol, comprised of two characters. The first looked like an antique version of the word *temple*, and the second was the word *way*. Temple...*ryu*, and way...*do*? Ryudo.

Keiko stomped her heel to keep from kicking the mirror. The son of a bitch had etched his *name* on her skin! What did he think she was? His property?

His mistress.

She curled her lip, and stepped back into the tub. Fuck him. If he wanted her, he'd have to come and get her. She sat down in the water. The small of her back burned. She hissed, sank into the water to her neck and endured.

Ryudo had done the same to Toku.

She snorted. Once Toku, young master of the house, and heir to his father's mega-corporation, got a look at Ryudo's name on his ass, he'd rip Ryudo a new butt-hole at the top of his lungs. A smile lifted her lips. Now *that* would be a sight to see.

Keiko pedaled her silver ten-speed through town with her green rattan staff strapped to her back. Traffic was very light, so she was making very good time. The staff's two leaves, sprouting from the last joint, waved madly in the breeze, right over her shoulder. She'd left the top of her *bo* case open so the battered leaves could get what little sunlight remained.

Her staff was doing quite well after spending the night and all day parked in front of her east-facing living room windows in a bucket of water and plant-food. She'd been worried that hitting all those ghosts might have hurt it, but apparently the rattan was just fine.

She had slept deeply and long, well into early afternoon. Unusual for her; she was normally an early riser. She utterly refused to think about the mark that had become a dark red scar at the small of her back; or the events that had caused it.

Keiko rolled into the dojo parking lot just as the sun disappeared completely behind the city's skyscrapers. She smiled. *Right on time.*

She dismounted and locked her bike to the rack, then pulled off her bicycle helmet and hooked it to the handlebars. There was a brisk nip to the air, so she left her black denim jacket half buttoned and the long-sleeved sweat jacket beneath it unzipped about halfway, exposing the bright red halter top.

She probably should have worn something warmer, but she wanted to make damned sure that she didn't have to expose herself if Shihan's friend wanted to see her scarred back. The halter top would let him see just about everything. If he wanted to see more, he could live without. She was not dropping her black jeans.

Her bike helmet under her arm, she climbed the steps to the

dojo. The door was locked. She knocked.

No answer.

She sighed, and sat down to wait.

The street lights buzzed on, flooding the parking lot with light, and the breeze picked up. Cherry blossom petals, blown from the trees along the right side of the building, looked bleached white.

A bright copper Nissan Murano, one of the newer styled sport-utility vehicles, slowed to turn into the dojo parking lot. Shihan had arrived.

Right behind it was a blue and yellow Kawasaki carrying two passengers. The first was male, and wore a very recognizable black and red leather jacket. Obviously that was Shido, but his passenger was smaller, slighter, and wore a decorative leather coat over a bright blue…skirt?

Keiko stood, and frowned. Shido and a girl? What were they doing here?

~ Twelve ~

The girl sitting behind Shido on the Kawasaki pushed up her helmet visor, and Tika grinned from within. She waved enthusiastically. "Hello, Keiko!"

Tika? Oh, yeah, they were dating. Keiko waved back. "What are you doing here? What about your party?"

Tika hugged Shido's back. "It doesn't start 'til later!" She rolled her eyes. "I left you a message that I was coming. Didn't you get it?"

A message? Keiko blinked. "No, I didn't." Her phone hadn't gone off all day… She winced. Because she'd forgotten to turn her cell phone back on after leaving the dojo.

The Nissan's driver-side window whirred down. Shihan smiled from the window. "Keiko! Ready to go?"

Keiko hefted her staff. "Coming, Shihan." Eyeing the two on the Kawasaki, she walked over to the Nissan's left side, and popped the passenger door open. She stepped up and leaned over the back of the chair to shove her staff across the backseat, then turned to sit in the roomy bucket seat. She turned to Shihan, behind the wheel on her right. Dressed in a dark blue v-necked long-sleeved sweater over dark gray pleated casual pants and white high-top sneakers, he looked very different. She'd never seen him in anything but the black *gi* he wore to teach class. "I like the…sneakers, Shihan."

Shihan grinned. "Very comfortable!" He lifted a foot for emphasis, then tromped on the clutch, and put the Nissan in gear.

She smiled and reached for the seatbelt. "Is Shido coming with us?"

Shihan nodded. "I asked him to join us." He eased the big Nissan forward, then turned around in the parking lot. "I thought it might be educational for him." He glanced in his rearview mirror. "Though his guest is...unexpected."

Keiko shook her head. 'Unexpected', was a good description for Tika. She peeked in the side mirror and watched the motorcycle roll after them. "Speaking of unexpected and educational, Shido got an education he wasn't expecting last night."

Shihan's brow lifted. "Oh?" He turned onto the street, cutting off a far smaller Toyota.

Tires screeched and horns blared.

Keiko gasped, and grabbed onto the door handle.

Shihan stomped on the gas. Tires squealing, he roared down the road.

Keiko eased back into her seat, and stared at her instructor. Shihan was a speed demon. Who would have thought?

Shihan wove through the early evening traffic, carelessly whipping past cars. "So! What did Shido see?"

Keiko smiled while subtly making sure her seatbelt was secure. "He caught me at the tail end of a ghost battle in the city park playground."

"Oh?" Shihan's mouth opened. "How did you do?"

Keiko's brows lifted. He hadn't asked if she'd gotten hurt, merely how she did, or rather, how well his training had worked. That certainly showed where his priorities sat. She smiled. "The green rattan worked beautifully. I kicked their butts. Every last one."

"Ah...good!" Shihan's smile was pure smug satisfaction.

Keiko rolled her eyes, and grinned.

"And what did Shido think?" Shihan whipped the car around a corner.

Keiko grabbed onto the door handle again. "Shido does not believe in ghosts."

Shihan's glanced at her. "Did he see them?"

Keiko nodded. "Oh, he saw them, all right. He just refuses to believe that they were ghosts."

Shihan pursed his lips. "Ah, so." His gaze narrowed and a small smile lifted his lips. "Then perhaps tonight will prove more interesting than he expects."

Keiko lifted her brow. Shihan was up to something.

Shihan grinned suddenly. "Do you like my new car?"

Keiko choked back a laugh. "It's a great car, Shihan. It's very…"

Shihan whipped around another corner and the car tilted, lifting on her side.

Keiko clung to the door handle, and bit back a small scream. She was absolutely positive the wheels were no longer on the road.

The car thumped down.

Keiko gasped. The wheels *had* left the road. "It's very fast, Shihan! Very, very fast!"

Shihan laughed. "Yes, it is! And it has a wonderful stereo, too!" He leaned over and pressed a button on the dash. American rock and roll exploded from the speakers.

Keiko winced.

Shihan began singing to the music with enormous enthusiasm, though without much attention to key, at the top of his lungs. "Born to be wild…!"

Keiko stared. One of the foremost, and respected, practitioners of the martial arts liked fast cars and loud rock and roll. The smile simply took over her face, and she could not stop herself from bursting into laughter.

Shihan's Nissan roared up a ramp and onto the expressway. In a matter of minutes, they were racing along the dizzying cliff heights that skirted the ocean.

Keiko watched the last of the sun disappear into the ocean, below the edge of the world.

At the speed that Shihan drove, it was not all that long before he turned the big Nissan onto a steep upward off ramp marked with a small sign announcing their arrival in the small town where the Whispering Forest and the Crimson Pavilion guesthouse awaited them.

The road narrowed, and a towering rattan forest closed in on them.

Shihan slowed his speed, and guided the Nissan up a narrow winding road that was almost too small for the big car. They passed under a bright red *torii* gate, and into the town proper. The Nissan's headlights washed across elderly post and plaster buildings. Shops were tucked behind sliding doors, with shuttered apartments above. The buildings crowded against each other and loomed close on either side of the indifferently paved lane.

Shihan turned onto the town's main street, and arrived in the middle of a night festival. Strings of paper lanterns laced between the rooftops rocked in the night breeze. Tiny booths made with cloth pinned to planks with tent roofs sat cheek to jowl, offering food, luck charms, fortunes told and trinkets of every kind. Laughing people were walking everywhere.

Shihan drove slowly, but blithely, right through the middle. The rock and roll blasting from his stereo caused quite a bit of subtle pointing, and a lot of giggling behind hands.

Keiko covered her face, and eased lower in her seat.

Just beyond the festival, the road curved sharply upward, and the town buildings gave way to elegant, single-story peak-roofed wooden houses peeking out from behind dense bushes and small trees. Wicker and bamboo fences held vegetable gardens and marked tree-lined walkways.

Shihan turned for no discernable reason, and bumped off the road between a pair of trees, his tires crunching on gravel. The Nissan climbed to the top of a hill, then scooted downward on the nearly invisible road. They passed under another *torii* gate, this one far simpler than the town gate, and unpainted. They rolled and bumped into a forest of enormous and elderly trees.

One hand on the steering wheel, Shihan leaned forward, and punched a button on his dash. The music died. "This is the park." He squinted at the dark road ahead. "One would assume that you brought a flashlight?"

Keiko looked out her window at the towering trees they were passing. When Shihan had said a 'walk in the park,' she had not expected the park to be forested, so had only brought her penlight. "I did, Shihan, but it's not large."

Shihan nodded. "Small is good, in fact, small is excellent."

Keiko winced. "It's very small, Shihan."

Shihan stomped on the breaks and grinned. "So is mine." He turned off the engine, and slapped his knees. "Shall we greet our hosts?"

Keiko blinked. "We're leaving your car in the middle of the road?"

Shihan pushed open the door, the interior overhead light washing across the trunks of trees around them. "Road? There is no road here." He hopped out of the car, and his sneakers crunched on gravel.

Keiko opened her door, and light spilled out into a circular space under the trees. She stepped out onto gravel. A single small picnic table with post stools sat at one edge of a broad gravel circle. They appeared to be parked in the middle of a picnic area completely surrounded by forest. There was only one exit. Leaves whispered far overhead, caressed by the night breeze. She zipped her jacket up to her throat and buttoned her coat over it.

Shido's Kawasaki roared up the gravel drive, and pulled up along Shihan's side of the Nissan.

Shido and Tika were still with them.

Damn. Keiko sighed and opened the back door. She had sincerely hoped that the festival would have distracted Tika into stopping to shop. No such luck. She reached into the back seat to get her staff.

"Think you'll need that?"

Keiko turned.

Shido frowned while strapping a second helmet to the back of his bike. His gaze followed her *bo*.

Keiko shoved her head, and arm through the shoulder strap, setting the staff's case across her back. "Did Shihan tell you who we were seeing?"

Shido straightened. "A friend of his, a monk."

Keiko lifted her brow at him. "Did he mention the monk's companion?" She closed the back door, and then the passenger door. The world went very dark.

"No. Damn, it's dark."

Keiko snorted. "Dark has been known to happen at night." She pulled her penlight from her pocket.

"Shido?" Tika's pouting voice carried clearly in the dark. "You brought a light, right?"

"I have one in my kit." There was rustling from his general direction. "Somewhere in here…"

Smiling, Keiko snapped on her penlight. A circle of light spilled around her feet, brighter than she'd expected, which meant that it was probably a lot darker than she thought. She was pretty sure her batteries were good enough for a few hours.

A second small circle of light appeared, and Shihan with it. "Shall we go?" He started walking.

Keiko hurried after Shihan. She could not afford to get lost—not with a ghost somewhere in these woods.

"Hey!" Tika called out from behind them. "Wait for us!"

Keiko trudged through the night black forest, less than two strides behind Shihan. Her small circle of light illuminated the leaf-littered forest floor, and the heels of Shihan's white high-top sneakers. It was still fairly early in the year, so the undergrowth was no more than ankle-height.

Tika let out a small squeal. "Is that a bug? Oh, icky!"

Keiko looked back at Tika, four strides behind them, and winced. *Merciful Lady, why did Shido bring Tika?*

Tika batted at her short blue skirt while trying to hang on to Shido's arm. "I hate bugs!"

Shido, juggling a rather large flashlight, collected Tika's hand and set it back on his arm. "No, it's just a leaf."

Keiko rolled her eyes, and turned to look firmly at Shihan's back.

She would not feel sorry for Shido. "You could have stayed home, Tika."

"What, and miss out on all the excitement? No way!"

"Excitement?" Keiko brushed at a hair that had gotten loose from her long braid. "What excitement? And you hate the woods."

Tika's boots crunched loudly. "Ow, a stick…You know; the cool creepy stuff that normally happens around you. It's always interesting with you around."

Keiko groaned, and dodged a bush. "The cool creepy stuff is dangerous, Tika, you know that."

"Well…okay." Tika released a long sigh. "But still, we haven't done anything, or gone anywhere, or seen anything, since you started your karate stuff. And what's with that stick you've been carrying around everywhere?"

Keiko untangled the said stick from a branch. "That's because you've only seen me going to, or coming from, the dojo."

Tika made a sound of complete disgust, followed by the sound of plant-life being whacked. "I noticed. Every day, right after class, you're heading off to the dojo, and when I can reach you on the phone, you're too busy doing studies to go anywhere."

Oh, shit… Keiko winced and glanced over her shoulder at Shido.

Shido's gaze narrowed toward Keiko. "You go to the dojo every day?"

"Except Sundays." Tika patted his arm, and smiled. "She's there twice as much as you."

Keiko hunched her shoulders and marched faster. *Gee, thanks, Tika; just what Shido needed to hear.*

Shido was conspicuously silent.

"My life has been so normal without you." Tika sighed heavily. "The last time anything interesting happened was during the house tour, last autumn, when you disappeared."

Keiko stiffened, but kept walking. Heaven only knew what Tika meant by that. She hadn't told her a thing about…anything that had happened there. "I wasn't feeling well. I went home in a taxi."

"So I heard, but I also watched you disappear through that wall." Tika tisked loudly.

Keiko hunched her shoulders. "I fell through a sliding panel. The staff found me." She absolutely, positively, was not going to mention Toku. Tika would have the rumors saying that they were dating, if not engaged to be married, overnight.

"I know. I watched the wall close behind you." Tika giggled. "So, did you see it?"

Keiko rolled her eyes. "See what?"

"You know, the ghost! Did you see that one too?"

Keiko sighed. "I don't want to talk about the house tour."

"Ha! You did see it! Was he cute?"

Keiko groaned. Only Tika would ask that.

"The stories say he kidnaps women every century or so and they become his lovers. He's got to be cute, if they stay with him. So was he?"

Shocked, Keiko tripped on nothing in particular. "Where on earth, did you hear that?"

"There was a whole book on the house's history in the school library." Plant-life rattled. "Damn, there's lots of this...tree-stuff."

Keiko sighed. "In case you haven't noticed, we are in a forest."

"Yeah, I noticed." A bush rattled. "So, did you see the ghost?"

Keiko stared hard at Shihan's back, wondering how he was taking this conversation. "I don't want to talk about it."

"Oh, come on, we both know you did, you might as well admit it."

Keiko sighed. Tika would keep nagging at her, right in front of Shihan and Shido, until she heard what she wanted to hear. "Yes, I did, yes, he was cute..." *Why did I say that?* "And nothing happened." *Liar, liar, pants on fire...* "Can we change the subject now?"

"Oh, no need to get all defensive." Tika groaned. "My feet are starting to hurt, can we stop?"

Great change in subjects. Keiko sighed.

Shido sighed as well.

Shihan abruptly lengthened his stride, walking faster.

Keiko stretched her stride to keep up with Shihan. "Come on, Tika, it can't be much further."

Tika groaned dramatically. "Right, fine, whatever…"

The back of Keiko's skull began to vibrate, and the hair stood on her neck. *Ghost…* The air chilled sharply. Her breath steamed out, and her hands turned icy. *Angry ghost…* They had to get out of there. "Tika, come on!"

"I'm coming! Shido, don't pull."

Shido sighed heavily. "What are you talking about?"

"Quit playing, and let go. Your hands are cold!"

"Tika, I'm not touching you."

"Huh? Then who…?" Tika gasped.

Keiko's heart thumped hard in her chest. She stopped and looked back. Although the night was perfectly black under the trees, Tika was clearly visible because something gray and glowing was wrapped all around her—a ghost.

~ Thirteen ~

Keiko stared at the silvery, almost gelatinous, mist wrapping Tika from head to toe. Why was a ghost anywhere near Tika? They normally avoided her like the plague. Tika's natural tendency to repel ghosts was the main reason why they had been close friends for so long. Keiko had been terrified to go anywhere without her—until she began carrying the rattan staff.

Guilt stabbed Keiko. Since she hadn't needed Tika to repel ghosts, Keiko had practically abandoned her friend.

His flashlight dimming to amber in hand, Shido stared at Tika's spirit-enveloped form. "What the fuck is that?" His breath steamed out.

"It's a ghost." Keiko licked her dry lips. "And it's pissed off. That's why it's cold."

Shido cringed back. "I've never seen anything like that."

Keiko smiled sourly. "Welcome to my world."

Tika threw up her head, and gasped in a deep breath. The glow disappeared. She dropped to her knees, abruptly and unnaturally, like a puppet whose strings had been cut.

Shido inched closer to her. "Tika?"

Keiko rolled the case of her *bo* over her shoulder and freed the ties. "Shido, get back." She slid her green rattan staff free.

Shido shot a glare at Keiko, and moved closer to Tika. "Tika, are you all right?"

"I'm fine." A giggle erupted from Tika. "Never been better." Her head snapped up, and she focused on Shido. "Hello, cutie." She held out her arms. "Give us a kiss?"

Shido reached for her.

Keiko raised her staff into a downward spear hold. "Shido, don't!"

Shido glanced at Keiko. "What is your problem…?"

Tika lunged off the ground, locked her arms around Shido's neck and covered his mouth with her lips.

Shido froze, then moaned and wrapped his arms around Tika. His eyes closed. Locked in her embrace, he slowly sank to his knees. His flashlight hit the ground. He topped backwards onto the forest floor, kissing her hungrily within the flashlight's pool of light.

Lip-locked, Tika threw her leg over Shido to straddle his hips and writhe.

Moaning, Shido's hands slid down Tika's body and under her short skirt.

Tika inched back and began tugging at the belt to his pants.

Keiko had no clue what to do, but she had to do something. She moved closer to the writhing pair. "Tika? Shido?"

Straddling Shido's hips, Tika reared up and twisted around to look at Keiko. "Back off!" Her eyes blazed with leaping blue flames. "He's mine!"

Possession… Keiko raised her staff. "Get out of her."

Tika smiled, and it was nothing like any expression she had ever worn on her face. "What are you going to do? Hit your little friend?"

Keiko tightened her hands on her staff. "Who are you?"

Tika raised a hand, and long black claws erupted from her fingertips. "Nobody you want to fuck with." She curled her lips back, showing a mouthful of black fangs, and smiled inhumanly wide. "Tell Keiko to go away, Shido, I want to have some fun."

Shido turned to look over at Keiko, his gaze unfocused. "Go away, Keiko."

Keiko frowned. "Shido?"

"Keiko. Come." Shihan's voice was soft, but commanding.

Keiko turned.

Shihan stood four strides away. "This way."

Keiko took a step toward him. "But..." She looked back at Tika and Shido.

The possessed girl had worked Shido's pants open. She pulled out his rather long and stiff cock. Her head dipped, then bobbed, busily and noisily, sucking him.

Moaning under her, Shido grabbed her head, and pumped his hips. "Fuck yeah, suck it. Suck it, baby..."

Keiko winced and looked toward her instructor. "Shihan, we just can't leave them...like this?"

"There is nothing you or I can do for them." Shihan shook his head, then turned away. "This is their lesson, not yours."

What? Keiko stared after Shihan. *What lesson could this possibly be?*

Shido writhed and gasped in the bushes behind her. "Oh, shit... Oh, fuck! I'm cumming!" He released a long, groaning sigh.

Tika slurped, and moaned with pleased satisfaction.

Shihan walked into the trees.

Keiko trotted after him "Shihan...!"

Shihan stopped and turned to face her, his gaze narrowed and his mouth tight. "Can you remove a possession?"

Keiko winced. "No."

"Neither can I."

Keiko looked back. "But we can't just leave them!"

Shihan leaned close, his gaze cold. "Keiko, that is not a common spirit, it is a demon. You of all people cannot afford to remain in its presence." He turned away and started walking. "Come, we have an appointment."

Keiko's skin crawled. "It's a *demon?*" She hurried to catch up to Shihan.

"Yes." Shihan marched, gazing straight ahead. "Rather than a mere spirit of the deceased, it's a soul that was ripped from a still living body." He wiped one hand down his side. "It's an enslaved ghost bound into service to a sorcerer."

Keiko felt the world shift under her feet. *Demons and sorcerers...*

And the demon had Tika. "Merciful Lady..." She barely knew how to deal with ghosts. She had no earthy idea how to deal with a demon— or a sorcerer. She slid her green rattan *bo* back into the cloth case, letting it settle across her back, and marched in Shihan's wake, her penlight spilling light right before her feet. "Where did you learn about demons?"

Shihan shoved one hand in his pocket and sighed. "That is a truly long story. Someday, perhaps I will tell you, but not tonight."

Side by side, they walked though the forest under whispering leaves. The trees became smaller, thinner and far more twisted. The undergrowth disappeared to become a broad carpet of thick springy moss. Light bloomed among the trees ahead. The scent of pipe smoke perfumed the air.

Keiko stepped from the trees, onto the bank of a rocky creek. Ten strides to her immediate right, the creek tumbled over several large stones and then washed past a rustic and rather small teahouse perched right at the water's edge. The sharply peaked thatched roof was barely visible under the trees.

A pair of round, and glowing, paper lanterns hung from the small porch over the guest entrance at the front. Light spilled down the white plaster walls and exposed natural wood post beams. The broad wooden window shutters were pinned partway up, revealing a sliver of light. There was a trace scent of burning charcoal from the small fireplace.

Shihan headed straight for it.

Keiko marched after him.

Just shy of the direct front of the house, flame flickered within a stone lantern. Light gleamed on a tiny pool of rainwater within the hollow at the top of the waist-high natural stone *tsukubai*. A long-stemmed bamboo dipper was positioned across the top.

Shihan stopped at the stone water basin, picked up the dipper, filled it and poured water over his hands. After making washing motions, he shook the water from his hands, refilled the dipper and looked over at Keiko.

Keiko sighed, walked over to his side and held out her hands.

Shihan poured the scoop of water over her palms for her ritual cleansing.

Keiko winced. The water was ice cold. She wiped her hands together, then shook the water off.

From the far side of the house, a man stepped from the shadows. Light from the paper lanterns gleamed brightly on snow-white hair pulled back into a tight tail, spilling over the shoulder of his deep black coat worn over a business suit of midnight blue. He lifted his chin, revealing mature yet arresting features, and a cool gaze above a sharp smile. The collar of his cobalt blue shirt was only a shade or so lighter than his suit, and his black tie had the shimmer of silk. Tobacco smoke wafted from the old-fashioned long-stemmed clay pipe in his hand.

Keiko abruptly shivered, and felt the hair on her arms lift. It wasn't quite the same as her awareness of ghosts, but she was definitely sensing something.

Shihan bowed showing a guest's respect toward his host. "It is good to see you, my old friend."

The man bowed; a host's acknowledgment. "My old friend, it is good to be seen." His voice was as soft as a whisper, and yet resonated in the night.

"This is the student I spoke to you about." Shihan clasped his hands behind him. "Keiko, this is Avatar Tsuke, of the Temple of the Black Lotus."

Keiko bowed a little more deeply than Shihan, expressing her lower rank, while trying to gain some control over her less than respectful expression. *A monk in a business suit?* Her long braid slid over her shoulder. "My respects, Avatar."

Avatar Tsuke abruptly focused on Keiko, and the heart of his midnight gaze danced with cold blue flame. He nodded. "Keiko."

Keiko took a long deep breath, and held very still. *I will not freak out, I will not freak out, I will not freak out...*

Avatar Tsuke turned toward Shihan, his expression warming, and lifted his clay-stemmed pipe. "Join me for a smoke?" He shoved his free hand into his pant's pocket.

Shihan nodded and approached the porch.

Keiko released her breath and stayed right where she was. She hadn't been included in the invitation, and that was perfectly okay with her. She discreetly stepped back toward the water basin, and snapped off her penlight. Hopefully, they'd have their little private conversation, and forget she was even there. A shiver slid up her spine and centered in the back of her skull. *Ghost...*

Keiko looked around sharply. Had Tika followed her?

Six long strides away, a soft radiance formed by the edge of the water. The glow condensed into a young man looking into the creek. His old-fashioned robes of blue and white seemed softly water-colored. Two swords were positioned in his deep blue sash, one a little higher than the other, and his hair was bound into an antique top-knot worn by *samurai* well over two hundred years ago.

Keiko held very still. Her staff was still untied, she could get to it if necessary, but she strongly suspected that this was Avatar Tsuke's companion, Ryujin.

He turned his head, and looked at her. "You are not afraid." The breeze of his voice carried the sharp clean scent of cypress.

Keiko released a soft breath, and bowed slowly, without taking her eyes off of the ghost. "Should I be?"

The ghost smiled, and nodded toward her, in acknowledgement. "Of me? No." He looked over toward the teahouse, and his smile faded. "But there are things that should not be taken at face value." He looked back at her.

Keiko inclined her head toward the tea house. "Some things are more obvious than one might think." A small smile lifted the corner of her mouth.

He smiled broadly, and suddenly seemed like any other young man her age. "He's that obvious, huh?"

Keiko slid her hand down her arm, and rolled her eyes. "Oh, yeah."

He looked off toward the trees, and took a casual step toward her. "You must be very sensitive."

Keiko stilled utterly, her heart suddenly pounding in her throat.

He stopped, and gazed at her. Blue fox-fire danced in the back of his eyes. "Are you?"

Keiko swallowed and fought to slow her heart. "I have the...gift."

His brows lifted, and his mouth opened on a sigh. "Do you?"

Keiko braced her feet, and lowered her chin, focusing on the ghost, measuring the distance between them, verses the length of her rattan staff. "And the means to protect myself."

He blinked and tilted his head, then smiled. "Is that so?"

Keiko nodded very slowly.

He turned his head, staring directly into her eyes. "Have you used this...protection, recently?"

Keiko frowned. There was something odd about his question. "Yes. Last night."

His brows snapped together, and he frowned. "Not tonight?"

Tonight? Keiko felt her temper stirring. "Then you know about that thing in the woods?"

"Yes." The ghost looked off into the trees, then focused on her. "Did you actually see it, or merely sense it?"

"I saw it." Keiko's hands fisted at her sides. "That...thing possessed my friend before I could stop it."

His eyes opened wide. "Possessed...?"

Keiko's jaw tightened. "Yes, possessed." She looked away. "When I left her, she was..." She swallowed. "Seducing her boyfriend."

The ghost glared at the trees. "It's feeding..." He abruptly set his hands at his sides, and bowed deeply toward Keiko. "Please forgive me, for...being unable to come to your assistance in your time of need."

Keiko's breath, and anger, left in a rush. "Do you know how to get it out of her?"

He nodded once. "I am Ryujin, companion to Avatar Tsuke, of the Temple of the Black Lotus." He smiled sourly. "Destroying demons is what we do."

She bowed to Ryujin. "I'm Keiko, and I could really use your help."

Ryujin strode toward her.

Keiko backed up hard against the stone basin, and reached for her staff. "That's close enough, thank you."

Ryujin stopped and scowled. "Do you want to know how to help your friend, or don't you?"

"I'm sure Keiko would indeed like to know how to help her friend, but first, I have a question for her." The voice was deep, resonant and sinister.

Keiko bit back a gasp, and turned to face the teahouse.

Avatar Tsuke stood on the porch within a pool of light cast by the hanging lanterns. With his thumb, he pressed tobacco into the bowl of his clay pipe, refilling it. A small cold smile played at his mouth.

Shihan stood at his elbow, also holding a pipe. He stared hard at Keiko, not smiling at all. All trace of the rock and roll singing speed demon was gone, as if it had never been.

Avatar Tsuke lifted his pipe, and snapped his fingers over the bowl. Flame leapt to life within the bowl.

A shiver slid across her skin. Keiko sucked in a sharp breath.

Avatar Tsuke glanced toward her, casually puffing while the flame remained under his fingers. He moved his hand away and the flame disappeared. He pulled the pipe from his lips, and blew smoke. "So, Keiko, whose mark are you wearing?"

What kind of question was that? Keiko frowned at Shihan.

Shihan held her gaze steadily, but made no motions.

Keiko swallowed. Something was definitely going on here. She took a soft breath and bowed her head just a little. "With all due respect, Avatar, I have dozens of marks." A small smile lifted the corner of her mouth. "I didn't stop to ask who they were when they put them on me."

Avatar Tsuke focused on her. "Is that so?" He turned to face her, and tucked his free hand behind his back. "May I see them?"

The hair on Keiko's neck lifted. She did not want to undress, and expose herself in front of this unnerving man. Her gaze drifted to Shihan.

Shihan didn't twitch a muscle, merely held her gaze steadily.

Keiko licked her dry lips and slanted a look at the unnerving Avatar.

His brows lifted, and his smile faded. "Keiko, I know you do not feel comfortable in my presence. As sensitive as you are, that's...unavoidable, considering what I am." He sighed. "I can only assure you that I do intend to help you, in every way open to me." He dropped his chin. "However, I cannot assist you until I know all of what you have been exposed to."

Keiko jolted with confusion. The Avatar's expression seemed sincere, but... "If I may ask, what are you?"

Avatar Tsuke's brows lifted. "You don't know?"

Shihan cleared his throat. "I thought I would leave such revelations to your discretion."

Avatar Tsuke rolled his eyes. "Merciful Lady, no wonder she's..." He chuckled and smiled. "I'm an adept, a mage."

~ *fourteen* ~

"You're a mage?" Keiko frowned at the silver-haired Avatar. "Is that like, being a wizard? You do magic?"

Avatar Tsuke's eyes crinkled with humor, transforming his face from something sinister to merely that of a handsome older man. "As Ryujin's host, I have access to, and use, what you would call magic. That is what you are sensing." He lifted his pipe toward her. "I'm not going to say that you should not be alarmed when you feel this way. You should. A rogue adept—a sorcerer, if you like—is just as much of a threat to you as a ghost, and for the same reasons. My duty, and that of my temple, is to guard against such sorcerers, and the demons they create." He smiled wryly and lifted his chin. "I really am here to help you."

Keiko sucked on her bottom lip. Shihan had brought her here specifically to gain his help with her…problem. She took a deep breath. She could at least see if he *could* help. She smiled. "It's a little dark to see my skin, Avatar." Not to mention chilly.

Avatar Tsuke turned to the side, and lifted his hand, palm up, toward the tea house. "By all means, come inside."

Keiko bowed again, and stepped up onto the thatch-covered porch. The wooden door of the teahouse was slightly open, and very traditional, meaning small. She had to crouch to go through it. The small size of the door was meant to show respect to any guests that might already be seated. Hovering upright while others were seated was impolite. Hopefully there wouldn't be anyone else in there. She'd had enough surprises for one night.

She crouched on the stepping-stone and pushed. The door opened, revealing the slightly raised alcove, on the immediate right, featuring a beautifully painted hanging scroll. A stick of incense burned beneath it.

An antique iron lantern hung in the center of the tiny room shedding fairly bright light on the four-and-a-half-*tatami*-mat-wide floor. Though the large windows on each wall had their shutters partially lifted open, the teahouse was surprisingly warm. A square fire-pit holding a steaming cast iron teapot occupied one whole quarter of the half-sized *tatami* covering the very center. A plain black cushion was set on the floor to her immediate right, directly before the alcove. On her left, just beyond the doorway, was another cushion.

The host's miniature door was at the far wall, with the host's seat, and the tea utensils arranged to one side.

Keiko crouched all the way to the lesser cushion and knelt on it, knees together. She tugged open her jean jacket, but with only her halter top under her jackets, she decided to leave her sweat-jacket zipped.

Shihan crouched through the door and knelt on the cushion before the alcove. He gave her a quick smile.

The tiny door at the very back of the teahouse slid open, and Avatar Tsuke crouched through it. He slid the door closed behind him, then took the seat in the host's place, decorously arranging his coat and jacket around him. He smiled. "So, shall we have tea first?"

Keiko looked at Shihan, the honored guest.

Shihan nodded gravely.

Avatar Tsuke went through the motions of the tea ceremony with surprising skill, and impressive speed. In a very short time, all three were sipping fragrant and near boiling green tea from small cups.

By the time Keiko finished her cup, she felt far more relaxed in the adept's humming presence. The dread she'd felt earlier had calmed under the quiet comfort of the familiar antique ceremony.

Avatar Tsuke set down his cup. "Are you ready, Keiko?"

Keiko took a deep breath. This was what she was here for; she might as well get it over with. "I am."

Shihan held out his hand for her teacup.

Keiko passed her cup to him, then unzipped her jacket. She pulled both jackets off, exposing her bright red halter-top, then turned around. She pulled her braid forward, letting it settle across her breast, presenting a nearly unblocked view of her scarred back.

There was a prominent amount of silence.

She peeked over her shoulder.

Avatar Tsuke frowned. "Would you be so kind as to sit in the center, directly under the light?" He smiled. "My old eyes are not as good as I'd like them to be."

He wanted her to sit closer? Mild alarm shivered across her skin, but she couldn't think of a reason to refuse him. Keiko nodded and scooted to the very center, taking the spot right next to the steaming pot sitting in the off-center fire-pit.

A shimmer of chill washed across her back, raising the hair on her entire body. She stiffened.

"Do not be alarmed." Avatar Tsuke's voice was calm, but commanding. "I am merely using a small amount of power to see what made such...injuries."

A shimmer of awareness thrummed in the back of her skull. *Ghost...* Alarmed, Keiko turned around sharply.

Ryujin smiled from where he was seated next to Avatar Tsuke. "Very sensitive." The clean scent of cypress colored his words.

Avatar Tsuke raised a brow at him. His palms were up and wreathed in a soft blue glow. "Indeed."

Keiko's brows lifted. That blue glow, was that magic?

Ryujin's gaze drifted lower, to her back, and his smile faded.

Keiko turned away. She didn't want to see his disgust at her hideousness.

"This damage is...unforgivable." Ryujin's voice was low and cold.

Chill bumps raced across Keiko's skin. The temperature was dropping. Ryujin was apparently getting angry. Her brows lifted.

Ryudo had reacted the same way, with anger. *Interesting...*

Avatar Tsuke cleared his throat. "Keiko, most of these are very old. When did these attacks begin?"

"In grade school." She studied the door across from her. "I was eight."

"You came into your gift in childhood?" Ryujin sounded appalled.

Keiko rolled her eyes. "It wasn't my idea!"

"Of course not, but you should have been put under protection after the first incident!"

A shiver attacked her. It was getting colder. Ryujin's temper was obviously getting the better of him. Keiko leaned closer to the warmth of the fire pit.

"I agree, the temple should have been notified." Avatar Tsuke sounded tired. "Do you have any marks anywhere else?"

Keiko shook her head. "They only scarred my back."

"Blood-drinkers." Ryujin's voice was hoarse with anger.

Keiko's breath steamed out. It was getting colder. Ryujin was showing quite a temper.

"Of course." Avatar Tsuke's coat rustled. "At that age, the other option was not available."

Keiko flinched just a tiny bit. *Ryudo...*

"However, there is this..." Avatar Tsuke sounded mildly curious. "And it's new."

A shimmer of sensation focused at the top of her butt, right under her belt. Keiko froze. Ryudo's mark. *Shit...*

Ryujin's scent of cypress became stronger. "Demon mark."

"It seems that we will be doing some hunting after all." Avatar Tsuke sounded distinctly amused.

Keiko stiffened. She didn't want them thinking Ryudo was a demon. He was a possessive and manipulative bastard, but he wasn't a clawed, fanged monster out to make her bleed. He didn't want to hurt her—just own her. "No." Keiko shook her head. "He's not a demon."

"Then you know where this mark came from?" Avatar Tsuke's

voice vibrated with quiet intensity.

Keiko flinched. No help for it now. "Yes." She looked over her shoulder at the two. "He is a pain in my butt, but he's not a demon. He's not out to hurt me." He merely wanted to keep her locked in his house for the rest of her life as his mistress.

Ryujin focused on her. "Keiko, an ordinary ghost cannot do this."

Keiko scowled. "He's not a demon. He's nothing like that thing in the woods."

Avatar Tsuke raised a brow, and blue fox-fire flickered in the depths of his black eyes. "Has this creature marked anyone else?"

Keiko dodged his penetrating stare. She was not bringing Toku into this. "My apologies, but I have nothing more to say on this subject."

Avatar Tsuke raised his brows at Ryujin.

Ryujin dodged his gaze and shrugged.

Keiko's hands fisted at her sides. "Look, I already took care of the problem. It's over."

Avatar Tsuke shook his head sadly. "Keiko, your soul is bound to this creature. As long as you wear this mark, you can be found—and subdued."

Keiko stiffened. *Subdued?*

Avatar Tsuke folded his hands together. "Would you like us to remove it?"

Huh? Keiko turned to look at them. "Can you?"

"Of course." Avatar Tsuke smiled very mildly. "Tell us where he is, and we'll remove his mark."

Keiko felt a shiver that had nothing to do with either the adept, or his ghost companion. "What are you going to do to him?"

Avatar Tsuke's brows lifted, and he looked off to one side. "If he's not demonic, as you say, then we'll merely bind him."

Bind Ryudo? Keiko stilled. "What exactly does that mean?"

Avatar Tsuke smiled and shrugged. "We capture the spirit, and bind them to an Avatar as a companion. Avatars and their attendant spirits work as a team to destroy destructive spirits, in service to humanity."

Ryujin looked away, and his hands slowly closed into fists.

She found herself shaking her head. She couldn't. She couldn't turn over Toku's hundreds of years old house guardian. "I'm sorry, but I can't tell you that."

"You can't?" Avatar Tsuke scowled. "Are you so enthralled by this creature that you cannot see beyond your own lust for it?"

Keiko jerked away, staring. "What?" Where the hell had that come from? "No! He's not mine to turn over!"

Ryujin's head came up, his brows lifted in clear astonishment.

"What?" Avatar Tsuke's gaze narrowed, and filled with blue fire. "Who owns this creature?"

Who owns Ryudo? Keiko bit back a sudden chuckle. She'd like to see someone try! She shook her head. "No one owns him, he's a house guardian."

Ryujin's eyes widened.

Avatar Tsuke rolled his eyes, and smiled. "Oh, I see. Well, now, that's very different." He patted his knee. "No need to worry, then, just tell me what house he guards and we'll take care of it from there."

Ryujin stared at the floor.

Keiko froze. "What?"

Avatar Tsuke leaned forward. "I'll gain the master's permission to do a blessing on the house, and collect your ghost in the process. Once he's bound into service, removing your mark will be simple."

Ryujin abruptly vanished.

Keiko stared. Bound into service as in, *enslaved!* Her heart thumped and the small house became stiflingly hot, and close. For all that Ryudo was a pain in the butt, she couldn't see him anywhere but in that house, and under that late summer cherry tree. It was wrong to take him from his home. She turned away, and shook her head. "Forget it. I'll deal with him myself."

"Keiko, a ghost that powerful should not be free."

"He's not free." Well, not technically. "He's a house guardian."

Keiko moved away and grabbed for her jackets. "He's been in that house for..." She had no idea how long he'd been in that house. She shoved her arms into her jackets. "You can't take him from his house. He belongs in that house."

"Keiko, I'm only trying to help you."

"Yes, I know." Keiko zipped her sweat-jacket and started buttoning her denim jacket closed over it. "But you can't take him from his house." It was where he belonged—with Toku. She'd just have to find another way to deal with Ryudo.

"Keiko, he's already bound you to him. It's only a matter of time before he finds a host he can manipulate and enslaves you both to feed his appetites."

Keiko froze. *Toku...* She snatched for her *bo*, lying on the floor against the wall. She had to get out of that teahouse.

"Keiko, where are you going?"

Keiko turned around and sketched a kneeling bow. "I need some air." She twisted around on her knees and shoved her way through the door.

Keiko stumbled off the porch and leaned over the waist-high stone water basin by the stone lantern. She closed her eyes and worked to stop the shaking.

"Keiko?"

Keiko gasped and whirled around, her sheathed staff up in a defensive stance.

Ryujin stood only three strides away just out of her staff's range.

Keiko relaxed her stance and set the end of her *bo* down. She gave him a tired smile. "Sorry, you startled me."

"I understand." He smiled just as tiredly. "Did you tell him where to find your house guardian?"

Keiko shook her head. "He belongs in that house. He belongs with his family."

Ryujin smiled. "If only my family had been half as...considerate." He looked away.

Keiko winced. Obviously he'd been someone's house guardian.

No wonder he had reacted with the same protective anger as Ryudo over her ghost attacks. She wondered what house he'd belonged to. "I'm sorry."

He shook his head. "It was done long ago." He lifted his eyes to regard her with his fox-fire gaze. "Your friend, the one possessed by the demon. Could she see ghosts, normally?"

"Tika?" Keiko's brows lifted. "No, not at all." Tika rarely saw past her own image in the nearest reflection. She frowned. "And ghosts normally avoid her. I've never seen a ghost—do that, to anybody."

"Demons are not true ghosts. They're bound souls. Their power comes from the sorcerer that holds them." Ryujin took a couple of steps to the right, and then the left, pacing before her. "To rescue your possessed friend, you must pull the ghost out and then destroy the sorcerer's seal within it to allow the soul to disperse." He stopped and faced her. "If she is not one who normally sees ghosts, then it must be done soon. She is not a suitable host for a spirit. It will warp her soul, and then her body. Eventually, it will kill her."

It would *kill* her? Keiko stilled. Could Toku be in danger too, from Ryudo's frequent possessions? "What about someone who *can* see ghosts, what if they are possessed?"

Ryujin sighed. "I'm not sure how it works, exactly, but for some reason, someone that can see spirits has the capability of protecting their soul from that of an invading spirit, even while under the spirit's physical control." He shrugged. "An adept can house a spirit and remain free from control." He looked toward the teahouse. "A skilled adept can bend the spirit to his will, even from a great distance."

Keiko frowned. "So as long as someone can see ghosts, they're pretty much okay if possessed?"

Ryujin lifted his brow. "Then your house guardian does have a host." It wasn't a question.

Keiko refused to look at him. "I don't want to talk about it."

"Has your house guardian bound his host, as he bound you?"

Keiko glared at him.

Ryujin smiled sadly. "I guess, 'yes'."

Keiko turned away. "Why is it so damned important to you and...?" She nodded toward the teahouse

"A ghost with both a chosen and a host bound to them is a very powerful creature." Avatar Tsuke stepped off the teahouse's porch. "And highly destructive."

Keiko scowled. "He's not like that. He's not a monster." She threw up her hand. "And what the hell is a 'chosen'?"

"That would be you." Avatar Tsuke smiled slightly. "I would like to offer you an honored place in the Temple of the Black Lotus, but as long as you are marked..." He shook his head sadly. "We cannot accept you, or protect you."

Keiko's hand tightened on her staff. "Thank you, but I don't need your protection. I can protect myself."

"Is that so?" Avatar Tsuke's brows lifted. "Are you saying that you volunteered for that mark?"

Shihan appeared at Avatar Tsuke's elbow.

Keiko glared at Avatar Tsuke. "Are you going to help me rescue Tika or not?"

Avatar Tsuke smiled. "Absolutely." He gestured toward the woods. "Shall we go?"

~ Fifteen ~

Shihan led the way back into the night shadowed trees with Avatar Tsuke at his side. Shihan had his penlight out. Avatar Tsuke didn't seem to need one.

Keiko, her staff bouncing against her back, followed a full length behind Shihan, her penlight shining on the heels of his white sneakers. Ryujin was nowhere to be seen. She could feel his presence nearby, but with Avatar Tsuke's presence jangling her nerves, she couldn't pinpoint exactly where he was. She scowled. It was like looking for a lit candle while standing next to someone with a high-powered flashlight.

The wind picked up, and chilled.

Keiko clenched her jaw. They were probably getting within range of the demon's ability to sense them. She reached over her shoulder for the green rattan staff.

Near a massive spreading beech, Keiko's awareness picked out a low and bitter scraping sensation. It wasn't like Ryujin's neck-ruffling presence, or Avatar Tsuke's sonorous and heavy hum. She concentrated on that odd and unpleasant impression, and it became a feeling of metal scraping against metal that ached in her teeth.

Shihan raised his hand and stopped. They stopped with him. "Here."

Avatar Tsuke peered up and nodded. He pulled out a cell phone, hit a button and set it to his ear. "Yes. Come." He pressed a button and pocketed the phone.

Keiko blinked. Short phone call.

Shihan looked back at Keiko, and pointed up into the branches of the beech.

Keiko looked up. An odd colorless glow was concentrated around something writhing against the trunk nearly concealed among the tree's branches. Long moving twisting limbs, like that of a gigantic octopus, were threaded around the trunk and among the branches. Her skin crawled. Definitely some kind of ghost. An icy breeze washed around her. Her breath spilled from her lips in a mist. The demonic ghost definitely knew they were there, and it wasn't pleased.

A soft moan drifted down.

Keiko frowned. It sounded like Shido. But if it was Shido, how the hell did he get up there? And how were they going to get him down? She inched closer, and stepped on something. She shone her penlight at her feet. Shredded clothing and shoes were scattered at the bottom of the tree. Shido's leather jacket lay in a crumpled pile. She picked up the jacket and looked up.

Shido and Tika were suspended by semi-transparent snaking and pulsing...tentacle things wrapped around them. Both of them were naked and locked belly to belly in an intimate embrace. Entwined, they writhed rhythmically against each other, their eyes closed tight in the throes of ecstasy—or agony.

Keiko frowned, then swallowed hard. The tentacles weren't just wrapped around them, they were inserted within them, too. Both of them had one shoved down their throats and it looked like one was in their navels. There were two moving between Tika's legs, with one clearly up her ass, and another was thrusting slowly but steadily in and out of Shido's ass. The demon was ass-fucking them both.

Shido threw his head back and stiffened. Every muscle in his body stood out in sharp relief, straining. A choked moan escaped his throat. The thing down his throat slid out, dripping. He collapsed against Tika, his head dropping against her neck while choking and gasping for breath. The stink of spent sex was thick in the air.

Keiko suddenly wished she hadn't looked.

Ryujin materialized less than a hand-span away, looking upward with his hands resting on the hilts of his swords.

Keiko nearly jumped out of her skin.

Ryujin smiled at her briefly, then frowned up at the thing in the beech tree. "We need to get them down."

Keiko grimaced. "Yeah, but how?"

"I go up there, and cut them free." He drew his swords from his sash.

"By yourself?" Keiko jerked back. "Ryujin, that thing is huge! It's all over that tree!"

Ryujin smiled at her, and backed away. He turned to Avatar Tsuke. "I am ready."

Avatar Tsuke nodded and raised his hands. Blue flame enveloped them. He glanced at Keiko and lifted his chin at Shihan. "See to them once they fall."

Keiko gasped. "Fall?" She looked up. They were halfway up the tree.

Shihan walked over to Keiko with his hands up. "Back. You need to get back."

Keiko tripped backwards, away from the tree.

Ryujin looked up at the tree, and spread his arms wide, with his swords upraised. "Begin!"

Avatar Tsuke made a complicated gesture with the fingers of both glowing hands, pointed at Ryujin, and shouted. A blinding bolt of blue fire lashed from his hands to envelop Ryujin's form. Ryujin exploded in a percussion wave of blue-white flames that lit the night to day.

Keiko ducked behind a tree and watched the wave pass through the entire forest at incredible speed in an ever-expanding ring of eye-searing brightness.

Blue flames gather tightly around Ryujin, stretching upward and outward into a massive scaled and ridged serpentine figure of blue and white flame. The mouth opened, revealing dagger-length teeth.

Merciful Lady... Keiko stared. A *dragon?*

The thing in the tree exploded into movement, unwrapping long snaking limbs that transformed into gigantic hinged scythes. It propelled itself higher into the tree, raised a pair of scythed legs and hissed.

Shido dropped from the tree, and landed on his back, his limbs flopping like a rag doll. He groaned.

Shihan ran and grabbed Shido under the arms.

Keiko ran from behind the tree and grabbed Shido's other arm. He was soaking wet and slippery. Together they lifted Shido onto his feet, and half carried the naked young man out from under the tree. They let him down to sit behind another large beech. Keiko knelt and set Shido's coat over his shoulders.

Shido turned his head away and clutched at his coat, trembling.

Keiko straightened and looked back. Tika was clearly visible, curled up and suspended within the demon's semi-transparent abdomen. "It still has Tika!"

Avatar Tsuke raised a ball of blue fire between his palms and shouted. "Ryujin! I can't seal it until it releases the girl!"

The dragon roared and launched itself up the tree on clawed limbs. "Let her go!"

"No!" The Demon screamed and wrapped the dragon in snaking limbs, slashing with long scythes. "Mine!"

The dragon twisted sharply, ripping with claw-tipped hands, the long ridges down its spine tearing the limbs that bound it. It sank its teeth into a thick supporting limb and ripped it away. The limb dissipated.

The demon screamed and lashed out with dozens of sword-length scythes. The dragon twisted out of the way and spat gouts of blue fire at the demon's heart. The demon retreated. The dragon pursued, grabbing another supporting limb in its fangs and tearing it away.

A bitterly cold wind whipped through the trees generated by the anger of both powerful spirits.

Shido shivered hard, and curled up very small with his eyes tightly closed.

Keiko shivered herself, praying that none of it was hurting Tika. Technically the dragon was a ghost, so its claws and teeth should pass harmlessly through her, but then, how was the demon thing holding her to begin with, since it was a ghost too?

The demon whipped out long snaking limbs, grabbing onto the trees around it. It pulled itself out of the tree, jumping into the next, like a gigantic spider. And then the next...

The dragon leapt after it, spreading scaled wings. Blue flame blasted from its open mouth.

"What's happening?" Keiko stepped away from her tree. "Why does it still have Tika?"

"It's fleeing!" Avatar Tsuke followed after the battling pair with his ball of blue light.

Keiko turned to Shihan. "We have to go after them!"

Shihan, stood over Shido, and folded his arms. "We are not prepared for such a battle."

Keiko's temper snapped. "Fine. You stay here." She bolted, chasing after the blaze of light in the trees.

"Keiko!"

Keiko ignored Shihan's shouts and kept running. She was not going to abandon Tika again.

The light behind the trees moved upward, then winked out.

Keiko was forced to stop and turn her penlight on. Following the bone-jarring hum of Avatar Tsuke, she proceeded at a trot. Hopefully the light disappearing was good news. She skirted a tree and very nearly ran straight into Avatar Tsuke, heading back. She skidded to a halt before him. Neither Tika nor Ryujin were with him. "What happened?"

Avatar Tsuke scowled and kept marching toward Shihan. "The demon is in flight and headed for the village. If it gets there it can burrow itself into any number of victims and disappear."

Keiko trotted at his side. "What about Tika?"

Avatar Tsuke shook his head. "We can only hope that Ryujin finds her abandoned. If so, he'll notify me immediately and we'll go collect her."

Keiko jolted. "You mean it still has her?"

"Yes."

Keiko trotted to catch up to him. "How can it do that? It's a ghost! It shouldn't be able to touch her, never mind carry her off!"

"It is not a ghost. It is a demon that has just fed on the combined lust of two humans."

Keiko stopped. "I have to find her."

Avatar Tsuke stopped and turned to face her, his gaze narrow and icy. "Ryujin is already searching, and I have also notified the local authorities to watch for her. What more would you have us do? Search the village ourselves?"

Keiko glared at him. "I can find her."

"Is that so?" Avatar Tsuke lifted his brow. "Do you have any idea which way the village is from here? Do you even know where *here* is?"

Keiko opened her mouth, then closed it. She didn't. She'd been tracking him. She looked away. "No."

Avatar Tsuke smiled tiredly and walked onward. "Your loyalty is impressive, but I'm afraid there's nothing more we can do than wait for contact from Ryujin, or the local police."

Keiko turned to stare at the trees that Avatar Tsuke came from. Guilt wrenched at her. She couldn't leave Tika behind, again. She turned to look toward Avatar Tsuke, but he was gone.

A small blue light appeared between the trees. "This way, Keiko."

Keiko stumbled through the trees after the blue light, muttering every foul curse she could think of, burning with angry frustration. It was better than tears.

Keiko tromped through the woods keeping two long strides behind Avatar Tsuke. She pushed past barely visible low branches until her knees ached and her eyes danced with exhaustion. The trees thinned and then parted to reveal a perfectly groomed lawn with a neat single story wooden house, completely surrounded by a long gallery porch. Lanterns glowed suspended from the overhanging porch roof. A pair of aged, and impeccably trimmed, conifers spread across the front of the house, arching together over the scarlet double doors.

She frowned. This had to be the guesthouse.

Avatar Tsuke stepped onto the curving slate path, one hand in his pocket and the other holding his phone against his ear.

Keiko didn't remember him even opening the phone. She sighed. Not that she remembered much from the past hour of walking.

Avatar Tsuke strode under the arching trees, stepped up on the porch, and shoved the front door open. He walked inside, leaving the door open.

Keiko's brows lifted. He'd left the door open. Apparently, he wanted her to follow him inside. She stepped under the trees and walked in, closing the door behind her. She toed out of her sneakers while trying to conceal a yawn, then stepped up into the main room.

The house was open and shadowed in the far corners, with highly polished wood floors, and distant whitewashed walls. The cedar foundation posts were painted a deep scarlet. Several of the bamboo wall screens had been pulled closed. The fire pit to her immediate left was lit, with a large iron kettle releasing curls of steam suspended over it on an ironwork tripod. Avatar Tsuke was nowhere in sight.

A middle-aged woman in traditional robes, probably the housekeeper, shuffled toward Keiko and bowed deeply. Her long hair was combed and bound in the old style with large wooden pins holding her bun at the top of her head.

Keiko bowed in return, and hastily covered another jaw-cracking yawn with both hands.

The housekeeper gestured that Keiko should follow, and started walking down a short hall to the right. She opened a sliding door on the right side, revealing a very small room nearly completely filled by a futon bed. A light sleeping robe in red was neatly folded at the end. A tiny old-fashioned washstand took up the far corner. The wall opposite was a pair of sliding glass doors that led onto the wrap-around porch. A bamboo and paper folding screen had been spread open across them to provide privacy.

Keiko's brows lifted. Apparently she was spending the night. She eyed the low washstand with its bowl of steaming water, small cake of soap and nubby white cloth. She smiled. Her bath.

The door clicked closed.

Keiko jumped and turned around. The housekeeper was gone.

Not bothering to hide her yawns, she stripped out of her clothes, freed her hair from its braid and washed as much as she could at the washstand. She stumbled to the bed. Too tired to bother putting on the robe, she climbed in and pulled the blankets over her. She was asleep in seconds.

Keiko walked through a shadowed hallway with a wall of frost-obscured windows on her right. Shadows hinted at trees on the other side. Onward the hallway went, endlessly. He was here, she knew he was. Where was he? She had to warn him.

The walls slowly moved, twisting to the right, and the floor moved with it, lifting under her bare feet. Tilted off balance, she slid to the side and fell against a frosted window. Pressed facedown, her palms chilled, and thawed circles in the frost. The window cleared right under her hands.

She saw him.

He was in the heart of a garden full of summer. In long flowing robes of snow white, he sat at the base of the cherry tree, one knee bent up, gazing at the branches overhead. His hair spilled in a cascade of black silk down his shoulders, to the grass.

Ryudo.

She had to warn him. She pressed against the frost, trying to clear a larger view, but the circle remained small, not much bigger than her two hands. She shouted, but nothing came from her throat. She pounded on the glass with her fists, but made no sound.

He didn't move. He didn't hear her.

A handsome young man walked into the garden dressed in a neat dark gray business suit. Shoving his hands in his pocket, he leaned

down to tell Ryudo something she could not here. They both smiled.
Toku.

She had to tell them both! They needed to know! They had to hear her! She shouted, she screamed, she pounded on the glass with both fists, but couldn't break the silence.

The frost spread, closing in, making her view smaller, and smaller...

Drowning in silence, she battered at the unyielding glass and inclosing frost, screaming without a sound. "They're coming!"

~ Sixteen ~

"Keiko?"

Keiko jolted awake, gasping. Her entire body shook. She couldn't see. Tears overflowed and ran down her cheeks. She clutched the blankets, hunching over them, trying to breathe while wiping her eyes.

"Are you all right?"

Keiko pushed her hair from her cheeks and looked up. The tiny room was dark but for the softly glowing figure of kneeling, one knee up, at the foot of her bed.

Ryujin's mouth was turned down and his fox-fire-lit eyes wide. His dark hair tumbled loose across his brow, and down his shoulders. His long robes were snow white, spilling around his ankles and loosely tied with a simple sash. "Keiko, you were screaming."

Screaming? Keiko covered her mouth with one hand. "Oh, my... I'm sorry! Did I wake anybody?"

Ryujin tapped his brow. "It was all within." He thumbed a long lock of his hair behind one ear. "What happened?"

Keiko looked away. "It was a dream."

"It must have been a bad one."

Keiko shrugged. "It was just a dream." She blinked...Ryujin! He was back! She turned to him. "Did you find Tika?"

Ryujin looked down, his hair falling about his cheeks. "No. She wasn't in the village, and neither was the demon. It must have used her to leave the town."

Keiko shook her head. "But where would they go?"

Ryujin shrugged. "If they were working together, they'd go where she felt the safest, but since she was taken by force, it's more likely that the demon is making the choices." He lifted his head, his eyes narrowed. "Or the sorcerer that created it."

Keiko gripped the blankets. "Then we have no way of knowing where she could be?"

Ryujin sighed and looked at the floor, his hair hiding his expression. "I can only offer my most sincere apologies for not stopping the demon."

Keiko shook her head. "I should have never let her come." She winced. Stopping Tika from coming would have been no easier than stopping Shido. She looked up. "How is Shido?"

Ryujin lifted his head and smiled slightly. "He's doing well. He's sharing quarters with an Advocate."

Keiko frowned. "An Advocate? Are they part of your order?"

"They are Avatars that have yet to complete their training. They have not..." Ryujin looked away and frowned. "Gained a companion to host."

Keiko lifted her brow. "How do you train to be possessed?"

Ryujin snorted and looked over at her. "Their training is in magecraft, and fighting skills. They are..." He lifted his shoulder and rolled his eyes, clearly searching for a word. "Subordinate to an Avatar." He looked down at the floor. "Advocates sustain their Avatars during a campaign."

Advocates *sustain* Avatars? That sounded a little strange. Keiko frowned. "Is this what Avatar Tsuke wants for me, to join the order as an Advocate?"

Ryujin shook his head. "Chosen cannot host a companion, or any other spirit. They cannot be Avatars."

"Then what are they?"

Ryujin rose to his feet and stepped back. "I bid you good night." He bowed and faded.

"Ryujin!" Keiko came up on her knees, clutching the blankets to her naked chest. "Tell me, damn it!" She slapped the bedding. "I am sick of all these secrets!"

Ryujin reappeared kneeling at her side, less than a hand-span away. The fox-fire in his direct gaze blazed white hot, and his lips slightly parted. "Have you not guessed?" His voice was as soft as a whisper and perfumed with fresh cypress. His robe had parted above his sash, revealing a pale and muscular chest.

Keiko could feel the thrum of his otherworldly body so close to hers, reaching toward her heart. If she touched him, he would be as solid to her fingers, as her own flesh. She had to tear her gaze away. "I haven't got a clue."

Ryujin leaned closer, his head rising above hers. "The Chosen are consorts."

"Consorts?" He could not have meant that the way it sounded. She leaned away; suddenly very aware that she was in a bed and completely nude. "To the Avatars?"

Ryujin's gaze focused on her mouth. "Their companions."

They wanted her to be the consort to a ghost. Keiko took in a single startled breath, then grabbed for the blankets. Twisting away, she tore herself from the bed to stand on the other side, by the paper wall screen. "No, forget it!" She struggled to get the blankets around her. "I'm no one's consort."

Ryujin gazed up at her from where he knelt beside her bed. "That mark you bear says otherwise."

Keiko shook her head. "He hasn't caught me yet."

Ryujin stood slowly. "He not only caught you, he's had you at least once."

Keiko jerked her gaze away, her cheeks warming.

"Ah, so more than once."

Keiko leveled a glare at him.

Ryujin frowned. "Did he rape you?"

Keiko looked away, sucking on her bottom lip. During her first encounter with Ryudo, her body had been more than willing. She had been practically frantic. When he had taken her, with Toku, she had told him point-blank to fuck her. Her cheeks heated fiercely.

Ryujin's brows lifted and a slight smile lifted the corner of his mouth. "So then, seduced."

Keiko turned to the side, looking anywhere but at the handsome young ghost, wanting desperately to hide her burning cheeks.

Ryujin tilted his head, and turned to the side. "Was it so terrible?" He folded his hands behind him and casually stepped toward the end of her bed.

"No, I…" Keiko dropped her chin, shook her head, and sighed. "It's not that." She stared at the wall. "I won't be kept, I won't be owned." She lifted her chin and shot a narrow look at him. "Not by anyone."

He took a step closer, dropped his chin and looked up from under the fall of his hair, from only three long strides away. "I understand."

Keiko fisted her hands among the blankets and her heart pounded. He was too close. She hadn't been paying attention.

Ryujin held out his hand. "Keiko…"

She leveled a glare at him. "Back off, Ryujin." For a ghost, he was amazingly nice and very handsome, but she had more than enough problems with ghosts already.

His outstretched hand closed and a sullen glare flashed very briefly across his gaze. He dropped his head and his hand, slumping, then sighed. He lifted his gaze and a small, sharp smile lifted the corner of his mouth. "Very well, I can wait."

Keiko angled slightly away, but kept her gaze on him. "You'll be waiting a long time."

Ryujin turned away, with a sad smile, and shook his head. "He'll find your house guardian, and his host."

Chills raced across Keiko's skin, raising the hair. "What?"

Ryujin jammed his thumbs into his sash and looked down at the floor. "In less time than you would believe, all three of you will be collected and bound in service to the temple—to Avatar Tsuke." He lifted his head and stared hard at her, his jaw tight. "And then you will discover what it truly means to be 'owned'."

Fear tightened around Keiko's heart, then anger came in a hot strengthening rush. She spoke through her clenched teeth. "That isn't funny."

"It was not meant to be." Ryujin looked away. "The moment he met you, your fate, and theirs, was sealed."

Keiko took a step toward him. "Get out."

He looked down, the silky fall of his hair hiding his cheeks, and began to fade. "I can only hope you will forgive me." He vanished.

As soon as his presence faded to the bare edges of her awareness, Keiko got dressed. It didn't matter what Ryujin had said, she would not bow to Avatar Tsuke.

But Ryudo and Toku? Her dream came back in a rush. She shivered. Had it been a premonition of danger, or something else entirely? She shook her head while buttoning her denim jacket over her zipped sweat-jacket. She didn't know.

Staff in hand, she slid open the door to the porch outside, and stepped out into the brisk night. Toku's father held a corporate empire. It was highly unlikely Avatar Tsuke would even think to look at that powerful a family anyway. He certainly could not touch the heir, and Toku would be sure to watch out for Ryudo. They should be fine.

Avatar Tsuke had already admitted that he couldn't take her with Ryudo's mark, so she was safe from him too.

Keiko snorted. Ryudo really was protecting her. Not that she would ever thank him directly for it. She smiled. Not in a million years. Slouched comfortably against one of the porch's broad support posts, her staff across her lap, she watched the night forest, listening to the crickets and waited for dawn.

Pale sunlight speared through the curling mist, clearing it away to reveal the surrounding forest and a robin's egg blue sky filled with pinked clouds.

A door slid open to Keiko's right. Yawing hugely, Shihan strode out onto the broad covered porch. He threw out his arms and stretched. He grinned at Keiko. "Ready to go?"

Keiko rolled up onto her feet with her staff. "When you are, Shihan." She brushed off her bottom.

Shihan nodded. "Very good. I will meet you at the front door." He ducked back into his door.

In her stocking feet, Keiko padded along the porch around the outside edge of the house. She didn't want to walk through the house, and chance meeting Avatar Tsuke, Ryujin, or Shido in the hall. She slipped into the front door and grabbed her sneakers from the shelf. She could hear Shihan presenting his goodbyes to Avatar Tsuke. She slipped back out, closing the door very quietly behind her. Avatar Tsuke was the last person she wanted to see. Ducking back by the arching tree to stay out of casual sight, she sat on the porch to put her sneakers on.

Shihan came out the front door with a small and bright red cardboard box and a pair of plastic bottles. He closed the door behind him, spotted Keiko and tilted his head away. "This way." He started walking down the slate path, heading for the woods.

Keiko slanted a glance toward the door and hurried after him. She caught up with him in the cool shadows of the spring forest and walked to his left.

Shihan held out one of the bottles. "Breakfast, yes?"

"Yes, thank you!" Keiko took the bottle, it was warm in her hand. She opened it and smelled dark Chinese Oolong tea. "Shihan, what about Shido? She took a timid sip of the pungent tea. It was just shy of seriously hot. *Perfect...* "Doesn't he have to go home too?" She took another sip.

Shihan dodged a low branch while rummaging through the red box. "Shido has decided to join the order."

Shido? She very nearly spit out her mouthful of tea. "He did?"

"Yes, as an Advocate." Shihan held out a large, hard-packed rice-ball rolled in sesame seeds. "It seems that Shido no longer has difficulty believing in ghosts."

Keiko winced. His incident up in the tree would have been a bit difficult to explain away. She took the double-fist-sized rice-ball from Shihan. It was semi-soft and warm. It must have been made that morning. "They accepted him?"

Shihan pulled another rice-ball from the box. "He has the talent. I'm sure his training will go swiftly." He took a huge bite.

Keiko stepped over a rock, nearly losing her slippery breakfast. "Will Shido be coming back to class?"

Shihan raised his half-eaten rice-ball. "If you are not going to eat that, I would be happy to do so."

"I'm eating." Shihan apparently did not want to talk about Shido. Keiko bit into the hard-packed cooked rice rolled in sweetened sesame seeds and chewed. It was going to be very strange not seeing him in the dojo. It was going to be even stranger not having Tika in class, at the university.

The mouthful of rice lodged in Keiko's throat. She swigged some tea to swallow it down and stared at her breakfast. "Shihan?"

"Ah?" Chewing, he looked over at her.

Keiko held out her bitten rice-ball. "I'm not all that hungry."

Shihan took the rice-ball and didn't say another word for quite a while.

Shihan's bulky copper Nissan, gleamed in the morning sunlight, a welcome sight. A double-chirp announced that Shihan had unlocked the doors. Keiko practically ran across the gravel lot. She was more than ready to go home.

Keiko popped open the front passenger door and leaned over the back of her seat to set her staff across the back seat. The two leaves on her staff, poking from the top of her case, looked very limp. She was going to have to cut a fresh staff once she got home.

Shihan opened his door and proceeded to climb in.

Keiko turned to sit and glanced over toward Shihan. Shido's blue and yellow Kawasaki, parked on Shihan's side of the SUV, glowed in the sunlight just beyond his open door.

Shihan closed his door, blocking the view of the bike.

Keiko swallowed, sat and fastened her seatbelt.

Shihan fastened his seatbelt, and started the car. Rock and roll screamed from the speakers. Slowly and carefully, he drove the Nissan out of the graveled picnic area.

Keiko stared into the side view mirror and watched Shido's motorcycle, sitting alone in the sunlit forest, disappear behind the trees.

Book Three

~Bamboo Leaves & Nightfall ~

~ Seventeen ~

The tiered circular lecture hall was silent, but for the whisper of pencils moving on papers and the ticking. All the way down at the bottom of the amphitheater, at the very front edge of the instructor's tall pine lectern, a small and old-fashioned double-bell alarm clock squatted menacingly.

Halfway up into the tiers, Keiko stared hard at the figures on her completed exam sheet. A trickle of sweat slithered down her back, dampening her cotton blouse. She had studied hard, but industrial history was not her strongest subject. She tugged at her straight black wool skirt. It was itching something fierce against the back of her knees. Whoever had pronounced wool as a good material for the school uniform had been either an idiot, or into torture. She folded one knee over the other and thanked Mercy that she'd skipped wearing stockings in favor of knee-socks. The annoying pull and rub of the nylons against her thighs combined with the over-warm wool would have driven her insane.

She fought the urge to look to her left. She didn't want to see the empty chair beside her, where Tika should have been sitting. Tika hadn't attended industrial history for the past two weeks. Rumor had it that Tika was attending classes, just not this one; the only one she shared with Keiko.

Keiko's hands tightened on her pencil. She hadn't seen Tika at all since the...incident. Tika wasn't answering her phone or replying to her messages either. She didn't know if Tika was still possessed or if the demon had finally left. She didn't know anything.

The alarm clock jangled loudly.

Keiko nearly jumped out of her chair.

Rustling, sighs, and groans erupted all over the classroom. The hour-long exam was over.

The instructor rose from behind his desk to shut off the alarm. His short-sleeved white dress shirt was rumpled and his black tie slightly crooked. He looked up and the glare on his black-framed glasses hid his eyes. "Please, set your pencils down, and pass your exams to the student before you."

Keiko sighed and lifted her paper, handing it to the boy sitting in front of her, one tier down. She collected her black fold-over book-bag from under her chair, then sat back down to fuss with her long black pony-tail. She'd tugged on it one too many times during the exam.

One more class and she could leave for the dojo, and then go home for the entire weekend. She'd quit the soccer club to do her karate classes, so she didn't have to come back to school for her sports club on Saturdays like everyone else.

The class-end bell chimed.

Keiko shoved up the armrest desktop, and got up. Shouldering her book-bag, she tugged her blazer from the back of her chair and folded it over her arm. *One more class, just one more...* She stepped into the main aisle and proceeded down the steps toward the door at the front of the lecture hall, along with all the other students.

Keiko shoved through the door and into the curved, industrial gray painted, windowless hallway. It was fitfully lit, full of shadows, and packed with students rushing to their next class. Knots of confused freshmen gathered in corners waiting on fellow students.

Remembering the trials from her freshman year, Keiko smiled wryly. Unlike ordinary school where classes were held in the same room with the teachers moving from room to room, University was a whole new environment. Not only did the students have to hunt for their individual classes, they were forced to interact with different students in each classroom. Very unnerving when one was used to being with the same forty students for six years at a time.

Keiko rolled her eyes. She would have been so lost without Tika, who knew every cute boy there was to know. She could get directions, if not a guide, in seconds. Tika, who no longer came to their industrial history class.

Keiko's smile slid away. She really didn't blame her. She had abandoned Tika to the demon. Mercy only knew how she had suffered. Tika had every right to hate her for that abandonment. She had failed her friend.

Keiko ducked her head and pushed past a knot of four junior boys.

One of the boys groaned. "Wish I could afford her every day!"

"She's expensive, but she's worth it. Tika gives great head."

Keiko froze mid-step. *Tika?* It couldn't be... She turned around.

A sophomore leaned close to the juniors with his hands jammed in his pockets. "Is she still doing it in the music wing's third practice room?"

The tallest boy snickered. "Oh, yeah! I got mine earlier today, with extras." He moaned in dramatic satisfaction.

One of the juniors frowned. "How is she getting away with it?"

"The music instructor is getting it from her too."

"Tika's doing anyone that asks." The tallest boy smirked. "As long as they have the cash."

Keiko frowned. Tika went through boyfriends the way an allergy victim went through tissues, but she didn't do...that! Not for money! She didn't need money.

"I hear she's seriously freaky after dark, too."

"Oh, she is, she is!"

"Damn! I got to get some of that!"

Keiko's temper flashed. It couldn't be her Tika, but there was only one way to find out. She headed straight toward the boys.

The tallest spotted her and grabbed onto his buddy's arm. "Uh oh, here comes Crazy Keiko!"

A boy shivered dramatically. "See any ghosts lately?"

Keiko froze. *Crazy Keiko...?* From grade school into junior high she had been teased constantly about seeing ghosts. It had stopped when she and Tika had transferred to high school and left those kids behind. So, how had these students found out? None of them were from her junior high. Who had told them?

One of the boys threw up his arms and moaned. "Boo!"

One of the boys ran behind the other and pointed. "Oh! I'm so scared!"

The entire group howled with laughter.

Students stopped in the hall to stare at them, then at Keiko.

Keiko's face heated to scalding. She glared at them, and her hands fisted at her sides. There was no way she could punch any of them without being tossed out of school. She turned on her heel and walked.

"Look! She's running away from the ghost!" Their laughter followed her down the hall.

Keiko slammed open a stairwell door and stomped down the industrial gray steel and cement steps. Who could have told those boys about her seeing ghosts? No one at the university knew.

Except Tika.

Keiko shook her head. It couldn't be Tika. She'd been Keiko's staunchest defender through grade and middle school. When they transferred to the high school it had been their deepest secret, with Tika covering for her when she had seen something, though she'd wanted a full report on it afterwards.

But Tika wasn't coming to industrial history class, the only one she still shared with Keiko.

Keiko slammed the fire-door open on the basement level hallway. The curved basement hall to the left, and to the right, was empty of students. The paper sign up on the wall before her indicated that the music wing should be to the left.

Keiko turned left and marched. There was only one way to find out what was going on. She'd have to find Tika and ask her. Hopefully Tika was still speaking to her.

Keiko's footsteps on the tile floor sounded oddly loud in the deserted hall. The narrow glass panes on the wooden class doors showed empty room after empty room. They were only empty for the moment. After classes, the rooms would be crammed with students in one student club or another.

The music wing was under the oldest building on campus, and that building had settled. The floor wasn't exactly level, and the walls were painted brick rather than cinderblock.

Keiko pushed through the double doors to enter the music wing, and froze. It looked no different from the hall she had just walked through; the same scuffed linoleum tile and steel gray brick walls with brilliant industrial ceiling fluorescents killing every trace of shadow.

And yet, every hair on her body shivered upright, and the back of her skull buzzed nearly painfully with awareness.

Something was in there; something...dead, and it was powerful.

Her heart slammed in her chest, and cold clenched around her stomach. It was too big for her. She could feel it. She had to get out of there. She turned to push back out the door.

"Keiko!" The voice was very familiar, and bitterly cheerful. "Long time, no see, girlfriend."

Keiko flinched, her hands clenching tight on the door's push bar. "Tika..." She turned to face her friend.

Tika threw up her hand in a jaunty flourish. "Here I am!" She was immaculately dressed in her school uniform, her chin-length hair neatly combed with a clip at her brow pulling her bangs to one side. She smiled and the dimple appeared in her cheek. "In the flesh!" She chuckled in a low sensual tone that became a liquid feline growl, and blue foxfire blazed in the heart of her eyes. "And then some."

Keiko sucked in a breath. Tika was still possessed. It was the demon's presence throbbing within Keiko's skull. "Tika, I..."

Tika lifted a brow. "You...what?" Her lips curled into a sneer. "You missed me?"

Keiko swallowed. "Actually, yes." She took a step away from the door toward Tika. "And, I'm sorry."

"You're sorry?" Tika stopped and her brows lifted. "For what?"

Keiko took a half-step closer. "I'm sorry I left you." She took a breath. "—possessed."

Tika laughed. The sound was sharp, high-pitched and brittle. "You honestly think you could have done something about it?"

Keiko winced. "I should have stayed and tried."

Tika's eyes narrowed. "Did you ever think that maybe I was glad you left? That maybe I didn't want you there to spoil it for me?"

Keiko jerked back. "Spoil it? What are you talking about?" She threw out her hand. "Tika, in case you didn't notice, you're possessed by a demon!"

Tika covered her mouth with her hands. "No shit, really?" She dropped her hands and rolled her eyes. "I got a special bulletin for you, Miss I'm-so-special-because-I-can-see-ghosts. I'm perfectly happy this way!" She took a step toward Keiko and her lips curled back in an inhuman snarl. "So why don't you go your merry way and leave me the fuck alone to enjoy it?"

Happy? Enjoy it? Was she insane? Keiko shook her head then held out her hands. "Tika, the demon will eventually kill you!"

Tika crossed her arms. "Yeah? So will smoking cigarettes and drinking beer. Big deal."

Keiko shook her head. "Tika, I don't get it, why would you *want* to be possessed by a demon?"

"Why? Why *not!*" Tika laughed. "Do you have any idea what I can do now?"

Keiko bit down on her lip and leaned back. "Uh, no, not really." If there was any truth to what she'd been hearing, she wasn't sure she wanted to know.

"Just for starters..." Tika folded her hands together and set them against her cheek. "I'm irresistible! I can seduce any man I want, any time I want." She sighed then waved her hand. "Oh, and I can walk into any store and have anything I want—for nothing! The clerks practically throw the stuff at me." She lifted a finger and leaned forward with a wink. "But best of all, I can fly!" She threw out her hands and looked up at the ceiling with a brilliant smile. "Anywhere I want to go, I just grab the wind, and go!"

Keiko folded her arms and lifted her chin. "At what price, Tika? What does the demon want in return?"

Tika turned her face aside as though slapped. She pressed her fingers to her lips and avoided Keiko's gaze. "Nothing I'm not willing to give."

"Really?" Keiko stepped toward Tika, her hands fisted at her sides. "Nothing you're not willing to give—to anyone that asks?"

Tika rolled her eyes and lifted her hand in a negligent wave. "It's just sex."

Keiko folded her arms. "Rumor has it you're selling it."

Tika snorted. "Oh, that." She shrugged. "Give a couple of guys a blow job and suddenly everybody wants one." She flipped up her hand. "I put a price on it to thin down the requests." She shook her head. "I don't need the money. Father makes sure I always had everything I need."

Keiko's hands tightened on her book-bag. "Then, why do it?"

"What, have sex?" Tika smiled. "Because I want to, silly. I like sex." She scanned down Keiko's body, then tilted her head to the side and pressed a finger to her chin. "You've got a nice body, Keiko. I never really noticed it before."

"Huh?" Keiko jerked back. "I didn't know you liked girls."

"Occasionally...depends on the girl." Tika folded her hands behind her, and shrugged. "I like kissing, and girls are better at kissing than guys." She took a small step closer. "I wonder..."

Keiko frowned. "Wonder what?"

Tika focused on Keiko, and her eyes flickered with foxfire. "Why I never kissed you?" She licked her lips. "I bet you'd taste really sweet."

Keiko backpedaled to the door. "Uh, I think I'll pass, okay?"

"Oh, don't be shy!" Tika glided a pace closer and smiled. "We're friends, remember?" Her hands came out from behind her and something barely visible sinuously writhed around them, like semi-transparent snakes. "I'll make it very pleasant for you. I promise."

Keiko sucked in a breath. *The demon..*

~ Eighteen ~

Icy panic doused Keiko from head to gut. She whirled around and slammed the door's release bar. The door swung open, slamming against the wall. Keiko tore back down the hallway, her shoes slapping loudly on the linoleum tiles. Her book-bag thumping at her side seemed to weigh a million kilos, slowing her down.

The demon's power filled the small hallway with whispering shadows. Giggling came from far too close behind her. "Where are you going, girlfriend?"

The back of Keiko's skirt was grabbed and pulled.

Keiko's feet slipped, and went out from under her. She gasped and fell to her hands and knees. "Ow, shit…" Her book-bag crashed to the floor and slid away along with her blazer.

Hands caught Keiko's shoulders and shoved her over.

Keiko landed flat on her back. "Hey!"

"Hey, yourself." Tika dropped onto her, straddling Keiko's hips. "Playing hard to get, Keiko?"

Keiko grabbed Tika's shoulders and shoved, but she couldn't budge her. She didn't know what else to do. She could punch her, but she didn't want to hurt Tika. "Tika, stop this!"

"Stop?" Tika grabbed Keiko's wrists and pinned them to the floor by her head. "What for?" She leaned down on top of Keiko, belly to belly and breast to breast. "Don't you want to kiss me?"

Shadow shivered along Keiko's skin and pulsed against her belly. Erotic heat flushed through her. Her nipples rose to sudden tight attention and her belly clenched with violent desire. She focused on

Tika's full lips. She did want to kiss her—but she didn't want to feed that demon. She closed her eyes and turned her head away, trying to grab hold of her scattering thoughts. "Tika, this isn't right."

"Oh, come on, Keiko!" Tika caught Keiko's chin and forced her to look up into Tika's foxfire eyes. "What's a little kiss between friends?" Her mouth pressed against Keiko's closed lips.

Keiko froze under Tika's soft, wet mouth. A wash of chill power danced against her lips, making shivers erupt all down her body. It was the demon's power. She jerked her head away. "Tika, no!"

"Kiss me, damn you!" Tika caught her chin, forcing her head back. She pressed her lips to Keiko's, her tongue sweeping against Keiko's closed lips. Her fingers dug painfully into the muscles in Keiko's jaw.

A whimper escaped Keiko, and her mouth popped open. Tika's tongue surged in and lapped hungrily. Chill demonic power slid along Keiko's tongue and speared down to pool in her belly. She closed her eyes and moaned in dismay.

Tika turned her head to fit her mouth to Keiko's and her kiss turned gentle, delicately exploring Keiko's mouth and tongue. Although Keiko could taste the demon on Tika's tongue, the kiss itself was persuading, and just a little playful. It felt affectionate. It felt like Tika.

Keiko found herself replying with gentle forays of her own. She had missed her.

Tika moaned in pleased reply. She pressed down along Keiko's body and rubbed, her hard nipples pressing against Keiko's breasts. Tika wasn't wearing a bra.

Keiko had never had someone's breasts rubbing against her. It was actually quite interesting, and rather erotically exciting. No wonder the guys liked it so much. She arched her back to press closer, to feel more, and briefly wondered what it would be like to taste the hard nipples she could feel.

Tika lifted her head. "That's much better." She licked her lips. "You taste…interesting, different from the others."

Keiko gasped for breath and sense. Mercy, what was she thinking? "Tika, please! You need to stop this!"

Tika's brows shot up. "Stop?" She smiled and reached down to tug up Keiko's black skirt. "We haven't even started." Tika nudged one knee between Keiko's thighs, and pressed up against Keiko's mound. She rubbed just a little, coming in contact with Keiko's clit.

Unexpected heat and pleasure clenched in Keiko's belly. She gasped and her hips lifted in automatic response. Her panties dampened against Tika's knee.

Tika licked her lips. "Mercy, you're a responsive little slut." She grabbed Keiko's blouse and jerked it apart, spraying buttons. "I bet you'll scream when you cum for me."

Keiko grabbed Tika's hands. "Tika, please! I'm your friend!"

Tika jerked her hands from Keiko's "And that means...what?" She grabbed the front of Keiko's bra. "That you love me?" She shoved the bra up, freeing Keiko's breasts.

Cold air washed across Keiko's bare breasts. She gasped and tears slid from her eyes. "Yes, Tika! I do love you!"

Tika stilled. "You love me?"

Keiko drew in a small breath and smiled, just a little. "Of course." She reached up and closed her arms around Tika's neck, slowly pulling her down into a hug. "I've always loved you." She pressed a kiss to Tika's brow. "You're my best friend."

Tika's arms slid under her, embracing Keiko. "I love you too." She pressed a kiss against Keiko's neck. "But I'm still going to fuck you."

Keiko giggled suddenly.

Tika froze. "What?"

Keiko turned to face Tika and smiled from a kiss away. "Tika, you're a girl. You can't fuck me, you don't have a dick."

Tika chuckled against her neck. "Wrong, girlfriend. I'm a demon, remember?" She lifted her head smiled. "I have as many dicks as I need."

Keiko's blood turned cold. "Tika..."

"And in your case…" Tika rolled her eyes and pursed her lips. "I think I'll use two." He gaze narrowed and her smile turned feral. "One for the cunt and one for the ass."

Panic washed through Keiko. "Tika, wait!"

"I love you, Keiko." Tika pressed a kiss to Keiko's brow. "But I have needs that you're going to satisfy."

"Fine, okay, all right…" Keiko caught Tika's face in her palms. "But don't use the demon."

Tika's bottom lip protruded. "But I like using the demon…"

"Tika, I…" Keiko took a breath. "You don't need the demon. I'll cum for you."

Tika pushed back and sat up. Her eyes narrowed. "You'll cum for me? Willingly?"

"Yes." Keiko pushed up onto her hands and swallowed. Merciful Lady, she was out of her mind. "I'll even do it myself, just don't use that thing on me."

Tika licked her lips and lifted a brow. "Will you let me touch you while you do it?"

"Anything you want." Keiko looked down and tugged her bra back down over her breasts. She glanced toward Tika. "As long as it's you, and not that thing."

Tika took a breath and looked away, frowning. "All right." She caught Keiko's gaze and smiled. "Deal." She stood up and held out her hand. "Let's go, girlfriend."

Keiko took Tika's hand, and was pulled up onto her feet. Merciful Lady, she hoped she hadn't just agreed to something supremely stupid. She pulled her shirt closed. "Where to?"

Tika jerked a thumb toward the empty classroom to their left. "This will do."

Keiko frowned at it. "Isn't it locked?"

Tika smiled. "Not for me." She flicked her free hand toward the door. There was a click, and the door eased open all by itself. "See?"

"Wait…!" Keiko turned back to get her book-bag and blazer lying in the middle of the hallway.

Tika's hand closed tight around Keiko's wrist. "No more waiting." Mouth tight and eyes narrowed, she swung Keiko through the doorway and into the deserted classroom, releasing her.

Keiko stumbled across the thin carpet, nearly falling. The small classroom was windowless and empty, but for some long gray folding tables leaning against the right wall, and a long row of stacked folding chairs along the back wall. She turned around to face her friend. "What now?"

"Now?" The door slammed closed behind Tika. She smiled. "Now you get naked."

Keiko took a steadying breath. She couldn't decide. Should she stall for time and hope for rescue, or just do it and get it over with?

Tika smiled, showing her dimple. "Just so you know, no one will come to rescue you. I have all the doors closed."

Keiko frowned. "I got down here just fine…"

"That was then." Tika stalked nonchalantly toward Keiko. "This is now." She tilted her head to one side. "And I'm getting impatient. Do you need help getting undressed?"

"No thanks!" Keiko stepped back and tugged her open blouse from her skirt. "I'll do it." She turned to the side and pulled her blouse off her arms. This wasn't anything like last time she was seduced by a ghost. She folded her blouse, glancing at the plain walls and worn carpet. No garden, no flowers, no…tea. She set the blouse on the carpet, bit down on her lip and unzipped her skirt. Not even a bed. She tugged the skirt down and stepped out of it, then folded it and set it on her blouse.

There was no question that she meant nothing beyond food—at least to the demon. She reached back to unfasten her plain white bra.

"Your back…"

"Huh?" Keiko lifted her head and looked over at Tika. "You've seen it before." She straightened and pulled off her bra. Her nipples tightened in the basement room's cool air.

Tika's eyes were wide and her arms folded with the fingers of one hand at her lips. "Yeah, but now… Now I know what it means."

Keiko smiled sourly. The demon must have told her. "It means that ghosts have been bleeding me, to feed on me, since grade school." She dropped the bra on her clothes. "Just like you're going to in a minute."

"No!" Tika shook her head, clearly shocked. "Not like that." She pointed. "I'm not going to do that!"

"Aren't you?" Keiko turned to face her in knee socks and panties. "What's the difference, Tika? You're still going to feed on me. You're still going to take a bite out of my soul, to feed your new best friend."

Tika scowled. "That's not fair!"

Keiko's brows shot up. "What's not fair? You told me to get naked. You want me to cum for you, and you're going to feed on me, Tika, when I do it."

Tika clenched her hands together. "I'm not going to scar you, just…"

"Just what, Tika?" Keiko set her hands on her hips, and tilted her head. "Just eat me from the inside rather than the outside? That's what you're doing every time someone cums for you. You're eating a piece of their soul."

"I have well over a dozen guys begging me to do them daily. They don't look eaten to me!"

Keiko threw out her hands. "Just because you can't see it doesn't mean you're not eating them!"

Tika crossed her arms and turned her face away. "Then why do they keep coming back for more?"

Keiko rolled her eyes. "Because they don't *know* you're eating them!"

Tika shook her head. "If they don't feel it, then I can't be hurting them all that much."

"Tika, you're *eating* them!" Keiko held out her hand. "Just like you're going to eat me."

Tika scowled and stomped her foot. "Fine. Have it your way. I'm a demonic soul-eating bitch and you're next on the menu." She pointed at the floor. "Drop the panties, on your knees, and spread. I'm starved."

Keiko sharply turned away. For just a moment, she'd thought Tika would give it up. The shock on her face from knowing what her scars actually meant had been very real. Tika didn't want to hurt her, but she wasn't going to stop either. She put her thumbs in her panties and pushed them down. There was no way out of this but to go through with it.

Keiko dropped her panties on her clothes and knelt.

Tika dropped to her knees right in front of her and looked down. "Spread real wide, so I can see."

Keiko spread her knees.

"Nice, really nice." Tika smiled. "Good. Do it." She licked her lips. "Touch yourself."

Keiko licked her lips and closed her eyes. She couldn't look at Tika and do this. She reached under to part her plump lips and explore her damp folds. She dipped her long finger into her warm wet body and rubbed along her clit. She jolted just a little. Sitting with her knees spread extended her clit a little and made it more sensitive. She rose up on her knees just a little to ease the sensitivity and rubbed.

Curls of erotic heat stirred under her fingers. She leaned her head back and released a sigh.

A hand curled around the back of her neck.

Keiko's eyes flew open.

Tika's blouse was open, showing her bare breasts and hard pink nipples. Balancing with the hand around Keiko's neck, she leaned down. Her other hand was in her panties, stroking herself. She closed her lips on one of Keiko's jutting nipples and sucked. Her tongue lashed the swollen tip expertly.

Erotic fire raced from her nipple to stab in her clit. Keiko jolted and gasped. Moisture slicked her hand and made her flesh slippery. In pure carnal reflex she leaned up, grabbed onto Tika's shoulder, and pressed her breast into Tika's mouth while rubbing at her clit. Heat coiled tight in her belly and clenched. Her body trembled in excitement. Her knees parted further.

Tika moaned in appreciation and her fingers tightened at the back of Keiko's neck. She sat up a little higher and her hips bucked against her fingers. Her mouth clamped tight on Keiko's nipple, torturing it with her wicked tongue.

Keiko moaned and her hips began to buck. She'd expected it to be hard to masturbate for Tika, but it was surprisingly easy. She closed her eyes and a groan slipped out. She was going to climax...

The door slammed hard against the wall. "Get off her!"

Keiko felt a hard shove on her shoulders and fell back, sprawling on the floor. Her head spun. "What...?"

Tika was on her feet facing the wide open door. "Who the hell are you?"

Toku held the door wide open with one hand while gripping Keiko's book-bag and coat with the other. His jaw was tight, and his lips curled back from his clenched teeth. "The last person you want to fuck with, demon."

Keiko frowned. "Toku?"

Toku's gaze didn't move from Tika. "Get dressed, Keiko, we're leaving. Now."

~ Nineteen ~

Keiko rolled over onto her knees and reached for her clothes. Her head wouldn't stop spinning. She dragged on her white blouse, not bothering with her bra.

Tika released an inhuman snarl. "How did you get in here?"

Keiko stilled. Good question. Tika had said she'd closed all the doors. She looked over at Toku.

Toku propped his hip against the door, holding it open, leaving his right hand free. His glare didn't waver from Tika. "Keiko, hurry up and get dressed!"

"I'm hurrying!" Keiko buttoned as fast as she could, snatched up her panties and dragged on her black skirt. She stomped into her loafers.

A chill wind lashed through the room. "I asked you a question." Tika's voice dropped into a low growl. "Dead man."

Toku smiled coldly. "Why, so you did." He held out his hand, fingers spread wide. "Ready, Keiko?"

Bra and panties in hand, Keiko scooted around Tika and rushed through the door.

Tika threw up her arms and an icy wind howled around her. "The bitch is mine!" Black force boiled around her.

With his right hand, Toku made a sudden gesture and shouted out three words. Blue white force radiated around him, blurring his image, as though seen through rising heat, then a ball of white fire exploded from his palm

The blazing ball slammed into Tika, knocking her off her feet and throwing her across the room to crash into the wall, making a hard impact dent in the cinderblock wall with her body.

Keiko gasped. "Tika!" She turned to Toku. "What did you do to her?"

"Never mind that!" Toku shoved Keiko's coat and book-bag into her arms. "We need to get out of here!" He grabbed her arm and rushed her down the hall.

Keiko jogged up the hallway at his side. "Toku, you hurt her!"

"I doubt it. I'm not strong enough to do any lasting damage to that thing."

Keiko jerked at his hand, but his fingers were too tight to budge. "That *thing* is my friend!"

Toku slammed his right hand against the fire door leading to the stairs. "That thing only *looks* like your friend—it's a demon!" A white flash exploded.

Keiko flinched back from the light. "She's possessed!"

Toku looked down at her. "She *was* possessed. There's nothing left in there that's human." He shoved her into the stairwell. "Keep going, we don't have much time."

Keiko went up two steps and turned back. "That's not true, she's still in there!"

"It *is* true! She's been consumed by the demon inhabiting her." Toku sketched a circular design on the door with his fingers. Blue light flared, igniting the entire sketch, then faded away completely. He turned to face her. "What are you waiting for? Run!"

Keiko started up the steps, but couldn't quite find the energy to run. Tika was gone?

Toku lunged up the stairs, took her by the arm and practically towed her upward. "Faster, Keiko."

Keiko grabbed onto the railing, trying to go faster. "Toku, she can't be gone. She didn't try to hurt me."

"She didn't try, she succeeded." Toku wrapped his arm around her, propelling her up the stairs. "Unless you don't think a bite is harm?"

Keiko tripped on a step. "A bite?" She pulled out her shirt and looked down at her chest where Tika's mouth had been. "She didn't bite me."

"Yes, she did." Toku dragged her upward. "The back of your neck is bleeding."

Keiko set her hand on her neck and it burned. She hissed, and her hand came away wet and scarlet. The red smears faded before her eyes. It wasn't heart's blood, something that could be replaced in an ordinary hospital, but the blood of the soul, something ordinary doctors couldn't even see. *Tika's hand...* Keiko's heart clenched hard and tears threatened.

"Keiko!" Toku hauled on her arm. "Keep going! My spell won't hold the door long. Go!"

"Huh?" Startled, Keiko blinked up at him. "Did you say *spell?*"

Toku bared his teeth in a snarl. "Never mind that! Keep going!"

The sound of tortured metal echoed loudly up the stairwell, then something exploded.

"Shit..." Toku grabbed onto the railing and pressed Keiko against the wall. The stairs shook under their feet.

Keiko grabbed onto Toku. "What the hell was that?"

Toku scowled. "Your friend." He grabbed her around the waist and raced up the last few steps, dragging Keiko with him. He slammed the door open onto the first floor. Panicked students and teachers filled the hall screaming and shouting about earthquakes. Papers and books were scattered all over the floor.

Toku turned Keiko to the right and wove through the crowd, keeping Keiko tight to his side. "Keep going, keep going..."

Keiko found it harder, and harder, to keep her eyes open, and her feet under her. She grabbed onto Toku's coat to stay upright. Toku's arm tightened around her. Among a river of frightened students and teachers, he half-carried Keiko through a pair of open doors, and outside. Without knowing quite how they got there, Keiko suddenly realized that they were in the preferred parking lot at the back of the campus.

Toku dug a set of keys from his pocket. A double chirp announced that a car had been unlocked. He opened the door to a silver Subaru, and shoved Keiko into the passenger's seat. "Put on your seatbelt and stay down." He shut the door and ran around to the driver's side.

Keiko shivered hard. It was cold. Her hands didn't want to work the seatbelt. They were shaking too hard.

Toku got in, shoved her book-bag and coat into her lap and started the car. "Keiko, your seatbelt?"

"I can't… I can't close it." Her teeth chattered. She was so cold…

Toku leaned over and fastened her seatbelt. He tugged her coat up over her. "Lay down."

Keiko curled up on the seat, her head by his warm thigh. She couldn't stop her shivers. "Where…where are we going?"

"Home." He put the car in gear and stomped on the gas. "My home." The tires squealed and the car lunged forward.

Keiko wrapped her arms around herself. His home; where Ryudo was. "I can't…go there."

"We don't have a choice. Ryudo is the only one that can stop your bleeding."

The perfume of chrysanthemums, summer warmth, and gentle hand stroking her hair and down her spine… "Keiko, love."

Keiko opened her eyes and found her cheek pressed against a knee covered in heavy white silk. Someone was stroking her hair. It felt wonderfully calming. She rubbed her cheek against the white silk and her eyes drifted closed.

"No, love, stay with us."

"Huh?" She frowned and opened her eyes again. She was sprawled facedown across someone's lap on a huge king-sized bed. One hand was curled under her. The palm of her other hand slid across the pitch black silk and down comforter. A massive high-tech entertainment system, framed by a pair of tall chrome floor lamps, occupied the full breadth of the dark cedar wall at the foot of the bed. She frowned. "Where am I?"

"You are safe."

She knew that voice. "Ryudo?"

"Yes."

She shouldn't be here, wherever *here* was. She needed to go. She pushed up onto her hands. Her knees sank into the thick comforter and her head spun. She closed her eyes and suddenly couldn't remember why she should leave. Sinking back down into the warm lap and sleeping was far more appealing.

"You may sleep afterwards." Warm hands closed on her shoulders. "Sit up." He eased her upright and gently pushed her long hair from her cheeks. "Stay with us, Keiko. I've sealed the wound, but you are not out of danger yet."

Keiko blinked blearily up his striking and familiar face. Black brows winged over deep black eyes that danced with fox-fire deep in their hearts. His silky hair was loose, spilling down the shoulders and back of his loosely tied white silk robes patterned with flowers…chrysanthemums. She could see the elegant line of his throat and the swell of his chest. He looked wonderful. She lifted her hand to his smooth pale cheek and smiled. "Hey, handsome."

Ryudo's eyes widened. "Keiko?" He covered her hand with his and closed his eyes briefly. He smiled and drew her hand from his cheek. With his other hand, he nudged her chin up and peered into her eyes. "How do you feel?"

Keiko thought about it. How did she feel? She pursed her lips. "I feel…okay. Like, I'm kind of…floating."

Ryudo's brows lifted. "So I see."

"Is she all right?"

Ryudo tilted his head to look past her and smiled. "The blood-loss has made her a bit light-headed."

Keiko turned to see Toku kneeling by a low teakwood table with a closed door to either side. He had changed from his suit into black silk trousers and a short and sleeveless belted robe. He looked ready for bed. On the table, a small hotplate held a steaming black glazed teapot with a red coffee mug waiting beside it.

Toku frowned at Keiko. "She seems a little...quiet."

Ryudo smiled. "It makes a nice change, don't you think?"

Toku scratched the back of his head. "Actually, it's kind of freaking me out."

Keiko looked the other way, past Ryudo. Tall, floor to ceiling windows spanned the wall on the far side of the bed. A heavy-looking black lacquer folding screen with pink and green jade dragons and clouds stood before it, blocking the view. They appeared to be sliding glass doors leading to the outside.

"Keiko, turn and sit this way." Ryudo encouraged Keiko to turn to the side, toward Toku, until her feet dangled off the side of the bed. He tugged at the robe she wore, covering her knees. "There."

Keiko looked down and plucked at the silk robe she wore. Her school uniform had been replaced with a light sleeping robe of scarlet with large white flowers...more chrysanthemums. "Where are my clothes?"

"Your clothes are being cleaned." Ryudo thumbed a lock of his long black hair behind his ear and turned to look toward Toku. "Is the tea ready?"

"Yes." Toku poured dark tea into a large red coffee mug, rose to his feet and walked toward Keiko with it. "Here."

Toku dropped to one knee in front of Ryudo's knees and offered Keiko the mug. "Drink this, it's medicine."

"Okay..." Keiko took the mug. She was thirsty. She sipped. The tea was not particularly hot, but it was very bitter, thick, and oily. It felt like it was curdling on her tongue. She pulled her mouth away and made a face. "Yuck! That's awful!" She held the mug out toward Toku.

Toku pushed the mug back toward her. "You need to drink it. All of it."

Keiko set a hand over her mouth. "If I drink that, I'll throw up!"

Ryudo smiled sourly. "That's why you need to drink it."

Keiko stared. "What?"

Ryudo set his hand on her shoulder. "You've been implanted with a seed from the demon. We need to get it out of you."

She frowned. "I have a...what?"

"A demon's larva." Toku pressed the cup toward her. "It's in your stomach."

She had a demonic dead thing in her *stomach*? Keiko's head cleared so fast it began to pound. "Give me that!" She pinched her nose to kill the taste, and started gulping the nasty oily concoction down.

Toku and Ryudo exchanged startled glances.

Keiko stuck out her tongue and shook her head, shuddering. "Merciful Lady, that's stuff is gross!" She pushed the cup back toward Toku. "How fast does it work?" Her temperature soared and an icy sweat rolled down her body. "Oh..." Her stomach suddenly roiled angrily. She crossed her arms over her belly and groaned. "Never mind. Quick, where's the bathroom!"

Toku held out a large steel mixing bowl. "Here."

Keiko eyed the bowl. There was a design etched into the bottom. "You're kidding, right?"

Toku shook his head. "Afraid not."

Ryudo stretched his arm behind her and rubbed her back. "We need to destroy it once we get it out of you."

Keiko lifted her brow toward him. "Flushing isn't enough?"

Toku looked away, bit his lip and scratched the back of his head. "Uh..."

Ryudo frowned at Toku and shook his head.

Toku winced. "Err...no, flushing is not enough."

Keiko's stomach gave lurched viciously. "Shit! Give me that!" She grabbed for the bowl and slipped off the bed, landing hard on the floor, on her knees and hands. "Ow!"

"Keiko?" Ryudo dropped to one knee on the floor behind her.

"Just give me that bowl!" Keiko snatched the bowl from Toku's hands, bent over it and made hideous retching sounds, horrifyingly embarrassing herself for several long minutes, while Ryudo kept her hair pulled away from her face. Suddenly, something large came up her throat, closing off her air. And it moved. Part of it wriggled nastily in her mouth.

It was alive! Keiko lunged back, shaking her head to get the hideous thing out. Her throat was too blocked to scream—or breathe.

"Keiko!" Ryudo grabbed for her. "Toku, its coming! Get the bowl!"

In a blind panic, Keiko pushed away from both of them. She had to get that hideous thing out! She grabbed her throat, trying to force it out.

Ryudo caught her wrists. "Don't squeeze your throat!"

Keiko twisted away. She had to get it out! She dug her fingers into her throat.

Toku snatched for her hand and missed. "Keiko, don't...!"

"Keiko, stop!" Kneeling on the floor, Ryudo grabbed her hands and twisted her arms behind her. "You will hurt yourself!" She bucked against him, her feet thumping on the floor. There was a whisper of silk and her hands were bound together behind her. Ryudo fisted her long hair and tipped her forward onto her knees, holding her head firmly over the bowl. "Ready, Toku?" He put one hand over her eyes.

"I am." Toku's voice was a hoarse whisper.

Sightless and terrified, Keiko felt the large wriggling thing stretch her jaw as wide as it could go. It left her mouth with a wet plop. Keiko gagged, sucked in a deep breath, and screamed in abject horror.

Toku gasped. "Blood and hell..."

Ryudo pulled Keiko away from the bowl. He uncovered her eyes to cover her mouth with a white towel, muffling her screams. He held her tight against his chest and looked over his shoulder at Toku. "Toku, quickly! Destroy it!"

Shocked beyond words, Keiko kept screaming despite the towel over her mouth. Bucking and twisting in Ryudo's arms, her heels hammered on the hardwood floor.

Behind them, blue-white light flashed. "Done!" Toku's voice was firm, and disgusted. "Gross, that was nasty."

"It is destroyed." Ryudo's hold was unbreakable, but his voice was gentle. "It is gone, Keiko."

Gone... The all-consuming panic in Keiko's mind abruptly dissolved. She collapsed against Ryudo, trembling violently. Tears slid down her cheeks. *Tika, I'm so sorry.*

~ Twenty ~

Ryudo took the towel away from Keiko's mouth, and eased the binding from around her wrists. "You're going to be fine, love…"

Keiko wiped her sleeve across her cheeks, but the tears refused to stop. That thing had come from Tika, but it was her fault Tika had gotten possessed in the first place. If only she had protected Tika better, or at least insisted that Tika not come with them, then the demon wouldn't have possessed her. *I'm an awful friend…* She leaned forward onto her hands, pulling from Ryudo's embrace, and staggered to her feet.

"Keiko?" Ryudo rose behind her, his hands out.

"No." Keiko held up her hand, motioning him to leave her be. "I…" Her entire body was one vicious ache, but she bit back the pain and fought to stay upright. The pain in her heart was far worse. She took a breath. "I just need…a minute."

Toku's voice was soft. "Is she okay?"

Ryudo hissed. "Cover that bowl!"

Wiping at her wet cheeks, Keiko sniffed and turned around. She eyed the blackened steel mixing bowl at Toku's feet. A white towel had been tossed over it. "So, what was it?" *What had Tika put in her?*

"It was nasty." Toku shuddered. "That's all you need to know!"

"That was a demon's larva." Ryudo sat down on the edge of the bed, and leaned back on his elbows, watching her. His hair spilled across the bed in a long black cloak of silk. His belt was missing and his robes fell open, showing a delicious amount of muscular chest and belly above the belt of his full pleated trousers. He crossed one knee over the other and his brow lifted. "And I would dearly like to know how you ended up with it."

Keiko averted her gaze from Ryudo's broad naked chest. How could she even think about Ryudo after what she had done to Tika?

"Keiko got it from one of the students at the university." Toku crossed his arms. "I found Keiko masturbating for it."

"What?" Ryudo sat up and frowned at Keiko. "You were feeding it voluntarily?"

Keiko felt the tears slip down her cheeks and her temper flashed. "She's my friend!" Keiko's crossed her arms over her stomach. "I told her that I would…" She focused on the floor. "I told her I would cum for her if she didn't use the demon on me."

Toku snorted. "Your *friend* lied."

"Keiko…" Ryudo rolled his eyes. "One cannot be friends with demons, only food."

Keiko shook her head. "She's not a demon, she's possessed by one. I don't think she knew what she was doing."

Toku curled his lip and pointed at the bowl. "This wasn't an accident."

Keiko glared at him. "Tika's possessed! She may not have known what the demon was doing!"

"Keiko." Ryudo shook his head. "The creation of a seed is not something done easily or in haste. This could only be a deliberate act."

Deliberate? Keiko trembled. *Why would Tika deliberately…?*

Toku picked up the blackened bowl and averted his face. "I suspect that this same demon is the source of all the recent activity at the university." He walked past them and around the end of the bed, carrying the bowl toward the glass sliding doors on the far side.

Ryudo turned to look at him. "Indeed?"

"The source…?" Keiko turned to look at Toku. "The source of what?"

Toku nudged the tall black folding screen to the side. "There has been an epidemic of minor demonic activity scattered about the university. I've been cleaning up pockets of...disturbances. Luckily, no one has turned up with one of these, though I figured it was only a matter of time."

Beyond the glass door, night darkened a small lantern-lit, enclosed garden with sculpted trees and pale flowers surrounding a bubbling stone jar fountain stained from moss.

Keiko frowned. When had night fallen? How long had she been there?

"But why seed Keiko?" Ryudo lifted his brow and frowned. "The demon must have known that Keiko was not an appropriate host."

"A better question is, why *only* Keiko?" Toku released the lock on the sliding glass door with a loud snap. "With all the students it had seeing it daily, you'd think it would have seeded half the school by now."

Ryudo frowned. "Indeed."

"Not an appropriate host?" Keiko shook her head. "And what is seeding, or a demon larva anyway?" She curled her lip in a sour smile. "Other than nasty."

Ryudo looked away. "A seeded host eventually gives birth to a half-demon, half-human larva that the parent demon can possess. The larva feeds on the host's soul as a chick feeds on the yoke of an egg during incubation. Naturally, the host dies with the creature's birth."

"Dies?" Keiko clutched her elbows and shivered. "Great Mother..." Tika had a long history of doing nasty things to her ex-boyfriends; sugar in gas-tanks being the least of her less than gracious acts, but Tika never tried to *kill* anyone. Maybe Toku was right, maybe she was gone? She looked up at the shadowed ceiling. *Damn it, Tika...*

Ryudo shook his head. "Once the demon consumes a host's soul, the body dies fairly quickly. The human body cannot live long with a soul that is not its own. Seeding is a way for a demon to gain a physical body that is capable of housing it for a full human life-time."

He frowned thoughtfully at her. "However, because of your nature, your body will not allow such a creature to germinate. Eventually you would have expelled it."

Keiko tilted her head. "Expelled it?"

Toku shoved the glass door open. "A demon larva nesting in a human is incorporeal, a spirit. In your body it has mass and weight, so naturally, your body would reject it."

Keiko's brows lifted. "You're saying I would have barfed it up anyway?"

Ryudo looked sharply away. "Not quite."

Toku smiled sourly. "Does the term 'tapeworm' bring anything to mind?"

"Oh, ewww!" Keiko cringed. "Thanks for the image Toku!"

"But there is no mistaking Keiko's nature, therefore it knew that she would expel the larva, so why seed her?" Ryudo twisted around on the bed to frown at Toku. "It defies logic."

Keiko wiped at her damp cheeks and shook her head. The Merciful Lady only knew why Tika had done it. Tika had never bothered much with logic.

Toku frowned at them over the blackened bowl. "I have no clue. You know more about these things than I do." He tilted his head toward the open door. "Excuse me while I dispose of this." He ducked outside.

Keiko frowned after Toku. "What is he going to do with it?"

"What must be done with all things demonic; burn it."

Keiko winced. "Oh."

"Keiko…" Ryudo leaned forward, pressed his fingers to his brow, and winced. "Why, in the name of all the holy ones, would you seek out a demon?"

"Tika is my friend! I wanted to help her." Keiko's gaze dropped to the floor. "It was my fault she was possessed."

Ryudo's brows lifted. "Your fault?"

Keiko sighed. "When it happened, I didn't do anything to stop it and then…" She closed her arms around her stomach and rocked unsteadily on her feet. "I left her with it."

Ryudo sighed and dropped his hands, setting his forearms on his knees. "Keiko, as talented as you are, only a mage or a sorcerer could have done anything to stop your friend's possession."

"That wasn't the point!" Keiko threw out her hands. "I should have at least tried, but I didn't. I just walked off and..." She pressed her hand to her brow. "And I left her there."

Ryudo shook his head. "There was nothing you could have done for your friend."

"I know, they told me." Keiko stared at the floor. "But I should have at least tried." She stilled. Maybe Tika *had* put that thing in her on purpose, knowing that Keiko wouldn't die from it.

The demon had no reason to be mad at her, and less reason to put that thing in a person that couldn't carry it, but if Tika was pissed at her, and knew that she'd eventually get rid of it—she just might. It was perfectly logical for Tika—which meant that Tika couldn't be gone yet!

Keiko stared at the door. She had to get back to Tika and remove that demon. She bit down on her lip. But she didn't know *how* to remove a demon!

Ryudo frowned at her. "Come and sit, before you fall."

Keiko's knees decided, in that very moment, that they didn't want to work anymore. "Maybe I should..." She took two steps toward the bed and felt her head spin. Her knees wobbled, and she tripped.

Ryudo was suddenly before her with his strong arms around her, steadying her. "I have you."

Keiko tried to push him away without staring at his naked chest. "I'm fine."

"You are not fine." He urged her to the edge of the bed. "Sit."

Keiko nearly collapsed onto the bed. Sheer stubborn will kept her sitting upright. "There, I'm sitting." She pushed at his hands. "Happy now?"

Ryudo sat next to her on the bed and set his arm behind her. "So, how did this possession come about?"

Toku stepped back inside, without the bowl. "That's what I'd like to know." He closed the sliding glass door behind him.

Keiko clasped her hands in her lap. "Shihan took me to me to meet a friend of his, an Avatar..."

"An Avatar?" Ryudo abruptly threw up his hands. "Blood and hell-spawned night, I should have known! Where there are demons, there is always an Avatar!"

Keiko frowned at Ryudo. "You know about them?"

"Know about them?" Ryudo scowled. "Those spiritual blights have meddled in my affairs more times than I care to recount."

Toku sat down on the opposite edge of the bed. "Are these the guys you told me about, the monk-sorcerers?"

"Yes." Ryudo leaned back on one elbow to look over at him. "They call themselves demon-hunters in service to humanity, but they tend to manufacture more problems than they solve." His gaze narrowed at Keiko. "Tell me about this...Shihan. How did he know this Avatar?"

Keiko leaned away. Ryudo looked seriously pissed. "Shihan is my karate instructor. He said that Avatar Tsuke was an old friend of his. Shihan told me that they could help me with my..." She glanced away. "My problem with ghosts."

"Is that so?" Ryudo rolled onto his side, his robe slipping down his shoulder. His brows dipped lower over his white-hot gaze. "And your friend's possession?"

Keiko leaned further back balancing on her hands. "It happened on the walk through the park to the meeting. I felt its presence, and then it was...already too late." She winced and looked away. "It happened so fast; almost the moment I felt it. I turned around and it was all over her." She closed her eyes. "And then it was in her. Then she started...doing her boyfriend right there in the woods."

Ryudo sighed. "So, it fed immediately."

Keiko nodded.

Toku cleared his throat. "And her boyfriend? What happened to him?"

Keiko tilted her head to one side. "He's with the Avatars. We were able to get him back, but she...she flew off."

Ryudo shifted with a whisper of rich silk. "So, the meeting with the Avatar came after the possession?"

Keiko lifted one shoulder. "Yes."

"This Avatar, did he notice my mark?"

"Oh, yeah, he noticed it." She took a breath and deliberately turned to face Ryudo. "And he said..." The words dried up in her mouth.

Ryudo was stretched out on the bed with his white robe open and spilling like milk behind him. His long hair fell in a wash of midnight silk across his muscular belly, his broad chest and his erect nipples. Both arms, from wrist to shoulder, were intricately tattooed with stylized dragons, blooming chrysanthemums and cherry blossoms.

She wanted to touch the bright colors of his tattoos. She wanted to touch him. She wanted to feel all that muscle and slide all that silky hair through her fingers. She licked her lips, then closed her hand into a fist. Ryudo was far too sexy, and much too close for her personal comfort.

Ryudo's fox-fire-lit gaze caught hers and his smile held wry amusement, and heat. "Keiko, what did this Avatar say?"

Keiko swallowed and focused on his handsome face. "He wants to collect you." She looked over at Toku. "And your host."

Toku stiffened. "What?"

Ryudo's brow lifted. "And yet, they have not come here."

Keiko shook her head. "I told them you were a house guardian, but they didn't know what house you guarded."

"Ah, well, it has been well over a century since my last encounter with them." Ryudo rolled back onto both elbows, his long hair sliding across his bare chest. "Apparently I have been forgotten." He shrugged and smiled. "Let me guess, they offered to rescue your possessed friend in trade for my location?"

Keiko turned to the side gave him a glance from the corner of her eye. "No."

Ryudo's brows lifted. "No?"

Keiko shrugged, then looked down at her lap. "They offered to remove your mark."

Ryudo stilled.

Toku leaned closer. "You didn't tell them…?"

Keiko clasped her hands in her lap and sighed. "No. He's not my family spirit."

Ryudo and Toku exchanged surprised glances, then Toku frowned at Ryudo. "Can they take you?"

"They have tried before, on numerous occasions." Ryudo suddenly smiled. "As you can see, they have yet to succeed."

Toku propped his chin on his upraised hands. "Okay… Well, I understand why they'd want you, they collect ghosts, or Keiko because of what she does for them, but why me?"

Ryudo looked over at Toku. "Any human that can see and therefore host spirits is highly valuable to them."

Keiko scowled at Toku. "At least you have a use beyond sex-toy."

Ryudo snorted. "That is not entirely true." He looked over at Toku. "The lesser ranking Avatars, the Advocates, service their superiors. This intimacy is considered proof of an Advocate's devotion to their order, as well as feeds their superior's companion ghost."

Toku's face blanched. "What…?"

Ryudo lifted a brow and smiled. "However, your level of talent for mage-craft is as unusual as Keiko's ghost-touch. Should they discover your talents, they will move heaven and earth to bring you into their order."

Toku cringed. "Great."

Ryudo chuckled and waved a hand. "Fear not, as long as you bear my mark, the order cannot claim you." He looked over at Keiko. "Either of you."

Level of *mage-craft…?* "Wait a minute…" Keiko turned all the way around and stretched out on her stomach to face Toku. "Toku, you're a mage? Since when?"

"Well, yeah." Toku shrugged. "You saw me open the lower level doors with mage-craft when I took you from the demon." He rolled over onto his back and folded one knee over the other. "Ryudo's been teaching me how to control it since grade-school."

"Ryudo's been teaching you?" Keiko sucked in a sharp breath. "Since grade-school?"

Ryudo snorted. "Purely self defense, actually." He smiled at Keiko. "Toku has a rare talent for unraveling very carefully wrought spells." He rolled his eyes. "He had pulled down fully half of the house's defenses before I realized that it was completely accidental and not an attack."

"Half the house's defenses?" Toku turned his head and grinned at Keiko. "All I did was wander through a couple of his hidden doors." He lifted his chin toward Ryudo and his smile broadened. "I ended up in his private chambers before he knew I was there."

Ryudo scowled. "I knew you were there."

Toku pursed his lips. "Did not."

Ryudo rose up on one elbow to face Toku and curled his lip. "Do not start with me, brat!"

Keiko frowned. "Ryudo, how do you know about magic?"

"Is it not obvious?" Ryudo dropped his chin. "I was a fully trained mage before I was a guardian."

Keiko winced. "Oh…" A sudden yawn stretched her jaw wide. She covered her mouth with her hand. "Oh, sorry."

Ryudo frowned at her. "Keiko needs to rest."

Keiko sniffed at her silk robe. She stank of sweat, and…other things. She curled her lip. "Keiko needs a shower."

"The tattoo is too fresh." Ryudo tilted his head. "Perhaps a sponge-bath?"

Toku's brows lifted. "A sponge bath?"

Ryudo sat up and glanced toward Toku. We will need a bucket and a stool, as well as a pair of sponges."

Toku grinned and lunged off the bed. "I'll be right back!" He dashed across the bedroom and yanked the door open. "Don't start without me!" He closed the door behind him.

"Tattoo?" Keiko frowned up at Ryudo. "What tattoo?"

~ Twenty-One ~

Ryudo rose from the bed in a wash of flowing white silk and stood by her knee. "Can you stand?"

"Of course." Keiko scooted to the edge of the bed and set her feet down on the floor. She rose, and her head spun. Her knees simply refused to work properly, and she teetered. "Maybe not."

Ryudo's cool, strong fingers closed around her elbow. "I have you."

Keiko leaned against his warm body, trying very hard not to look at all that exposed skin. "Ryudo, what tattoo were you talking about?"

Ryudo looped his other arm around her waist and guided her across the hardwood floor "When Toku brought you home, you were unconscious from the loss of your soul's blood." He angled her toward a closed door to the right of the entertainment equipment, very near the sliding glass door to the garden. "I sealed the demon's bite to stop the blood-loss." He released her elbow and waved his hand.

The door opened and the light winked on, revealing a spacious white tile and chrome bathroom. A white tiled counter and marble sink took up most of the left wall ending with a glass door led into a large shower-stall. The room's entire far end held a huge round traditional cedar tub big enough for four. The entire right wall was windowed showing the enclosed night-filled garden. A low wooden table centered on the window held towels.

Keiko frowned up at Ryudo. "Are you saying that you fixed the bite with a tattoo?"

"Yes." Ryudo gently pushed her toward the long wall mirror over the sink. "The wound was spiritual, not physical. Tattooing is the traditional method for spiritual protection."

"Oh, that's right." Keiko frowned up at him. "Then the tattoo is real, I mean visible?"

"As real and visible as the scars you bear." Ryudo turned her back to the mirror and waved his hand. A hand mirror materialized in his hand. "See for yourself." He pushed her black mane over her shoulder and held the mirror before her eyes.

Keiko stared into the small oval mirror reflecting the wide mirror behind her. Exquisitely drawn across the back of her neck was a nearly photographic rendition of three chrysanthemum blooms in shades of yellow, orange, and scarlet. Her mouth opened. "Oh, wow."

Ryudo looked down. "Do you like it?"

"Like it? It's gorgeous!" Keiko took hold of his wrist to steady the hand-mirror, then tilted her head from side to side to see it all. "Your work?"

Ryudo tucked his other hand behind his back and dropped his chin. He nodded.

She whistled softly. "You're an incredible artist."

Toku leaned against the doorframe with his arms folded and grinned. "I was impressed too." He held up a wooden bucket and a small square stool. "I've got the sponges and the bucket. Ready to get naked?"

"What?" Keiko clutched the collar of her robe together. "I can bathe myself!"

"Bathe yourself?" Toku walked past her and opened the shower door. "Now where's the fun in that?" He set the wooden bucket and the low stool on the white tiles.

Keiko leaned back against the counter. "No really guys, I don't need help bathing."

"Of course you do." Ryudo stepped back and gestured. His hand-mirror winked out, like a blown candle. "Keiko, you are clearly exhausted. You can barely stand." His white robes slid from his shoulders, fluttering to the floor and out of existence. He smiled.

Keiko turned her face away, but couldn't quite take her eyes off his magnificent chest. "I can sit on a stool and use a sponge just fine!"

"Relax, Keiko." Toku turned to face her and tugged the belt on his black robe free. His robe opened revealing a sleek muscle and smooth skin. "It's not as if we haven't seen you naked before." The black robe slid from his shoulders.

Toku had a point. Keiko licked her lips. He had a really, really nice chest, too. They both did.

"Well, are you going to lose the robe?" Toku unknotted his black trousers, and let them slide down. He was firmly and impressively erect. He was also intimately shaved.

Keiko's mouth watered, and her nipples tightened. She'd never seen anything like it. His bare cock and ball-sack looked...lickable.

Toku smiled and lifted his brow. "Keiko?"

"Huh?" Oh, Merciful Lady, she was staring! She closed her eyes to get a grip on her runaway libido. "Can't I just do this myself?" Her voice sounded small and tight.

"Keiko, give it a break; it's just a bath!" Toku sounded disgusted.

"Keiko, are you afraid?" Ryudo's voice held humor.

Afraid? Keiko opened her eyes and glared at Ryudo. "I'm not afraid of a damned thing." Except maybe all that sleek muscle only a few inches away. Merciful Lady, he was way too handsome. She took a breath to steady herself. A mistake; Ryudo smelled way too good too. *Shit, what had he asked?*

Ryudo's brow rose and his lush mouth lifted in a sarcastic smile. "Then what are you waiting for?"

Oh yeah, he'd asked if she was afraid. *Bastard.* Grimly, she lifted her chin, and untied the robe's knotted belt. Holding his gaze, she let her robe fall open, then slide down her arms.

Ryudo's gaze dropped to her breasts, then he tilted his head, clearly looking lower. His gaze lifted to hers and he smiled.

"Excellent."

Though her cheeks heated ferociously, Keiko clenched her jaw and fought the urge to cross her arms over her breasts—or touch him. She held up her robe and lifted her brow in defiance.

"Thank you." Ryudo gestured and the robe rose from Keiko's fingers, sailed to her left, past Toku. The robe and landed on a peg to hang beside Toku's clothes.

Staring wide-eyed, Toku licked his lips. "Whoa, Keiko, I keep forgetting how hot you are."

Ryudo glanced toward Toku. "I did not." The ties on his trousers unraveled and the white silk slid downward and disappeared.

Keiko's gaze was drawn down Ryudo's muscular belly. Rising from a nest of dark hair was the smooth column of his jutting erection. Her core clenched hard and moisture slicked her thighs. She'd never actually seen him completely naked. She'd never seen either of them completely naked. On that stormy afternoon she had been blindfolded, and then in the alley, Toku had dropped his pants, but otherwise, he'd been fully dressed. They were both breathtakingly beautiful men.

"Tight nipples." Toku smiled. "I think she likes what she sees."

Ryudo turned his head slightly to glance over at Toku. "From the scent of lust rising from her skin, I am inclined to agree."

Keiko snapped out of her daze. *The scent of lust?* She scowled. "I think you're both perverts."

Toku snorted. "You obviously don't know what real perversion is."

Ryudo tilted his head and smiled. "Perhaps later we can show her?"

"Now there's a thought!" Grinning, with his impressive erection waving before him, Toku stepped into the shower stall. He turned away and pulled the spray nozzle from the wall, extending the long hose. His entire back, from the top of his neck down to the arch of his butt-cheeks, was tattooed with a massive dragon coiled among clouds in every color of the rainbow.

Keiko stared. She'd had no idea he had a tattoo. In fact, there was very little she actually knew about either of them.

Ryudo held out his pale hand and raised his brow. "Shall we?"

They were naked, and she was naked; it was too late for a change in plans. Keiko took his hand and let him lead her into the shower. The tile was warm under her feet, and wet. She sat on the small wooden stool and both men towered over her. It was more than a little intimidating.

Ryudo lifted and coiled Keiko's hair. "Hold your hair up for us, Keiko."

Keiko lifted her hands to hold her hair.

Toku turned toward her, the spraying nozzle in his hand, and smiled. "Chin up, and eyes closed."

Keiko did as asked. Her breasts lifted with her movement. Water, just on this side of bearably hot, spilled across her feet. She gasped softly. The spray rose, spilling over her knees, her thighs, her lap, and across her chest to spatter up her neck and chin.

"Coming around, don't freak out." Toku's voice came from her right side.

Keiko snorted. "I'm not going to freak out." The water moved around her right, across her arm, then all down her lower back to her butt.

Toku sighed from behind her. "There, that should do it." The water stopped.

A hand closed on her left shoulder.

She stiffened.

"Calmly, Keiko." Ryudo's voice was as soft as a breath in her left ear. "You may open your eyes."

Keiko opened her eyes to see Toku kneeling on the white tiles in front of her, pouring liquid soap on a natural sponge. He was painfully handsome, and wet. And erect. His cock arched only inches from her knees. He smiled. "Ready for your bath?"

Keiko smiled back, and said the first thing that popped in her head. "Do me, baby."

Toku leaned back on his heels and choked out a laugh. "Now you're brave?"

Ryudo leaned over her shoulder to frown at her, his long hair spilling past his shoulder. "Do me?"

Keiko felt her cheeks heat. "Never mind!"

Chuckling, Toku attacked her feet with the sponge. "Too late now!"

Keiko watched a dripping sponge rise from the bucket. The bottle of liquid soap lifted from the floor by Toku. Both floated behind her. She shivered.

Ryudo's hand closed on her left shoulder and a damp sponge brushed across her back. He sighed. "I missed this particular pleasure."

Toku frowned. "Ryudo, are you actually holding that?"

Ryudo held the sponge out past Keiko's shoulder, and squeezed it, spilling water and suds down her shoulder. "As long as I am in contact with Keiko, I have physical existence." He scrubbed down her arm, leaving suds in his wake.

"Really?" Toku tugged Keiko's foot out and swept his sponge up her calf. "How physical?"

Ryudo set the sponge on the floor and held out his hand. "See for yourself."

Toku set his sponge down, leaned toward Ryudo and grasped his hand. "Shit, you're really there!"

Ryudo snorted and released his hand. "I've always been 'really there'." He retrieved the sponge. "Keiko's talent merely allows me to have a semblance of life, such as a body."

Keiko frowned, thinking of when Ryudo had been in Toku's body in the alley. "Then how did you and Toku…?"

Ryudo chuckled. "How did I take you while possessing Toku?"

Toku lifted a brow. "That's what I want to know."

Ryudo sighed. "One would think the answer obvious. I can choose to be physical, or not."

Toku pursed his lips and scrubbed up Keiko's thigh. "That's

convenient."

"It can be." Ryudo scrubbed down Keiko's other arm. "However, physical existence is not without physical inconveniences."

"Inconveniences?" Kneeling between Keiko's spread thighs, Toku switched to scrubbing and soaping her other leg. "Like what?"

Ryudo chucked. "Such as an erection. I had forgotten how very distracting one can be, especially when one's love is literally in one's hands." He leaned close to Keiko's ear. "Especially when her arousal is so very evident."

Keiko stilled. *His love...*

Toku stopped scrubbing Keiko's thigh and suddenly focused on her crotch, only a kiss away. "I see your point." He looked up and focused on her breasts, specifically her nipples, and grinned. "And hers, too."

Keiko jabbed him with a toe. "Okay, so you're both hot. It's not like I can ignore it!"

Toku leaned to one side to grin at Ryudo. "Hear that? She thinks we're hot!"

Keiko scowled. "Oh, give it a break!" She poked him with her toe again.

Toku grabbed her foot and grinned. "Play nice."

Ryudo chuckled, then leaned over Keiko's shoulder. "Kneel up on the floor, and don't release your hair."

Keiko eased off the stool and came up on her knees. The stool slid to the side until it rested against the shower wall.

Ryudo lifted his chin. "Toku, shall we continue with our hands?"

Toku smile slipped away and his gaze heated. He tossed the sponge in the bucket. "Absolutely."

Their hands? Keiko sucked in a breath. That couldn't mean what it sounded like "Uh, guys...?"

~ Twenty-Two ~

Kneeling directly in front of Keiko on the wet shower tiles, Toku grabbed for the soap bottle. Staring hard at her, he squeezed soap onto his palm and licked his lips.

Ryudo leaned close to Keiko's cheek. "Don't let go of your hair."

Keiko slanted an uneasy glance toward the handsome ghost. Kneeling between both men, naked and wet, with her hands on top of her head, she was completely at their mercy. Not that her libido minded a bit. In fact, the warmth coiling low in her belly was making it very difficult to remember why she was supposed to be resistant to their attentions.

His hand on Keiko's arm, Ryudo rose up on one knee, leaned past her and held out his hand to Toku. "May I?"

"Sure." Toku tipped the bottle, releasing a thick dollop of the pearly liquid soap onto Ryudo's palm. The warm scent of masculine arousal mixed pleasantly with the sandalwood soap.

"My thanks." Ryudo retracted his hand and knelt behind Keiko.

Toku rubbed his palms together creating thick suds.

Ryudo's hand swept down her back, slick with cool soap. He released her arm to use both palms against her back, rubbing firmly in circular motions.

It felt wonderful. Keiko leaned back into his hands and sighed. *Damn, I should have a bath like this more often.*

His hands swept down to her buttocks and kneaded.

Keiko bit down on her lip. It felt good, really good, but... *No need to panic, it's just a bath.*

Toku leaned forward and set his palms on her belly, he rubbed. Staring straight into her eyes, his mouth serious, he moved upward to brush against the bottom of her breasts.

Keiko held perfectly still. *It's just a bath; it's just a bath...* Her nipples tightened to hot, aching points and anticipation clenched in her belly. She closed her eyes. *No, really, it's just a bath.*

Behind her, Ryudo's fingers slid between her thighs and soaped his way up.

Toku swept upward to cup her breasts in his soapy palms, brushing against her hard nipples.

Erotic heat seared her nipples then stabbed downward. Her core pulsed in awakening hunger. Suddenly and violently, she found herself wishing it was more than just a bath. A soft moan escaped.

Ryudo's fingers slipped down into the seam of her butt cheeks and over the tight bud of her anus. He dallied, rubbing and pressing lightly.

It was a little alarming, but not uncomfortable. *No need to freak out, it's just a bath, damn it.*

Toku lathered her breasts, and inched closer. "Lift your chin." His voice was barely more than a whisper.

She lifted.

His hands spread soap along her throat, avoiding the back of her neck, then slid back down to her breasts.

Her mouth opened on a sigh. *Mother of Mercy, he's good with his hands.* She took a deep breath. The perfume of sandalwood soap and summer chrysanthemums, mixed with the potent musk of two heavily aroused and incredibly sexy men.

It didn't have to be 'just a bath' if she didn't want it to be.

Ryudo's hands slid under to cup her mound, then dipped between her plump outer lips, exploring her intimate folds, yet evading her clit.

Under a rush of spiraling heat, Keiko sucked in a breath. Hunger cleared her mind of all thought but of the erotic appetite their hands were stirring. She arched her back, pressing her breasts into Toku's palms while spreading her thighs just a bit more for Ryudo's inquisitive explorations.

Toku's breathing deepened and his fingers closed on her nipples.

Ryudo brushed his fingers across her clit.

Pleasure stabbed low and fierce. She jolted, and her core clenched violently. She gasped.

"Enough." Ryudo pulled his hands from her intimate flesh, settling them on her hips.

Toku took a deep breath and pulled his hands away from her breasts. "All right." His eyes were wide and dark, and his mouth tight. He leaned to the side and reached for the sprayer.

A soft moan of frustration escaped Keiko. Damn it, she'd just made up her mind to let them seduce her, and they quit? It wasn't fair!

Toku stood and turned the hot spray on her, sluicing the white suds from her skin. He stepped to the side to reach her back, then came back to stand before her, the water rinsing the soapsuds gathered at her knees. His cock bobbed only inches from her lips. She could clearly see a tiny pearl of moisture at the tip.

Keiko leaned forward that extra bit and lapped at the tip of Toku's cock. The taste of salty musk exploded on her tongue.

Toku gasped, then groaned. "Keiko, if you start, I'm going to finish!"

Keiko licked him again. "Good."

Toku grasped the base of his cock. "Then open wide, because I've been dying to be in your mouth since the day I met you."

Keiko lifted her brow at him. It was not a particularly romantic thing to say, but by the tightness in his jaw and the flush in his cheeks, he was completely sincere. She opened her mouth and sucked him in as deep as she could. He was not a small man, and she couldn't quite get all of him. She lashed him with her tongue.

Toku choked, grabbed her shoulders and pushed straight down her throat. "Oh, shit!"

Her nose pressed against his belly, Keiko swallowed to keep from gagging on the cock in her throat.

Toku groaned and pulled back. "Shit, I almost came right there."

Keiko felt a spurt of feminine triumph. She released her hair, letting it fall over her breast so she could grasp Toku's muscular butt with one hand and caress his denuded balls with the other. His pouch was slightly cool and a touch fuzzy, like a soft peach, in her palm.

Ryudo lifted up on his knees, and pressed against her back. His erection was a hot hard bar resting in the seam of her butt-cheeks. "That looks very entertaining. Mind if I join you?" His arms came around her, and he cupped her breasts, then squeezed.

Delight spiraled straight to Keiko's clit. She moaned, and gently squeezed Toku's balls.

Toku threw up his head and hissed through his teeth. "Keiko, be really careful, I'm already hanging on by a hair."

Keiko released his balls to grasp the base of his cock, and swirled her tongue around the head of Toku's cock. Tongue extended, she looked up and smiled.

Toku snorted. "Pleased with yourself?"

Keiko nodded without losing tongue contact with his cock.

"Of course, she has you right where she wants you." Ryudo released one of Keiko's breasts, sliding it down her belly and then lower. "But then, so do I." He cupped her mound. His fingers delved into her intimate flesh. He groaned with obvious pleasure directly into her ear. "You're wet, very, very wet." He found her clit, and flicked.

Delight clenched voraciously in her belly, pushing her to the very edge of a quick climax. Keiko whimpered just a tiny bit, dug her fingers into Toku's butt, and sucked his cock into her mouth as deep as she could get him.

Toku's fingers tightened on Keiko's shoulders and he groaned. "Oh, fuck!"

She let him slide back, then suckled.

Toku gasped and trembled. "Son of a bitch, I was right the fuck there!" He looked down, watching Keiko pumping him slowly in, and then out, of her mouth. "Ryudo, whatever it was you did, please by the powers, do it again!"

Ryudo chuckled. "Are you sure? You know what will happen when you release."

"I don't care! It's for a good cause!"

"Very well, then..." Ryudo pressed his fingers to Keiko's clit and captured her nipple. He tugged and flicked at the same time, and continued.

The delicious throbbing in her nipple and clit was a pleasure so intense it was very close to pain, but it didn't send her over the edge. Moaning, Keiko bucked hard against Ryudo's hand, and hungrily sucked Toku deep into her mouth. She wanted to cum, damn it!

Toku panted and came up on his toes, pumping into her mouth.

Ryudo continued to put his hands to torturous use on Keiko's intimate flesh.

Trembling under jolt after jolt of intense delight, Keiko dug her fingers into Toku's butt, pulling him into her mouth to suck him deep, and then releasing him to suck him deep again. At the same time, she pressed back against Ryudo's hard hot cock, writhing against it, begging for more than just his fingers.

Ryudo groaned and rubbed his cock against her backside. "This...physical urge is difficult to control."

Toku choked out a laugh. "Tell me about it."

"Fuck!" Ryudo closed his arm around Keiko's waist and pulled one hand back. His cock slid down the seam of her butt and under. Hot, hard flesh rubbed against soft, wet flesh.

He was going to fuck her.

Keiko released Toku's cock and spread her knees wide, arching back to meet the cock searching for entry into her core. She groaned in encouragement.

Ryudo found her and nosed into her. "Yes!" He pulled hard, bringing her down onto his spread knees, and impaling her. He choked.

Keiko threw up her head and gasped. He was larger than she'd thought. He filled her and then some, stretching her. She ground against him and moaned.

Ryudo closed his arms around Keiko, holding her still. "Oh, the glorious sensation of flesh around flesh…"

"Poetry?" Toku snorted. "Okay…"

Ryudo tisked. "Wretched peasant! You would not do well among the court."

Toku came down on his knees and licked his lips. "I do just fine in the boardroom, thank you very much. I leave the politics to Father." He leaned back on his hands and spread his knees, his erection rising strong and curved from his lap. "Keiko, love, I really need your mouth."

Gently, Ryudo pushed Keiko forward onto her hands, and came up on his knees behind her. "Go to him."

Keiko didn't care one way or the other. Poetic or not, she finally had a cock in her cunt and one looming before, waiting to be milked. She opened her mouth and plunged down over Toku's lap, sucking his hard length in, then retreating, sucking every bit of the way. She reached the flared edge of his cock head, lashed her tongue and plunged back down, then again, and again.

Toku panted and pumped up to meet her downward plunges. "Blood and night, she's good at this."

"Of course." Ryudo's fingers closed around Keiko's hips. He eased most of his length from her. "She needs to feed."

Keiko hesitated. *Feed?*

Ryudo thrust, and groaned.

His cock struck against something utterly delicious deep in her, jolting her toward the promise of nirvana. She moaned around Toku's cock, and it pulsed on her tongue.

Ryudo pulled back.

Keiko followed, seeking to hurry his thrust.

"No, love." Ryudo's hands tightened on her hips, stilling her. "My control is not enough to withstand your…encouragement."

"Neither is mine." Toku coiled his hands into Keiko's long hair and groaned. "Slow down, babe!"

Keiko arched her back, pulling against their hold. She didn't want to slow down, she wanted to hurry up. She moaned in protest.

Ryudo groaned "Impatient..." He bent over her to curl his arms around her, holding her still for his unhurried thrusts.

Keiko sucked hard at the cock sliding in and out of her mouth. She needed him to cum, damn it.

Toku gasped for breath, his hands fisted in her hair to hold her head still for his cock. "Shit, shit, shit...I'm about done."

Toku was close. She could taste it on her tongue. Keiko pushed against the tile floor, urging them faster.

Ryudo held her firmly under him, and slowed his thrusts. "Just a bit more patience."

Damn it! She wanted to cum, but she needed them to cum first. She needed them to cum. She needed...them. She needed them both. Something embarrassingly close to a whimper escaped.

It was Ryudo, he was controlling the pace. She needed to get him closer to the edge. Something niggled at the back of her mind; a way to make a man cum while he was in her body. Something she could do without hands. Something Tika had mentioned. *Ah, yes!* Keiko closed her eyes to concentrate, and clenched her inner muscles around the cock lodged in her.

Ryudo choked, stilling on a thrust.

Keiko clenched again, squeezing him within her. Then again, and again...massaging his cock with her inner muscles.

Ryudo trembled and, gasping, thrust harder, and faster, pushing her onto Toku's cock. "Mother Night!"

Toku panted between thrusts. "Ryudo?"

Ryudo gasped over her, thrusting fast and hard. "Done, I am done..."

"About damned time!" Toku moaned, and thrust wildly up into her mouth.

Yes! Keiko kept steady, firm suction on Toku while clenching, and releasing, clench, then release... Using her muscles was pushing her back, away from orgasm, but they needed to cum more than she did. She would cum after theirs. No, she would cum during theirs. She didn't know how she knew this, but she was very sure that it was so.

And they were right there.

Somewhere, distant, thunder rumbled.

Ruthlessly, she squeezed her inner muscles around Ryudo's cock.

Ryudo's breath caught and he froze. He choked, and thrust hard, then sucked in a deep breath and thrust again. "Fuck!" His arms closed tight around her and his breath released on a choked cry.

Keiko felt the pulse of his cock within her body. *Yes!*

Abruptly something dark and powerful vibrated in the air. A hot summer wind where there could be no wind washed across Keiko's skin carrying the rich scent of chrysanthemums.

Keiko inhaled deeply and felt the shimmering darkness soak right into her skin and into her heart, filling her belly with summer heat.

"I can't hold it!" Toku came up on his spread knees bringing Keiko partially up with him.

She locked her arms around his waist, and sucked. His cock pulsed on her tongue, seeping salty liquid musk.

Abruptly something bright and powerful trembled in the air. A cool autumn wind swept across her back, bringing the smoky scent of fallen leaves.

Toku froze, his cock deep in her mouth. "I'm cumming, shit, I'm cumming..."

Ryudo came upright on his knees, still locked within her, and grabbed Toku around the neck, pulling Toku's mouth to his open mouth.

His lips locked to Ryudo's, Toku groaned and thrust his cock into Keiko's mouth.

Salty musk spurted into her mouth, and spilled past her lips. Keiko moaned in satisfaction, and pulled her mouth off his cock. She spat to clear her mouth and inhaled deeply. The trembling brightness soaked into her. Autumn cool closed gently around her heart, then filled her belly.

The two natures, dark and light, Summer and Autumn, life and death, entangled within her, combined—and exploded, delivering a fiery wave of euphoria to big for her body to hold. She screamed, pushing it back out, and into the men embracing her, and each other.

Both men threw back their heads, shouting.

Lightning flashed and thunder crashed over the house.

The bathroom lights went out.

Ryudo groaned in the darkness. "It is done, finally."

Rain hammered on the roof.

~ Twenty-Three ~

Keiko frowned at the remains of a completely charred dress in the middle of the university hallway.

Tika walked over to stand on the far side of the dress. She clapped her hand to her cheek. "Oh, no! Keiko, you ruined it!"

"Me?" Keiko looked up at her. Shock washed through her. Tika was a complete mess. One sleeve to her school blazer had split at the seam, to the point that it was barely attached. Her blouse was rumpled and her tie was missing. Her skirt had dark stains. Her shoes were missing, and one knee sock, leaving one foot bare and dirty.

Keiko held out a hand toward her. "Tika, what happened to you?"

Tika lifted her gaze. Her lips had lost all color. There were dark circles under her eyes, and her black eyes had a hazy bluish wash over them, like she was blind. Or dead. She scowled. "That's not the point!"

"Huh?" Keiko's brows lifted. "The point? I was asking what happened to you!"

Tika raked dirty fingers through her dusty and tangled hair. "Never mind that. The point is, you've ruined everything!" She held her hand out toward the dress. "How am I supposed to do anything with that?"

Keiko frowned. "It's a dress, or was a dress. You can get another one."

Tika frowned ferociously and her hands fisted at her sides. "No, stupid, not the dress, the scissors!"

Keiko shook her head. "Scissors? What scissors? You're not making any sense!"

"That's because your head is so thick!" Tika shook her head. "The scissors were in the dress! I was waiting for the dress to get finished so I could use them, but you burned the dress before it was done and melted the scissors!"

"Okay…" Keiko scratched at the back of her head. "What did you want the scissors for?"

Tika rolled her eyes. "I needed those scissors to get rid of these!" She raised her arms and peered under them. Long semi-transparent strings, like oversized spider webs, hung loosely from her elbows and wrists. She dropped her arms and groaned. "Now what am I going to do?"

"Since I ruined yours, you can use mine." Keiko shoved her hand into her blazer pocket, and pulled out a tiny pair of thread snips. Rather than the modern scissors used with the finger and thumb, they were in the antique style, like traditional shears. Squeezing the u-bend handle brought the blades together. Gold-handled and silver-bladed, copper scrollwork chrysanthemums were etched all over the entire piece. The small snips gleamed brightly under the hallway lights.

"Here." Keiko smiled and held her thread snips out to Tika. "They're my favorites."

Tika scowled. "Those won't work."

Keiko frowned. "Yes, they will. They're very sharp."

"You're so thick headed!" Tika shook her head. "Those are no good."

"You're thick headed!" Keiko stomped her foot and waved the snips at Tika. "They're perfectly fine!"

"I'm thick headed?" Tika crossed her arms. "Look at them! They're all wrong for what I want."

Keiko frowned at her gold and silver snips. "There's nothing wrong with them." She glared at her friend. "They're exactly what you need!"

Tika curled her lip. "How would you know what I need?"

"My snips are perfect for cutting thread!" Keiko spotted a long nearly invisible thread sticking to one of her jacket buttons. "Here, I'll show you." She grasped it and discovered that it was sticky, and made the hairs on her arms rise. It felt like a really thick spider web. "Oh, gross...!"

Tika frowned. "Keiko, what are you doing?"

"Give me a second." Keiko frowned. The sticky thread wasn't attached to her jacket. She opened her jacket to find what it was attached to. It went inside her shirt. She opened the buttons over her belly. The thread spread out to cover her navel, and there was something moving in it. She curled her lip. "Eww, that's disgusting!"

"Keiko!" Tika leaned forward and squinted. "What are you doing?"

Keiko looked up and raised her snips. "Here, I'll show you how well my snips work—on this!" She snipped at the thick thread. It began to fray apart.

"Keiko, no!" Tika gasped and reached out across the dress toward her. "Don't do that! Stop!"

Keiko stepped back and kept snipping. "See? They're nice and sharp. They're cutting through this like it's made of floss." The thread parted, and became dust. She lifted her head and smiled. "There, it's all gone."

"You stupid bitch!" Tika's face began to crumble into powder. At the same time, the university hallway dissolved around her; the walls and floor running like a chalk drawing under a rainstorm. "Look!" Tika threw out hands that were turning to ash. "See what you've done?"

Keiko sucked in a sharp breath. "Tika! What's happening to you?"

Tika shook her head and the ash fell away from her skull, revealing a face that looked as though it was made of charred wood. It opened eyes that blazed with blue flame and a mouth full of long black fangs. "You broke my toy!" Ash continued to fall away, revealing a tall, char-blackened, emaciated man buried underneath the shambles of Tika.

Keiko stepped back. "Tika?"

"Gone!" The charred man spread his arms and long black talon blades extended from his fingertips. "All gone!" He pointed a bladed finger at Keiko. "And you did it! You ruined everything!"

"I don't understand!" Keiko stepped back and watched everything around dissolve into a misty, empty, grayness. "What's going on?"

"You just couldn't leave it alone, could you? You had to mess with it!" The charred man continued to crumble, his body falling apart like an over-burned log. "You broke it! You broke everything!" He collapsed in a soft tumble of blackened coal powder onto the charred dress. A breeze whisked across the pile of coal dust blew it all away.

She gripped the snips with both hands and stared. He was gone, the dress was gone, Tika was gone… She turned all the way around and saw…nothing. "Tika? Where are you?" Everything was gone. "Tika? I'm sorry!" She shouted into the nothing all around her. "Tika, please! I'm sorry!"

Keiko gasped awake in darkness, nearly buried under a silk comforter. She was sandwiched, skin against skin, between two large and over-warm naked bodies, with no clue how she'd even gotten there.

A small golden flame flickered to life in the far left corner. The light brightened revealing that it was within the tall glass chimney of an antique Victorian oil lamp and sitting on a small table. The light spilled upward and outward, casting shadows across an overlarge television set in an entertainment center, and across the black silk comforter.

She was in Toku's room, in his bed.

"Keiko?" On her right, Toku turned toward her, rubbing his eyes. "You okay?"

Ryudo, on her left, sat partway up, the black comforter rolling down his bare chest.

Keiko wiped at her wet cheeks and looked from one to the other. She was in bed with...both? Ryudo was a ghost, what was he doing in a bed at all? She sighed. Why did Ryudo do anything? She suddenly remembered that Toku had asked her a question. She looked over at him. "I'm okay."

Ryudo sat all the way up and pressed his palm to her damp cheek. His hand was surprisingly warm. "You are...weeping?"

Toku stilled. "Weeping?"

Keiko wiped at her cheeks. "I was dreaming."

Ryudo frowned. "A dream made you weep?"

Toku exchanged a quick glance with Ryudo. "Why don't you tell us what you were dreaming about?"

Keiko hunched down, dragging the covers up to her chin. "Do I have to?"

Toku propped his elbow on the pillow, then set his chin on his hand, and smiled. "If you're having bad dreams about us, we probably ought to know. Don't you think?"

Keiko's earlier dream flashed through her mind, but she did not want to talk about that one. She lifted one shoulder. "I was dreaming of Tika."

"Ah..." Ryudo's brows lifted and he looked over at Toku. "Then, I think perhaps you should most definitely tell us."

Keiko bit down on her lip. "It was really weird."

"Well, of course." Toku smiled and set his hand on top of the covers, over Keiko's hip. "It was a dream." He swept his palm downward and patted her buried thigh. "They're always weird."

Ryudo slid down and onto his side, facing her. He propped his elbow on his pillow, then set his chin on his palm, echoing Toku's position in reverse. "So?"

Keiko looked from one to the other. "Okay." She looked up at the shadowed ceiling, and told them. Oddly, it wasn't as difficult to relate the dream to them as she expected it to be. In fact, it was rather nice to have someone to share it with.

Ryudo fished for her hand under the covers. "Do you understand what your dream was telling you?"

Keiko closed her eyes. "Tika's gone."

Toku sighed. "Keiko, I'm sorry…" He squeezed her thigh. "But Tika was gone when you last met her."

A fist tightened painfully around Keiko's heart. She didn't want to believe that. She didn't want to believe that she'd never had the chance to apologize, or say…goodbye. She closed her eyes against the hot ball of regret aching within her. Tears escaped anyway.

"Oh, hey…" Toku wrapped an arm around her and pulled her up against him, and pressing her cheek to his warm chest. "I'm sorry, Keiko." He pressed a kiss to her brow.

Ryudo inched closer, refusing to give up her hand.

Keiko took a breath and then another. "It's not your fault. You didn't do it."

Toku caught her chin and made her look up at him. "Neither did you."

Keiko flinched.

"Keiko." Ryudo sat up and released her hand to press his palm to her cheek. He thumbed away the tears. "You cannot blame yourself for something you could not prevent."

She turned to look at him. "But I could have…"

Ryudo shook his head. "Only a fully trained mage could have stopped it from happening in the first place."

Toku turned her to face him. "When was she possessed?"

Keiko frowned. "A bit more than two weeks ago."

Toku's brows lifted. "Two weeks ago?"

Ryudo shifted closer. "Could she see ghosts before it happened?"

Keiko shook her head. "Ghosts normally avoided her."

Toku winced and looked away. "Then she was a willing host."

Keiko pulled away. "She couldn't have been…"

"Keiko, there is no doubt." Ryudo shoved his hand into his long hair, pushing it back over his shoulder. "True possession, the kind that consumes the soul, cannot happen without consent."

Keiko stilled. "Consent?"

Ryudo held her gaze. "Someone who cannot normally see spirits has a closed soul. They are not made to interact with spirits. A demon may enter, but it cannot remain for more than an hour. Their closed soul will not allow the demon to feed, driving it out of the body or face starvation. For a demon to remain, they must deliberately open their soul to it, consenting to its presence."

Keiko closed her eyes. "That's impossible!"

Toku sighed. "Keiko, the demon should have been driven out of Tika after only an hour, but it was still in her two weeks after her possession. She must have wanted it there."

Tika's words came back with the force of a hammer blow. "*I got a special bulletin for you, Miss I'm-so-special-because-I-can-see-ghosts. I'm perfectly happy this way! Do you have any idea what I can do now?*"

Keiko pulled her knees up and wrapped her arms around them. They were right. Tika had wanted her demon. "I see."

"But why she would choose to be possessed is beyond me." Ryudo looked toward the foot of the bed. "It defies logic."

"Not really. Not for Tika." Keiko set her cheek on her upraised knees and took a deep breath. "Tika thought I was special, because I could see ghosts." She closed her eyes. "She wanted to be special, too."

"Special?" Toku frowned. "Did she know what ghosts normally do to you?"

"She knew." Keiko glanced briefly toward Ryudo then sighed. "She even saw the marks happen a couple of times. But, she couldn't see the ghosts doing it, or the blood…"

Toku scowled. "Because the blood came from your soul, not your veins."

Keiko nodded. "So she never made the connection." Not even when Tika was doing it herself.

Ryudo shook his head. "Denial. She saw only what she wanted to see." He leaned up to look over at Toku. "However, clearly there is more to this matter than the random possession of a schoolgirl."

"More?" Toku lifted his chin. "What makes you think that?"

Ryudo lifted a brow. "Do you not find it curious that this demon not only seeded Keiko, but also placed a thread?" He smiled at Keiko. "Which you rather easily cut."

Keiko blinked. "Was that good?"

Ryudo nodded slowly. "Very. In your dream, you broke the demon's connection to you. Without a seed, or a thread, it cannot find you."

Keiko frowned. "Find me?"

Toku leaned up and frowned. "Huh... The demon knew that the seed would eventually be expelled, so the thread means it wanted to keep track of Keiko once it was gone." He rubbed at the back of his head. "So, why waste a seed, knowing she would lose it? Why not just place the thread all by itself, and save the seed for a better host?"

Ryudo looked toward the foot of the bed. "An excellent question."

Keiko frowned. "In my dream, the thread was practically invisible. The only reason I noticed it was because I was looking for something to cut."

"Now that I think about it, I missed the thread completely. I only noticed the seed." Toku's brows lifted. "A diversion?"

"It seems likely." Ryudo looked over at Toku. "But without a seed, for what reason would the demon wish to monitor Keiko?"

Keiko frowned, puzzling over her dream. "The demon had threads on it too. A bunch of them, and it was obsessed with scissors, but it didn't want to use mine. That still doesn't make sense."

Toku gripped Keiko's hand. "It had threads? Of course..." His chin lifted and he focused on Ryudo. "The demon isn't operating on its own."

Ryudo frowned at Keiko, his brows dipping low. "Ah..." His lip curled. "Then it is not the demon that holds interest in Keiko, but the demon's master—the sorcerer that made it."

~ Twenty-Four ~

Keiko stared at Ryudo in shock. "Are you saying that a sorcerer is after me?"

Ryudo smiled slightly. "It would seem so." He lifted his chin and locked gazes with Toku. "Preparations will need to be made."

Toku nodded. "The house is already pretty tight, but it couldn't hurt to reinforce what's already there."

"Preparations?" Keiko looked at one, then the other. "For what?"

Toku shrugged. "This is your last known location. The sorcerer will come here looking for you."

Keiko scowled toward the foot of the bed. "How do I fight a sorcerer? A ghost I can handle, but I don't know anything about magic." Then again, she'd never dealt with a ghost that could become a giant spider-thing, like the demon in the forest, or even one that could be come a dragon, like Ryujin.

"Don't worry, we do." Toku stroked his hand down her hip. "We'll keep you safe."

Ryudo smiled, to chilling effect. "Do you honestly believe that we would allow anyone to take you from us?"

"Wait just a minute, you mean you want me to stay here?" Keiko pushed away from Toku, clutching the covers to her breasts. "I can't stay here, I have a life!"

Toku rolled his eyes. "Oh, right...I'll arrange for an instructor to come here so your grades won't suffer."

Keiko clutched at the blankets. "What about my karate classes?"

Ryudo patted her hand. "You may train with me."

Keiko eyed him. Train with a real samurai? It was a tempting offer. She shook her head. "I still need my own clothes and my private stuff…"

Toku shrugged. "I can have the staff bring what you need here."

Keiko scowled. "What are you going to do, move me into your bedroom? I don't think so!"

Ryudo lifted his chin at Toku. "The Peach Blossom Suite on the other side of this garden is unoccupied."

Toku smiled. "See? Everything's covered."

Keiko hunched her shoulders. "What did you do, plan this?"

Ryudo looked away and covered his mouth.

Toku rolled his eyes. "No, I didn't plan for a sorcerer to send a demon after you, okay?"

"Okay, okay…" Keiko scowled. "But, I can't stay locked up in your house forever!"

Ryudo smiled. "Why not?"

Toku shot Ryudo a narrow glare, then smiled at Keiko. "You don't need to stay here forever. Just long enough to deal with the sorcerer, as a guest."

"A guest?" He was going to let her leave after…? Keiko's indignation abruptly bled away. "Oh."

Ryudo rubbed his bottom lip. "We *could* keep her…?"

"No, we can't." Toku glared at Ryudo. "Kidnapping may have been fine in your era, but it's not done in this one."

Ryudo flopped back on the pillows, folded his arms and scowled.

Toku rose up on his elbow. "Ryudo, are you pouting?"

Keiko looked over at Ryudo, and her brows lifted. "You *are* pouting!"

Ryudo scowled deepened. "I do not pout." He lifted his chin and the corner of his mouth twitched upward. "I plot."

"Save your plotting for the sorcerer." Toku abruptly yawned. He covered his mouth with his hand. "Oh, yeah, I forgot. It's the middle of the freaking night." He rolled onto his back. "We need to get some sleep. We have a lot to do tomorrow."

He had a point. Keiko slid down under the covers.

Ryudo sighed. "Alas, yes." He leaned toward Keiko and pressed a quick kiss to her lips. "Sleep well."

Toku frowned at Ryudo then leaned over Keiko to press a quick kiss to her lips, too. He smiled. "No more nightmares, okay?"

Keiko smiled in spite of herself. "I'll do my best."

Both men nodded, then dropped back onto their pillows and fussed with the covers, jostling Keiko in the process.

"Hey!" Keiko shoved at them both. "You're squashing me, here!" She sat up. "Why do I have to be in the middle?"

Ryudo lifted a brow at Toku and smiled.

Toku froze then flopped onto his back to stare at the ceiling. "Keiko, I, uh, prefer you there, if you don't mind."

Ryudo eased the covers up to his chin and gave her a coy smile. "I am perfectly happy to have you between us."

Keiko snorted. *I'll just bet.* Securely sandwiched between them, she wouldn't be able to move from the bed without the both of them knowing. She eased back down under the covers, and sighed. "Fine, sure, whatever...."

The flickering lamp in the corner went out.

She listened to the darkness. Outside, a very soft rain was falling. She could hear it pattering on the leaves in the garden, right outside the sliding glass doors.

She frowned. She'd forgotten to ask about what had happened earlier, in the bathroom. She could have sworn she felt...magic.

Keiko vaguely felt a hand moving on her belly, stirring warm curls of erotic heat. She sighed and arched up into the gentle touch. Another warm hand on her left hip pushed, urging her to roll onto her right side.

She rolled against a hard male body facing her. An arm draped over her waist. Lips met the base of her throat, and then a warm wet tongue. She lifted her chin to offer the rest of her throat.

The offer was taken, and tingles followed the upward path of the tongue. A knee nudged between hers, and then a firm, hot erection pressed against her belly. The hand on her belly moved up to cup her breast, and squeezed.

Heat pooled in her belly, and moisture slicked her thighs. She sighed, and swept her hand across a warm chest, her fingers encountering an erect masculine nipple.

Behind her, another male body pressed up against her spine, and the hard hot line of a rigid erection seared her buttocks.

Keiko moaned and opened her eyes to see the top of Toku's head. He was kissing her throat. Watery gray light spilled through the tall windows past the standing screen. Outside, in the garden, rain was falling.

Toku lifted his head and smiled from a kiss away. "Good morning."

Lips pressed against Keiko's spine, then a tousled Ryudo looked over her shoulder. "A very pleasant awakening." Under the covers, his hand swept down her bare hip and he smiled. "Toku, is the lube still in the drawer?"

Toku stilled, his eyes wide. "The lube?"

Ryudo rolled his eyes. "Two men, one woman…?" He lifted a brow. "One of us is going to need lubrication."

Toku blinked, then released a breath. "Oh…yes, it is."

"Good." Ryudo leaned up on his elbow and pointed past Toku at the nightstand on the far side of Toku's huge bed. The drawer opened and a small white tube with a garish purple label lifted from the drawer. Ryudo gestured and the drawer closed. The bottle flew through the air and smacked into his upraised hand. He peered at it. "Ah, yes, that will do nicely."

Keiko frowned at the lube in Ryudo's hand. "What are you planning?"

Ryudo rolled onto his back and grinned. "Exactly what you think we are planning." He shoved the covers down, revealing his muscular belly and strong, thickly veined erection. He gave her a wink and uncapped the tube.

Toku wrapped his arms around Keiko and rolled her on top of him. He pressed a quick kiss to her lips and smiled. "Don't tell me you've never had anal sex?"

Anal sex? Keiko's heart slammed in her chest with alarm. "Uh..." She glared down at him. "Don't tell me you have?"

"If you must know, I have." Toku shoved the blankets down off of them. "Don't worry, Ryudo knows what he's doing."

Ryudo smiled and squeezed clear gel onto his palm. "Why, thank you, Toku."

Keiko looked over at Ryudo in alarm. Anal sex, with his big dick?

Toku lifted his head and captured Keiko's nipple with his lips, then lashed the tip with his tongue. He palmed her other breast and tugged the nipple to firm attention.

Delight blazed a path from Keiko's nipples straight down to pool in her clit, washing her thoughts away under a ferocious rush of erotic fire. She moaned and writhed against the hot cock on her belly. His teeth worrying her nipple put her right on the edge of begging for it.

Ryudo turned onto his side, propping his elbow on his pillow, and set his chin on his palm. Fisting his cock with slow pulls, he watched them with a smile on his lips and fox-fire flickering in his half-lidded gaze. "Ah, the joys of the flesh, and the two of you in which to indulge them."

Toku stilled. His gaze slid to Ryudo's, then dropped to the hand working his cock. "Don't get any...weird ideas."

Ryudo bit down on his bottom lip and smiled. "Toku, are you feeling shy?"

Toku clenched his teeth, and a soft pink blush seeped into his cheeks. He glanced up at Keiko, then looked over at Ryudo. His eyes narrowed. "Do you mind?"

Keiko looked from one to the other and frowned.

Ryudo shook back his long black mane and smiled. "And I was thoroughly convinced that I had removed any trace of innocence you had left." His brow lifted and his smile became feral. "I'll have to do better next time."

Toku scowled and his cheeks became a deep pink. "Enough, Ryudo."

Keiko lifted her brow at Ryudo. "Just what have you been doing to Toku?"

"Keiko!" Toku lunged up and bit down on her nipple.

Keiko's swollen nipple protested, and yet a hot throb speared her core. She yelped.

Ryudo pushed up onto his knees and focused on Toku. "You didn't tell her?"

Toku released her nipple with a tiny lick. "I did, but..." He licked the other nipple, refusing to lift his gaze. "Not in any...detail." He licked again.

Highly distracting curls of delight spiraled from Keiko's throbbing nipples and settled in her throbbing clit. She moaned. Damn, he was good with his tongue.

Ryudo's brow shot up. "I see." He smiled. "Toku, you're going to need to raise and spread your knees."

Toku's cheeks turned decidedly red, but he nodded, then lifted his knees, spreading them wide.

"Good. " Ryudo moved to kneel between Toku's feet. "Keiko, take him into you, nice and slow. I want to watch."

He wanted to watch? Keiko felt her cheeks heat ferociously. Well, it wasn't as if she could stop him. She brought her knees forward and came up onto them. She leaned forward, splaying one hand on Toku's broad chest. She reached back with her other hand to grasp his cock. It was hot and hard in her palm. Her body clenched in hungry anticipation.

Toku groaned and reached up to cup her breasts.

Keiko rubbed the broad hot head of Toku's cock against her wet cleft. She pressed down, urging Toku into her. The head spread her flesh deliciously. She groaned.

Toku's lips parted. "God, yes..."

Ryudo sighed. "How lovely, the spreading gates of heaven."

Keiko stilled, feeling very exposed by his attention, yet also feminine pride in his compliment. Her conflicting feelings stirred a curling roll of violent arousal and need. She pressed downward.

Ryudo's hand closed on her hip. "Wait."

Keiko froze with her hand around Toku's shaft, Toku's cock-head barely within her. A hot, velvety tongue swept the very back of her cleft, then along her intimate flesh stretched around Toku's cock. She sucked in a breath. The caress was startling, and alarmingly stimulating.

Ryudo's tongue moved from her flesh, then abruptly, brushed against the edge of her hand wrapped around Toku's shaft.

Her lips parted in surprise. To reach her hand, he had to be licking Toku's cock. It was a painfully exciting thought.

"Oh, shit..." Toku went rigid and trembled under her. "Ryudo!"

Keiko smiled. Apparently she was right. *Wicked Ryudo...* She licked her lips. Too bad she couldn't see it from this angle.

Ryudo chuckled softly. "Delicious." His tongue moved upward to swirl around Keiko's anus, delivering shivers. The point of his tongue stabbed, pushing partway in.

Keiko fought to hold back her startled cry, and dropped her head, her hair spilling across Toku's chest. His tongue, where no tongue had been before, felt incredibly wicked and devastatingly exhilarating. He persisted in his explorations, and a tiny sound escaped her.

Ryudo pulled back and replaced his circling tongue with a broad, gel-slick finger. He pressed against the tight forbidden rose. "Push out against me, Keiko."

Keiko bit down on her lip. What he was asking for was rather embarrassing. "I..."

Ryudo's hand tightened on her hip. The pressure on her anus increased. "Keiko, this is only my finger. I assure you my shaft is much larger. Push out."

Toku stared up at Keiko, his eyes wide and very dark. He captured both her nipples and tugged. "Do it."

Keiko whimpered in erotic torment, and pushed. Her body released tension and the finger slid into her. She gasped with surprise.

"Ah, there we are." Ryudo slowly pulled his finger out, then pumped it back into her.

She moaned. It wasn't uncomfortable. In fact, it felt oddly stimulating, but the sensation was not something she was used to feeling.

"Very hot, very tight." Ryudo sighed. "You are going to feel wonderful around me."

Toku's cock jumped and hardened just a hair.

Keiko sucked in a breath. Apparently Ryudo's anal debauchery was exciting Toku.

Toku licked his lips and rubbed her nipples between his fingers.

Keiko moaned. Between Ryudo's inciting finger up her ass and Toku's torturous fingers on her nipples, she could barely think beyond the wickedly pleasurable tension coiling within her.

Ryudo pulled his finger outward and pressed a second finger to her anus. "Now, Keiko. Take him."

Keiko gripped Toku's shaft and pressed down, pushing down onto him, driving his cock into her and Ryudo's two fingers into her ass. Achingly tight and wickedly erotic, she gasped, and kept pushing.

Toku groaned and arched upward to meet her, his eyes closing and his heels digging into the mattress. His hands opened wide on her breasts, then closed, his fingers sinking into her soft flesh.

Behind her, Ryudo sighed. "Yes, exquisite…" He set his hand against Keiko's back, encouraging her to lean forward while driving his two fingers ever deeper into her ass.

Keiko released the hot, firm flesh of Toku's shaft and arched over him, gripping his shoulders. She pressed down, taking him in and moaning softly every bit of the way. She sat, straddling his hips and sheathing him completely within her.

"Yes, very good." Ryudo came up on his knees, against Keiko's back and pressed a kiss to her shoulder. "How does it feel?" He moved the fingers within her.

Keiko couldn't think of a single thing to say. Instead she pushed forward, letting Toku's cock and Ryudo's fingers slide outward, then pushed back. The snug delight of Toku's cock moving within her mixed with the odd pleasure-ache of Ryudo's fingers in her butt. She bit back a groan. "Tight."

Ryudo chuckled. "Good."

Keiko's head lifted. "Good?"

Ryudo pressed against Keiko's back to look over her shoulder. "Toku, can you direct the resulting flow into the helix to strengthen the house's perimeter's defense?"

"What?" Toku turned his head to stare at Ryudo with his eyes dilated wide and his cheeks flushed. "You want me to spell-work the helix in the middle of this?"

~ Twenty-Five ~

*R*esulting flow? Spell-work? Helix? Keiko frowned down at Toku, intimately connected, his cock hard and strong within her, her fingers digging into his shoulders. "Wait…you mean magic?"

Toku nodded.

"Very much so." Ryudo withdrew his fingers from Keiko's butt and reached back to grasp the tube of lube. "Because of what we are, a manifestation of spiritual power is unavoidable, especially when we are in intimate contact." He leaned up against her back and pressed a swift kiss to Keiko's cheek. He looked down at Toku. "Spiritual power that can be diverted into the established defenses to protect the house, and all who dwell within, from an attack that will come very soon."

Toku scowled. "There is no way in hell that I'll be able to concentrate on the helix while fucking!"

Ryudo rolled his eyes. "You need only touch the helix with your talent, and remain connected. I will regulate the distribution." He lifted a brow and smiled tightly. "I do not have your difficulty concentrating while fucking."

Keiko turned to look at Ryudo. "Wait a minute… Are you saying that we make magic every time we have sex?"

Ryudo smiled. "Yes. Our first joining gave me flesh, but I am still a spirit. Toku is a mage, born with the talent to direct the energy of the spirits, but he is still a living man. You, my love, are spirit given living flesh. You are both the bridge between us, and a living source that empowers us."

Keiko frowned. "You're saying I'm the battery you guys plug into to make your lights work."

Toku winced. "That's one way of putting it."

Keiko's brows lifted. "Then what I felt in the bathroom last night, was that magic?"

Ryudo turned his head, breaking eye contact. "Yes."

Keiko frowned. "Was there a spell?"

Ryudo licked his lips and dropped his gaze. "Your soul had been drained. You needed the power we could manifest."

"Keiko."

She turned to look down at Toku.

"What he said is true; you did need the power, but there was a spell, too." Toku held her gaze. "It was a binding that connected your soul directly to ours."

Keiko felt a cold chill snake down her spine. "A binding?"

Toku nodded slowly. "If you are ever in danger again, or hurt, as you were by that demon, we will know and come to you."

Keiko closed her eyes and looked away. "You're saying that you'll always know where I am." The fierce chill of betrayal poured through her.

Toku took her chin and made her look at him. "When I saw you trapped by that demon, I…I lost it." He swallowed and smiled. "I can't handle you being hurt, not when I can stop it."

Warmth closed around Keiko's heart. They'd bound her, tied her soul to theirs, to protect her. But there was no question that they also wanted her for reasons that had nothing to do with care, and everything to do with power. It wasn't her they were protecting, but what she could do for them. She jerked her chin away from his hand. "I don't need your help. I can protect myself!"

Ryudo spat out a sound of disgust and grabbed a handful of her hair, jerking her head back. "Foolish! Ordinary spirits, yes, from those you can protect yourself, but not a demon or a trained mage. Not by yourself! Not even Toku can stop either by himself. And it is demons and their sorcerers that seek you!"

Keiko winced and grabbed his wrist. "Ryudo!"

"Listen to sense, not your pride!" Ryudo tugged on her hair. "Together we are strong enough to defend us all!" He released her hair and crossed his arms, scowling.

"Ouch, damn it, Ryudo!" Keiko rubbed at her scalp. "Watch that temper!"

"That was nothing." Toku chuckled. "When I brought you in last night, unconscious and bleeding, Ryudo about had a heart attack. I swear the whole house trembled until he had you back in one piece."

Keiko suddenly recalled Toku's words from their time in the park under the cherry tree. *"Ghost or not, I know rage and grief when I feel it."*

"I do not have a heart that can have an attack." Ryudo looked away and tightened his crossed arms. "And I did not lose control."

"You *did* lose it." Toku reached out to grab Ryudo's wrist. "And you do have a heart. I saw it breaking as you fought to tattoo her life back into her body. Ryudo, I watched you use your own blood in the inks."

The image of Ryudo's beautiful tattoo seared Keiko's mind. He had used his own spirit blood, his soul?

"I'm really beginning to think he's in love with you."

A fist closed tight around her heart. Lady of Mercy... What if Ryudo *had* fallen in love with her?

Ryudo closed his eyes and dropped his chin. "I am a spirit, not a man..."

"Spirit or man..." Toku tightened his hold on Ryudo's wrist. "Does it matter which?"

"Ghost or not, I know rage and grief when I feel it."

A shaft of pain stabbed through Keiko's heart. She closed her eyes and set her palm over her aching heart. Ryudo *was* in love. Yes, he was a spirit, but did that change what he felt? No. No it didn't.

She shook her head. "Not to me." She turned to face Ryudo. "It doesn't matter to me."

Ryudo looked up, his eyes wide and his lips parted. "What?"

Keiko snorted. He wasn't getting the message. She grabbed a handful of his hair and tugged his open mouth to hers. She swept her tongue against his, kissing him.

Ryudo's arms unfolded and wrapped around her tightly. He groaned and kissed her back, his tongue sparring ferociously with hers.

Keiko angled her mouth to kiss him more thoroughly, tasting the shadowy essence that betrayed that he was indeed a spirit, but also the masculine arousal of a man. He was both, and he loved her.

He released her from the kiss. "It seems that I do have a heart." His eyes closed, and he pressed his brow to hers. "It resides in you." He opened his eyes, curled his lip and glared at her. "And I will do everything in my power to protect it. Is that understood?"

Keiko sighed and rolled her eyes. "Oh, all right."

Toku snorted. "Gee, how disgustingly sweet. I think I'm about to get a cavity."

Keiko turned to look at Toku, and lifted her brow. "What? Do you want a kiss, too?"

Toku crossed his arms and stuck out his bottom lip. "Think you can spare it?"

Keiko bit back a smile and leaned over him. "I'll see what I can find." She leaned down and brushed her lips against his.

Toku looped his arm behind her neck, pulling her down to plunder her mouth with a hungry tongue. He moaned and cupped her butt with his free hand. He rose under her, grinding his cock up into her and pressing directly—and deliciously—against her clit.

Keiko moaned under a fresh onslaught of erotic tension.

Ryudo came up on his knees behind them. Leaning over her, he snaked his arm around her waist, his broad chest pressing against her spine.

Keiko automatically turned to seek his lips.

He kissed her with delicately light touches of the tongue and pressed against her anus.

Keiko pushed out against the pressure and felt the ache of

something rigid and too broad to be his finger. Alarmed, she opened her eyes and gasped.

Ryudo tightened his arm around her, and pressed his mouth firmly against hers, holding her mouth captive while staring straight into her wide eyes. His fox-fire bright gaze was hot with intent. He pressed harder, his entire body tense with urgency and demand.

Keiko struggled to accept him. He was big and solid, his cock-head stretching her well past the point of comfort. She closed her eyes and moaned.

Toku's hands closed on her breasts and tugged at her nipples. The erotic ache created by his fingers burned downward, entangling with the very physical ache of Ryudo's unrelenting shaft pushing for entry into her butt. Abruptly, Keiko's body gave way and Ryudo's cock-head surged into her.

Ryudo released her lips and gasped. "Ah…" He leaned over her, pushing her forward, over Toku. His other hand came from behind her to grasp Toku's shoulder. He pulled, and ruthlessly drove into her, sliding up against Toku's cock already within, and only a thin membrane away.

All three of them groaned.

Keiko gasped for breath. With both of their rigid lengths in her, she felt brutally full.

Ryudo licked his lips. "Yes…" He released Toku's shoulder and slid his hand between her body and Toku's. His fingers delved until they found her clit, then rubbed, lightly and quickly.

Pulses of erotic fire jolted Keiko. She trembled with sudden and ferociously building tension. A small cry escaped.

Ryudo flashed a smile. "Toku, begin."

Toku closed his eyes and threw out an arm, letting it hang over the edge of his bed, as though reaching for something beyond him. He opened his hand, whispered too softly to hear, then closed his hand into a tight fist. "I have it."

Ryudo slowly withdrew his cock from Keiko, his fingers dancing on her swollen clit while his arm held her in position, mounted on

Toku.

Fierce delight scorched her clit and at the same time, his withdrawal delivered a decadent pleasure she was not used to feeling. She gasped, startled.

At the very edge of her body Ryudo stopped. His arm tightened around her, and he pushed back in, just as slowly. The fierce ache of his resurgence squeezed a small pained sound from her throat. His inciting fingers did not relent. She trembled from bolts of fierce delight stirred even as her body ached with fullness.

Toku shifted under her, deliberately withdrawing his cock even as Ryudo buried his length within her. Both cocks passed one another, rubbing against each other, one going in and the other going out, the dull ache of her stretched flesh mixed with voluptuous pleasure forcing another gasping cry from her lips.

Toku reached the end of her body just as Ryudo's buttocks pressed against her, his cock fully seated. They reversed, Toku surging back in while Ryudo pulled back out.

The decadent pleasure of Ryudo's cock leaving her ass mixed with his fingers on her clit, and the delicious surge of Toku's cock into her body. Keiko sucked in a deep breath and released it on a small keening cry.

Toku's lips pulled back from his teeth and the muscles in his neck stood out in strain. "Shit, I can't…I can't concentrate." He panted for breath. "I have…I have the helix, but…I can't…" He groaned. "I'm going to cum. Shit, I'm going to…cum."

Ryudo bared his teeth. "It is too soon!"

"I know! I know!" Toku tossed his head against the pillow. "I can't hold it!"

"Then I will hold us all." Ryudo trapped Keiko's arms against her body, and pulled upright.

The bright hot ferocity of Ryudo's cock surging up into her ass forced a gasp from Keiko's lips. Darkness surged against Keiko's spine. Within her something responded, blooming and spreading from her belly outward.

Toku's eyes flew open. "What are you doing?"

Ryudo lifted his chin and took a deep breath. His voice rolled out on a wave of darkness. "Manifestation."

A hot sultry wind carrying the scents of late summer caressed Keiko's skin, and blew her long hair across her eyes. The sound of rain on the tiles became loud, and thunder rumbled far away.

Fingers brushed against her thigh, then a hand grasped it. Another hand grasped her other thigh. A mouth closed on her breast, and a tongue made wet circles around her tender nipple. Hot, moist breath whispered across her other nipple, and then a tongue, and yet someone's mouth still lapped at her other breast.

Keiko gasped in confusion, even as arousal clawed its way through her. It felt like before, like the first time in Ryudo's bed.

Thunder rumbled much closer and the rain out in the garden fell harder.

Beneath her, Toku gasped. "Ryudo! I don't need..." He choked.

Ryudo's voice rumbled, filling the room with whispers she could feel on her skin. "But you do need, and our need is too great to rush headlong without control."

She shook her hair back, clearing her vision.

Toku's chest, arms, and thighs were bound by what looked like semi-transparent ropes of differing entwining thicknesses, glowing with a soft gold incandescence. Finger-thin ropes defined the ridges and hollows of his straining muscular body. Slender tendrils curled around his nipples. He groaned, writhing among them, his head back and his mouth open.

Carnal hunger quickened and clenched in her belly. He looked so...beautiful.

A sharp pinch to her nipple made her gasp, and finally notice the glowing golden ropes binding her thighs, and her breasts. What she had thought were mouths on her nipples were actually counterworking filaments. Their gracefully entwining movements simulated the impression of lips and tongue to perfection.

She couldn't help but respond to the seditious and deliciously urgent ardor they stirred. She moaned softly and shifted, stirring the cocks within her, and found that while small movements were possible, she was actually securely bound in place.

Erotically imprisoned... A wicked thrill raced through her.

His arm tightened around her. It was the same soft nearly transparent luminous gold as the ropes. She had realized that the ropes must have come from him, but still, it was an unexpected sight.

And chillingly familiar.

Shivers of alarm raised the hair on her arms. The semi-transparent ropes coiled around her and Toku looked a lot like what the demon had wrapped around Shido and Tika in the tree.

Ryudo's lips caressed her throat. "Do not be afraid, Keiko." He released her waist and swept his palms across her belly, then over her thighs to insinuate his long fingers between her body and Toku's. With both hands, he rubbed against her intimate flesh.

A hot wash of rapturous delight drowned her alarm. She arched back and moaned. "Ryudo." She turned her head to look at him.

His face was familiar, but luminescent gold, and his eyes had become orbs of bright sunlight. His hair floated behind him and around her in long golden strands, lifted by a current she could just feel. The tattoos on his arms had unraveled from his skin to become the ropes and filaments that bound, and caressed, her body and Toku's.

Unlike the demon in the forest, Ryudo was still human in shape, his cock was still very much lodged in her ass, but there was no mistaking that she was in the arms of a powerful spirit.

His mouth tight, his expression became serious. "I will not harm you."

She smiled and kissed his glowing cheek. "I know."

Ryudo's golden lips curved in a smile.

"Ryudo..." Toku groaned beneath them. "Must you have a vise-grip around the base of my dick?"

Ryudo's chuckle echoed among the room's pooled shadows and brushed against the skin feather light. "You needed assistance, I have supplied it." He leaned forward, pressing Keiko before him. His hair floated around them, silky fingers caressing wherever it touched. "Shall we continue?"

Toku groaned. "Fuck, yes!"

The cock in Keiko's ass slid outward. Combined with hundreds of intimate caresses, a finger here, a squeeze there, the firm pulls on her nipples, and the flicking of her clit... The wash of combined pleasure took her hard and fast to the edge of sanity. She cried out.

Toku groaned and dug his heels into the mattress pushing up hard into Keiko's body, then withdrew. Ryudo surged into her body faster and harder. Toku withdrew on his stroke. Stroke and counterstroke, they pumped in and out of Keiko, gaining in speed and force, until flesh slapped loudly against flesh, and sweat slicked both Keiko and Toku. Cries of both excruciating delight and striving hunger escaped their throats.

Around Toku's fist, threads of gold shimmered into existence and rayed outward forming a web of golden light all the way around the bed. The threads pierced the walls and disappeared.

Keiko writhed and shuddered in Ryudo's hold, overwhelmed by the carnal intensity of her body's surging and building urgency.

Ryudo sighed. "It is time."

Toku choked on a laugh. "About fucking time! I need to cum so bad, my balls are on fire!"

Ryudo lifted a brow. "Then, by all means, have your release." Golden tendrils snaked across Toku's belly and tangled around his nipples, then arm-thick incandescent ropes whipped around Toku's wrists and pulled them above his head.

Toku jerked at his wrists. The webbing in his clenched hand vibrated with his struggles. "What are you...?" His eyes opened wide, then his mouth. He threw back his head and choked, his body arching up from the bed. "Shit!" His eyes closed tight and he bared his teeth. "Ryudo, get that...out of me!"

Ryudo reached out with a golden hand and set it over Toku's breast. "You wanted release, now you shall have it." He surged forward and into Keiko's ass, brutally fast and achingly hard.

Keiko gasped. Ryudo's ruthless thrust should have been painful. Instead, it sharpened and tightened the coiling rapture building within her belly.

Toku choked and groaned. "You sadistic son of a bitch…"

Ryudo's eyes narrowed. "Sadistic?" His lips curled back from his teeth. "Very well, then…" He drove hard into Keiko's ass again.

Keiko moaned, writhing on Toku's cock.

"Shit!" Toku gasped and arched up off the bed, thrusting up into Keiko. He came back down only to thrust back up, then again, and again, hammering up into her body.

Toku's slamming strokes struck something blindingly delicious deep within Keiko. "Yes." Ryudo stroked in complete opposition to Toku's thrusts, taking her just as hard. A smile curved his lips. "Much better…"

Bound between them, Keiko could only surrender. Thrust followed thrust. Sweet ache, then brutal delight, then forbidding decadence, then wicked pleasure… Over and over and over… Gasping cries fell from her lips.

Without warning, white-hot climax rushed upward and crested. Driven to the very edge of a rapture too big for her body to hold, her breath stopped. She trembled, teetering on the razor's edge.

Toku moaned and twisted under her, held firm by the golden ropes snaked around him.

Ryudo's summer-hot breath caressed her throat. "Now!"

Toku opened his eyes, and green flame leapt in their depths.

The perfume of summer flowers abruptly became tinted with the smoky scent of autumn leaves. Ryudo's streamers of soft gold were suddenly joined by streamers of deep green rising from under Toku.

Toku shouted. The green and gold threads twisted into a single snake and stabbed straight into Keiko's chest.

Keiko gasped, and felt warmth close around her heart. It wasn't painful, just startling. The warmth abruptly spilled outward from her heart and spread throughout her body. She could almost see traces of gold and green racing under her skin. Heat collected in her belly. Green life and golden death, living shadow and spiritual light, coiled tight within her and erupted.

Climax exploded in a fiery wave, arching her back and dragging her into a pounding spiral of agonizing rapture. She threw her head back and shrieked her joyful agony. Ryudo's mouth closed over her lips, stealing her cries and taking her breath.

Beneath her, Toku writhed and bucked, pulsing deep in her body, Ryudo's hand over his mouth, smothering his frantic cries of release.

Ryudo groaned, his voice echoing with shadows. He threw back his head and his mouth opened. "Yes, my hearts! Yes!"

Lightning flashed, and thunder shook the entire house.

~ Twenty-Six ~

Whatever she was sleeping on was incredibly lumpy—and breathing. Keiko opened her eyes. She was draped all over Toku's naked, sweaty and sticky body. And she was just as naked, sweaty and sticky. With the black silk comforter tossed over the two of them, it was way too warm for comfort.

She shoved the covers back a bit and pushed up. Her arms shook. She groaned and dropped back down onto Toku's chest. She was completely wrung out. She smiled. *Damn....that was some good sex.*

Toku yawned and stretched under her, then lifted his arm and draped it around her waist. He opened sleepy black eyes and smiled. "Good morning."

Keiko felt a smile creeping across her lips. "Didn't we just do that?"

Toku snorted. "What, you're asking me to think after all that?"

Keiko grinned. "You poor baby." She glanced about and frowned. "Ryudo's gone."

Toku kicked at the blankets covering them, shoving them further down. "He's probably checking the house's defenses."

Keiko struggled to sit up, then winced and hastily shifted to the side. Her butt was too sore to sit on. "Your helix something or other?"

"The helix is the base spell woven into the house." Toku pushed up and propped himself semi-upright with his hands. "The defenses are threaded through it, but the helix does more than just defend the house from attack, it's kind of like the glue that holds everything together." He winced and propped one knee up, leaning slightly to one side. "Ow, my ass…"

"Your ass?" Keiko bit down on her lip to keep from grinning. "Then Ryudo really was…?"

Toku rolled his eyes and pushed off the bed to stand. "Come on, we both need a shower."

"No kidding, I'm sticky all over." Keiko shoved off the bed and onto wobbly knees.

Toku grabbed her elbow, grinning. "And I was happy to help get you that way."

Keiko rolled her eyes. "Oh, gee, thanks." She stuck out her tongue.

Toku snorted. "Don't go sticking that tongue out unless you plan to use it."

Keiko winced. "Not right now, honey, I have a butt-ache."

Toku snorted and led her into the bathroom. "Funny… Me, too."

After a mutual scrub under the shower using enormous amounts of soap, Keiko and Toku rinsed off and stepped out.

"How about a soak? We didn't get the chance last night." Toku walked over to the huge wooden hot tub and shoved the wooden cover off and to the side. Steam curled up.

"A soak? Mercy, yes!" Keiko coiled her hair, fastening it to the top of her head and walked over to peer at the blue-green water. "That is a big tub."

"Most of the house is still original, but I wanted a modern tub." He grinned. "Complete with jets!" He hit a switch. The water swirled and bubbled as though boiling. He offered her his hand.

She took Toku's hand and he helped her down into the deep, steaming bath. It was deliciously hot. She groaned in delight. "I bet this comes in handy after all your marathon sex sessions."

"Marathon sex sessions?" Toku stepped into the water. "Not hardly."

"No?" She sloshed to the far side and sat on the edge of the sunken seat. The heat dug into her sore muscles. The bruises and strains she'd acquired from that morning, the night before, Tika the day before, and also, the past week's long exam sessions, eased from agonizing knots to manageable annoyances. Her butt felt better, too.

Toku sloshed after her. "I soak after my training sessions. Magic takes a lot more out of the body that you'd think." He sat down beside her, spread his arms across the tub's rim and let his head fall back. "Sex isn't something I do here."

She lifted a brow at Toku "Then you *have* been having marathon sex?"

Toku rolled his eyes. "Don't blame me. Ryudo has been doing all the driving." He looked over at her. "Possession, remember?"

Keiko frowned. "Ryudo has been *making* you have sex?"

Toku shrugged. "I told you in the park, Ryudo was pissed at me for letting you go. Apparently he thought I should know what he was missing out on, so he's been taking over my body and..." He swallowed. "Last night was the first time I actually had sex without Ryudo driving from the inside."

Keiko's brows lifted. "You didn't want to have sex?"

"With you?" Toku grinned. "Oh, hell yeah, I did, but you're the only girl I've..." He looked away and sighed, his smile fading. "You're the only girl I've wanted to, uh..." He sank a little deeper into the water, then lifted his shoulder in a tiny shrug. "You're the only girl I...like."

"Oh." Keiko felt her heart warm, and smiled. If she wasn't careful, she could really fall for him. She closed her eyes and her smile faded. *Oh, yeah, let's beg for heartbreak, shall we?* She lifted her feet up onto the bench, raising her knees, and closed her arms around them.

Toku shrugged. "So, in case you'd like to know, you're the first person that's been in my bed."

She lifted a brow at Toku. "Not even Ryudo?"

Toku curled his lip and snorted. "No. The only reason he was in it was because you were in it, too."

"Really?" Keiko bit back a sudden smile. "Ryudo waited all this time to take advantage of you?"

Toku turned to stare at her. "What?" He scowled and his cheeks flushed a dull red. "What exactly are you trying to say here?"

"I was saying…" Keiko smiled as innocently as she could. "That I just don't see how he could have resisted making a love-toy out of a pretty-boy like you."

Toku sat up and gaped. "A what…?" He glared and spoke through his clenched teeth. "I am not a pretty-boy!"

Keiko grinned. "Have you looked in the mirror lately?"

A gentle knock sounded.

Toku's eyes widened and he looked toward the door. He winced.

Standing in the doorway was a handsome older gentleman with neatly trimmed salt-and pepper hair in semi-formal traditional *kimono* robes of rich forest green over white with red silk hanging ties. Bamboo stalks and leaves were embroidered on the shimmering silk. He smiled pleasantly. "Good morning, Son."

Uh, oh… Keiko sank very slowly into the water to her chin.

Toku cleared his throat and glanced at Keiko. "Good morning, Father."

Toku's father folded his hands behind him. "I see you have a guest." His brows lifted in clear question.

Keiko whispered her family's name to Toku.

Toku stared at her and his brows lifted. "That's your family name, seriously?"

Keiko nodded.

"Huh…" Toku lifted his chin toward his father and somehow succeeded in making a formal introduction, with her full name while sitting in a bubbling hot tub.

His father's brows lifted "Indeed?" He smiled and nodded. "Ah, an excellent choice, Son, I quite approve."

"Thank you, Father, I'm glad you approve." Toku's voice came out tight and high-pitched.

Toku's father smiled and clasped his hands before him. "I will have one of the staff bring your Keiko the appropriate attire for breakfast immediately. Your mother will be very pleased to meet your new fiancé." He nodded. "Welcome to the family, Keiko."

Keiko's heart turned over in her chest. She barely remembered to nod politely in return. "Thank you, sir." *Fiancé?*

Toku's father waved his hand in dismissal. "Oh, no, no, Keiko, you must call me Father." He nodded at Toku. "Don't be too late, Son. Your mother likes to wait until we are all seated before she lets anyone eat."

Toku swallowed loudly and spoke in a strained voice. "Yes, Father."

Toku's father walked out of the bathroom, his steps completely silent.

Keiko turned to Toku. "Fiancé?"

Toku wiped a hand down his face. "Don't ask me, I just live here!" He stood up and held out his hand. "Come on. If I know Father, the staff will have a full outfit ready and be here to dress you in less than five minutes."

Keiko stood up. "They're going to dress me?"

Toku bit down on a smile and helped her out of the tub. "My parents like to appear traditional at home, which includes formal breakfast on Saturday mornings. Mother says it's in keeping with the house's noble status." He handed her a fluffy towel. "We're supposed to be nobles, so we should act like nobles."

"What?" Keiko took the towel with nerveless fingers. "Your... Your family is noble? You're related to the emperor? "

"Way far down the line, and only by marriage." Toku dropped a towel over his head. "Anyway, that was a long time ago. Our money comes from Father's business." He scrubbed. "What are you worried about? Your family line is more illustrious—and older—than mine."

"Illustrious? Oh, yeah, right..." Keiko leaned over and rubbed the towel against her skin to hide the heat seeping into her cheeks. "It's my mother's family name, not my father's."

Toku laughed. "Of course! Your family doesn't name the

daughters after the father. It's traditional among priestesses."

Keiko froze. "Priestesses?"

Toku pulled the towel from his head and frowned at her. "You mean you didn't know that you're from a priestess line?"

Keiko shook her head. "Mom never told me anything like that."

"Really?" Toku swept the towel across his broad chest. "No one in your family mentioned your heritage at all?"

Keiko looked away. "I don't know anyone from either side of my family. Mom raised me by herself. I don't even know my father's name." Her cheeks heated. "I don't even know if they were married."

Toku snorted. "As far as I know, the priestesses of your family line didn't marry, at least not often. I guess it was easier to keep track of all the daughters if the family name never changed. Anyway, your father must have done something awful to make your mom leave him when you were too little to remember him. Any idea why she left her side of the family, too?"

Keiko looked up cautiously. "Mom won't talk about her family, or my father, at all."

"Oh…" Toku shrugged. "Well anyway, now you know why you have ghost-touch. You're descended from a really old shaman priestess line that's legendary for talking to the dead."

"Really?" Keiko stilled. She'd inherited her curse? Could she have relatives with her problem with ghosts?

"Really." Toku took her towel and tossed it over the shower door. "Your family history goes way back. Technically your family has served the Emperor longer than mine."

She frowned at him. "How do you know all this?"

Toku grabbed her hand and tugged her into the bedroom. "Father thinks it's educational for me to know the histories of all the noble houses." He pulled her toward a large mirrored dresser on the wall opposite the windows. "We have a huge library that dates back to the feudal age." He rummaged in a drawer and pulled out a pair of dark blue cotton robes. "Ah… That's what we need." He held one of the robes out to her. "There's a whole book dedicated to just your family history, up to the second Great War."

"There's a book?" Keiko took the robe and shrugged into it. It was his of course, and too large, nearly dragging on the floor. She knotted the belt. "You have a book on my family?"

"Oh, yeah, I read it a while back." Toku shrugged into his robe. "Your family is famous for all kinds of spiritual things." He knotted the sash and smiled. "I'll see if I can find it for you."

Keiko blinked. A whole book about people like her? Maybe she wasn't so alone after all. "Thank you. That would be wonderful."

Someone knocked on the bedroom door.

Toku opened the door. Two women in traditional robes entered with their hair piled and restrained with decorative wooden pins. They looked at Keiko, bowed and smiled.

Keiko bowed politely back.

Toku nodded at the ladies. "Keiko will be staying in the Peach Blossom suite across the garden."

More bows were exchanged, with giggles behind hands added, then the women towed Keiko out into the hall. Two other women were waiting with their arms full of silk. Keiko was hustled down hallways and through sliding doors across empty rooms floored with *tatami* matting.

In less time than Keiko imagined, she was ensconced in a spacious but spare room painted with blooming peach trees and bright with morning light. A door on the left led to a small bath suite, and the corner niche on the right wall, by the door, held a tall pale green vase with several sprigs of blooming peach beneath an antique scroll detailing a poem to love and tranquility.

Keiko rolled her eyes. Since when was love tranquil?

She was towed to the room's very center and placed facing the wall of windows, and the garden, and Toku's suite. A folding screen was spread before the window and her robe was whisked off, revealing her scarred back. Keiko bowed her head and waited for the sounds of horror.

There was a single long moment of silence, then the women

grabbed Keiko and positioned her with her arms out. Old-fashioned split-toed socks were set on her feet and house sandals of braided silk offered. Then they began draping her with layer after layer of silk. A knee-length red under-robe, then a very long, floor-draping white robe, then a pale green robe embroidered in gold, nearly as long as the white, then another white robe, this one heavier but draping only to her ankles, with pale pink swirls and embroidered with sprigs cherry blossoms.

Keiko stood there, stunned. They hadn't said a word. Not one.

The women worked with incredible speed. They had one robe folded across her breasts and tied, then suddenly the next one was on her. They folded the wide sleeves back in layers to show each of the sleeves beneath.

A deep red and gold *obi* was placed around her waist. The heavily padded wide sash was tightened snugly around her middle, from the bottom of her breasts to her waist, and tied in a massive and reinforced bow at her spine. A white silk rope was decoratively knotted around the red sash, with a pale green jade pendent dangling from it.

Made entirely of silk, the whole thing looked crushingly expensive. It was an incredibly feminine outfit, and really, really binding around the legs.

All four of them attacked her hair with a will and large combs. They pulled Keiko's hair straight up on the sides and combed the rest straight back from her brow, then gathered the length into a tail, binding it back with a tasseled red cord.

They ooh'ed and ah'ed, nodding and smiling at each other over their job well-done for maybe three whole seconds, then grabbed Keiko by the elbows, turned her bodily toward the door, and hustled her back into the hallways.

As her knees were bound nearly together by her clothing, Keiko was hard pressed to do anything beyond a very quick prancing trot. It was so silly a gait that after turning the second corner, all of them at the same prancing trot, Keiko began to giggle. By the time the women stopped before a pair of red sliding doors, all of them were giggling.

The doors opened and Keiko was summarily shoved into a gorgeous breakfast room painted with spreading mulberry trees. Morning sunlight spilled through the wall-to-wall open doors showing a magnificent formal garden. The rain had been replaced by blue skies and fluffy clouds. The air smelled very fresh and was just a touch chilly.

Keiko was suddenly very glad for all the layers of silk.

Directly before the wide-open garden doors was a low black table where Toku's father, mother, and Toku himself, all in formal dress, knelt on pillows.

Keiko stared, stunned, then hurriedly bowed, her hands on her knees. "Please forgive my lateness."

A handsome older woman seated facing the garden, turned around to smile. "Good morning and welcome!" She held out her hand and indicated the pillow to her left and directly across the table from Toku sitting by his father.

Keiko struggled to cross the room in her over-long and binding clothes, but somehow managed to get to the table and down on her knees without falling over on her face.

And then the staff began to carry food into the room. They set down steaming heaped platters, bowls of rice, and small plates of delicacies in the center of the table for everyone to take from.

Toku stared at her, eyes wide.

Keiko blinked at him. *What in heaven's name...?*

A touch of chrysanthemum perfume wafted and Ryudo shimmered into existence kneeling at Keiko's left elbow. He was dressed in his flowing white robes again and his hair fell black as spilled ink down his back and over his sleeves. He leaned close, his lips nearly brushing her ear. "Remember, no one can see me but you and Toku."

Keiko kept her head facing forward and glanced only slightly at Ryudo. She whispered very softly. "What are you doing here?"

Ryudo smiled. "You look lovely in traditional attire."

It was a sweet compliment. Keiko dropped her chin, smiled and whispered. "Thank you."

Ryudo lifted his chin toward Toku. "You've impressed Toku."

Keiko looked toward Toku.

Toku smiled and nodded very slightly.

Keiko felt heat rush into her cheeks, and looked down at her lap, and folded hands.

Ryudo faded away, then reappeared sitting casually on the edge of the porch behind Toku and his father, yet positioned between them where he could watch Keiko from under the waving branches of a blooming peach tree.

And then breakfast began.

Somehow Keiko managed to keep her sleeves from getting in the food and didn't dribble her tea, but it was a battle. As long as she kept her movements slow, and her other hand at the ready to grab for draping material, she was able to collect food from the selected plates, get it into her bowl, and actually eat it. This was a very good thing, as she was starved.

Toku carefully fielded most of the politely nosy questions that came up from his family. They were fellow students at the university, which was true, though they didn't share classes. They met in the park the day his other fiancé decided on other pursuits, which was also true, to some degree. Keiko mentioned her interest in feudal history. This was met with more approval than she expected, but then this was a historic house.

Toku carefully kept conversation away from Keiko's lack of immediate connection to her apparently historic family.

All in all, it was a very pleasant, if rather alarming, meal.

The plates were cleared away by the staff, and replaced by a pot of tea, a pot of chocolate and another of coffee.

Keiko stuck to sipping tea. Coffee and chocolate were notoriously difficult to get out of silk and her battle with her sleeves was not conquered yet.

Toku's mother abruptly leaned over to peer at Keiko's hands. She frowned and turned to look at Toku with an uplifted brow.

Keiko looked at Toku in confusion. Had she done something wrong?

Toku frowned. "Mother?"

His mother sighed and set her hands on the table. "She's not wearing the ring."

Keiko winced. The engagement ring. *Oops…*

Toku flushed, then lifted his chin. "I didn't want to give Keiko a ring worn by another woman."

Behind Toku, Ryudo stood up and rolled his eyes. He faded out of sight.

His mother nodded. "Oh, I see." She smiled. "How romantic!"

Toku's father lifted a hand, not quite hiding his indulgent smile.

Toku merely nodded sternly and picked up his cup of tea. He sipped.

"And when exactly is the wedding day?" Toku's mother leaned forward.

Toku nearly spit out his tea. He swallowed hard and choked, just a little. He slammed a fist into his chest. "The wedding day?"

Keiko had to cover her mouth to keep from laughing out loud. Kind of hard to decide on a wedding day when Toku's father was the one who decided they were engaged to begin with.

Ryudo suddenly appeared at Toku's elbow. He leaned close to Toku and whispered something.

Toku frowned, and looked down at his lap. "Oh, well, the wedding day. I, uh, figured that we would wait until the…" He glanced at Ryudo. "The betrothal dinner with Keiko's family, and let you and her mother decide."

Toku's mother and father stared at him.

Toku looked from one to the other. His brows dropped. "What?"

"You are going traditional for your wedding?" Toku's mother clapped her hands together. "How wonderful!"

Toku's father rolled his eyes. "How expensive!" He turned to look at Toku. "You could elope?"

"Don't you dare!" Toku's mother shook her finger.

Toku's father leaned over the table and jammed a thumb in Toku's direction. "Wife, between her illustrious family, our extended families, and then my business associates, do you have any idea how big this wedding could be?"

"But, Husband…?" Her bottom lip trembled.

"But, Wife…!"

Toku cleared his throat. "I wanted to ask permission…"

Both his parents stopped in mid-breath and turned to look at him, eyes wide. Toku's father frowned. "Son, are you feeling all right?"

Toku's brows lifted, and he blinked at them. "What?"

Toku's mother patted the table and smiled. "It's just so refreshing to hear you ask for permission for anything!"

"All right, okay, I get it already." Toku rolled his eyes and shook his head. He turned to his father and held out his palm. "I wanted permission to give this to Keiko."

Keiko frowned. Give her what?

Toku's father looked down at Toku's palm and frowned. "Where did you find that?"

Toku's jaw tightened. "You told me you did not want certain answers coming out of my mouth."

Toku's father looked up at Toku and stared for about two whole seconds. "I see. You have my permission." He sat back. "Actually I am quite pleased to witness your presentation." He nodded and picked up his cup of coffee.

Toku's mother frowned. "Presentation of what?"

Toku leaned back. "You mean, right now?"

"Is there a reason such a beautiful morning will not do?" Toku's father smiled at him.

Toku's mother stared from one to the other of her men. "Do for what?"

Keiko looked over at Ryudo, still kneeling at Toku's side. He was grinning broadly. What was he up to now?"

~Twenty-Seven~

Toku sighed and pushed up from the table. He walked around the table and shot a glare at Ryudo in passing. He came to Keiko's side and dropped to one knee. He looked over at his father and offered his palm to Keiko.

Keiko looked at him in confusion. *What?*

Toku huffed a hair from his brow and whispered softly. "Keiko, give me your left hand."

"Okay…" She gave him her hand.

Toku held up a thick gold ring heavily enameled in red and orange flowers. It was clearly very old. "Keiko, will you be my wife?"

Keiko froze, and every thought in her head evaporated.

Toku frowned. "Keiko?"

Ryudo appeared at Toku's elbow. "The answer is, 'I will'."

Keiko sucked in a sharp breath. She leaned close and whispered. "I can't accept this!"

Toku whispered right back, his gaze intent. "Yes, you can."

Ryudo set his hand on her arm. "Just say 'I will', Keiko. It's not that difficult."

Toku glanced at Ryudo and spat out a sound of disgust. "Really, Keiko, I won't make that bad a husband."

Keiko felt a smile creep up on her. "I know. I'm sure you'll make a wonderful husband."

Toku froze then smiled. "Good!" He raised his brows and gestured with the ring. He cleared his throat. "Then will you be my wife?"

Keiko sighed. "Okay." She glanced at Toku's staring and stunned parents. "Uh, I mean, I will."

Toku slid the ring on the third finger of her left hand, and stared up into her eyes. He clasped both her cold hands in his warm palms and leaned forward, his lids drifting downward, clearly about to kiss her.

Keiko leaned in to meet him and their lips touched. It was a perfect moment. There would probably never be a more perfect moment in her life. Her eyes burned, and she closed them, but the tears slipped out anyway.

She knew she couldn't actually marry him. He was the very modern heir to a business fortune, and she was a scarred-up, bad-tempered, poor university student. He deserved a wife that was well-connected, sweet-natured and beautiful. But for this one moment, everything was absolutely perfect. She would keep the beautiful memory in her heart, and treasure it forever.

Behind Keiko, the sliding doors to the breakfast room clacked closed. She jumped and turned sharply around to stare at the closed doors. She was standing in the hall? She couldn't remember how she'd gotten there.

She could not remember a single thing beyond Toku's kiss. Everything after it seemed to be a total blank. She was pretty sure that Toku's parents had chatted happily around her, but for the life of her, she couldn't remember what anyone had said.

Toku's perfect kiss…

Keiko raised a hand to her lips, and spotted the enameled gold band on her finger. Her engagement ring. Yellow, red and orange chrysanthemums encircled it, bound by a bright green ribbon. His family crest was detailed and upraised like a document seal. This was an antique wife's seal.

From around the corner the flock of brightly-colored women from earlier, suddenly appeared. They collected Keiko and hustled her down the hall, tip-toeing at top speed, chirping away at how lucky Keiko was to be marrying the son of the house.

Keiko winced. They had no idea it wasn't possible.

Back in the peach suite, Keiko was stripped down to the skin, given proper underwear and then redressed, again at top speed. A short white kimono of heavy cotton, with sleeves far less difficult to manage, was folded over her chest and tucked into bright red hakima pants, also of heavy cotton and fuller than any skirt she'd ever worn. Immeasurably more comfortable than the previous outfit, the clothes were masculine in style, but perfectly fitting with the house's antique air.

A folded fan was tucked into the belts knotted high on her waist, and the women stepped back, their arms full of the silks she'd just worn. They bowed.

Keiko bowed. "Thank you so very much."

The women bobbed another bow, and exploded into giggles. Keiko was showered with congratulations and praise on just how wonderful it was to be married to such a handsome and rich young man. She must be very special indeed.

Keiko's cheeks heated. Oh, she was special, all right; she had the scars to prove it.

The women abruptly flocked to the door and left in a swirl of giggling colored silk.

Alone in the empty and silent room, Keiko stared at the closed door. What a strange morning. A cool spring breeze washed across her back.

"I thought they'd never leave." Ryudo's sarcastic voice came from right behind her.

Keiko jumped and turned.

Ryudo leaned against the open door to the garden with his bare and muscular arms folded across his broad chest. He was in the thoroughly modern black muscle shirt, black leather pants, and heavy boots she'd seen him wearing in the alley. His hair was pulled back into a long tail.

Keiko's brow lifted. "Practicing your 'tall, dark, and intimidating' look?"

He dropped his arms and walked toward her. A smile curved his sensual mouth and his black gaze held leaping blue flames. "Perhaps."

Keiko automatically took a half-step back, then stopped. "What?"

Ryudo shook his head and lifted his hand, jerking his thumb over his shoulder. "Time to collect your belongings before anyone knows we have you."

Keiko's jaw tightened. "You don't have me."

Ryudo reached out and caught her left hand. He rolled the ring on her finger between his finger and thumb, and smiled. "Don't we?" He released her hand and strode toward the open door to the garden. "Toku is waiting for us in his rooms, on the other side of the garden." He hopped off the edge of the porch.

At the stairs leading down into the garden, Keiko stopped and stared at the damp grassy lawn, and the scattered rain puddles. "I can't walk across the garden, I don't have any shoes!" She wiggled her stocking toes in her indoor silk sandals.

Ryudo's brow lifted and his smile broadened. He turned back and walked to the edge of the porch. "I'll carry you." He reached down and scooped her up into his arms.

Keiko gasped. "Ryudo…!" His mouth took hers in a ferocious kiss, silencing her protests, and every thought in her head. He released her lips and she couldn't think of what she was going to say.

He nodded. "Much better." With a grin, he carried her into the garden. His long strides rushed her past flowering trees, then he hopped onto the porch on the other side. "There." He set Keiko back on her feet.

Keiko straightened her full pants back out and smiled sourly. "Thank you."

Toku stepped out onto the porch in black jeans and a black muscle shirt identical to Ryudo's. "Let's get this done quickly." He walked into his room and picked up her loafers from the floor by the door. "You might need these." He held them out to Keiko.

Keiko took her shoes. Too late to back out now. "Thanks."

"Come on." Toku grabbed his car keys from the dresser, a set of dark glasses, and led the way out into the hallways, then into the narrow servants' access halls. In a matter of minutes, they emerged in the huge and somewhat cool garage.

Keiko jammed her shoes on and hurried after them, past several luxury cars to where Toku's silver Subaru was parked.

Toku raised his keys and the car chirped, unlocking the doors. Keiko was set in the back while Ryudo took front passenger seat, and Toku took the driver's seat. They drove out into bright morning sunlight with heavy metal throbbing on the sound system.

Traffic was very light on the streets, but a little heavy on the speedway with families going out to the country for visits and picnics. In far less time than Keiko expected, they were on her street, and then easing into the alley behind her apartment building moving cautiously past parked cars.

She frowned. Well, at least one mystery had been solved; how Toku had had time to leave the park, shower, and then come back with Ryudo to catch her in the alley.

Toku parked the car against the side of the building, between a rusty Honda and a slightly dented Toyota. He opened his door and got out, with Ryudo only a beat behind him.

Keiko stepped out of the car on the street side, and something suddenly occurred to her. "I need my house keys! They're in my school book-bag."

"Got it covered." Toku opened the trunk of his car. "Your book-bag is right here." He pulled it out and smiled.

"Oh, good." Keiko took her bag, and fished her keys from it.

Toku closed the trunk. "Ready?"

Keiko took a breath and nodded. In complete silence, both men followed her to the front of the building and up the multiple staircases to her apartment. She unlocked the door and froze. She couldn't remember if she'd left the house a wreck or not. She sighed and stepped back to let them in. *Too late now.*

She pulled off her loafers at the door, stepped up into the hall, turned left into the hall then took an immediately right, walking into the living room. The house wasn't too bad. A peek into the kitchen showed that she'd remembered to wash her dishes, but her study books were still scattered all over the low black lacquered table, along with a mound of papers covered in notations. The sitting pillows were every which way. She sighed. It was a good thing she didn't own a whole lot; she was a bad housekeeper.

She dropped her book-bag on the table and her cell phone slid out of it. She picked up the phone. She needed to call her mom to tell her where she was going to be staying, and ask her to toss the food in the fridge. The battery was dead. She walked over to the far left wall and jammed it into the charger plugged in by her tiny stereo and TV.

The guys wandered into the living room and looked about, examining her movie posters—her samurai movie posters. There were eight of them, all framed, with photos of weapons and armor scattered between them. Ryudo peered closely at one movie poster in particular, chuckled and shook his head.

Keiko cringed and turned her back. All of her posters featured samurai, and Ryudo was a real samurai. She did not want to know his opinion on her favorite movies.

"Ah!" Toku walked over to the bucket by the living room windows holding her two rattan staffs in water. They had sprouted leaves. Her third staff was still at school, in her locker with her gym bag. He fingered the wrist-thick stalks. "We will definitely take these with us."

"Living weapons against the dead." Ryudo joined him by the window, but didn't touch the rattan. "Clever."

Keiko smiled. "Toku's idea."

Toku shrugged and looked away. "It just seemed logical, considering that she didn't have magic to work with."

Ryudo set his hand on Toku's shoulder. "It was an excellent idea."

Toku rolled his shoulders and stepped out from under Ryudo's hand. "It was nothing, really."

Keiko rolled her eyes. Toku was being shy. "It might have been nothing for you, but it was a big deal for me."

Toku turned away, shoved his hands into his pockets and shrugged. "I'm glad I could help."

Keiko shook her head. "I'm going to go get my stuff." She stepped out of the living room, took a left and opened her hall closet where she kept her two suitcases. She lugged them the half a dozen steps and to the left, into her bedroom. A quick look showed that she'd remembered to put her freshly washed clothes away, but her bed was still unfolded, with the blankets rumpled. There was no time to make it now.

She opened the two cases on the floor by her closet, slid open her closet door and started heaving folded clothes into them. She left her university uniforms hanging in the closet. The guys weren't going to let her go back to school, not while Tika was there. She hoped Toku was serious about a tutor, or she was going to be in real trouble with her grades.

The clothes in her dresser by the window were next. She had every stitch of clothing she owned packed fairly quickly, and there was still room for a few of her favorite books. She frowned at the two suitcases. Did she really own so very little?

At the last second, she grabbed the framed picture of her mom from off the top of the dresser. Her fingers tightened on the silver frame. Why hadn't her mom told her that she was from a family of priestesses? If her mom had been raised in such a family, then she must have known that Keiko would have problems with ghosts. But, she'd never said anything, not in all those times she'd been in the hospital. Why? What was her mom hiding? She tossed the picture in her last open case and closed the lid.

Keiko left her cases on the bedroom floor, and went into the bathroom. She shoved the tub lid to one side. The water was still a little warm. She pulled the plug so the tub could drain. She looked through her bath supplies, but didn't see anything beyond her toothbrush that she might need.

Toothbrush in hand, she went back into the living room.

Ryudo was poking at the books scattered across the living room table, and Toku knelt by her tiny stereo, leafing through her CD collection. She snorted. "You guys are a lot of help."

Toku rose to his feet with a grin. "As if you'd let us decide what you're going to bring?"

Keiko shook her head. "Okay, you have a point." She smile and jabbed a finger his way, and then Ryudo. "But you can cart it down all those stairs for me."

Toku rolled his eyes. "Yes, dear."

She felt a silly grin creep onto her lips. *Yes, dear...* It was something one said to one's wife. But she wasn't going to marry him. She couldn't do that to him. He deserved someone better... *Better than me.* Pain stabbed her through the heart. She turned away and walked over to the table to deal with her books.

Ryudo lifted his chin. "Where are your trunks?"

Keiko blinked. *Trunks?* Oh, her suitcases. Well, a century ago, they would have been trunks. "In the bedroom." She shoved her toothbrush, books, and papers, into her book-bag. They barely fit. She walked over to her stereo and collected her CD case. Her player and headphones were in her bag already. Music would come in handy while studying. Finally, she turned and picked up her phone and unplugged the charger. She stared at the blinking light on her tiny phone.

Toku looked over her shoulder and frowned. "Messages?"

Keiko nodded and flicked the phone open. There was a message with Shihan's number, one from Shido, and one from Tika. Her hands went cold. "There's a message from Tika."

"The demon?" Toku's jaw tightened. "You better check it."

Keiko punched in the message code.

"You have three new messages... Message one, Friday, eleven twenty-three p.m..."

Keiko looked up at Toku. "She left the message last night after eleven."

Toku nodded. "That would have been about the time we purged the larva."

Keiko punched the skip button to get to the message.

"Hi, Keiko, this is your best friend." The voice sounded a little high-pitched and strained, but it was definitely Tika's. The familiar tones punched Keiko straight in the heart. "You naughty girl, throwing away my present like that." She giggled, and it sounded awful. "Anyway, I just wanted you to know, I know where you are. See you! Kiss-kiss, bye-bye!"

I know where you are. See you. Keiko slammed the phone shut with shaking hands. *Kiss-kiss, bye-bye!*

Toku grabbed her hands. "Keiko?"

Ryudo stalked into the living room, with both her suitcases. "What happened?" He set the suitcases down.

Toku looked up at Ryudo. "The demon left a message on Keiko's phone."

Ryudo frowned ferociously. "And?"

Keiko tugged her hands from Toku's and walked back over to the table. "She said, 'I know where you are, see you'." She viciously shoved the charger and her phone in her shoulder bag with her books. Her hands tightened into fists. *Damn it, Tika!*

"I'll get that." Toku took the bag from her, and set the strap over his shoulder.

Ryudo crossed his arms. "Keiko, you already knew that your demon would come. What has upset you?"

"I know, I know! It's just that..." Keiko closed her burning eyes and wished her chest didn't hurt so much. She had to take a breath to speak past the ache. "It's just that it sounded just like her." She looked over at Ryudo. "It sounded like Tika, not like a demon."

Ryudo sighed and dropped his gaze. "Keiko, demons steal the memories of the person they inhabit. It was not your friend. It is simply not possible.

Toku set his hand on Keiko's shoulder. "I'm sorry, but he's right.

No human could survive this long."

"I guess." Keiko crossed her arms over her chest and turned her face away. But somehow, she knew he was wrong. She just knew it. Tika was still in there. She had to be.

Ryudo picked up her suitcases. "We are done here." He turned and carried them out to the front door.

With her over-stuffed book-bag over his shoulder, Toku walked over to the bucket, plucked both green staffs from it and strode after Ryudo.

Keiko had no choice but to follow. They were done; it was time to go. She walked out to the area before the door, shoved her loafers on, and followed them out the door. She turned and locked her apartment. At the bottom of the staircase, she followed them around the corner and into the alley, trying very hard not to imagine that she'd just shut a door on a chapter of her life.

Toku chirped his car unlocked, then opened the trunk. Ryudo tossed in her suitcases and Toku shoved her book-bag in on top, then closed the trunk.

Keiko shoved her staffs across the back seat floor and climbed in.

Ryudo and Toku climbed into the front seats, and Toku started the car. "Seatbelts, people."

Ryudo fastened his with a grin.

Toku glanced in his mirrors, then pulled forward, heading up the alley.

Keiko fastened her seatbelt and looked behind her, up the alley toward the front of her apartment building. Mercy only knew when she'd see it again.

At the far end of the alley, a bright yellow and blue Kawasaki motorcycle pulled into the alley and stopped. The driver wore a black full-face helmet and distinctive red and black leathers.

Keiko started. *Shido?* Toku turned to the right, and her view of the motorcycle was gone. Keiko sat forward and frowned. What was Shido doing out here?

Toku lifted his chin and grinned into the rearview mirror.

"Anyone up for cheeseburgers?"

Ryudo lifted his hand and grinned. "Yes!"

Keiko stared. "You eat food?"

Ryudo snorted and folded his arms. "When I am embodied, all physical functions work."

Keiko frowned, trying to imagine Ryudo eating a burger and fries. "Really?"

"Oh, yes, really." Toku laughed. "You should have seen him trying to manage a toilet."

Ryudo batted a hand at Toku's head. "Rude boy!"

Toku flinched. "Hey, I'm driving here!"

Keiko suddenly had an image of Ryudo on the toilet reading a newspaper and giggled. "That is just scary."

Ryudo turned all the way around to scowl at her.

Book Four

~ Cypress Needles & Mist ~

~ Twenty-Eight ~

Toku pulled out of the bright red and yellow fast-food restaurant drive-in, and a debate over who ordered what ensued.

Keiko was eventually handed the bag with her small cheeseburger, small fries and her child-sized soda. She peeled the yellow waxed paper off and sank her teeth into meaty-cheesy, pickle and catsup heaven. She chewed and moaned, then grabbed for a napkin. Damned white kimono sleeves…

Burger in one hand and steering wheel in the other, Toku frowned at his side mirrors. "I think we're being followed."

Ryudo took a huge bite out of his burger and nodded. "Um-hmmm."

Toku frowned at Ryudo. "You know?"

Ryudo sucked on his straw, taking a gulp of soda. "The young man on the motorcycle? Of course. His presence has been with us since leaving Keiko's apartment."

Keiko looked sharply around. Sure enough, Shido's Kawasaki was about three car-lengths behind them. "It's Shido, from my karate class."

Ryudo lifted a brow. "A student of your Shihan?" He smiled. "Ah, then clearly a spy for the Avatars."

"The Avatars?" Toku curled his lip and shoved his burger back into the white paper bag. "I should be able to lose him…"

"Let him follow." Ryudo fished Toku's burger back out of the bag and held it out to him. "He does not have the power to take the car, and no one can take the house. The demon—and the sorcerer that owns it—are our true concerns."

Toku took the burger from Ryudo and frowned. "You can tell from here that he can't take the car?"

Ryudo snorted. "I am a guardian spirit. Even encased in flesh, my radius of influence is considerably larger than this tiny vehicle. I assure you, he does not have the power." He bit into his burger and chewed, then smacked his lips and sighed. "I love this century."

Keiko leaned forward. "Take the car?"

Toku lifted his chin. "With magic."

Keiko sat back. "Oh." She bit into her burger and turned around to watch the yellow and blue Kawasaki.

Silence filled the car, punctuated by rustling burger wraps, sipped sodas and heavy metal. The car turned onto the highway, and the motorcycle followed.

Toku frowned at Ryudo.

Ryudo stared out the window at the passing scenery, and sucked loudly on his straw.

Toku peered into his side-view mirror. "Ryudo, are you sure we should…?"

Ryudo crushed the empty cup in his hand. "Yes. This way they do not know we are aware of their scrutiny."

The silver Subaru turned into the gate and continued up the drive leading to the expansive and sweeping mansion. The Kawasaki and its lone passenger passed by without stopping.

A hard shiver wracked through Keiko.

Ryudo looked back at her. "We have just passed the barrier."

Keiko shook out her hands. "Gee, thanks for the warning."

Toku drove into the garage and parked by the door into the house. He popped the trunk from the dashboard, pulled his keys from the ignition and sighed. "Well, that's done." He and got out with Ryudo only a beat behind him. They both went to the back end of the car.

Keiko climbed out of the car and pulled her rattan staves after her.

Toku pulled the two suitcases and the book-bag from the trunk. He slid the strap to the book-bag over his shoulder and closed the trunk. Ryudo picked up both cases. Both men started walking toward the house door.

Keiko stared at her suitcases in Ryudo's hands and trotted after them. "Ryudo, if you're solid enough to eat, then other people can see you, right?"

Ryudo lifted a shoulder. "If I care to be seen."

Toku opened the door leading into the house. "Hey, I didn't even think of that!" He tugged off his boots. "You can finally prove to Father that I was telling the truth...!"

Ryudo shook his head. "No." His boots abruptly disappeared, and were replaced by slippers. He went up the stairs and stepped into the hallway.

"No?" Toku followed on his heels. "What do you mean, no?"

Keiko stopped on the stairs to pull off her shoes, then shoved her feet back into the silk slipper sandals she'd worn earlier. Shoes in one hand and her green staves in the other, she hurried up into the house.

Ryudo stood in the hall, shaking his head.

Toku scowled at Ryudo. "Why the hell not?"

"Because I said so." Ryudo started up the hall.

"What?" Toku dogged his heels. "What kind of crap is that?"

Ryudo refused to even look his way.

"Damn it, Ryudo..."

Ryudo dropped the cases and rushed at Toku, slamming his hands against the wall to either side of Toku's body, pinning him. "Stop!" He glared at Toku, eye to eye, from barely a kiss away. "I will not reveal myself to your father. Accept it and be done with it."

Toku's jaw clenched. "Tell me why and I'll drop it."

"I have my reasons, Kentoku." Ryudo took a deep breath, turned his face away and stepped back. "That's all I can say." He picked up the cases.

Keiko frowned. *More secrets.* Every time something made sense, another secret surfaced. She shook her head and followed them down the plain narrow hall. How many more secrets could there be?

Several winding and narrow hallways later, they stepped into the main hall near Keiko's suite.

Toku opened the door to Keiko's suite and stiffened. "Oh, hi, Mother." He looked back and shot Ryudo a glare.

Ryudo grinned, and set the cases down against the wall.

Toku's mother? Keiko backed away.

Ryudo dropped his hand on her shoulder and shoved, pushing Keiko past Toku and through the door.

Keiko stepped into the room, and her mouth fell open. The polished wood floor had a brilliant nearly wall to wall carpet in scarlet, gold, and flame. Tall, cast iron Victorian standing lamps with embroidered tasseled shades of rich cream occupied all four corners of the room. A large and thoroughly modern desk, complete with built-in bookcase, occupied the left wall. The folding screen, normally sitting before the sliding glass windows, had been partially folded back to the right corner to make room for a tall black lacquered table with two matching high-backed chairs. Three closets on the right wall were open. A huge rolled futon and folded bedding occupied the center closet; the other two were empty.

Keiko spotted Toku's mom, dressed far less formally in a midnight blue, ankle-length kimono, in the far right corner and bowed hastily.

Toku's mom walked over and smiled. "There you are, dear. Since you'll be with us for a while, I thought you might need some furniture."

Keiko stepped further into the room. "Thank you, but this wasn't necessary." She wasn't going to be there that long.

"Don't be silly." Toku's mom waved her hand then turned to look over the room. "You're going to need the desk at the very least, especially for your exam studies."

Keiko's blood ran cold. *Her exams? But that was months away!* She took a deep breath and worked to calm her pounding heart.

There was no way in hell she was staying that long.

Toku stepped up beside Keiko, smiling tightly. "Father works fast."

Toku's mom nodded. "Being alumni, he is allowed the occasional favor."

Keiko glanced at Toku. His *father* had arranged for the tutor?

Toku's mom turned back to Keiko. "The tutor will be by Tuesday afternoon with your lesson schedule."

Keiko bowed. "Thank you, ma'am."

Toku's mom reached out and patted her hand. "Such an agreeable daughter." She smiled. "Now then, is there anything else you'd like for your suite?"

Daughter? Keiko jerked a smile up on her face. *Merciful heavens, she really expects Toku and I to marry?* "This is wonderful, really, thank you."

Toku's mom positively beamed. "Well then, I will leave you to do your unpacking." She walked toward the door. "Toku, if you would accompany me?" She proceeded out into the hall.

Toku rolled his eyes. "Yes, Mother." He took off the book-bag and handed it to Keiko. "Be good!"

Keiko blinked at him. "Who, me?"

Toku rushed out the door after his mom.

Ryudo appeared leaning against the wall just inside the door. "Yes, you." He stepped away from the wall to tower over her.

Keiko's heart thumped hard, for no apparent reason she could think of.

He smiled, leaned down and pressed a soft kiss to her lips. Power surged against her heart. His clothes became flowing white robes that floated around her on a breeze she could almost feel. He released her mouth and his smile was gone. "Welcome home." He faded into mist.

Keiko stood perfectly still for two whole breaths. Welcome *home?* She scowled up at the ceiling. "Hey! I don't live here yet!" Shock washed through her. *Yet?* She clapped both hands over her mouth in alarm. She hadn't meant to say that.

Soft laughter and the scent of chrysanthemums drifted through the room.

Keiko unpacked and had her clothes put away in the closets fairly quickly. There really wasn't a whole lot. She picked up her toothbrush and carried it into the bathroom on the far side of the bookshelf beside her desk. There was a small, enclosed closet for a very modern commode just inside the door and to the left. She walked past it and into the bathing facility. It wasn't nearly as large as Toku's, but there was a garden window and the round tub was modern enough to have a heater installed to keep the water hot once it was filled.

Under the sink, she found a plastic bucket. After a thorough rinse, she filled it with water and carried it out into the bedroom to post it next to her desk in full view of the window. Both her staffs fit nicely. She leaned the green rattan against her desk and spent several long minutes in front of the open door plucking green shoots from the stalks.

She set her mother's picture on the desk then dumped her bookbag out on the table. Her homework assignments were all mixed up together. Sorting through the pile of books and papers, she found her cell phone. There were two unchecked messages still on it.

Keiko punched in the message code and jammed the phone next to her ear, striding to the edge of autumn bright carpet to the other, then back.

"You have two new messages... Message one, Saturday, eight forty-seven a.m..." It gave Shihan's phone number.

Keiko stopped pacing to punch the button to skip to the message, then started pacing again.

"You were not in class Friday." Shihan sighed heavily. "I...understand. Please forgive me."

Keiko winced. She had planned to go to class, but then Tika...

She sighed and bowed her head. Perhaps it was probably better this way? It wasn't as if Toku or Ryudo would let her attend karate class with someone associated with the Avatars. She looked up at the ceiling. Still, she ought to call him and tell him… What?

She shook her head and punched for the next message.

"Message two, Saturday, two thirty-three p.m…" It gave Shido's phone number.

Punch. Skip. Pace…

"Hey, Keiko, do you know where Tika is? I can't reach her, and she hasn't been home. Call me."

Keiko pulled the phone from her ear and stared at it in shock. Shido didn't know about Tika? Hadn't the Avatars told him? She closed her phone. She wouldn't return his call. She absolutely, positively, did not want to be the one to tell him that his girlfriend had been consumed by a demon. A fist closed tight around her heart. She'd done enough to him already.

Keiko walked back over to the table and plugged her head phones into her small circular CD player. *I can't help Shido.* She unzipped her small nylon CD case and searched for the loudest, angriest music she had. *I can't help Tika.* She slid the rainbow-hued disk from the plastic sheath and jammed it into the player. *I can't help Shihan.* She closed the player with a snap.

She looked up and stared out the window toward Toku's suite, where she'd spent the night intimately entwined with a mage and a ghost. *I can't even help myself.* She pressed 'play', then 'repeat all'. Angry German rock music howled into her ears. *I don't want to think about any of this any more.* She began sorting through her papers and books.

Keiko pushed the last book into alignment on the desk's top shelf and flopped down into her desk chair. She finally had all her homework assignments tagged, sorted and back in the right order. She squinted at the notes on her ledger pad. She could barely read her own handwriting. The light had gone too dim. How late was it? She turned in the chair to look out the window.

The sky had gone dark with fast moving storm clouds and a stiff wind whipped the branches of the carefully groomed trees. Shredded blossoms tumbled across the manicured lawn and white pebble walk.

The light was on in Toku's suite.

Keiko got up and turned on the tall standing lamp closest to her desk. The light bloomed in the room, flickered, then went out. She frowned. A bad bulb?

A broad streak of lightning filled the sky, then thunder slammed so hard it drowned out the music blaring in her ears. The floor vibrated under her feet.

What in the heavens...? Keiko tore off her headphones and tossed them on the desk. Thunder rumbled and the back of her head crawled with awareness. She snorted. Somewhere in the house, Ryudo was in a seriously pissy mood.

"Miss Keiko?"

Keiko yelped and whirled toward the door.

A small woman in very plain gray maid's livery and holding a blue plastic flashlight, bowed in her open door. "Please excuse me, Miss, but you have a visitor."

Keiko set her hand over her pounding heart. "Me? I have a visitor?" But no one knew she was there. She hadn't even called her mother yet.

The woman bobbed. "Yes, Miss, at the front door. She says she's a fellow university student, a Miss Tika."

The demon that was killing her best friend had arrived.

Cold determination washed through Keiko. "I see. Thank you." She walked around the far side of the desk and plucked one of the green staffs from the water-filled bucket. She strode toward the door. "I'm ready, take me to her."

~ *Twenty-Nine* ~

Keiko followed the maid through the candle-lit and starkly shadowed hallways. The power in the entire house was out. Thunder shook the rattan sliding walls and lightning glared beyond rice paper screens. The angry weather suited Keiko's mood just fine. Ryudo wasn't the only one in a foul temper.

The front double doors were huge, heavy oak affairs, painted a bright green, with enormous brass locks—standing wide open. Wind and driving rain from outside whipped into the broad foyer. No one was there.

Keiko frowned. "I thought you said…?"

"I did." A sweet, soft giggle broke out.

"What?" Keiko turned, her staff up in the downward spear position.

"Man, this is so much fun!" The maid straightened and smiled in a fashion completely unsuited to her face. "This maid was so easy! She took me straight to your room!" Her body melted into shadows. "And did she ever scream when I showed her my favorite scary face! She even dropped her flashlight." The shadow reformed into a smiling and perfectly groomed Tika, still in her school uniform. "Nice house, Keiko. What did you do, marry the heir?" Her lip curled and her smile soured. "Or just screw him?"

White fury burned up the back of Keiko's skull and she clenched her teeth. Demon or not, this was definitely Tika being her spiteful self. She took one step toward her best friend. "You…" She lashed out with her palm, right across Tika's right cheek. The smack was loud and sharp. "Stupid idiot!"

Tika yelped and fell back onto her butt. Knees splayed and eyes wide in clear astonishment, she set her hand against her cheek.

"You moron!" Keiko balled her stinging hand into a fist. "Since when is killing yourself *fun?*"

"You..." Tika pooled into black shadow with blue-fire eyes, then reformed in back into herself in a standing position. "don't understand anything!"

Keiko was so pissed she had to yell through her clenched teeth. "You're right, I don't understand!" She pointed at Tika. "Why did you let yourself be possessed? How stupid can you be?"

Tika turned her head, glaring at Keiko from the corner of her eye. "I just wanted..."

"What?" Keiko raised her fist. "You just wanted what? To be special? To be different? To not belong anywhere? To never be able to...?" Her temper became a throbbing ache in her head and in her heart. She dropped her hand and turned away. "To never have a normal life."

"Normal, huh?" Tika crossed her arms. "What's so fun about being just like everybody else?"

"You idiot." Keiko sat her hand on her hip and scowled at Tika. "Normal people can have a job, a family or anything else they want! Normal people can go anywhere, or do anything!" Tears were streaking down her cheeks but she just didn't give a damn. "Normal people can be with other people without being called...crazy." She turned her face away. *Normal people didn't get scarred up by things that couldn't harm anyone else.*

"Oh, whoop-dee-do." Tika rolled her eyes. "Why would anyone want to be around normal people? They're boring!"

Keiko pointed a finger at her friend. "You spoiled little brat! You had everything, looks, money, a future... Everything I ever wanted!" She tossed out a hand. "And you go and do...this?" She stomped her foot. "What is *wrong* with you?"

Tika's hands fisted at her side. "I had everything?" She raised her fist and opened her hand, splaying her fingers. "I had nothing a million other girls didn't have!" She lifted her chin and pointed at Keiko. "You had what nobody had! You had magic powers!" She scowled. "Well, now I have them, too!" She set her hands on her hips. "And they're better than yours!"

Burning with fury, Keiko bared her teeth. "You stupid, spoiled, little bitch."

Tika's eyes blazed blue-white and her voice dropped to a low growl. "What did you call me?"

Keiko leaned in. "I called you a stupid, spoiled bitch." She straightened and thumped the heel of her green staff on the foyer floor. "And you know what? I think you deserve exactly what you've gotten, too."

Tika curled her lip, showing black fangs. "What the hell is that supposed to mean?"

Keiko took a step to the right, leaving Tika on the left side of the wide foyer. "It means…" She lashed out with staff, swinging it with both hands around the end, like housewife swatting at hanging spider with a broom. "Get out of my house!"

The staff caught Tika across the back and propelled her out the door—and into the downpour just beyond it. She flew, hands first, down the steps, flipped gracefully once and then landed on her feet in a backwards-skidding crouch, with one hand clawing the ground. Her heels and hand dug furrows into the drive.

"It means…" Keiko tromped to the doorway and pointed her staff at her. "You're not my friend anymore!"

Tika straightened slowly. "Fine!" Bright blue foxfire boiled up around her body in curling waves, drying and straightening her clothes for her. "Be that way." Rain sizzled against the waves, but did not touch her. She tugged at her school blazer and smiled. "I have a new best friend who loves me, just the way I am."

Keiko set her hands on her hips and lifted her chin. "Yeah, right! Who'd want to be best friends with anybody as selfish as you?"

Tika threw out her arms. "Why, my one true love, of course!" Blackness exploded around her and lunged upward, forming into the monstrous semi-transparent spider-like tentacle shape Keiko remembered from before.

Keiko knew damned well she should have been scared out of her mind, but she was just too pissed off. She crossed her arms, raised her brow and curled her lip. "Oh, yeah, I can see that he's a hottie." She snorted. "If you're into squids."

"What?" Tika glanced over her shoulder and stomped her foot. "No! Not that one, the other one! Show her the other one!" She crossed her arms. "What? Oh, please." She rolled her eyes. "She's not even a black belt!"

Keiko's brows shot up. "What, is your demon scared of me?"

Tika turned to face Keiko. "He's not scared of a girl with a twig."

"Really?" Keiko smiled and leaned on her staff. "I don't know. He looks pretty spooked to me."

The demon abruptly condensed downward into a very slender young man in a black suit and tie. His long black hair was bound into a tight tail. He gripped the naked blade of a long sword in his right hand and frowned.

"Hmmm…" Keiko tilted her head to the side and sucked on her bottom lip. *Interesting…* The ghost seemed to be outside Tika's body. Could she get them further apart? Could she…separate them? "I think Shido's way cuter than he is."

Tika jabbed a finger at Keiko. "You shut up about Shido!"

Keiko's brows shot up. "What?" Her mouth tightened into a smile. Did she actually care for that vain pain in the ass? She eased back on her heels. "By the way, he's looking for you."

Tika stiffened. "So?"

Keiko shrugged casually and looked away. "Just thought you might like to know." Just how pissed off could she get Tika? Enough to make her run away from her ghost? Keiko watched Tika from the corner of her eye. "He left a message on my phone, you know."

Tika scowled and hunched her shoulders. "How did he get your number?"

Keiko waved her hand in dismissal. "What do you care? You have a new boyfriend. Oh, wait..." She touched her finger to her bottom. "He's a ghost." She lifted her brow. "You can't fuck a ghost, can you?" She put on her smuggest smile. "You can't even kiss him."

Tika's face went cold white, then flushed blood red. Her lips peeled back from her teeth and she took a step toward her. "You shut up!"

"Your one true love? Ha! You can't do a thing with him." Standing on the door's threshold, Keiko propped one hand on her hip, set one foot behind her, and leaned toward her, grinning viciously. "But I can. I can touch him. I can kiss him, and you *can't*."

"Bitch!" Tika screamed and ran toward Keiko. The ghost was right on her heels, sword upraised for a classic heart stab.

Keiko waited and felt time slow down for her. The soft rush of perfect calm came from nowhere, easing her heart and clearing her mind. With all the time in the world, she waited for Tika to mount the stairs and come to her.

It wasn't something she'd planned, just a spur of the moment thing that seemed too good an opportunity to waste.

Casually, Keiko reached out, grabbed the front of Tika's shirt and pulled her right past, throwing her into the house behind her. She swung up the bottom end of her green and living *bo*, catching it in both hands to hold it across her body. She slammed the right end under the blade of the sword coming for her, blocking it, then lashed out with the left end. She nailed the ghost clean across the chest and pushed hard with her feet fully braced, knocking him back off the porch and down the stairs to sprawl on the drive below.

It seemed the most natural thing in the world, to just jump down the entire flight of stairs, after him, her *bo* held in a downward spear's thrust.

Somewhere far away, someone was screaming.

The ghost oozed into black shadow and reformed upright, sword out in another classic sword-thrust position. His mouth was open, black teeth bared, blue eyes blazing.

Keiko's sailing leap took her right past the naked sword blade.

The point of her green and living staff punched straight through the ghost's chest with an almost delicate pop. Her upraised knees slammed into him, knocking him back.

In slow motion, the ghost tumbled backwards, his mouth open, his eyes wide.

Staring into his ghost-blue eyes, Keiko rode his body down to the ground, her knees firmly against his chest. And they fell.

The ghost crashed to the ground, and her *bo* pushed all the way through him and slammed into the pebbled drive below. Her knees slipped off his chest, and suddenly she was straddling his hips.

Time slammed to normal speed.

Ice-cold rain sluiced down onto Keiko, soaking her instantly. She ducked her head to keep the rain from her eyes. Something hot slid down her cheek and dripped onto her arm. Blood. His sword had cut her. Not a wound of the body, but of the spirit. Her soul was bleeding.

Under her, the ghost gasped and gagged, then stiffened. A wash of blue fire slammed up from the black suited ghost and into Keiko. Suddenly there was a young man in pale blue robes sprawled under her. He stared at her in complete shock, then grabbed for the staff, his sleeves falling back from his forearms. His hands clasped the staff. He cried out in obvious pain and released it.

Keiko winced.

He grabbed Keiko's shoulders and howled in her face.

The sound rattled Keiko to the bones, but she wasn't letting go of the staff pinning him. She turned away from the sound, not that it did any good, and saw a highly detailed four-armed and fanged humanoid beast, an *oni* demon, tattooed on his left forearm.

The ghost stopped screaming and closed his eyes, falling still. He turned pale white and began to dissolve into mist at the edges, unraveling into nothing.

Someone screamed, high-pitched and terrified. "No!"

A clinging weight slammed against Keiko's back. She didn't think, she just elbowed the weight hard, throwing it off her.

"Stop!" Tika scrambled around to Keiko's side and grabbed for the staff. "You're killing him!" Her uniform was no longer pristine. It was stained and torn, the sleeves parting from the shoulders at the seams. One sock and both shoes were missing. Her hair was a matted and filthy mess. The rain had no problems soaking her, but there was no disguise for the tears streaking down her cheeks. "Please stop!" Sobbing hysterically, she pulled at Keiko's staff. "He's dying!"

Keiko stared at her in shock, and her heart broke clean in two. "Tika, he's dead. He's been dead all this time."

Tika shook her head. "No! He's not!"

"Yes, love, I am." The fading ghost turned his head to look at her with barely a trace of blue in his gaze. "I am dead, and soon I'll be gone."

Tika gasped and sobs exploded from her. "No, please, you can't...you can't leave me?"

"I need to go." The ghost smiled. "I...want to go."

"No!" Tika wailed, trying to grasp him, her hands passing right through him to the ground below. "You can't go! I can save you! Let me save you!"

The fading ghost slowly shook his head. "I am beyond saving, and if you try, you will die."

Keiko felt her heart twist in her chest. The ghost didn't want Tika to die?

Tika scrabbled in the pebbled drive, trying to touch him. "Then let me die with you!" the tears shook her entire body. "I can't live without you. Please...?"

Keiko's knees pressed down into the pebbles of the drive. The ghost was nearly gone. She could feel a part of her heart going with him. "He's too weak to possess you. It's over."

Tika grabbed onto Keiko's arm. "Then make him stronger! I know you can!"

Keiko shoved her away hard. "What? No!"

"Please!" Tika crawled back. "Just make him strong enough to come into me."

"Tika!" Keiko gasped. "You're insane! You'll die too! Do you want to die?"

"Yes, damn you!" Tika sat back on her butt and held out her filthy hands. "Do you think I want to live—like this?" She pulled at her uniform, showing an emaciated shoulder and gray skin. "Please, let me die with him." She turned to look down at the nearly dissipated ghost. "Wait, where is he? Is he gone? No!"

Keiko sniffed. "No, he's still there."

Tika tugged Keiko's arm. "Please! I want to go where he goes! I want to go with him!"

Keiko shook her head. "Why, Tika? Why do you want to die with him?"

Tika threw her head up and wailed. "I love him! Oh, God, I love him and I don't want to live without him!"

Hardly knowing what she was doing, or why, Keiko pulled her staff from the ghost's chest. She smeared her fingers across her bleeding cheek and let her soul's blood drip down on the misty faded form of the ghost.

The ghost flickered slightly into being. It opened pale blue eyes and sighed.

"Oh!" Tika moaned and fell over him. "I'm here! Right here!" She took a deep breath

The ghost disappeared.

Tika's eyes opened wide. She choked and collapsed onto the drive, rolling onto her side, facing Keiko, her hands curled into fists. She groaned and then a smile flickered. "Oh... Okay." Her lids dropped halfway down, focusing on nothing in particular. She smiled and her dimple appeared in her cheek. "I love you too." Her palm opened in a puddle. A soft sigh left her lips and the blue dimmed from her eyes, to nothing.

Kneeling in the mud by her best friend, and soaked to the bone, Keiko gasped for breath past the pain burning in her shattered heart, her eyes full of boiling hot raindrops.

She barely heard the roar of the motorcycle coming across the lawn, straight for her.

~ Thirty ~

Icy rain hammered down on Keiko's head and slithered into the collar of her kimono top. Kneeling and shivering on the pebbled drive, she could feel cold mud soaking into her pants from splayed shins and thighs to her butt. She could care less.

Sprawled before her was her best friend, who had chosen to join a ghost in death rather than stay among the living.

Keiko could barely breathe past the huge and hollow ache in her chest.

But someone was yelling, and there was this irritatingly loud growling sound intruding on her. Out of sheer irritation, Keiko looked up.

The headlight to a blue and yellow Kawasaki cut through the rain and night, the bike skidding and spraying wet gravel. It was coming straight for her.

Keiko lifted her arm to block the light from her aching eyes. She was too bone-tired and empty to bother moving. If it ran her over, then perhaps all this pain would…stop.

Power exploded around her in a blaze of golden fire. Thunder clapped right over her head, making the ground tremble. Lightning blazed sharp and blue white. A golden figure draped in billowing robes of blinding white appeared practically on top of her. The figure flung out his arms, a naked sword in each hand. "Stop!"

The Kawasaki lunged upward, rearing up on its back tires, screaming. The leather-clad driver was flung from it, landing hard then rolling to a collapsed facedown sprawl on the soaking ground.

The bike crashed onto its side, tires spinning, screaming for two breaths, rattled, and died.

Ryudo sneered. "Fool..." He turned around and knelt at her side. "Keiko, what are you doing out here?"

Keiko didn't think, she just wrapped her arms around Ryudo's neck, clutching him tight.

"Keiko, love?" He eased her back to look into her eyes, then tilted her face up and set a thumb against her burning cheek. "A *sword's* cut?" He pressed his palm to her cheek and the burning stopped. "There, it is closed. What happened?"

He was a watercolor of brightness from the rain in her eyes. "I...I had a fight."

"I can see that. The cut was from a ghost blade." He turned and frowned at Tika. "Who was this?"

Who *was* this?

Keiko couldn't take a breath. *Tika.* She was gone. Gone for good. Gone forever... She closed her arms around her waist and gasped, trying to hold in the pain clawing to get out.

Ryudo leaned over her. "Keiko?"

Toku came running across the yard, his soot black and tightly buttoned caped trench coat flying behind him in the storm's wind. "Good god! What is Keiko doing out here?"

"I have no idea." Ryudo lifted his head to look at Toku. "There are so many Avatars hammering at the barrier, I felt nothing beyond that she was in danger." He sat back on his heels. "Can you take her?" He turned to scowl at the young man in black leather, climbing to his feet over by the fallen motorcycle. "The Avatars are breaching the outer ring."

Toku knelt at Keiko's side, his hair rain-soaked, and windblown, his eyes glowing a bright unearthly green. "I'll see to it." His breath steamed from his lips. He hastily unknotted the belt of his the long coat and unbuttoned it.

Keiko felt his warm hand on her shoulders. "I'm... I'm coming." She leaned forward and pushed up onto her knees. She'd sat on her butt long enough.

Toku grabbed her under the arms and helped her up onto her feet. "You're ice cold… How long have you been out here?"

Keiko leaned against Toku's deliciously warm chest. He smelled wonderfully of clean soap, and slightly of autumn leaves. "Not long. Not really." She pressed her cheek against his warm, bare throat.

Toku wrapped his coat around Keiko, closing her tight against him, and frowned at the still small body on the drive. "Who was that?"

Keiko sniffed and wiped rain from her cheek. "Tika."

Toku stared down at her. "Tika?"

Ryudo's brows lifted. "The demon? It must have been small. I did not feel its presence past the Avatars."

Toku scowled fiercely. "The demon would come when we had a bunch of hostile Avatars surrounding the property."

Ryudo frowned at the fallen body, then looked over at Keiko. "What happened here?"

Keiko took a deep breath and looked down at the body. "I got the demon out of her, and…"

"Wait…" Toku choked. "You got it *out?*"

Keiko nodded. "But she wanted it back." She clenched her fingers in his shirt. "It was almost gone, but she wanted it back anyway. I told her it would kill her. She said…" It hurt. It hurt to say it. "She wanted to die with it, rather than live without it." She looked over at Ryudo. "She said…she loved it."

Toku stared at Ryudo. "Suicide?"

Ryudo looked away. "Apparently so."

The body on the ground suddenly shifted. A soft blue mist rose from it and the torn clothing sank onto the wet pebbles, empty.

"Shit!" Toku stepped back. "What was that?"

Ryudo made a sound of disgust. "The demon, dissipating. It consumed everything, leaving nothing to bury, not even ash."

Keiko leaned against Toku. It was over. Everything was over. Including her reason to stay. Emptiness yawned black and fathomless in her chest.

The young man in black leather stumbled toward them. "Tika?" He tore his helmet from his head and tossed it to the ground. Shido stared at the small pile of torn clothes, his eyes wide, clearly in shock. "Where is she...? What did you do with her?"

Toku glared at him. "The demon is gone. Destroyed."

Shido's wide-eyed gaze lifted to Keiko. "I saw you fighting. You did this. You...killed her." He blinked under the downpour, his face bone white. "You murdering..." His hands fisted at his sides and he took a step. "Bitch!"

Keiko just stared at him. She was just too damned empty to care what Shido thought.

Ryudo pointed his sword at Shido and scowled. "No closer, Avatar!"

Shido stared at Ryudo and stepped back. "Demon!"

"He belongs here. You don't." Toku's arms tightened around Keiko. "Get off my property!"

Shido took another step back and pointed at Keiko. "This isn't over, bitch!"

Toku bared his teeth. "I said..." The wind rose around him, blowing his coat wide. "Get off my property! *Now*!" Thunder cracked, and a bolt of lightning slashed to the ground only yards away.

Shido gasped and stumbled away. "Sorcerer..." He turned and bolted, snatching his helmet from the ground. He hastily levered his bike up from its side and climbed on. The bike started with a snarl and skidded off, spraying driveway pebbles.

Ryudo smiled briefly. "Temper, temper, Toku."

Toku bared his teeth at Ryudo. "Get them off my property!" Thunder rumbled again. "Do what ever it takes."

Ryudo abruptly bowed. He straightened, frowning grimly. "I will do what I can." He opened his arms and dissipated into golden mist, mixing with the rain and the rising wind.

"Keiko, damn it..." Toku tightened his arm around Keiko under his coat and hauled her up the steps. "Why did you leave your room?"

Keiko scowled. "Because Tika came inside to get me."

"What?" Toku stopped in the dark foyer and released her, both of them dripping on the floor. "She got in?" The doors slammed closed behind them.

Keiko bent to peel her soaked slippers and socks off. "She turned into a house maid. But I threw her out."

Toku sat to drag his boots off and grinned. "You threw a demon out of the house? Wow, I'm impressed." His boots thumped to the foyer floor, and he nudged them to the side.

Keiko smiled and felt the ache loosen around her heart. She shivered violently.

Someone gasped.

Keiko looked up.

Holding a very fine cut crystal oil lamp in one hand, Toku's mother rushed to them in a rustle of midnight blue silks. "What in the realm of Paradise were you two doing out in this storm? Keiko! Where is your coat? You're both soaked!"

Just beyond the foyer, a narrow sliding door opened. A pair of maids in drab gray with plain white aprons, carrying flashlights, poked their heads out.

Toku grabbed Keiko's hand and strode for the open servants' door. "I will need a pot of hot tea, fresh towels, and dry clothes for Keiko in my suite!"

Toku's mom raised her hand to her cheek. "Your suite?"

Toku's jaw tightened. He stopped at the door. "Not now, Mother."

Toku's father came up the hall in plain black robes, carrying a cut crystal lamp matching his wife's. "Wife, leave be."

"But, Husband...?"

Toku's father smiled. "Wife, who are we to stand in the way of love?"

"Oh!" She giggled. "Yes, dear."

Toku's father nodded at Toku. "On your way, Son. Try not to drip on the antiques?"

Toku smiled tightly. "Yes, Father." He started down the narrow servants' hallway, his warm hand locked around Keiko's cold fingers.

The door closed behind them, leaving them in the dark. Toku stopped and lifted his hand. A small glowing sphere appeared in his palm, lighting the hallway enough to walk without bumping into walls. He tugged her onward.

Keiko lifted her brow. "Magic?"

Toku smiled. "It does have the occasional practical use." He strode forward.

Keiko trotted in his wake and felt an unexpected giggle well up. She tried to suppress it, but it refused to stay down.

Toku turned a corner. "What?"

Keiko smiled. "Your parents, they think we're in love."

Toku glanced back, frowning. "Well, aren't we?"

Keiko stared up at him, at his expression. *He looks so...serious.*

The door slid open before him. Toku led her out into a broad hall and turned left. The door closed behind them. He smiled grimly. "Almost there."

Keiko looked back at the door and watched it slide closed. No one was there. She frowned. "Who opened the door?"

Toku snorted. "Ryudo."

Keiko frowned. "But I don't see him."

Toku shook his head. "Keiko, haven't you figured it out yet?"

"Figured out what?"

Toku smiled. "Ryudo isn't just the ghost that lives in the house; he *is* the house, itself. That's what a house guardian is; the sentient soul of a house."

Keiko nearly tripped. Ryudo was *the house?* The *entire* house? *Whoa...*

Toku's bedroom door opened, and Toku towed Keiko straight into the dark bathroom. He tossed his tiny light up and it floated, shedding warm gold luminescence within the bathroom. Shadows stretched in every corner.

"We need to get you warm." Toku peeled out of his coat and dropped it on the floor. Squelching every step of the way, he went into the shower and started the water. Steam wafted up toward the ceiling. "Good, the boiler is still working."

Leaning against the sink's counter and shivering, Keiko worked to undo the knots on her pants with chilled and nerveless fingers.

"Hang on, I'll get that." Toku came over to Keiko, knelt and brushed her fingers away. He jerked at her belt ties, freeing them, and pulled the pants down. "You are seriously soaked." With near violent haste, he undid her kimono top and peeled it off her. He stopped, staring at her breasts.

Keiko's nipples were tight with cold.

He leaned down, opened his mouth and sucked her nipple into his boiling hot mouth.

Keiko leaned back against the counter and groaned. "Hot, your mouth is hot!"

He released her nipple and smiled. "No, your skin is that cold." He frowned. "Too cold." He towed her into the glassed-in shower.

"Wait!" Keiko pushed at him to get him back out. "Toku, you're still dressed!"

"So?" He shoved her under the running shower, soaking himself while he was at it.

Needles of heat scorched Keiko's skin. "Oh, shit, that's hot!" She pushed away from the water.

Toku shoved her back under. "Stay there, it's not hot, really. It just feels that way." He stepped back. "I'll be right back." He stepped out of the shower stall and started peeling out of his wet shirt and jeans.

Keiko rubbed the burn from her skin and set her palm on the wall to watch the breathtaking sight of Toku's bunching, writhing muscles in action. Her breath caught. He was so beautiful. She bit her lip. And kind, and funny, and dedicated to his family. He would make a perfect husband.

His parents thought they were in love. Apparently, so did Toku. *"Well, aren't we?"*

Keiko stuck her head under the water and pressed her palms to the wall, letting the water streak down her cheeks. *I am. I am in love with Toku.* She had been in love since their kiss in the park under the cherry tree. She had felt it in that first sharing of breath.

And Ryudo?

Her heart twisted in her chest. Merciful Lady, she was in love with him too. She wasn't quite sure how that had happened, but she could feel it. Like two hands gripping her heart to make one fist, she was in love with both of them.

And it hurt. It hurt... Because she had to leave. There was no reason for her to stay. The demon was gone—and she could not marry Toku.

Toku deserved a perfect wife, and she wasn't it. She didn't know anything about managing a house this large, or being a corporate wife. She did know that corporate wives didn't talk to the dead. Or sleep with the dead either. *Ryudo...*

One didn't have two men in their lives. It wasn't done. Could she stop being Ryudo's lover to be Toku's wife? She shook her head. She couldn't do that to Ryudo, he loved her. The hurt squeezed around her heart into a snarled mess.

She closed her eyes. She had to leave. She had to. If she stayed, she'd ruin everyone's life. But, Mercy help her, she loved them, which meant she needed to leave while she could still do it.

Toku stepped into the shower, and reached past her, grabbing for the soap.

She looked up at his clean profile. Pain and desperation gripped her heart. This might be their last moment together. She turned and caught his face in her palms.

He blinked, startled.

She pulled him down to her and pressed her chilled lips to his scorching hot mouth, kissing him with all the love she had. He opened under her lips and she sought him, stroking against his hot tongue. He tasted slightly of ozone from the lightning storm, and fresh clean rain.

Toku groaned into her mouth and his arms came tight around her, pulling her against his strong, hot body. He pushed her back against the warm wet tiled wall. His hand cupped her butt and pressed her tight against the rigid length of an erection.

Keiko locked her arms around his neck. Want and need lashed her in a storm of heat and desire. She rubbed her hard nipples against his broad chest and rocked her hips against his in hungry urgency. Hot moisture slicked her thighs.

A shiver of awareness shimmered at the back of Keiko's skull, and the hairs on her neck suddenly rose. *Ghost…* She gasped and pulled her mouth from Toku's.

Toku frowned, "What…?"

A seam formed in mid air, right next to them. Ryudo stepped out as though from behind a screen—of nothing. His white robes and long hair floated in a soft wind Keiko could almost feel. "Good, I caught you in time."

Toku bared his teeth, and his arms locked around Keiko. "Ryudo, we're busy!"

Ryudo frowned, his lips tight and grim. "I need you both. Now."

"What?" Toku dashed the water from his face. "Now? Right now?"

Ryudo's mouth lifted in a chill smile. "Your father has just allowed one of the Avatar sorcerers into the house."

Toku froze. "What?"

~ Thirty-One ~

"It seems that one of the Avatars reached your father by telephone and asked for an invitation. Apparently your father granted it." Ryudo sighed. "He is still master of the house. There is nothing I can do to stop him from entering."

Keiko frowned. What had Tsuke said, back in the teahouse?

"I'll gain the master's permission to do a blessing on the house, and collect your ghost in the process..."

Keiko dug her fingers into Toku's bare wet shoulders. "They're going to ask permission to do a house blessing." She stared at Ryudo. "It's to...collect you."

"A house-blessing is actually a cleansing... Shit!" Toku smacked the wet tile wall. "We can hold off outside attacks, but if they're already inside...?"

Keiko frowned at Ryudo. "What can we do?"

Ryudo stared hard at her. "I need your combined power in the house's spiritual helix to keep the secret places hidden."

"All right." Toku scowled and leaned over to shut off the water.

Keiko wiped dripping water from her cheeks. "Wait, where is this helix? How fast can we get there?"

Ryudo arms opened. "We can be there in one breath." Power surged, hot and dark. His ghost-white robes fluttered up, then wrapped around Keiko and Toku, blinding and engulfing them breathlessly tight.

Toku gasped and grabbed Keiko around the waist. "How about a warning before you do that?"

Surrounded in blinding whiteness, the world tilted and a hot wind wrapped around them, rushing in Keiko's ears. The ground disappeared from beneath Keiko's feet. She closed her eyes and wrapped her arms tight around Toku's neck. Her heart slammed in her mouth. His arms around her waist, and his water-slick body against hers the only reality left to cling to.

Toku's lips brushed her cheek. "Relax, we're perfectly safe."

Keiko moaned. "Where are we going?"

The hot wind calmed and they floated in complete darkness. Power swelled around them, wrapping them in a thousand invisible supporting hands. Wings fluttered in the darkness around them.

"We are there." Ryudo's breath whispered against her other cheek. "Deep in my heart, where you belong."

She couldn't feel Ryudo's body, only Toku's, but he was there just the same, all around. Ryudo breathed in the warm moist darkness that held them; the air itself was Ryudo.

"Keiko…" Ryudo's hot breath brushed against the side of her throat, then seemed to caress her everywhere at once. "Take us."

Keiko felt Toku's hands cup her butt, holding her, lifting her. His hands slid downward to part her thighs, spreading her and pulling her up against the heat of his rigid cock. His lips sought hers, and they kissed.

The thousand supporting hands became exploring fingers and licking tongues. Hands cupped her breasts and squeezed. Lips fastened onto her nipples and sucked. A wriggling tongue explored her intimate flesh and the tight rose of her anus.

Passion burned white hot in her belly, need rising in a sudden and violent fever. She gasped and wrapped her legs around Toku's hips and writhed, seeking the heat of his cock, seeking his possession, seeking fulfillment, perhaps for the last time.

Toku moaned and trembled. His cock-head nudged inward, seeking entry. He slid up into her, spreading her flesh to accommodate. Thick, hard, powerful, filling… He gasped. "God, Keiko…"

She groaned. He felt so good.

Toku thrust hard, sheathing himself deep in her slick channel, all the way to the root.

She rocked with the impact and moaned.

The tongue at her anus became a fiendishly slippery finger that wriggled into her ass. "Fuck us..."

She tightened her arms on Toku's neck and writhed, releasing a soft whimper in dismay. It wasn't painful, merely, shocking.

Toku shifted slightly and thrust again, striking something high and in the back.

A bolt of near rapture forced a gasp from her, and her entire core clenched. The finger in her ass surged sinfully deeper. She moaned and writhed, automatically seeking more.

Toku's hands tightened around her thighs, his fingers digging into the soft flesh. He pulled nearly all the way out and thrust, hard, slamming into that delicious spot again.

Rapture flared and sparks danced behind her eyes. She cried out.

Toku moaned. He thrust, withdrew, thrust, and withdrew...striking that spot perfectly again, and again, and again...in an agonizingly slow rhythm.

The finger in her ass lengthened and thickened with each of Toku's strokes, becoming a slick yet rigid length, broadening and filling her, until it matched the size of the thrusting shaft in her core.

She gasped and groaned with the fullness stretching her flesh. The brutally snug and slick length in her ass withdrew partway, and thrust in opposition to the shaft in her core, each rubbing against the other. The sensation fired white-hot bolts up her spine, a pleasure that was closer to pain.

A thousand hands, fingers and tongues swept across her skin, stroking her, tasting her, squeezing and nipping at her flesh. The two shafts thrust and withdrew, advancing and retreating, slowly, yet greedily fucking her ass, even as Toku rapaciously fucked her cunt. Thrust, and thrust, and thrust...

"Love us..."

The slippery yet tight ache of the scandalous shaft debauching her ass mixed with the deliciously thrusting shaft within her core, sharpening both into a profane mix of unholy stimulation that threatened to take her sanity.

She howled her depraved delight.

Toku howled with her.

Pressure in her core built and tightened. Her heart hammered in her chest. The blood rushed in her ears. Heat flushed her body. She couldn't take it. It was too much. "Please!"

Toku cried out against her cheek.

Ryudo sighed in her other ear. "Yes, my loves…" A hand between their bellies became a finger slipping among the intimate folds of her flesh where her body joined Toku's. Lips brushed her cheek, right by her ear. "Cum for me." The finger very lightly touched her clit.

Keiko's core clenched violently.

Toku gasped and went rigid against her.

Something intense and potent trembled in the air.

Ryudo sighed against her cheek. "Cum…" The finger pressed against her clit. "Now."

Keiko's entire body went rigid. Her toes curled, her spine arching, and her breath stilled. It felt as though her heart stopped.

Toku choked and thrust, hard.

Riding the momentum of his stroke, something electrifying, volatile and potent slammed into her core. It impacted within her and erupted. Release unfolded in a boiling rush of carnal ferocity that cascaded into a wash of pleasure so fierce she couldn't contain it. She shrieked.

Blue-white electrical current erupted from her skin to dance all along her body, lighting a writhing, moving darkness. Tiny bolts of lightning arced and lashed across Toku, his eyes wide and still locked within her. Toku shuddered, and howled.

The crisp scent of autumn leaves, summer chrysanthemums and electrical ozone sizzled in the air.

A crash of thunder shook the entire world and green-tinted

lightning flashed all the way around them, illuminating a gigantic pale gold web that seemed to be holding them suspended and entwined. The web ignited into white-hot incandescence too bright to look at.

They screamed.

Keiko opened her eyes and lifted her head from Ryudo's shoulder. *Huh?* She was sprawled across Ryudo's body from shoulder to foot.

The garden, forever locked in late summer, spread around them. Ryudo sat with his eyes closed and one knee drawn up, his back against the trunk of the cherry tree swaying over head. Sunlight shadows patterned his white robes. Strands of his long silky black hair floated on the soft breeze.

Keiko pushed to sit up. A rich crimson kimono embroidered with birds in black and white silk thread had been draped over her like a blanket. Toku was nowhere in the garden.

Ryudo opened his eyes and smiled.

She clutched at the crimson robe and looked around. "Where's Toku?"

Ryudo brushed a stray hair from her brow. "His father called to him. It seems that we have succeeded in sufficiently annoying the Avatar with one too many places he could not delve into. He wished a guide." He tilted her chin up. "And so, I have you all to myself." He pressed his lips to hers in a gentle kiss that tasted of fresh water, spent passion and lingering shadows.

The flavor of a ghost that was yet a man.

His robes had parted and her palm rested on his chest, where his heart would have been, if he had been a living man. And yet a soft thump pressed rhythmically under her fingers.

Heat flushed in her belly, sailed up into her breasts, hardening her nipples, and spilled up into her cheeks. To her body, he was very much a living man, with blood, and bone, and passion.

And love. He loved her. She could feel it squeezing against her heart. And she loved him too. *But...* She loved Toku, too. How could she love two men? She pulled the robe closer and pushed up. "I should…"

"Stay." Ryudo's arms closed around her, holding her to his chest. The curve of his smile slipped downward. "You should stay. With me."

Keiko stared into his black eyes, where blue flames danced in their depths. She sighed and dropped her gaze. She had no clue how to put her mixed feelings into words. "Ryudo, I…"

His finger pressed against her lips. "Can you not accept love when it is given to you?"

Keiko shook her head in frustration. "But there are two of you!" She covered her mouth in shock. She hadn't meant to say that.

Ryudo cupped his hand under her chin and made her meet his gaze. "Yes. And we both love you. Is it so terrible to be loved by two men?"

Keiko felt her heart crack. "But I don't want to choose!"

"Choose?" Ryudo smiled. "When we already share true intimacy with each other? How silly."

Keiko's fingers on his chest curled into a fist. "But if I marry Toku…" Mercy, she couldn't believe that she was even contemplating it.

Ryudo smiled. "*When* you marry Toku, you shall have to resign yourself to two husbands."

Keiko looked up at him. "*Two* husbands?"

Ryudo snorted. "One would assume it was obvious?"

Keiko frowned and looked away. "You make it sound so simple."

"It is very simple." Ryudo pressed his palm between her breasts. "Listen to your heart, Keiko. Your heart already knows."

She stared up into his handsome face as though seeing it for the first time. Her heart did know. He was in love, painfully in love, with her. And she was just as much in love with him, and Toku, too.

Two loves wrapped around her heart, squeezing it tight.

There was no escape. She loved them…both. Unable to put what her heart felt into words, she lifted her lips to his and kissed him. The tears came from nowhere.

His eyes closed and his mouth opened above hers, releasing a soft moan, his tongue reaching out to stroke gently against hers, a warm velvet caress.

She closed her eyes and tasted the essence of shadows and arousal on his tongue. Her hand opened over his heart.

He lifted his lips, his midnight and lightning eyes opening. His hands cupped her face, his thumbs stroking the tears from her cheeks. He sighed. "Now, will you stop your running?"

Keiko smiled through her tears. "Will you stop chasing me?"

He laughed and pressed his brow to hers. "Perhaps I was chasing you, a little."

"A little?" Keiko smiled and pressed forward to lay her head on his shoulder. "What am I going to do with you?"

He pressed his cheek to her hair and his hand swept down her back. "Love me. That's all I ever wanted."

Her hands clenched in his white robes and her eyes closed. "I do. I do love you."

His arms tightened around her. "Then I have all I need."

The perfume of chrysanthemums drifted on the late summer breeze accompanied by the sound of buzzing cicadas and the soft chirp of small birds. It was a perfect moment…

Ryudo gasped and his entire body went rigid. The sky wavered and darkened. The blue sky smeared and thinned to reveal hints of a ceiling of plain cedar; reality showing through the illusion. The sounds of summer vanished. "Toku, you fool!"

Keiko sat up in his lap. "Ryudo?" She looked around. "What's happening?"

Ryudo closed his eyes tight and bared his teeth in a grimace of pain. "I am being called." He set his hand on the tree and pushed against it to rise to his feet.

Keiko rose with him and slid her arms into the sleeves of the crimson robe. "What should I do?"

Ryudo clasped her in his arms. "Hold me. Do not let go."

Keiko locked her arms around his waist, unsure of what else to do. "I've got you."

Ryudo threw out his arms and power exploded outward in a blaze of gold brilliance too bright to look at. "Do not let go!"

Keiko was forced to close her eyes against the brilliance. "I won't!" The floor disappeared from under her feet. Wind rushed in her ears and the world shifted around her.

And they fell.

Keiko gasped, clutching Ryudo to her.

Ryudo groaned and folded around her, locking her in his embrace. The falling stopped. The perfume of flowers was overpowered by the scent of fresh cypress.

"Ah, there you are." The voice was deep and frighteningly familiar.

Keiko opened her eyes. In the darkened shadows of the large audience chamber, she hung suspended in midair, held tight in Ryudo's luminescent gold embrace. He had become a creature of energy and light, his hair and robes floating around them both. Her crimson robes and long black hair was also floating, buoyant on his power.

On the floor directly below them, stood Toku, dressed in black slacks and a black dress shirt with the sleeves rolled up over his forearms, though barefoot. "There, I called him. Are you satisfied?"

"Impressive…" Avatar Tsuke, in a suit of midnight blue, stood before him. He looked up at Ryudo and his brow lifted. "Spirit, why don't you set the young lady down?"

Toku scowled. "Ryudo, don't you dare let Keiko go."

Ryudo's arms tightened around Keiko. "Yes, Master Toku."

Keiko lifted her brow at Ryudo. *Master?*

Ryudo winked a sun-bright eye.

Tsuke smiled. "Spirit, he is not master of this house."

Ryudo scowled down at him. "To me he is master, sorcerer."

"Be that as it may, he does not have true authority to command you—or to hold you." Tsuke raised his hand, palm up. A blue sphere of light formed in his hand. "Come to me. I will give both you and your chosen an honored place in my temple."

"As your slaves? I think not." Ryudo smiled. "I have met your kind before, sorcerer."

Tsuke's mouth tightened. "Have you now?"

Toku hands fisted at his sides. "You are not taking either of them."

"Am I not?" Tsuke parted his hands, and the blue sphere became a ball of writhing lightning.

"I said no, and I meant no." Toku threw his hands out, a sphere of shimmering green light exploded outward, encompassing all three of them.

"Very nice." Tsuke spread his hands and lightning danced between his palms. "However, you do not have the power or the authority to keep this spirit from me. You are not master of this house."

At the far end, the audience chamber's massive doors slammed open, and Toku's father strode in. "But I am, and I do."

~ Thirty-Two ~

Toku's father held Avatar Tsuke's chill gaze, his brows lowered over his dark eyes. His casually formal black robes shimmered with green highlights cast from Toku's magical sphere. He lifted his chin. "Avatar, I gave permission to bless my house. I did not give you permission to disturb my son, his fiancé, or my house spirit."

Toku stared at his father and his mouth fell open. "Father, I thought you didn't…?"

His father glanced at him. "Not now, Son."

Tsuke's hand closed into a fist, extinguishing the blue sphere. "Sir, you wish to leave a demonic ghost in residence?"

Toku's father looked up at Ryudo and smiled briefly. "He is troublesome on occasion, but we have grown quite accustomed to his presence." He folded his hands behind him. "Will that be all, Avatar?"

Tsuke's jaw tightened and his hands fisted at his sides. "If you are quite sure?"

"I am." Toku's father lifted his hand. "This way, Avatar, I believe we have entertained you and the rest of your associates quite enough for today."

Keiko's brows rose. Apparently Toku's father knew about their earlier battle, too.

"Of course." Avatar Tsuke bowed briefly and strode for the door.

Toku's father led him out into the hallway and slid the doors closed behind them.

Toku dropped his hands and the green sphere evaporated. "What a total…!" He threw up his hands and snarled out a wordless sound of sheer anger.

Ryudo drifted toward the floor, his golden mien dissipating. "A bastard?" His robes shifted into white silk and his features regained their human appearance.

Toku nodded. "Yeah, a bastard, that'll do."

"Speaking of the bastard..." Ryudo set Keiko on the tatami-covered floor. "Toku, calling me into his presence was beyond foolish!"

Toku scowled at Ryudo. "He was only two doors away from the heart of the house's helix before I could stop him. It was a choice of letting him find it and tearing it apart to get to you out of it, or leading him elsewhere and calling you with the helix still intact and accessible."

Keiko frowned at Toku. "Okay, so what does all that mean, so I can understand it?"

Toku sighed. "It means that Avatar Tsuke was spiritually tearing the house apart to find you two." He glared at Ryudo. "Even with all the power we shoved into the helix, he very nearly succeeded in reaching you. I called Ryudo so he would still have a fighting chance if I couldn't hold him off."

Keiko tilted her head to the side. Okay, that made sense. "So, now that Tsuke has been told point blank that you and Ryudo are off limits, does this mean that the Avatars won't bother you anymore?"

Ryudo crossed his arms. "One can hope."

"We're good..." Toku stepped close and reached out to take Keiko's hand. "But you're still on their hunting list."

Keiko rolled her eyes and groaned. "Great."

"No big deal." Toku smiled and tugged her close. "Once we're married, you'll be off-limits, too." He dropped a quick kiss on her lips.

Keiko lifted her brow at him. "So, I marry you and that's it, happily ever after?"

Toku grinned. "Why not?"

Keiko clutched his hand. "But I don't know how to be a wife!"

Toku shook his head. "Don't worry. Knowing Mother, you'll get a very thorough education."

Keiko covered her eyes with her hand. "Wonderful."

Toku tugged her into his embrace. "I swear, you'll be fine. Okay?"

Keiko looked up at him. "If you're sure you want me?"

Toku's smiled disappeared. "I have never been surer in my life."

Keiko smiled up at him. Maybe it wouldn't be so bad.

Toku's father opened the doors to the audience chamber and strode in, wiping his hands together. "Now that our unwanted guest and his lingering associates have left..." He smiled. "You had a question, Son?"

"I do, Father." Toku's hand tightened around Keiko's. "You knew about Ryudo all this time?"

Toku's father smiled. "Of course."

Toku threw out his hand. "Then why did you let everyone think I was crazy, or lying, when you knew I was telling the truth?"

Toku's father shook his head. "Despite the truth of certain matters, a spirit cannot serve as an excuse to those who cannot believe in them, such as the staff." He raised a brow. "Or your mother." He shook his head and sighed. "Much as I love you, Son, to remain head of my household and my company, I could not profess to believe in what others could not, or I would be labeled unfit to run either."

"Oh." Toku slumped and dropped his gaze. "I...understand."

Toku's father rolled his eyes. "Finally." He sighed. "Son, unlike you, I don't have the skill for..." He fluttered his fingers. "Hocus-pocus that you seem to possess. Normally I can barely see our house spirit, Ryudo." He lifted his brows at the white robed ghost. "Though for some reason, he seems quite solid right now."

Ryudo nodded and smiled.

Keiko suddenly found the autumn scene on the wall screen to her left very interesting.

Toku frowned at the floor. "One more thing, Father." He lifted his gaze. "About that Avatar, did you know...?"

"Of course I did." Toku's father snorted. "All the family's interactions with the Avatars are in the histories, Son, which is why I had you read them."

"I don't get it." Toku shook his head and set his hands on his hips. "If you knew, then why...?"

"If I knew about the Avatars, why did I let one in?" Toku's father rolled his eyes. "Son, he asked for an invitation. It would have been impolite to refuse a holy man."

Toku winced. "Oh."

Toku's father smiled. "If I have answered all your questions...?"

Toku nodded. "Yes, Father." He lifted a brow. "And if I have more?"

Toku's father shrugged and smiled. "If you have more questions, I can arrange to talk in my private office. In the meantime, I suggest we call it a night. Your mother has plans to spend the day with her new daughter to get acquainted." He rubbed his brow. "And begin preparations for a rather expensive traditional wedding."

Keiko winced. "My apologies, sir."

Toku's father smiled. "No need. I assure you, my wife will enjoy it immensely." He lifted his chin. "Oh, and Ryudo, would you mind restoring the power? Charming though all the candles are, I prefer my bath water hot without having to boil it on the stove."

Ryudo bowed. "Of course."

The lights flickered on in the hallway, then remained lit.

"Thank you." Toku's father nodded. "Now, I believe I will bid you all a good night."

Toku folded his arm around Keiko, pulling her close. "Good night, Father."

Keiko nodded. "Good night, sir."

Toku's father rolled his eyes. "Oh, please, call me Father."

Keiko smiled. "Yes, Father."

He smiled. "Good night, Daughter, Son, Ryudo." He turned and headed toward the doors.

"Blood and hell, I'm tired." Toku started up the audience

chamber, headed the other way with Keiko under his arm.

Keiko's belly rumbled. Heat filled her cheeks. Well, at least her stomach had waited until Toku's father had left.

Toku lifted his brow at Keiko. "Hungry?" The door ahead of them slid open.

"Starved." Keiko stepped into a hallway lined with windows showing a night-dark enclosed garden. She frowned. "I think we missed dinner."

"I think you're right." Toku stepped through the doorway into the hallway and waited for Ryudo. "Tell you what, Ryudo can take you back to my room and I'll go hit the kitchen and meet you there." He looked over at Ryudo. "Do you mind?"

Ryudo stepped into the hall and the door closed behind him. "Do I mind spending time alone with our betrothed? Not at all." He took Keiko's hand and folded it over his arm.

"*Our* betrothed?" Toku blinked, then smiled. "Well, I guess she is." He grinned at Keiko. "Think you can handle two husbands?"

Keiko bit down on her lip. "You don't mind sharing me?"

Toku grinned broadly. "Are you kidding? I'm not doing the sharing—he is!" He lifted his brow at Ryudo. "Possessive bastard."

Ryudo raised his chin. "I am willing to make any sacrifice necessary to keep her."

"What?" Keiko scowled up at Ryudo. "Keep me?"

Toku raised his hands and backed down the hall. "On that note, I'm heading for the kitchen!" He waved and jogged to the right, his chuckles echoing behind him.

"This way." Ryudo led Keiko to the left and down the hallway.

Keiko frowned up at him. "Has anyone ever introduced you to the concept of 'husband abuse'?"

Ryudo chuckled. "No, I can not say that anyone has."

Keiko snorted. "Any more of that 'keeping her' routine and I'll make sure to give you an up close and personal demonstration of the concept in action."

Ryudo leaned close and smiled. "Promises, promises…"

The walk to Toku's chambers was not long, though it took several turns to get there. Finally they reached the doors to Toku's suite. Ryudo waved open Toku's door. "Here we are, and in one piece, no less. Try not to get into any more difficulties?"

Keiko frowned up at him. "You're leaving me?"

"There is a small but immediate concern I must see to. I will return soon." He dropped a kiss on Keiko's brow and vanished.

Keiko walked in and eyed Toku's huge bed. The yawn came out of nowhere. Since there was nothing better to do, she climbed up on top of the bed and sprawled out. She set her forearm over her eyes, just for a few minutes...

"Now that's what I like to see, a semi-naked woman waiting in my bed."

Keiko sat up dazed. She must have actually fallen asleep. "Huh?"

Toku walked into the room holding a square tray with covered dishes and a steaming teapot. "Sorry about the 'naked' comment. It just...popped out of my mouth." His cheeks pinked and his gaze dodged hers.

Keiko raised her brow. Was he actually blushing? "Ryudo's obviously been a bad influence on you."

"You have no earthly idea." Toku rolled his eyes and winced. "When he's in my head, his way of thinking gets all mixed up with mine, and some of it ends up coming out of my mouth when I don't expect it." He kicked the door shut and lifted the square tray. "Anyway...I brought food. Of course, it's only leftovers from dinner earlier."

Food! Keiko's stomach growled, loudly. "Good, I'm starved. Wait, from earlier? There was hot food without power?"

"Yep." He grinned. "We still have the original hearth ovens and wood stove in the kitchen, and Cook is very creative."

Keiko frowned. "Does the power go out often?"

Toku winced and walked over to the low table by the windows. "The power goes out whenever Ryudo and I have to throw a lot of magic around." He set the tray down by the oil lamp. "It blows the house's fuses."

Keiko's brows lifted. Come to think of it, the power had gone out when she first got there, right after she, Ryudo, and Toku had finished sex… She clutched at her scarlet robes. *Oops…*

Thunder rumbled, but not near as loudly as it had before.

Keiko winced, only a little, and glanced at the windows. "Is magic making the thunderstorms?"

Toku sighed. "It does that too, on occasion." He pulled the covers off of the bowls. Steam wafted up, delivering mouthwatering aromas. "Big magic generally screws with the weather; that's how we can tell if something magical is happening." He shoveled food into bowls.

Keiko came up on her knees and sniffed appreciatively. "That smells fantastic." She slid from the bed. Two steps took her to the table.

Toku held out a bowl. "Here, eat."

Keiko folded the robe around her, took the bowl and knelt on one of the big cushions. She shoved a bite into her mouth and nearly fainted from the savory flavor of the herbed chicken. "Wonderful."

Toku poured tea from a small black pot into white egg-sized cups, adding sips of tea to the sounds of utensils clicking against bowls, and soft moans of delight. After several long minutes of hurried eating, Toku set his bowl down, lifted his cup, slurped tea and sighed. "I was hungrier than I thought." He smiled. "Sex with you certainly builds up an appetite."

Keiko raised her tea to cover her warming cheeks. "So, what are we going to do about not blowing the power every time we do it?" A shiver of awareness shimmered at the back of Keiko's skull, and the hairs on her neck suddenly rose. *Ghost…* She looked up.

"To preserve the electricity in the house…" Ryudo eased into existence only three steps away. "You may want to consider changing our sleeping arrangements."

"To what?" Toku scowled. "I am not willing to sleep alone."

"You're not willing to sleep alone?" Keiko set her tea cup down.

"We're not even married yet!"

Toku grinned. "So?"

Ryudo snorted and crossed his arms. "I also, am not willing to sleep alone."

Keiko smiled sweetly. "So, sleep with each other."

Toku spit out his mouthful of tea, and gave Ryudo a wide-eyed glance.

Ryudo lifted his brow at Toku in clear amusement.

Keiko grinned into her tea.

Ryudo shook his head. "Might I suggest moving into my personal chambers?"

Toku looked up in alarm. "Your chambers?"

"All of us, Toku." Ryudo rolled his eyes. "The rooms surround the heart of the helix. Power discharged by our activities will be directly absorbed without interruption of the far more delicate electrical wiring."

"Oh..." Toku lifted his brow. "Are you going to let me update that antique bathroom of yours?"

Ryudo sighed. "Oh, very well..."

Toku grinned. "Excellent! We'll take it" He winked at Keiko. "Ryudo has the biggest suite in the house."

"Of course." Ryudo sat down on the bed and eased onto his side, resting up on one elbow. "My chambers were the original master's suite."

Keiko frowned. "I've only seen that one room."

Ryudo nodded. "That is the heart. There are a number of larger rooms around it."

Toku rose from the cushion to sit on the side of the bed. "You realize Mother is going to want to decorate?"

Ryudo rolled over onto his back and threw an arm over his eyes. "That woman and her decorating..."

Keiko rose to her feet. "Is she that bad?"

Ryudo and Toku exchanged a speaking glance. Toku looked over at Keiko and smiled. "You'll find out tomorrow."

"Oh…" Her yawn nearly cracked her jaw. She hastily covered her mouth. "Oops, sorry."

Ryudo patted the bed. "Come, we should all sleep."

She looked out the window toward her prepared room. "Shouldn't I…?"

Both men spoke simultaneously. "No!" As a team they latched onto Keiko's arms and hauled her onto the bed. In a matter of moments she was stripped of her robes and lying spread with the two of them on hands and knees over her, holding her down on the pillows.

Keiko scowled up at them. "Hey! Am I the only one getting naked here?"

Ryudo rose up on his knees, lifted a brow at Toku, and unknotted his sash. His white robes slithered in a whisper of silk from his broad shoulders. The silk pooled around his knees and evaporated.

Toku sat back on his heels, scowled and jerked at his shirt buttons. "Show-off." He had to turn to the side of the bed to peel his jeans down his very fine butt.

Keiko came up on her elbows to watch.

Toku tossed his clothes at his dresser, letting the fall in a heap on the floor. He turned around, displaying a partial erection. Under Keiko's eyes, he stiffened and rose. Toku smiled and crawled back onto the bed. "See anything you like?"

She smiled. "You realize that if we all have sex, we're going to blow the power out again."

Toku froze, then glared at Keiko.

Keiko put up her hands. "Hey, don't blame me!"

"But Keiko, you *are* the cause." Ryudo leaned over to lounge across her legs, setting a hand and his chin on her rounded hip. "Neither Toku nor I generate that much power during sex."

Keiko lifted her brows. "So you guys can have all the sex you want, but if you do it with me, all the lights go out?"

Ryudo chuckled. "You are very potent, my love." He stroked her hip with his long fingers. "Quite realistically, Toku and I generate wind and rain. You add the thunder and lightning. How do they say it in this century?" He pursed his lips, then smiled. "Ah, you are overloading the system."

"Oh, great." Toku flopped onto his back and groaned. "Most people need a condom to have sex. We need a surge protector."

"Poor thing." Keiko set her arms behind her head and smiled. "You could always masturbate."

Toku leaned up on his elbow. His eyes narrowed and hot, he smiled at Keiko. "I will if you will."

Ryudo pushed up on one hand and presented Keiko with a distinctly lascivious smile. "That does sound rather entertaining."

Keiko looked from one to the other. "What? Masturbation?"

Ryudo licked his lips. "You, masturbating for us."

Keiko blinked. "Me?"

~ Thirty-Three ~

Keiko sat up among the pillows piled against the headboard, and spread her knees, opening herself. *How did I get talked into this?* She spread the plump outer lips of her feminine flesh with her left hand and licked the index finger of her right.

Toku sat up on his knees and focused on her displayed flesh. "Nice…" He reached down, wrapped his hand around the base of his shaft, and slowly stroked upward.

Ryudo, lounging on his side with his chin propped up on his palm, an arm-length away, reached down to cup his balls, then curled his hand around his cock and stroked as well. He lifted his gaze to hers and smiled.

The sight of both men stroking their cocks triggered a hot wet throb in Keiko's core. *On second thought…* She reached down and pressed her wet finger to the mouth of her core and explored the gathering cream. She rubbed lightly on her clit, encouraging small bolts of delight and the tiny bead of flesh to swell.

Toku leaned back on one hand, his cock hardening and swelling with each pull. His breathing deepened and his cheeks flushed. His cock-head darkened to plum and moisture seeped from the very tip. He palmed the head, took a deep breath and smeared the wetness down his shaft, lubricating himself.

Ryudo licked his lips and rubbed the pad of his thumb against the head of his cock, then stroked with strong, smooth pulls. His cock lengthened and swelled to full erection. His nipples tightened to hard points. He released a sigh and his gaze narrowed.

Keiko licked her lips watching both men becoming heavily aroused. She was doing this to them. They were getting excited from watching her. She took deeper breaths, and her finger on her clit worked just a bit faster. Her nipples tingled, and tightened. She settled deeper among the pillows and her hips began to rock with her finger's movements. She couldn't remember the last time she'd gotten this excited, this fast.

Toku lifted his chin and groaned, his hand working his cock a bit faster.

Ryudo glanced over at him and smiled.

Keiko lifted her chin and her eyes became heavy. Erotic delight tightened in her belly. She loosed a soft gasp.

Toku leaned forward and inched closer.

Keiko eyed the thick cock in his hand and spread her knees wider. She wanted to see him cum. She wanted to see him cum…on her. "Toku…"

Toku crawled between her legs, jerking his cock at top speed. He groaned and rose up on his knees. "God, Keiko…"

Keiko lifted her chin and licked her lips. "Cum on me, Toku."

Toku gasped, and leaned over her, one hand planted among the pillows by her waist, the other pulling on the hard shaft of his cock. "God, yes…" He choked and his eyes closed. "Fuck, I'm cumming." A moan came from deep in his chest. White ropes of cum jetted from his cock, spattering hot and wet across her belly. He leaned down and kissed her hungrily.

Keiko felt the spark of orgasm tighten within her.

"Keiko."

She released Toku's mouth and turned to her left.

Ryudo knelt at her side. He grabbed the headboard with one hand and rose up on his knees, pulling on his cock with the other. He took a deep breath and shook back his long hair, then smiled. "May I have a taste?"

Toku jerked back to sit on his heels between her knees. "A taste?"

Ryudo smiled. "Of her honey."

"All right." Keiko lifted her wet fingers from her flesh and held them out to Ryudo.

Ryudo leaned forward, his gaze locked to hers. He sucked her fingers into his mouth and stroked them with his tongue, sending shivers through her. "Mmm…"

Keiko groaned. She pulled her fingers back and stroked her clit with them.

Ryudo watched the fingers that had just been in his mouth stroking her flesh. His eyes widened. "Oh, yes…" He took a deep breath. His mouth opened and he leaned over her, groaning. Thick white ropes of cum erupted from his cock and spattered across her breasts. He swooped down and took her mouth, moaning the last of his orgasm.

Keiko's belly tightened, then released with the white-hot bolt of delight that wasn't quite orgasm. She arched her back and loosed a small groan of frustration.

Toku lifted her leg and set it over his shoulder, then leaned down, setting one hand on the bedcovers.

Ryudo released her mouth and his brows lifted.

Toku licked his lips. "Move your hands, Keiko."

Keiko frowned, and moved her hands from her feminine flesh. "What are you doing?"

"I'm going for the honey pot." Toku smiled. Knees spread wide; he hunched low. "You haven't cum yet, but we have. It should be safe enough." He spread her flesh with his fingers,

Ryudo grinned. "Clever. I had not considered that."

Toku turned a vicious grin on him. "You snooze, you lose." He leaned down and pressed his mouth to her in a searing and intimate kiss.

Keiko arched back against the pillows and grabbed onto his shoulder. Hot, his mouth was so hot… The touch of his lips and tongue was light, gentle, exploring. He lapped at her folds, her seeping core, and then focused on her clit, making her twitch with jolts of fierce pleasure. His tongue strokes became more adamant, the pleasure he delivered more intense.

Keiko gasped and rocked against his mouth. Urgency began to coil with every tiny bolt of delight that danced up her spine. Over his shoulder, her toes curled.

His tongue swirled around her clit, then he sucked strongly, and loudly.

The pleasure sensation was so severe she dug her fingers into Toku's shoulder, threw her head back and cried out. Climax rose and crested ferociously...

Ryudo leaned over her and sucked a nipple into his mouth, then bit down.

Her breath stopped. She choked and climax slammed her in the gut, then rampaged through her in violent tremors. She shouted and writhed under the mouths of both men.

Both men sat back and wiped their mouths.

Toku grinned. "Now that was nice."

Ryudo smiled. "I found it quite entertaining."

Keiko panted, boneless and wrung out among the pillows. "Oh, yeah, that was... That was...very nice." She looked down at the cum smeared all over her and winced. "Can I have a towel?"

Morning began far too early with the maids knocking on the door, wanting to get Keiko dressed for the day.

Ryudo dropped a swift kiss on Keiko's cheek and vanished.

Toku dropped a quick kiss on Keiko's other cheek and ran into the bathroom.

"Keiko sat up, clutching the blankets. "Abandoning me?"

Toku laughed from the safety of the bathroom. "Who me? No! I have to go to the office with Father. Enjoy your breakfast with Mother!"

Three maids in simple gray uniforms and white aprons came into Toku's bedroom in a giggling horde. They tossed a robe on Keiko, hustled her out of bed and escorted her through the corridors and to her suite.

Keiko was allowed a few minutes for a quick shower then they attacked her with towels and the blow-dryer. After drying, combing and binding her hair into a long straight tail, they folded a short white *kimono* top across her breasts and tucked it into full pleated *hakima* pants of deep plum. Split-toed socks and a pair of house sandals finished her outfit. Smiling and laughing, they hauled Keiko off to a private breakfast with Toku's mother.

And so began a very long morning that included a whirlwind tour of the house's back corridors, introductions to the staff, and long-winded dissertations on the more mundane workings of the household. Completely out of her depth, Keiko smiled and nodded through all of it.

Chatting happily, Toku's mother led her back into the breakfast room where an antique blue china tea service waited on them. Toku's mother knelt down on the cushion by the open garden door and smiled.

Keiko gratefully knelt on the cushion on the opposite side of the table, and reached for the teapot and poured the dark Chinese Oolong into the tiny cups, like a good soon-to-be-daughter–in-law should. Her feet were killing her. The house was freaking huge. They had to have walked through miles of corridors.

"Seems like a lot, yes?"

Keiko didn't quite miss the teacup she was filling. She looked up at Toku's mother and bit down on her lip. "Truthfully, I really don't know if I'm capable of doing all this." She held out the cup.

Toku's mother took the offered teacup with both hands and chuckled. "I didn't think I could either." She winked. "Don't worry. You won't have to do this alone for a very long time yet."

Keiko sighed. "I hope not!"

Toku's mother sipped her tea and sighed. "Now, shall we discuss the plans for your wedding?"

Keiko almost spit out her tea. "I'm sure whatever you decide will be fine."

Toku's mother beamed. "Such an agreeable daughter."

Keiko ducked her head and hid behind a sip of tea. *If only she knew...*

Escorted to her bedroom door by the maids, Keiko bowed her sincere thanks, then closed the door on them with a groan of sheer exhaustion. Moaning, she stumbled over to her unrolled *futon* bed, and flopped facedown onto the scarlet coverlet. *What a morning...* She tugged the band from her hair, freeing the long tail from its tight binding.

Knocking at the door brought Keiko upright in her bed. She rubbed at her eyes. *I must have fallen asleep.* "Yes?"

The door opened and a maid in gray poked her head in. "Miss? You have a visitor."

Keiko's heart nearly stopped. A visitor? *Not again?* She stared at the neat young lady and hoped she wasn't dealing with another possessed housemaid. But Tika was gone, and the Avatars had left. "Who is it?"

"It's a young man named Shido. He says he has a message from Shihan? He's waiting at the gate in the Peach Garden."

Keiko scowled. Shido, who was working with the Avatars, but he wasn't an Avatar yet. He had a message from Shihan? Her jaw tightened. *Right.* Like she was going to believe that? He probably just wanted to bitch. She rose from the bed and straightened her *kimono* and rumpled *hakima*. "I'll come." But there was no way she was going off the property. He could bitch at her through the locked gate, and the house's barriers. Ryudo would probably pop up when she got close to the door anyway.

The maid nodded. "Yes, Miss."

Keiko followed the maid through the main corridors. The maid stopped at a sliding door leading into a large walled garden, and bowed Keiko through the door into the enclosed garden.

Keiko stepped down onto the grass, then followed the maid

through the pruned trees. A strong breeze moved through the tree branches and lifted her hair. She was led toward a huge round moon-gate doorway occupying the tall plastered outer wall. One large wooden door of a pair painted bright scarlet stood open, revealing a barred gate.

Keiko frowned. She was pretty sure Toku's mother hadn't shown her this gate.

Shido, in his customary motorcycle leathers, lounged against the gateway's inner arch on the other side of the iron bars, his motorcycle parked on the side of the street only a few steps from the gate. His face looked a little pale and he had lost weight. The bones in his face were a little too prominent.

Keiko scraped her blowing hair back from her cheeks. "Shido."

He nodded back, and dodged her gaze, refusing to look her in the eye. "Keiko."

She swallowed. "So, what do you want?"

Shido straightened and hooked his fingers into the gate. "Are you going to let me in?"

Keiko smiled sourly. "I don't think so."

Shido snorted and his mouth twisted into the semblance of his cocky smile. "Afraid of me?"

Keiko leaned back on her heels and crossed her arms. "How about, 'not my property, not my decision to make'?"

"But it will be." He looked down at his boots. "I hear you're marrying the heir."

Keiko looked away. "Wow, word got out fast." Then again, Toku's father had told Tsuke to his face that she was Toku's fiancé, so of course Shido would know. She crossed her arms. "Why are you here, Shido?"

"Why did you kill her?" His fingers clenched on the gate's bars and his mouth tightened. "Why did you kill your best friend?"

Keiko reeled as though struck. She set her hand on the wall for balance. "I didn't kill her. She killed herself."

"Bullshit!" His fist slammed into the gate. "I saw you…!"

Keiko shook her head. "You saw me hit the demon possessing her—not Tika."

"What demon? I saw her on the ground and I saw you leaning over her, and then she was dead!"

Keiko sighed. He must have missed the beginning of the fight. "Shido, she was possessed. I got the demon out of her and just about killed it, but she wanted it back. It was dying, and it...killed her, when she took it back."

Shido shook his head and laughed softly, but it sounded more like a sob. "That is the biggest pile of bullshit I have ever heard..."

"Shido, she was possessed in the woods. You were there when it happened."

"Yeah, right, whatever..." He rolled his eyes. "She was possessed. So what?"

"So what?" Keiko's mouth fell open in shock. "It was killing her, Shido! When I took it out, she took it back and it consumed her until nothing was left but a pile of rags!"

"It killed her..." Shido chuckled and then sucked in a breath. "It was killing her..." A soft sound of pain escaped. "I've *been* possessed." He bared his teeth in something that wasn't even close to a smile. "But I'm not even close to dead."

Keiko shook her head. "Shido, she wasn't like you. Her body can't handle it the way yours can..."

Shido set his hands on his hips, smiled and shook his head. "You're still not listening to me." He threw up his head and laughed painfully. "You never listened to me."

"Shido, please..."

"No! You will listen this time, bitch!" He pointed at her. "Tika is dead because of you! I watched you do it!" He slammed the gate with his hand and shouted. "You *killed* her!"

"She killed *herself!*" Keiko stilled and let the tears fall. "Shido, I pulled out the demon and stabbed it. Tika could have lived, but she didn't want to let it go, so she took the dying demon back—and died with it." She wiped at the tears streaming down her cheeks. "Tika deliberately chose to die as a demon, rather than live as an ordinary person."

Shido nodded. "So you finally admit to killing her." He threw out his hand. "Do you plan to kill me, too?"

"Shido, stop it!" Keiko stomped her foot. Why wasn't he paying attention? "You're not possessed!"

"Oh, but I am." He smiled and stared straight into her eyes. "Seriously, Keiko, I really, really am." His eyes burned with flickering foxfire.

Keiko froze. "What?" She jerked back from the gate.

Shido shook his head and smiled sourly. "You know, I didn't want to do this. I was completely against it." He shook his head. The barred gate swung open and Shido walked into the garden.

Keiko tripped back, away from him. How did he get through the barrier?

"But you know what?" Shido lifted his chin curled his lip and brought his palms together. "You fucking pissed me off!" He threw his hands wide. A blade of light shot from his belly, washed through the closed gate, and exploded in Keiko's face.

There wasn't time to scream.

~ Thirty-four ~

Keiko moaned. Her head...hurt. There was cement under her cheek and belly. She opened her eyes. What was she doing on the sidewalk? She turned her head and frowned. She was not only on the sidewalk, she was on the wrong side of the garden's moon-gate. *How did I get out here?* She tried to push up, but her hands were fastened behind her, and it felt like someone was sitting on top of her. "Get off me!"

A palm pressed between her shoulder blades. "Do not try to struggle."

Keiko stilled. She knew that voice. "Ryujin?"

Ryujin caught her arm and pushed her onto her side and then over onto her back. He knelt straddling her thighs, then sat. "Yes." His handsome face was tight with concentration and practically colorless. His pale blue robes seemed a bit ragged, as though drifting at the edges. Compared to Ryudo's rich presence, he seemed barely there.

She winced and tried to shift. He had her legs pinned under him, proving that he was there enough to keep her from moving. "What are you doing?"

"Taking you."

Keiko smiled bitterly. "Idiot. I'm a lousy hostage. Ryudo is *samurai*. His loyalty is to his house first. He is not going to come out of it to get me." She sincerely hoped to the he wouldn't be stupid enough to come out to get her. Thank the heavens Toku was safe at his father's office.

Ryujin smiled. "I know. I'm counting on it." He unknotted the ties to her pants and jerked them open. He tugged her kimono free, exposing her belly.

Keiko gasped. "What are you doing?"

Ryujin pulled a short dagger, a sleek *tanto* from his sash. "Carving out his seal to separate you." He pressed his hand over her heart. "Do not move. This could kill you as easily as a heart stab."

Keiko stared at the bared blade and every hair on her body stood. "What? Why? You won't get him out of the house this way."

"Tsuke wants him for the order. I just want you." The blade shimmered into pale blue transparency. Mist curled up from its edge. "This will cut your spiritual connection with only slight damage to your flesh. You must not move. If I cut too deep, I will separate your soul from your body." He leaned hard on the hand over her heart, immobilizing her. He set the point of the dagger to seam under the swell of her belly.

Keiko's heart pounded in her ears. She couldn't move, he had her legs trapped under him and had her body pinned down by the hand on her heart. He was going to do this, and she couldn't stop him. Her throat squeezed tight. "No!" Her voice came out in a tiny whisper. "Please, don't!"

"I am sorry, but there are things I must do, and you're the only one that can help me do them." He pressed and the dagger slid into her.

Cold, the blade was ice cold. Keiko's breath escaped on a whimper. "It hurts."

"I know." He slid the blade across, right under her belly, from hip to hip.

She felt it, the snap of a thread, the unraveling of something tightly coiled – and loss, crushing loss, then emptiness, as though a part of her had gone missing, or died.

"Done." He pulled the dagger out and stared down at her. "You are mine."

Keiko sucked in a breath and screamed.

Ryujin dropped over her, his mouth covered hers, sucking the breath from her lungs and the terror from her heart in a cold rush.

Keiko remembered this feeling from before. From the ghosts that had cut her. They had bled her and sipped the screams from her until she lay in a bleeding stupor, unable to feel anything at all. He was drinking her fear, like every other ghost—but one.

Ryujin lifted his mouth from hers.

She stared up at him. Her fear was gone, devoured, consumed, taken from her. All that was left was the feeling of loss, and the tears slipping down her cheeks. "I hate you."

"I know." He lowered his gaze, then covered her eyes with his hand. "Sleep."

Keiko surfaced from the black abyss of sleep and gasped. She'd just had the absolute worst nightmare about Shido and Ryujin. She opened her eyes…and couldn't see a thing. She was fairly upright with her arms spread wide. She seemed to be reclining in some form of mesh chair. And she couldn't move. She twisted and pulled. She couldn't move anything at all. *What the hell?*

A ball of pale blue light flickered into existence right over her head.

She winced against the sudden brightness then sucked in a breath. She wasn't in a chair. She was suspended off the floor in the dead center of a stone-walled room, bound with some form of semi-transparent silver rope that stretched from her to the stone walls all around her.

She stared closer at the ropes and a chill raced down her spine. The ropes around her limbs were passing through her clothing as though her clothes weren't even there. The ropes were clearly spiritual. A ghost had done this.

Hopefully this was a new game of Ryudo's and her brief vision of Ryujin only a lingering nightmare. "Ryudo!" She jerked hard and the bindings stretched. She relaxed and they went right back into shape.

"Shit." She threw back her head and screamed. "Ryudo, this game isn't funny!"

"Your Ryudo is not here." Ryujin materialized, floating directly before her, his robes fluttering in a wind she couldn't feel. "Nor will he come here. Without his seal, he will not find you."

Keiko shivered. It hadn't been a dream. It had been real. Oddly, she could not dredge up any real fear. She scowled. His kiss had drained it all out of her. "Where am I?"

Ryujin held out his hands and a square black lacquered tray lifted from somewhere near the floor. It held a small teapot, a single cup and a plate with small bite-sized pieces of vegetables and fish rolled in sticky rice. "You are in a secret place, very deep in the earth."

"Is this…" She tugged at the silky ropes. "An illusion?"

"Not for you." One of the bites of food rose to her lips. "Eat."

Keiko was starved, breakfast was hours ago, but she didn't trust him. She turned her face away. "Why am I here?"

The bit of food drifted back to the plate. "I brought you here because it is unknown to the Avatars."

She glared at him. "Do you plan to kill me?"

"No." He smiled and gestured, making the teapot rise and pour steaming and fragrant jasmine tea into the cup. "Nor do I plan to drug you. The food and tea are quite safe. You will be released, to do as you will, once I have what I need."

Keiko eyed the tea. She was really thirsty. "What do you want?"

He lifted his palm and the cup rose to her lips. "Drink, you must be thirsty."

Keiko sipped at the tea. It tasted just fine, though it was a bit cool. She drank the cup dry before she knew she was going to.

Ryujin gestured the empty cup back to the tray. "I want your cooperation to destroy Avatar Tsuke."

Keiko froze. That couldn't have been right. "Wait, you want, *what?*"

"In the past year, Tsuke has bound the ghosts of three Avatars into service by ripping souls from their still living bodies."

"Their *still living* bodies...?" Keiko shook her head. "Isn't that murder?"

Ryujin nodded. "He murdered them to make demonic slaves of their spirits." He stared hard into her eyes. "The demon that took your friend, the one you destroyed, was one of them."

Keiko frowned. "He was an Avatar?"

Ryujin nodded. "I was his companion ghost for over thirty years. Tsuke murdered him to gain his spirit."

Keiko stared at Ryujin and finally felt the chill in the room. Her breath steamed out. Ryujin was very, very angry. She shivered. "Then this is revenge?"

He looked down and let the tray float away. "There is more."

Keiko frowned after the tray. "More?" She looked back at him. "More than murder?"

Ryujin floated toward the edge of the room, his back to her. His body shed a soft, blue, misty glow. "Avatar Tsuke has been using his demons to murder middle-placed government officials and then offering the higher-placed officials Avatars as body-guards."

Mother of Mercy... Killing other people, too? "He's doing this for money?"

Ryujin shook his head. "For something far more potent; influence over the laws and regulations being made. He is making demons to gain control of the country."

Keiko frowned. For a *Samurai* like Ryujin, or Ryudo for that matter, only the Emperor had the divine right to rule the country. Anyone else was...heresy. "What about the police...?"

"Your police cannot handle a fully trained sorcerer such as Tsuke. No jail is capable of holding him." He turned to face her. "Also, how do you explain murder by demonic attack, or death through the loss of a soul, to those who do not believe in ghosts?"

He had a really valid point. "Merciful Lady..."

He bared his teeth and the temperature dropped. "There is no mercy in these acts.

Keiko shook her head. "So, why me? Why did Tsuke send a

demon after me?"

Ryujin snorted. "He didn't."

"What do you mean, he didn't?" Keiko tugged at her bindings. "It came to the school! It came to the house! I killed it myself!"

Ryujin sighed, and turned away. "The demon acted on its own. It should not have approached you after the night in the forest. Once we discovered your mark, the demon was ordered to free your friend. We still don't know why it didn't let her go."

But Keiko already knew that answer. *Tika...* "The possession was deliberate."

"Yes. Tsuke planned to offer rescue as leverage to gain your submission to the order."

Keiko ground her teeth. Fear was hard to grasp, but anger was very close at hand. "Conniving bastard."

Ryujin smiled sourly. "Very much so." He floated toward her and his smile disappeared. "Tsuke must be stopped from making any more demons."

Keiko shook her head. "How? I can't do anything."

He reached out and cupped her face. "I need your power." His palms warmed, and pink tinted his lips.

She jerked back from his hands. She didn't want to give him anything, not even that small amount. "You want me to feed you."

He hovered closer, and focused on her lips. "Yes."

Keiko looked away. "You could just bleed me. I can't stop you."

"No." He sighed. "I have drunk your fear. It will not give me what I need."

She smiled bitterly. "Are you asking for my love?"

He caught her face and forced her to look into his fox-fire bright gaze. "If you can't give me your love, give me the love you feel for your Kentoku and Ryudo."

Keiko stared for a whole breath. "That's insane!"

"Is it? Consider this, Tsuke will eventually capture your Kentoku, just as I caught you…"

Keiko shook her head. "His father will never turn him or Ryudo over."

"Do you honestly think that will stop Tsuke?" Ryujin smiled grimly. "Compared to the murders he commits, kidnapping is child's play."

Kidnapping... Keiko shivered. She had been taken while still on the property. Toku spent hours in the office where there was even less protection. It *was* possible.

Ryujin stared hard into her eyes, his mouth tight. "On Toku's capture, your Ryudo will try to rescue him and be captured as well. Ryudo will be bound to the temple to serve as a companion ghost, but if Tsuke cannot gain Toku's fealty to the order, Tsuke will not hesitate to rip out his soul, murdering him to gain his ghost."

Fear was suddenly a strong and viable thing clawing in her chest. "No!" She tried to turn away.

Ryujin held her face captive in his warming palms. "Yes, Keiko. If your Toku will not swear to the order, he will die, and how he dies will make him a demon, a creature of foul evil and a slave to Tsuke's will. Once Toku's spirit is bound, his comatose body will be carried out and left somewhere public for the police to find."

Keiko closed her eyes tight. "No, that can't be right. That's impossible!"

"It is possible. It is how Tsuke has done all three of his last murders."

"No! All of this sounds impossible." Keiko opened her eyes and glared at him. "The demon never mentioned Tsuke. How do I know you're not feeding me a load of bullshit just to get into my pants before you laugh in my face and turn me over to play temple whore to every ghost in your order?"

Ryujin sighed and released her face. "I have proof, but I assure you, it will not please you."

Keiko bared her teeth at him. "Bring me your proof."

Ryujin drifted back and bowed. "As you wish." He dissolved.

Keiko tugged at her bonds. Ryujin was clearly insane. She squinted into the shadows. The room appeared to be plain gray stone blocks and square in shape with no windows, though there seemed to be a doorway to her far right with stairs leading up. She had to get out of this trap.

She tugged and twisted, she kicked and bucked. Her bonds stretched, but once she stopped straining, they merely returned to their original shape.

She kept trying.

And trying…

And failing.

Her heart found a shred of fear. She squashed it under her anger, and started screaming. "You sorry sack of shit, let me go!" He voice echoed in the empty chamber.

There was no answer.

She screamed out every foul expletive she ever heard.

No answer.

Exhausted, and her throat sore, Keiko dropped back into her imprisoning web. It didn't matter how crazy Ryujin was, she wasn't going anywhere. There was no escape. She closed her eyes. "I want to go home."

~ Thirty-Five ~

"Keiko?" The echoing voice came from her right.

Keiko opened her eyes. She knew that voice. "Shihan?" She frowned and turned to look down at the doorway.

The narrow beam of a penlight traced the lower steps, then Shihan in a white sweater and dark gray slacks, stepped down into the room. His white sneakers seemed to glow in the shadows. "Keiko?" He looked up and his brows lifted. "Oh, my..."

Keiko smiled hopefully. "Could you get me down from here?"

Shihan put his hand out to one of the ropes, and his fingers passed right through it as though it wasn't there. He looked up at her. "I'm afraid not."

Keiko's temper flared white hot. "This fucking sucks!" She jerked on the ropes, kicking ands twisting. They vibrated, but that was all. "Piss!" Bleak futility slammed her hard. Her eyes ached with sudden tears. *I will not cry, damn it!* She lifted her chin and blinked at the shadowed ceiling. *I'm tired of crying.*

"Keiko?"

She sighed and looked down at him. "Shihan." Then she frowned. What was he doing here? "How did you find me?"

Shihan walked into the room, passing through the ropes as though he was the ghost. He looked up at her, hanging about an arm-length above his head. "Ryujin said you would not help us without proof."

"Us?" Keiko's heart stuttered in shock. "You're part of this too?"

Shihan pulled the sleeve up on his arm. "Do you recognize this?"

He turned his hand palm up so that she could see the four-armed fanged beast, an *oni*, tattooed on his forearm.

"Yeah." Keiko frowned. "That was on the demon's arm."

"Because your demon was once an Avatar." He pulled his sleeve back down and looked away. "Just as I was an Avatar, once."

"Shihan?" Keiko couldn't have heard that right. "Did you say that you were…an Avatar?"

Shihan took a deep breath and released it. "A demon destroyed my companion while he was still within me. When I recovered, I could still see ghosts, but that was all. All of my talent for magic was gone." He shrugged. "And so, I was released from active service." He rubbed his arm. "The *oni* marks the fact that my soul is bound to the temple. Upon my death, no matter where, or when, or how I die, my spirit will return to the temple that I may serve once again, as a spirit."

Keiko blinked. He was bound to the temple after death? "Can you break it? The binding?"

"No." He looked up at her. "Nor do I wish to."

"What? Why not?"

"It is a very great honor to serve life, even beyond death." He stepped closer to her and looked up. "Avatar Tsuke is an abomination. He does not serve life, he serves himself."

Keiko stared down at him. "Then what Ryujin said… It's true?"

"It is true that Tsuke murders those who would have served beyond death willingly, and with honor; turning them instead into demons that he sends after the living."

Keiko fisted her hands. "If Tsuke is so awful, then why did you ever let him meet me? That doesn't make sense!"

Shihan sighed and looked away. "Tsuke eavesdropped when I spoke to Ryujin of your unique talent to touch and empower the dead. To cover for our blunder, we of course had to insist that we were discussing how best to approach him with the news of your discovery." He looked down and shrugged. "I warned Tsuke that you would not easily accept service to the temple. He turned to look back up at her. "And so he set a trap to encourage you into the sect."

Keiko spat out a sound of complete disgust. "My cooperation in trade for Tika's rescue."

Shihan shook his head. "Your cooperation for Shido's rescue; the demon was supposed to take Shido."

Keiko jerked in shock. "Shido?"

Shihan looked down. "Your friend's possession was an unfortunate accident that should never have happened. Shido should not have brought her."

Keiko's thoughts jumbled in her head. "Wait, you set up *your own student* to be possessed?"

Shihan scowled. "Shido's possession would not have been fatal." He waved a hand in dismissal. "Of course your mark linking you to your house guardian fouled all of Tsuke's plans."

Keiko felt the slow rolling boil of anger, tinged with the sharp edge of betrayal. "Shihan, Tika died because of these…plans."

Shihan frowned. "Tika should not have been possessed for more than an hour. She died because of her own foolishness."

Keiko closed her eyes. He was right, of course. She'd said as much to Shido. But Tika would not have been possessed if someone else hadn't plotted a possession in the first place. A possession designed to trap her into doing what Tsuke wanted.

What they *wanted*…

Yes, Tsuke had set the trap that took Tika, but *this* trap, her kidnapping, was not of Tsuke's doing. She stared down at her teacher and frowned. And what did Shihan, a man who had once possessed magic want, really? He was destined to return to those powers at his death…

What they *wanted*…from the beginning.

Keiko felt the heat of anger boiling in her heart. "This has nothing to do with saving your order or the country. You want me to help Ryujin stop Tsuke because you want to save yourself from becoming a demon. You didn't set Shido up, you set *me* up, from the beginning, to save *your* sorry ass from Tsuke!"

Shihan dropped his head and folded his hands together. "I had thought I was forgotten, that I would pass before Tsuke noticed my existence, but..." He sighed and turned away. "Tsuke found me last spring. I have made myself useful in offering training to his advocates. Tsuke has since been a most accommodating, and close, benefactor."

Keiko stared. "Your students? They're all Avatars?"

Shihan shrugged. "Not all, but more than a few." He looked up at her his hands clasped before him. "Without your help, there is no escape from my fate at Tsuke's hands."

Keiko scowled. "So you admit it. You sacrificed me to save your ass, you selfish bastard."

Shihan turned his head as though slapped, then turned on his heel and walked away, heading for the stairs.

Keiko stared after him. He was abandoning her, just as he had made her abandon Tika. "Shihan, I trusted you. I believed in you." She closed her eyes against the burn of bitter tears. "How could you do this to me?"

Shihan stopped at the foot of the stairway, but he did not look back. "Be aware, Keiko, that should Tsuke take me, I will not be the last casualty that you personally know." He lowered his head and climbed the stairs, disappearing into the darkness.

Keiko closed her eyes against the tears. "Damn you..."

"Keiko..." Ryujin shimmered into being right before her. "I told you my proof would not please you."

Keiko looked away from his handsome and determined face. "I want to go home."

Ryujin floated closer and his hands dropped onto her shoulders, and passed through her robes as though they did not exist. His cool fingers made contact with her skin. "You will, when I have what I need from you." His hands slid down from her shoulders to cup her breasts. His thumbs stroked against her nipples, lightly, gently.

Her nipples tightened in spite of the despair burning in her heart. "Ryujin, please... Don't do this to me."

"The choice to give was never yours to make." His lips brushed against the side of her throat. "There is no one else who can destroy Tsuke but I, and no one who can give me the power to do so but you."

Keiko closed her eyes and turned away. "I will hate you for this."

"I know." His hand slid downward, invisible under clothes but warming against her skin. "Know this also, Tsuke will come for you and he will not stop until he has you, your house guardian, and your mage. I am Tsuke's companion, he is my host. I alone can reach Tsuke's soul to destroy him. I am your only chance of escape from the fate Tsuke has planned for all of you." His palm opened on her belly. "Think of them, instead of yourself."

Keiko stilled. Was she being selfish? Was she denying the only chance of keeping Toku and Ryudo safe? She trembled under his hands. "I can't give you what you want, Ryujin. I don't love you."

"But you love your Kentoku and your Ryudo." He enclosed her in his arms, and pressed his body against hers, a warm and solid weight. The shadows within him reached into her and moved against something sleeping within her. "Give me the love you have for them."

She couldn't feel her clothing, or his, only his skin moving against hers, stirring her to enticing urgency. Her heart pounded and something within her unfolded, responding. Heat awakened under his palm and spilled outward, and into her blood. Anticipation coiled in her core.

"Yes..." His lips moved across her throat, stirring shivers. "Your gift awakens. It is time."

The light winked out and utter blackness wrapped around them like a blanket. The ropes around her arms and legs came to sudden writhing life, becoming fingers that skimmed across her skin, exploring her. A palm settled on her breast, and squeezed gently.

Tongues and fingers bloomed and traced across her skin. The hand on her breast became a mouth with a flicking tongue. Hands slid down her back and cupped her butt, pressing his belly to hers. A very human erection rubbed against her.

And her body responded, tightening with warm, wet interest.

Ryujin sighed in her ear. "Love them, Keiko. Love them with everything in you." Fingers delved between her thighs, encouraging her thighs to part. Wet, velvety tongues explored her intimate folds. Another finger explored the crease of her butt and became a tongue that swept with indecent interest across the tight rose of her anus. "I need all the love you are capable of giving."

A thousand hands, fingers and tongues swept across her skin, stroking her, tasting her, squeezing and nipping at her flesh.

Heat flushed her body. She sucked in a breath to hold back the growing excitement coiling within her, but it was a losing battle against his determined seduction. She could feel the cream of her arousal slicking her thighs.

The broad head of his cock slid downward and nudged against the slick entrance of her body. A mouth bit down on her swollen nipple.

Fire lanced down into her core. She cried out and writhed, instinctively pressing against the cock nudging at her. The cock-head slid inward, spreading her damp and welcoming flesh.

"Yes..." His arms tightened around her, and he thrust, burying himself within, striking something within that curled her toes in sinful delight.

Keiko moaned. He was in her body, and her body was perfectly happy to have him there, despite the ache in her heart.

He pulled back and thrust, then again, and again...

Her arms were freed and she grabbed onto his shoulders, her fingers digging in to sweat-slick warm flesh. She couldn't stop herself from rocking against him, from wanting and reaching for the climax he was stirring.

The tongue at her anus became a wicked and slippery finger that twisted its way into her ass. She gasped and writhed, but the finger only delved deeper, then circled, and circled within her, stirring shivers of fiendish pleasure.

Ryujin moaned against her throat. "Forgive me, but I need all of you."

The finger in her ass lengthened and thickened with each of his strokes, becoming a slick, hard length, broadening and filling her, until it matched the thrusting shaft in her core.

She gasped with the fullness stretching her to the edge of discomfort.

The brutally snug and slick length in her ass withdrew partway, and thrust in opposition to the shaft in her core. A white-hot bolt of brutal pleasure fired up her spine.

She could not stop her body from bucking, and seeking more.

The two shafts thrust and withdrew, advancing and retreating. The tormenting ache of the shaft debauching her ass merged with the delicious bolts of erotic fire from the thrusting shaft within her core, creating a fierce mix of intense and cruel pleasure. Thrust, and withdrawal, thrust, and withdrawal, thrust...

The pressure in her core built and tightened fiercely. Small helpless sounds of need boiled past her lips. She was going to cum.

Ryujin sighed in her ear. "At last." A finger slid among the intimate folds of her flesh where their bodies joined. The finger touched her clit very lightly.

Keiko's core clenched violently. She tried to hold back. She didn't want to cum for him.

Something powerful and compelling trembled in the air.

"Cum for me." His lips brushed her cheek. "Cum for us all." The finger pressed against her clit.

Keiko's entire body went rigid. She couldn't stop the tide from rising. Her fingers dug into his shoulders, her toes curled, pulling at the ropes that held her, and her spine arched. Her breath stilled and her heart tried to stop. "No..."

"Yes!" Ryujin thrust, hard.

Riding the force of his stroke, something exhilarating, explosive and dynamic slammed into her core. It impacted within her and erupted. Release unfolded in a blistering rush of carnal ferociousness that surged in a wash of horrifically vicious pleasure. She screamed out in denial of her depraved delight.

Ryujin howled with her.

Blue-white lightning erupted from her skin and danced all along her body, lighting the writhing, moving darkness. Tiny bolts of lightning arced and lashed across Ryujin above her, illuminating his expression of tormented rapture.

A deafening crash of thunder shook the stone room and blue-tinted lightning flashed all the way around them, illuminating the gigantic blue web that held her suspended and entwined. The web ignited into a white-hot incandescence that was too bright too look at.

She shrieked. Ryudo's image, alone in the garden under the tree, flashed like summer lightning and burned across her inner eye. She reached for him, across the darkness. *Ryudo!*

Ryudo seemed to turn, his eyes opened wide and he reached for her. *Keiko!*

Ryujin's mouth covered hers, his tongue plunging in to steal her screams, her breath, the lightning from her skin, and the dream shattered within her.

The web of light winked out, plunging them into utter darkness. The crisp evergreen scent of cypress, and electrical ozone sizzled in the air.

Keiko moaned in exhaustion, and tears burned down her cheeks. She'd felt him, Ryudo. She was sure of it. Which meant he'd felt her, too—and her betrayal with Ryujin.

Ryujin hissed. "Woman, what have you done?"

Keiko scowled in the dark. "What now?"

A small light shimmered into being above her, showing Ryujin, his cheeks newly flushed with color, his lips a deep red and his robes a deep cobalt blue. He was definitely looking better.

He grabbed a handful of her hair and tugged her head forward and to the side. His finger brushed across the back of her neck. "Blood and fire, a second mark!"

Keiko winced in his hold. "Ow, shit! What are you talking about?"

Ryujin released her hair and drifted back, floating before her. His brows dropped low over his fix-fire lit eyes. "The tattoo on the back of your neck was made with your Ryudo's blood. I can feel it."

Keiko frowned. "Yeah, so? He did it to seal the demon's bite."

"It is also a second mark, and it carries traces of your Kentoku's power." He spread his arms wide, his brilliant blue robes floating around him. "We must return you immediately, before your Ryudo and Kentoku do something foolish."

The bindings around her unraveled from her arms and legs, until she could sit upright, supported but free. She rubbed at her wrists. "Foolish, like what?"

"Like follow the release of your power here—and fall into one of the traps Tsuke has laying in wait for them."

Ryujin caught Keiko around the waist and the supporting web dissolved into mist.

"Whoa, hey!" Keiko felt the net go and grabbed for his neck.

"Hold on." Ryujin descended toward the floor, the golden globe of light following at Keiko's shoulder. He twisted in mid-air and sped toward the stairs with Keiko tight in his arms. They soared up the long darkened stairwell in a blinding rush, and emerged from the sub-basement of a half-destroyed factory building.

Keiko took a quick glance around and discovered that they were on the industrial edge of town, on the abandoned side of the railroad tracks. Black storm clouds swirled angrily overhead.

Shihan's copper Nissan was parked just outside by a pile of rubble. The karate instructor stood by his open car door, his cell phone pressed to his ear. He snapped the phone closed and turned to face them, his mouth tight. "They have them."

Ryujin spat out a sound of disgust and set Keiko on her feet. "Impatient fools!"

Keiko tugged at her short *kimono* top and full *hakima* pants, straightening them. "What's going on?"

Ryujin lifted his chin at Shihan and pushed Keiko toward the Nissan. "You will take us there."

"Of course." Shihan climbed into the Nissan, leaned over and opened the front passenger door.

Keiko climbed up into the Nissan. "You're taking me back now?"

Ryujin shoved her over, forcing Keiko to share the big bucket seat. "No."

Keiko pulled her pants up to give Shihan access to the gearshift. "Wait a minute, what do you mean, no?"

Shihan started the SUV and slammed it into reverse.

Ryujin set his hand on the dashboard and wrapped his other arm around Keiko, pulling her tight to him. "We are going to the Avatars."

Shihan rammed the SUV into first gear, and then immediately into second, bumping from the torn parking lot and screaming out onto the service road. Gravel spat from under the wailing tires.

Keiko grabbed onto Ryujin's arm. "What? But you said you were going to take me back…?"

Ryujin scowled down at her. "Your Kentoku and Ryudo did a very foolish thing. They went after Tsuke to rescue you. They've been taken. They are going to need your help to escape."

Keiko turned in her seat and scowled at Shihan. "Can't this thing go any faster?"

Shihan smiled grimly and changed gears. "Watch me."

~ Thirty-Six ~

Shihan's Nissan roared onto the parkway along the dizzying cliff heights that skirted the ocean. He lunged through the early evening traffic...

Keiko watched the last of the sun disappear into the ocean. Storm clouds obliterated the emerging stars.

Shihan spun the wheel and turned the big Nissan onto a steep upward off ramp marked with a small sign announcing the Whispering Forest, and the Crimson Pavilion guesthouse. The road narrowed, and a towering rattan forest closed in on them. Shihan did not slow down. The tires threw gravel and bamboo leaves slashed at the windows.

Shihan turned the Nissan and roared up a narrow winding road. They passed under a bright red *torii* gate, into the town proper. The Nissan's headlights washed across elderly post and plaster buildings. He turned to the right and took a small gravel and dirt road that skirted the very edge of town. He stepped on the gas. The Nissan rocked and swayed on what was clearly a narrow farm road.

Keiko held onto Ryujin for dear life, but she was not about to tell Shihan to slow down.

The road curved sharply upward, and the town gave way to small homes, and then to forest. Shihan turned again, and bumped off the road between a pair of trees, his tires spitting gravel. The Nissan climbed to the top of a grassy hill, then scooted downward on the nearly invisible road. At the tall plain wood *torii* gate on the edge of the forest of enormous and elderly trees, Shihan stopped the truck.

He sighed and turned to them. "I can go no further without alerting them."

Keiko stared out the dashboard window. "We're too far away, we'll never make it."

"We will." Ryujin opened the door and stepped out. "Come."

Keiko stepped out of the car and closed the door. "It's going to take all night to walk there."

Ryujin smiled. "Which is why we will not be walking." He threw his hands wide and was engulfed in a surge of power that blazed blindingly bright.

Keiko flinched back and threw her arm up to shield her eyes.

Ryujin's power snaked out and coalesced into a long, sinuous shape. The light died down to a soft glow, revealing the shimmering scaled and ridged form of a pale blue and slender dragon, as tall as a horse, and as long as six of Shihan's Nissans. The fanged head was crowned with a pair of split antlers, and enormous wings sprouted from the shoulders to arch overhead.

Keiko stared. "Wow... I forgot you could do that."

The dragon lowered its huge, fanged head. Brilliant blue eyes focused on Keiko. "Sit behind my head and take hold of my horns."

Keiko walked over and grasped the proffered horn. She lifted her leg and stretched to mount. He was warm under her, the scales surprisingly soft. She grasped his other horn and locked her legs around the dragon's throat.

The dragon arched its neck and lifted his head.

Dizzied by the sudden change in height, Keiko sucked in a breath and looked down at Shihan. "Lady of Mercy..."

The dragon turned to look down on Shihan. "Follow us, slowly."

Shihan nodded sharply, his eyes wide. "Slowly, yes." He clawed for his car door, staring at the dragon. "Very slowly. Very, very slowly."

The dragon began walking forward, the body snaking sharply, but his head rocked only slightly. Abruptly, he leaped forward in long, bounding jumps.

Keiko hunched down and hung on with every ounce of strength she had.

The dragon made a strong upward leap. His wings snapped out and he soared into the evening sky.

Keiko panicked and yelled in spite of herself.

The dragon chuckled, vibrating under her. "Afraid?"

Keiko squinted against the wind, watching the forest passing below them. "Yes, damn it!"

The dragon's flight smoothed into gentle ups and downs, following the tide of warm air rising from the forest and the rhythm of his wing-beats. Keiko took a deep breath and her terror eased down to merely a slight case of panic.

The forest passed blindingly fast. Abruptly, a clearing appeared below them and Keiko realized that she was seeing the lights of the guesthouse blazing in the darkness below.

The dragon landed on the grass at the forest's edge and dropped his head with a snap.

Keiko lost her grip and tumbled from his neck. She yelped in fright, then without even thinking, she rolled back onto her feet. Pissed and scared at the same time, she turned on the dragon. "Hey! How about a warning when you stop?"

The dragon thinned out into Ryujin standing before her. He threw out a hand. "Forgive me." A bolt of light lashed out from his hand and stabbed her in the heart.

Keiko's breath whooshed out of her, and her sight thinned down to a narrow black tunnel. She collapsed to her knees. "What...?"

"They will never accept that you came willingly." Ryujin knelt over her and waved his hand across her eyes. "Sleep. Now."

Sleep crushed her under.

Keiko awakened on her knees, held up against a warm body by a hand wrapped around her hair. Her hands were tied behind her. The bright blue robes she could see from the corner of her eye and the scent of cypress gave away that it was Ryujin's completely tense kneeling body that held her. She could just make out the sheathed long and short swords thrust through his sash.

They were in the half-lit main room of the guesthouse.

Ryujin whispered very softly against her cheek. "Do not make any sudden moves. I have a knife to your throat."

Keiko froze. *A knife?* She spotted Toku bound, arms wide, between two house supports. His clothes had been torn, his hair mussed, and a bruise marked on cheek. A hulking solid black and lion-fanged smoking demon held a glowing black sword to Toku's belly. Ryudo, in his jeans and black muscle-shirt, stood stiffly within a glowing and sickly yellow and puke orange counter-rotating double circle. The colors mixed badly with the tattoos on his arms. They both stared at Keiko, eyes wide and their mouths white with tension.

Keiko stared at the circle around Ryudo. She swallowed and pitched her voice to a soft whisper. "What are they doing to Ryudo?"

Ryujin breathed in her ear. "It is merely a cage. The living may not touch the dead, and the dead may not touch magic made by the living."

Keiko shifted her weight slightly and discovered that her hands were only loosely bound. She could escape this hold, but then what? What could she do?

Tsuke, neat and tidy in his midnight blue suit, stepped in front of Toku. He had the dull edge of a naked long sword, a *katana,* resting casually on his shoulder. He looked toward Keiko. "I told you Ryujin would find her, and bring her." He faced Toku. "Give me your oath and all of you may go home."

Toku's lip curled. "To await your summons?"

"Of course." Tsuke turned to look at Keiko then Ryudo. "I have much to accomplish and you three will be quite useful to my plans."

Ryujin looked down at her and then looked directly at Ryudo.

Keiko blinked and followed his gaze to Ryudo, trapped in a cage of living magic. *The living may not touch the dead, and the dead may not touch magic made by the living...* But she was a bridge between life and death. She could free Ryudo.

She eased the bindings from her hands and slowly moved one hand into position under Ryujin's upraised thigh for throwing leverage.

Ryujin watched her, and loosened his hold on her hair.

Tsuke lowered his sword from his shoulder. "Kentoku, have you decided?"

Keiko twisted away from the knife at her throat while tugging Ryujin's thigh with her, tossing him backwards and sprawling onto the floor. She grabbed for the hilt of his short sword and the *wakasashi* slid free of its scabbard. She lunged onto her feet and bolted to Ryudo's glowing prison. All she had to do was cross the magical line...

The demon guarding Toku came for her, claws outstretched and black fangs bared. She ducked under its slashing claws, turned and slashed Ryujin's ghostly blade across its stomach.

The ghost released a high-pitched scream and divided neatly in half, like a sheet of paper.

Keiko ducked away from the dissolving demon and dove into the circle of magic grabbing Ryudo around the waist with her free arm. The spell exploded around them, throwing Keiko to the floor with Ryudo sprawled on top of her.

Ryudo shouted down at her. "Why in hell did you do that? That spell could have killed you!"

She grabbed the collar of his robes and dragged his mouth down to hers for a fast, but ferocious kiss. She let him go and shouted into his dumbfounded face. "Because I love you, you idiot!"

"I love you too." Ryudo grinned and exploded in a wash of golden light, opening wings and stretching upward into the shape of a huge lion dog with a thick mane and wings made of leaping flames.

A massive silver dragon filled the room and faced the flaming winged dog. Roars and screams filled the suddenly crowded room.

Keiko bolted behind them along the cedar wall and came up behind Toku.

He turned to her, his eyes wide. "What are you doing?"

"Trying to free you, you idiot!" She slashed her ghostly blade at the rope binding him between the pillars. The blade passed right through as though it wasn't there. She looked at him. "I can't cut them!"

"The ropes are spell-charged." Toku tugged at his wrists. "I could break the spell, but they drained my power."

He needed *power...* She grabbed him around the neck and kissed him, pouring all the love she had in her heart for him and Ryudo straight into his mouth. A spark of energy leapt from her tongue to his, forcing them apart.

Toku gasped. "Ow, shit! What did you do?" He frowned and the ropes dissolved. "Holy shit, it worked!"

Keiko smiled. "Of course it did. I love you."

He grinned. "I love you too." He grabbed her hand. "Let's get out of here!" He towed her across the room, dodging past the dragon and the firedog, heading for the door.

Tsuke turned to see them. "No!" He threw out a hand and a ball of blazing red energy zig-zagged for them.

Toku turned and threw a bolt of green lightning, diverting the path of Tsuke's spell. Both spells crashed into the front door. The door exploded outward.

Toku and Keiko threw up their arms and ran through the falling debris, and kept running across the lawn under the stars. Light exploded behind them. They turned to look back.

The silver dragon and the howling fire-dog leaped up through the roof without disturbing a tile, their wings shedding brilliant light, their writhing battle turning the night to day.

Tsuke bolted out the door and ran screaming for Keiko and Toku, his sword upraised.

Toku threw up his hands and released a blazing green bolt of power.

Tsuke batted Toku's bolt away with his sword, then raised his blade and released a bolt of fire from the tip.

Toku shouted, threw up a glowing, bright blue-white sphere around himself and Keiko. The force of Tsuke's bolt hit the sphere and shoved them back, making deep drag furrows in the grass.

Tsuke slammed out another fiery bolt.

Toku kept his hands up. The shielding orb was driven back again, vibrating and screaming. Toku winced. "Shit! He's too fucking strong!"

The roaring dragon came blazing out of the sky with the baying fire-dog right behind him.

Tsuke shouted in triumph.

The firedog wheeled in the air, snapping at the dragon's wing and ripping it.

Keiko threw out her hand. "Ryudo, stop! Don't!"

Ryudo hesitated, stopping in midair.

The dragon flew over Toku and Keiko. "My sword!"

Keiko tossed Ryujin's shining *wakasashi* upward.

The dragon turned sharply, catching it in his teeth, then turned again and headed for Tsuke.

Tsuke stared up at the dragon barreling straight for him. "Ryujin! What...?" He shot a bolt of power at him. "Betrayer!"

The dragon opened its mouth and swallowed the power whole, then dove straight into Tsuke's chest, and came roaring out the other side—dragging Tsuke's transparent and screaming soul with him.

Tsuke's body dropped to its knees, then slowly, slowly fell to the side.

Ryujin vanished into the night sky and silence descended.

Keiko took a deep breath. It was over.

Toku's blue shield dissolved.

Ryudo dropped from the sky and became a man in ragged black jeans and blowing hair. He ran to Keiko and Toku. The three embraced, crushing Keiko between them.

Keiko shoved at them. "Guys! I'm being squashed here!"

Both men pulled back and began shouting furiously.

Toku jabbed a finger toward her. "Why did you leave the house?

Ryudo threw out his arms. "The barriers stopped at the house walls!"

Keiko threw up her hands. "I didn't know the barrier stopped at the walls!"

"You could have gotten killed!"

"Have you no concern for your own safety!"

"We didn't know where you were!"

"How dare you make us worry like that?"

"You deserve a severe beating!"

"What?" Keiko gasped in shock. "A beating?"

Toku crossed his arms. "At the very least!"

Keiko bared her teeth. "I'd like to see you try it!"

Ryudo smiled grimly. "There's two of us and one of you."

Keiko balled her fists. "Fine! I'll kick both your asses!"

Behind them a copper Nissan drove out of the trees. The horn honked. Shihan stuck his head out of the car window. "Anyone need a ride?"

Shihan eased his Nissan out of the Whispering Forest with Keiko in the backseat sandwiched between both of her men. All three of them had their arms crossed and scowls on their faces.

Shihan eyed them warily from the rearview mirror. He jerked the wheel to the side and the Nissan rocked hard.

Keiko was thrown hard to her left, into Toku's lap.

"Whoa!" Toku caught her by the arms. "I got you." He pushed her upright.

Keiko stared up into his face and her fingers clenched in his torn shirt. She'd almost lost him. She'd almost lost them both. Her heart stuttered in her chest, and the pain made her gasp and her eyes ache.

His brows lifted. "You okay?"

Keiko nodded. She couldn't speak past the sudden lump in her throat. She pushed back upright and locked her hands in her lap.

Toku looked past Keiko, over at Ryudo, frowning.

Ryudo leaned close against her right shoulder and set his hand on her knee. "Keiko?"

She refused to look at him. She loved him, and she'd let Ryujin... Her breath stopped. She lifted her knee out from under his hand, and crossed her legs. She wanted to touch him, but she was afraid to. She didn't have the right to anymore. "I...I'm sorry." Her voice came out in a breathless whisper. A tear streaked down her cheek.

"Keiko!" He leaned up, grabbing the back of the seat before him to look in her eyes. "What is this?"

Keiko dropped her chin, letting her hair screen her face, and her burning tears.

Ryudo looked up at Toku, then spat out a sound of disgust. He caught her chin in his hand and forced her to look at him. "Keiko, what is this? Tell me, now."

Keiko tried to pull her chin away, but he wouldn't let her go. She curled her hands into her belly and closed her eyes. "I let Ryujin..." She couldn't even say it. "I'm sorry."

"Keiko." Ryudo's palms cupped her face, his thumbs rubbing away her tears. "I doubt you let Ryujin do, or have, anything without a fight."

She opened her eyes and looked up at his handsome face. "I couldn't stop him."

Ryudo sighed. "He is a very powerful spirit. Of course you couldn't stop him." He looked down and set his hand over hers. "Any more than you were able to stop me."

Toku leaned forward and frowned at Ryudo. "Ryujin? What did he do?"

Ryudo sighed. "He fed from her, and she's attempting to take the blame for it."

Toku shook his head. "But that's stupid! Ryujin is almost as strong as you are."

Ryudo sighed. "Actually, he is far stronger. He's older than I, by at least a century."

Keiko looked at Ryudo and then over at Toku. "You don't hate me for…giving in?"

Ryudo snorted. "Of course not."

"Hate you?" Toku scowled and grabbed her other hand, squeezing it. "For something you couldn't control? That's stupid."

"Keiko." Ryudo leaned close. "We can not hate you, we love you." He pressed a kiss to her brow.

Toku pressed a kiss to her other brow, and smiled. "Nice try, but you are not getting out of this marriage that easily."

Keiko chuckled through her tears. "Good."

Toku looked up at Ryudo. "Oh, and by the way, I told Mother about taking over your suite." He grinned.

Ryudo groaned. "Oh, heaven forbid…" He slapped his free hand over his eyes. "That woman will have my rooms redecorated overnight!"

Keiko looked up and noticed Shihan's reflection in the rear-view mirror. He was smiling, just a little sadly.

Book Five

~ Petals, Leaves & Wind ~

~ Thirty-Seven ~

Shihan stopped his copper Nissan at the stone and ironwork gate that marked the entrance drive to Toku's sweeping and ancestral mansion.

Keiko climbed out on Ryudo's side, nearly stumbling to the pavement. More than a little tired and achy, she was seriously looking forward to a long shower and a soak.

Shihan stuck his head out of the driver's window. "Keiko?"

She looked up at him. "Yes?" Toku and Ryudo came up beside her, silent and clearly waiting.

Shihan's face seemed lined and careworn, all his youthful cheer drained away. He dodged her direct gaze. "Please, can you forgive me?"

Keiko stared at her teacher, the man that had taught her to defeat ghosts. He had betrayed her and Shido, and gotten Tika killed in the process. But he was also just an ordinary old man trapped between powers no ordinary human would normally face, with the threat of a horrific fate hanging over his head.

She would not have made the choices he'd made. She would not have even considered sacrificing someone else to save herself.

But to save Toku or Ryudo? She looked up at he starkly beautiful faces of her men. What would she have done to save them?

Anything. She sighed and wiped her hand down her face. "I understand what you did, and why you did it, and in the long run, it was probably the right thing to do. Tsuke was a monster, but…" She looked at him. "How can I ever trust you again?"

Shihan shoulders drooped. "I understand."

Ryudo lifted his brow. "There is always penance?"

Keiko looked up at him. "Penance?"

"It is a Christian doctrine." Ryudo smiled. "Your Shihan can atone for his sins, by donating his services."

Keiko frowned up at him. "In what way?"

Ryudo lifted his chin toward Shihan. "You still need to finish your fight training, though I will expect it to continue under my roof where you can be watched over."

Shihan sat up and nodded. "I would be most honored to do this...penance."

Toku nodded at Ryudo. "That's a great idea." He turned and smiled at Shihan. "How does Tuesday suit you? That's when Keiko's other tutor arrives. We can set up a schedule then."

Shihan smiled. "Tuesday will suit me just fine."

"Tutor?" Keiko's mouth fell open. "Wait just a minute! Now that all this is over, I can go back to school...!"

Ryudo dropped a hand on her shoulder. "We will see."

Keiko turned to glare at him. "Look here, you big bully..."

"Keiko." Ryudo dropped both his hands on her shoulders and pushed slightly, encouraging her to step back. "It would be best if you remained under guard for a while just yet."

Toku waved at Shihan. "See you Tuesday! Come for lunch!"

Shihan waved back. "I will! Thank you!" The Nissan pulled away, and loud rock and roll erupted from the SUV's open windows.

Toku chuckled and shook his head. He trotted up to Ryudo and Keiko. "Okay, that's done, so what is Keiko fussing about now?"

Ryudo continued to push Keiko backwards up the drive. "She is protesting remaining under our protection, again."

Toku shook his head. "It's not safe for you to go off the property alone, Keiko."

Keiko turned toward the house and folded her arms, marching stiffly between them. "I'm not helpless, damn it."

Toku's brows dropped low and his jaw tightened. "I'm not saying you're helpless, I just don't want to take any chances that you might run up against something you can't handle. I don't want a repeat of what happened today!"

Keiko threw out her hands in exasperation. "I didn't go off the property on purpose! I was kidnapped! Remember?"

Toku scowled. "Which is why you're not going off the property without at least one of us with you. On purpose or by accident, I don't want anything happening to you."

Ryudo patted her shoulder. "In fact, should you leave the house without one of us to escort you, you will be punished."

"What?" Keiko jerked to a stop. "Punished for leaving the house?" She turned to look at Ryudo. "Are you serious?" She looked over at Toku.

Toku crossed his arms. "Don't look at me. I'm with Ryudo on this one."

Keiko turned back toward the house in a huff. "That is so unfair!"

Ryudo smiled at Toku. "Life tends to be a bit unfair."

They walked up the stairs and into the house, stepping straight into mild pandemonium.

Four maids in formal *kimonos* and antique hairstyles converged on Keiko en masse, snatching her from Toku's hands the moment she pulled her ruined sandals from her feet. "Miss! Miss! You must change at once! At once!"

A pair of young men dressed in deep gray service *kimonos* latched onto Toku and started tugging on him as well. "Master Toku, this way! This way!"

"Hey!" Toku was trotted down the hall after Keiko and her maids. "What's going on?"

Keiko turned back to look at him in bewilderment. "I have no idea!"

They parted company at a cross hallway, each being ushered away at a trot.

Keiko was hustled into her rooms, stripped and thrust into the shower for the fastest scrubbing of her life. She shut off the water and was practically attacked with towels and the hairdryer, then rushed into the main room where she was posed, arms out and dressed in layer after layer of formal silks; deep red, then overlong white, then sheer pink... At the same time, a pair of maids yanked her hair into submission and piled it on the top of her head with heavy wooden pins to keep the hair on top where it belonged.

The broad red sash, her *obi,* was yanked tight and knotted into a massive butterfly bow over a snowy pink and white peach blossom embroidered formal *kimono.* Keiko gasped for breath. "Ladies! Ladies! What's going on?"

They stopped and looked at each other. "You mother is here, with your esteemed grandfather."

Keiko choked. "My mother?" Then the rest of the statement hit her. She blinked rapidly. "Wait a minute, did you say my *grandfather?*" She'd never met her grandfather. She hadn't known she'd had one. *What the hell...?*

One of the maids smiled and bobbed. "They're here with your marriage contract."

Keiko nearly fell over. "My what?"

Holding up her flowing robes with both hands, Keiko was trotted through several back halls, and stopped at a narrow blank door. They slid the door open and pushed Keiko through.

Not quite tripping on her overlong robes, Keiko stepped into a long room with windows all down the left wall showing a night-dark formal garden glowing with lanterns. The rest of the long room was lined with wall screens of black silk painted with graceful gold and silver bamboo stalks.

A large yet perfectly square low table of highly polished cherry graced the very center of the room. Toku's father and mother knelt on large pillows with their backs to the windows. Across from them, Keiko spotted her mom, in a plain gray suit. Next to her was an older gentleman with long white hair spilling over the shoulders of his blue robes. He had two tasseled ropes of red prayer beads around his neck. He looked like a monk, except that he hadn't been shaved bald. The far side of the table was unoccupied.

Directly in front of Keiko on this side of the table sat Toku with an unoccupied cushion on his immediate right.

Toku's mother smiled and set down her tiny blue teacup. "There you are, dear."

Everyone turned to Keiko, each holding a small porcelain teacup of deep rich blue.

Keiko froze, completely unsure of what she should do. If they had already been served tea, she was obviously very late for something.

Toku turned, spotted her and smiled tightly. He patted the cushion beside him.

Keiko stepped deeper into the room and dropped down onto the pillow. "My apologies for being late."

Toku took her hand and grasped it tightly. He leaned a little close and lifted his teacup to cover his whisper. "Watch out for the old man, your grandfather. He's a fierce old geezer." He lifted a brow at her. "Now I know where you get it from."

Keiko squeezed his hand back and gave him a slight smile.

A young man walked in from a side door, wearing blue robes very similar to Keiko's supposed grandfather. He knelt on the unoccupied side of the table, and unrolled a very formal looking document.

Keiko leaned close to Toku. "Who's that?"

Toku smiled slightly. "Your grandfather's lawyer. You're supposed to be some kind of heiress."

Keiko blinked at him. "I am?"

Another young man walked in from the same side door wearing a pitch-black three-piece suit. He knelt beside her grandfather's lawyer and unrolled a document of his own. He smiled tightly at Grandfather's lawyer.

Toku leaned close. "And that's my father's lawyer."

A maid came in with a tray holding a large steaming teapot of bright green. She placed a cup before the two lawyers, poured them tea, then walked around the table refilling teacups. Keiko was provided with a cup and tea, but she was too nervous to touch it.

The two lawyers began to drone at each other in excruciatingly formal phrasing. Occasionally one would stop and ask the other an incomprehensible question. An answer would be delivered, then the back and forth droning would begin again.

Suddenly Grandfather's lawyer stopped to look at Grandfather. "There is only one clause unfulfilled."

Grandfather lifted his chin in clear inquiry.

The lawyer folded his hands in his lap. "Proof of heritage."

Keiko's mother scowled. "There is no question of my daughter's legitimacy!"

Grandfather turned to her and patted her hand. "Of course not, there were witnesses to her birth, but we are speaking of the family legacy."

Keiko frowned. Legacy? What legacy?

Grandfather leaned forward to smile at Keiko. "Would you be so kind as to show us the proof of your gift?"

Her *gift?* Keiko went cold. *Her curse.* She had proof all right, all down her back. She lifted her teacup and whispered behind it. "I am not taking my clothes off." The hair lifted on the back of her neck and awareness shimmered at the back of her skull.

Ryudo misted into existence behind her wreathed in the perfume of chrysanthemums, his white robes floating around him. "No, you most certainly are not removing your clothing." He set his hand on her shoulder, and Toku's. Power rippled across from Toku's hand to hers, then up her back into Ryudo's hand. Electricity sparked between all three of them.

Keiko shivered hard.

The room's lights flickered. Beyond the windows, a sudden wind rushed through the trees, blowing leaves against the glass. Lightning cracked and thunder rattled the windows.

Ryudo's hand weighed heavily on Keiko's shoulder and his robes settled, weighted by gravity. He took a deep breath, and looked up the table. "Am I proof enough?"

Toku's father's lawyer gasped.

Toku's mother's eyes rolled up in her head and she fell, unconscious, into Toku's father's lap.

Keiko's mother dropped her teacup. The fragile cup didn't break, but tea spilled across the table.

Grandfather laughed and clapped his hands.

Grandfather's lawyer made a notation on the unrolled document. "Clause fulfilled."

Toku's father shook his head, and smiled crookedly while holding his unconscious wife close. "I did tell her." He shrugged. "I guess she didn't believe me."

Keiko walked through the shadowed hallways escorted by Toku and Ryudo. She was more than a little stunned. "I'm a priestess?"

Toku looped her arm over his. "That's what your grandfather said. He also mentioned something about ancestral property."

Ryudo looped her other arm over his arm. "It also appears that you will be gaining yet another tutor, this one provided by your grandfather."

Keiko rolled her eyes. "Great…"

Toku sighed. "A shame about your mother."

Keiko looked at the floor. "She didn't have my…talent, so she couldn't deal with living with a family who did. She thought they were crazy, and delusional." She sighed. "So, she left."

Ryudo shook his head. "And then you manifested the family legacy, and she still refused to believe, allowing you to grow up unprotected."

Toku grinned and patted her hand. "But now you have us!"

Keiko smiled. "Yes, I do." She frowned. "I wonder why she still won't talk about my father?"

Ryudo patted her hand. "I'm sure she will someday."

Toku snorted. "Are you kidding? Mother will get it out of her, and in time for the wedding, just you wait and see."

Keiko cringed. "That's what I'm afraid of." They turned a corner and she frowned at the hallway. It looked eerily familiar. "Where are we going?"

Toku smiled. "Ryudo's apartments. Mother told me that they're ready."

"I saw." Ryudo smiled sourly. "At least she tried to make them to the specifications I gave you."

"Difficult to do with all my electronics." Toku shook his head.

Ryudo lifted his brow. "Which is why they have a room of their own."

They stopped at a magnificent pair of carved doors. Keiko looked up at the swirling clouds and flowers. A pair of carved lion-dogs snarled at the top of the doors. "Wow, I don't remember this at all."

"Of course not. You have never been here." Ryudo stepped forward and pushed open the doors. "Enter, and be welcome to your personal abode." He stepped to the side.

Keiko stepped into an enormous room, obviously meant to be some kind of audience chamber. It was completely without furniture, covered in *tatami* mats and lined with wall screens of pale yellow painted with summer flowers. The ceiling was draped with orange and red silk. A set of double doors stood open on the left. There were another set of doors on the right, though closed.

Toku stepped in and looked around. "Mother says she's still looking for some of the other things you wanted." He lifted a brow at Ryudo. "She says she has to get the..." He glanced at Keiko. "Specialty stuff from China."

Ryudo nodded and walked across the room toward the open double doors. "Of course, that was where I gained the originals."

Keiko looked up at him. "Get what from China?"

Ryudo smiled and pushed her toward the open double doors. "Your wedding gift."

Keiko grinned. "A wedding gift? All the way from China?"

Ryudo nodded. "And I will ask you not to disturb the workers while it is being prepared."

Keiko's brows lifted. "Workers?"

Toku frowned at Ryudo. "Are you sure you want...?"

Ryudo reached out to press his fingers over Toku's lips. "More than you could possibly imagine."

The double doors opened onto a huge cedar-walled bedroom commanded by an enormous Victorian four-poster bed of carved teak. The mattress was three full body-lengths wide, and two full body-lengths long, spread with gold silk, and heaped with tasseled cream damask pillows. It pretty much took up the entire room. Keiko stared at it. "This bed is big enough for an orgy."

Ryudo chuckled. "Yes, actually. It belonged to a friend of mine who was quite fond of multiple and simultaneous bed partners."

Keiko raised a brow at Ryudo. "Did you ever...participate?"

Ryudo grinned. "How do you think I obtained it?"

Keiko covered her smile with her hands. "Oh, you naughty boy."

Ryudo lifted his chin and gave her a superior smile. "You have no idea."

The windows all along the far right wall opened onto an enclosed garden gone completely wild. Toku peered through the glass. "I see the housemaids were able to get the window glass clean, but the gardeners are going to have quite a time returning that garden back to its proper state. They didn't even know it existed."

Ryudo smiled. "Of course not. No one has seen any of these rooms in over a century."

Toku grinned. "Mother was certainly surprised."

Ryudo set his hands on Keiko's shoulders. "Toku, shall we open our gift?"

Toku focused on Keiko and rubbed his palms together. "That sounds like a great idea."

Keiko looked from one to the other. "What gift?"

Ryudo leaned down, his lips brushing against her cheek. He tugged at the ornate bow on her back. "Why, you, of course." The bow unraveled and her heavy *obi* slithered from around her waist to the polished floor.

~ Thirty-Eight ~

Two pairs of hands delved into Keiko's robes and two sets of lips followed in their wake. Ties were pulled and undone, ribbons unknotted. Silk whispered to the floor, the heavy pink and white followed by the sheer pink, then the sweeping snow white and finally the deep crimson.

Palms and fingers followed the path of the silk down her limbs. Lips followed the path of fingers, across her shoulders, and down her body.

Toku knelt to rub his cheek across her belly and tug her panties down while Ryudo stood behind her to pull the pins from her hair, setting it free to fall down her back.

Keiko sighed and shivered under their fingers.

Ryudo pressed his lips to her brow, then stepped to the side and moved around to Toku.

Toku stood, and Ryudo pulled at Toku's sash.

Toku grabbed his wrists. "Ryudo?"

Ryudo stared down into his eyes. "Are we not all lovers, all three of us?"

Toku swallowed. "Yes."

Ryudo pushed Toku's hands away. "Then let us be lovers." He unknotted Toku's midnight blue sash. It slipped to the floor. Ryudo stepped close, only a breath way and slid his hands into Toku's robes. His fingers skimmed Toku's shoulders, and he pushed the vibrant blue kimono from Toku's broad shoulders, baring the tattoo that covered his back, a massive dragon coiled among clouds in every color of the rainbow. The silk pooled at their feet on the floor.

Ryudo reached down and tugged the ties on Toku's full and pleated black *hakima* pants. The pants dropped, revealing Toku's round butt, strong thighs, and his firm erection.

Keiko's breath caught. It was incredibly arousing to see both her men together like this. Her thighs trembled and her core clenched hungrily. Cream slithered downward.

Ryudo stepped back and waited.

Toku swallowed, then licked his lips, staring at Ryudo. He took a single step toward Ryudo, lifted his hands and tugged at Ryudo's sash.

Ryudo smiled.

Toku's hands visibly trembled as he repeated Ryudo's actions, his finger skimming Ryudo's skin to push the silk from his shoulders, showing the brilliant flowers and clouds tattooed from his shoulders, all the way down his muscular arms to his wrists.

Ryudo captured Toku's hands and pressed them down his chest, over his erect nipples and down his belly. "I desire Keiko, but I desire you as well, Kentoku. I desire and love you both." He stopped Toku's hands at the ties to his white *hakima.*

Toku sucked in a deep breath and shuddered.

Breathless with the pounding of her heart and the clenching in her belly, Keiko leaned back against the monstrous bed. They were so beautiful, the both of them together.

Staring into Ryudo's eyes, as though trapped by his gaze, Toku reached down and untied Ryudo's hakima. The white silk dropped to the floor, revealing Ryudo's equally rounded butt, muscular thighs and upwardly curved erection.

Ryudo leaned close and tilted his head. Toku lifted his chin just a little and his lips parted. Ryudo covered his lips, kissing him. Toku jerked, clearly startled. Ryudo's arms closed around Toku, holding him still for his kiss. Toku's eyes fluttered closed and his arms closed around Ryudo. He moaned, his fingers digging in.

Ryudo released Toku's mouth and smiled.

Toku blinked as though coming out of a dream. His cheeks

flushed a deep pink and he dropped his gaze.

"Still a trace of innocence left?" Ryudo dropped a quick kiss on his brow. "How sweet." He looked over at Keiko. "Feeling neglected?"

Keiko took a breath. "Who, me? Oh, hell no, that was...wow." She licked her lips. "That was incredible."

Toku ducked his head, smiled and flushed a deeper pink.

Ryudo suddenly dropped, wrapped his arms around Toku's hips and stood, hefting Toku over his shoulder.

Toku gasped. "Ryudo!"

"Yes, Toku?" Ryudo grinned at Keiko. "Shall we all go to bed?"

Keiko grinned and turned to climb up onto the huge expanse of gold silk and cream damask pillows.

Ryudo took two steps and tossed Toku onto the bed.

Toku spilled onto his back, scattering pillows. He yelped in surprise.

Ryudo chuckled and leaped onto the bed, agile as a cat. He walked across the silk expanse wearing a truly feral smile.

Keiko crawled over to Toku's side and pressed a kiss to his open mouth. He moaned and his tongue parried hers enthusiastically. His arms came up and around her, pulling her down onto him.

Ryudo dropped down on his belly at Toku's side and reached under the pillows. He pulled out a familiar small white squeeze tube with a garish purple label.

Keiko shivered.

Toku released her mouth and frowned at her. "What?"

Ryudo leaned up on his side. "She saw me pull out this." He held up the lube and grinned. He dropped his arm over Toku's waist and propped his chin up on his hand, kicking his feet up behind him. "Toku, would you like to take the garden entrance this time?"

Toku lifted his brow at Keiko.

Keiko swallowed and inched back. She wasn't sure she really wanted Toku up her butt. He was not a small man, by any means.

Toku smiled and snatched for the tube. "Sure."

Keiko sat up. "Hey! Maybe I don't want a dick that big stuffed in my butt!"

Ryudo lunged right over Toku's body and tackled Keiko. "Relax, Toku knows what he is doing." He shot a grin toward Toku. "I taught him the intricacies of debauchery, quite thoroughly."

Keiko's brows lifted. "Did you?"

"Oh, yes." Ryudo dropped his head and kissed the side of her neck. "He seemed to quite enjoy it too." He pressed his open mouth to her throat. His stroking tongue sent shivers and coils of heat straight down her spine, stirring an erotic buzz that brought up the small hairs on her body.

Trembling under the sensual assault, Keiko grabbed onto Ryudo's shoulders, groaned and lifted her chin. She wrapped her legs around Ryudo's hips and pressed up to rub her throbbing clit against Ryudo's firm cock.

Ryudo groaned in encouragement and bit down on the long muscle in Keiko's neck.

Erotic fire lashed down Keiko's spine. She whimpered and writhed up against Ryudo's cock. Mercy, she needed that strong length in her.

There was a suspicious squirting sound, followed by a soft squelching.

Keiko's breath caught, and she froze. Toku was clearly lubing his cock.

"Keiko, pay attention to me." Ryudo closed his arms around her and rolled onto his back, taking her with him. He leaned up, sucking her nipple into his mouth.

Delight stabbed straight from where his mouth worked to her clit. Keiko choked and looked down.

Ryudo's fox-fire-lit gaze focused on her and his long pink tongue flicked against her swollen nipple.

A tiny bolt of erotic lightning struck from her nipple to her clit. She groaned and shuddered.

Ryudo's hands closed around her upper thighs. He looked up at her. "Take me."

About damned time! Keiko was desperate to have him in her. She reached back, and found his hot hard shaft, closing her hand around its curving length.

He groaned and sighed, his eyes closing. "Yes, yes…" His hands moved to cup her butt-cheeks.

She centered him on her body and rubbed the tip against her moist, hungry flesh.

He gasped and his fingers dug into her ass. "Enough of this torture! Take me!"

She smiled. "Suffer."

His eyes opened and he bared his teeth in a cruel grin. "Suffer?" He arched partially off the bed, locked an arm around her waist and reached down to find her hand around his cock. He closed his hand over hers and quite firmly centered his cock on her wet flesh. "I think not." He closed his arm tight around her waist, pulling her down onto him and thrust, sheathing himself in her.

Her back arched and she choked, stiffening with a strangled moan.

Ryudo groaned, raised his knees, and bucked hard under her. "Yes!"

Keiko dug her fingers into his shoulders and rocked on top of him, pressing down on her clit while grinding down on his delicious cock. Fire lanced up her spine. In this position she would cum very, very fast.

Ryudo closed his arms around her stopping her. "Not so quickly."

Keiko released an anguished moan, and then felt wet, firm pressure on her anus.

"Push out."

"Huh?" Barely able to think past the haze of lust boiling in her body, Keiko turned to look over her shoulder.

Toku up on his knees between Ryudo's spread thigh, smiled thinly. "Forget me already?" His mouth tightened. "I need to lube you." The pressure on Keiko's anus increased. "Push out."

Keiko didn't argue, she couldn't get think clearly enough do more than groan and push. Her anus abruptly relaxed, and a thick, slippery finger slid into her ass. Then it moved, circling the interior edge. And circling it, and circling it…encouraging the flesh to open wider. Shivers raced up Keiko's spine making her tremble. It was definitely pleasurable, just a pleasure she wasn't used to feeling.

A second finger was added to the first, stretching her wider, and pushed deep.

Keiko sucked in a breath. It was almost uncomfortably tight. The fingers moved within her, circling. That oddly pleasurable tingling sensation returned. She squirmed, just a little.

Ryudo moved under her, and his cock hit something deep within.

Her core clenched tight and the hair on her body rose. She gasped, her toes curling, and her back arching in erotic delight.

Ryudo grinned. "She definitely enjoyed that."

"Good." Toku leaned against her back and wrapped his arm around her waist. Keiko, push out, hard."

The pressure on Keiko's anus was back. She grabbed Ryudo's shoulders and tensed. The pressure increased. Something hot, hard, slippery and uncomfortably wide was forcibly spreading her anus. It burned sharply. She gasped and jerked away from it. "Shit!"

Toku tightened his arm around her waist, holding her still. "Relax, Keiko, and push out."

Desperate to stop the sharp pain, Keiko pushed. Her anus spread, and spread. The burning receded, but his violently hard and atrociously hot cock moved into her butt and lodged there. She arched and moaned. "You're too big!"

Toku grunted against her spine. "No, you're just not used to it yet." He pushed against her back, shoving his cock deeper. "Keep pushing."

Keiko groaned and pushed. Toku's cock slid against Ryudo's cock, within her.

Toku pushed against her back, pulling at her waist, until he was completely seated against her butt with his cock buried to the root.

"There, I'm in." He groaned. "You are squeezing me like a fist."

Keiko gasped for breath. With Ryudo's cock sheathed up against Toku's cock, her ass felt profanely full. "You both feel like a pair of hot iron bars."

Ryudo groaned under them and arched his hips, moving his cock within her. "I think you both feel delightful!"

"Yeah, right..." Keiko whimpered just a little, and shifted her hips in an effort to ease the fullness. Not that it did much good.

"Keiko..." Ryudo looped his arm around her neck and pulled her down for a devouring kiss.

Keiko stroked her tongue against his and moaned.

Toku leaned forward against her back setting his hands on the mattress, and kissed her throat, delivering shivers. He pulled back.

The cock in Keiko's butt began to retreat. It actually felt pretty good. She released a breath, only to feel Ryudo rising under her. He retreated, and Toku's cock surged back in, slowly.

She groaned. The burn was back in her butt, but not anything like before. She tried shifting to ease it.

Both men groaned. Ryudo locked his arms around her shoulders, and Toku locked his arms around her waist, holding her still between them.

Ryudo surged in hard, suddenly putting pressure on that, delicious hot spot deep within her, the one that made her clit throb and her belly clench with eagerness.

Keiko groaned, and tried to push down harder on his cock.

Ryudo smiled. "Ah, there it is." He retreated.

Toku surged into her butt and sighed against her back. "Does this mean we can go faster now?"

Keiko shivered hard, her body a tangled mess of aches and fiercely growing need. "Faster?"

Toku retreated.

Ryudo surged in faster—and struck that heavenly spot within Keiko.

The thrust jolted Keiko deliciously, the strike echoing in her clit.

Her core clenched voraciously. She choked and pushed down to meet it.

Ryudo groaned. "Yes, follow my strokes." He pulled back. Toku thrust, and retreated. Ryudo thrust, just a little harder, and a little faster. Toku echoed his speed. And again, and then again...

Keiko trembled between them, held tight in their arms, the delicious jolts of pressure in her core steadily increasing the coiling delight boiling in her belly. The erotic clenching gained in intensity until her moans became choking cries and her toes curled.

Ryudo closed his eyes, and his back arched, his upward strokes coming harder and faster, the muscles in his body flexing under her, and standing out with his efforts.

Toku's hands shifted up to Keiko's breasts, squeezing them, his hips striking against her ass with sharp damp smacks.

Ryudo choked out a cry. His eyes opened wide, and ignited into orbs of golden fire, and his skin began to bleed into pale golden light. The tattoos on his arms unraveled into streamers of gold.

Toku grinned against Keiko's cheek. "Ooo... Looks like he lost it."

Ryudo sighed, then grinned up at them. "Did I?" Golden tendrils snapped out and wrapped around them both. He licked his lips. "Why don't you join me, Toku?"

Power crackled in the air around them, laced with green flares.

Toku gasped and arched. "Shit! He's bringing up my power!"

Keiko felt the shiver of her own inner lightning trying to come up from under her skin. She gasped.

Ryudo sighed and licked his lips. "You are in my heart of hearts, the helix center, my source of power. Let's have a little fun, shall we?"

Keiko shivered hard under sensory overload. "If I have any more fun, I think I'll die!"

Ryudo groaned. "You will not die from pleasure." More golden ropes unraveled from Ryudo and wrapped around them, binding them together.

The bed under them began to retreat. Keiko gasped. The bed

wasn't retreating, they were floating upward.

Toku groaned against her back and bright green tendrils joined the gold, wrapping all three of them securely. Slowly they turned in mid-air.

Ryudo sighed, then thrust.

Keiko moaned with his powerful entry.

Toku gasped, his hands clenching on Keiko's breasts. "Oh, sneaky bastard!" He Threw up his head. "So, you want to play that game? Then we'll play." He waited on Ryudo's retreat then thrust slowly, but just as powerfully, groaning long and hard.

Ryudo gasped, his eyes closed and he arched back groaning.

Toku shuddered against Keiko's back. "There, how do you like a cock jammed up your ass?"

Keiko jolted. Was Toku actually *in* Ryudo? She couldn't see how, he was definitely still in her butt.

Ryudo writhed under them then smiled. "I am not the innocent in this game, Toku. By all means, let us continue with this…power-play."

Keiko frowned. Power-play? Her eyes widened. Toku must be using his ropes of power the same way that Ryudo used his, as an extra cock. A slight smile lifted her lips. Ryudo was having his own game turned on him.

Toku groaned and retreated. "Mercy, the both of you are tight!"

Ryudo thrust hard and fast, grunting.

His cock struck that spot within her again, making her belly clench with violent hunger. Keiko choked out a cry.

Toku cried out with her. "Oh, fuck!" He thrust just as hard and fast against Ryudo's retreat.

Keiko moaned with the fierce ache that had somehow become an odd form of extreme pleasure.

Ryudo gasped and grinned. "Oh, yes, just right!" He thrust swiftly and hard, retreated for Toku choked reply in kind. Then again, and again, swifter and harder…

Their ecstatic gasps and cries sounded in Keiko's ears, and she wailed between them, held still as they took her, and each other. Twisting and writhing while floating over the bed in a knot of flesh, lust, and entwined power.

Erotic heat within her surged to a violent, hungry boil. She was going to cum…

Power charged the air around them. The scent summer flowers and autumn leaves filled the room. A crisp bright, almost sharp scent became increasingly present. Barely able to think past the ferocious sensations and voracious rise of climax rampaging through her, she though she recognized the odd scent. It almost smelled like…snow.

Climax crested, taking her breath. Her body clenched tight. She was there, right on the edge.

Ryudo gasped and shuddered under her, then slammed into her. Toku choked and slammed into her as well.

Her body released, unleashing a cascade of howling delight. Keiko cried out, releasing everything within her and pushing it out. Lightning danced along her skin and shimmered all through the green and gold tendrils that bound them.

Keiko closed her eyes, shrieking out her rapture.

Both men howled with her…

Keiko moaned awake, her body wonderfully sated and tangled among a pile of warm, lumpy pillows.

The lumpy pillows groaned under her.

"Whose elbow is that in my ear?" It sounded like Toku.

Keiko rolled to the side. Apparently she was right on top of him.

A pair of sweaty arms reached out to capture her. Hands closed on her breasts. "Oh, hello, Keiko." That was definitely Toku. He rolled on top of Keiko and kissed her directly on the ear. Loudly.

Keiko squealed and shoved him over.

Ryudo groaned and stretched at the far end of the bed. "I believe I am going to quite enjoy being married to you two."

Toku moaned. "If we live that long." He stretched, a long an interesting display of muscle in motion. "Sex with you is an extreme sport."

Ryudo grinned and got up on his hands and knees. "What a nice thing to say." He crawled over to them and flopped face down between them.

Toku wriggled to make room for him.

Ryudo threw an arm over him, and over Keiko. "Stay."

Toku groaned. "We have a bed almost the size of the room and you want us all in one big, sweaty pile?"

Ryudo lifted his head, turned to Toku and dropped his mouth on Toku's, kissing his protests into moans. Toku reached up to clutch at Ryudo's shoulders.

Keiko chuckled.

Ryudo lifted his head and frowned at Keiko.

Keiko laughed and twisted away.

Ryudo pounced and covered her mouth too, his tongue sweeping in to seduce her into releasing a few moans of her own. She could taste Toku on his tongue.

Ryudo lifted his head and smiled, then rolled over onto his back and tugged both Keiko and Toku up against his sides.

Sleep descended heavily.

~ Omake ~

The largest hall in the venerable mansion was festooned with bowls of flowers and tall Chinese vases with long knotted branches covered in peach and cherry blossoms.

Voluminous skeins of peach and pink silk swayed from the ceiling in the fresh spring breeze that came rushing through the row of open doors leading out into the property's outlying gardens. Pavilions in festive colors were scattered all around the lawn, providing food, drink and places out of the bright spring sun.

Guests in crushingly expensive traditional robes of every shade and color wandered everywhere mixing with guests in equally expensive dark Armani business suits.

At the very back of the hall, Keiko sat in state in her heavy and incredibly complicated wig, with an even more complicated white silk boat-shaped hat under her long sheer veil. She was forced to sit very straight in her very confining wedding silks of heavy scarlet with gold embroidery over layers and layers of white. "Thank Mercy they have all the doors open or I'd be roasting in this get-up."

Toku, kneeling on his oversized cushion right next to her, and rendered nearly as immobile in his midnight blue and gray multi-layered wedding finery, turned to smile at her. "You can always drop the temperature if it gets too bad."

Ryudo appeared before them. "I would advise against it. This early in the spring, Keiko still has a tendency to make very sudden snowstorms."

Keiko blew at her veil. "How was I supposed to know that the reason I make lightning around you two is because you're both the warm end of your seasons while I'm the dead of winter?" She rolled her eyes. Hot verses cold made for severe thunderstorms and lightning. "I didn't even know I *had* a season."

Toku smiled grimly. "That priest sent by your grandfather had no clue either. That winter prayer he taught you made a snowstorm that lasted the whole week."

Keiko sighed. "I just wanted it to snow for the winter festival."

Toku rolled his eyes. "It snowed, all right! I don't think it's snowed that deeply since the last *shogunate.*"

Keiko scowled. "Husband-to-be..."

Toku smiled tightly. "Wife-to-be...?"

Ryudo rolled his eyes and knelt. "How about I placate the both of you with this?" He held up a black sake bottle and a matching flat dish to drink from.

Toku grinned. "Oh, yeah, I could really use a drink to relax."

Keiko looked over at Toku. "You get to pour. I don't have hands in this outfit." She raised her hands, buried deep under yards of layered sleeves.

Toku smiled sourly. "I'm not much better off! I swear there are nine layers to this. And then there's this..." He pointed to his tall black silk pointed hat intricately tied to his head. "I swear it's determined to float away on the next sneeze. Mercy help me at dinner tonight."

Ryudo smiled. "I will pour for the both of you." He tipped the clear and lightly steaming heated rice wine into the dish. "You will be pleased to know that the Shinto priest has arrived." He knelt close to Toku and let him have the first, and hottest, sip.

Keiko smiled. "Has he? Good. I am more than ready for this wedding to be done with."

Toku slurped and smacked his lips. "Oh that was nice!" He smiled. "I feel better already."

Ryudo poured more wine into the dish. "His lover will be playing the wedding *kagura* on the flute for your ceremony."

Keiko lifted her long veil, revealing her heavily painted moon white face. "Since the flautist is in love, that ought to make the music very sweet."

Ryudo lifted the dish to her lips. "I believe that was the idea. Drink the whole dish, love."

"The whole dish? All right." Keiko slurped discretely and licked her lips carefully. She didn't want to smear her oh, so carefully applied red lipstick. A warm glow started in her belly, and her nervousness faded.

Ryudo smiled. "You missed a drop." He leaned forward and licked the corner of her mouth.

Toku looked out at the guests. "It looks like your grandfather emptied the ancestral island for your wedding."

"I now have more relatives than I know what to do with." Keiko looked down at her hidden hands. "My mother is still a little weirded out about the whole 'spiritual' thing being real."

Toku turned to her and set his hand over hers. "I'm sorry that your father couldn't leave his order to come to the wedding."

"That's perfectly okay with me." Keiko curled her lip. "I've had enough Avatars in my life, thank you very much." No one had been more shocked than Keiko to discover that her father was an Avatar monk living on one of the outer islands. Apparently he and her mom had had a whirlwind romance, and then she'd left him without warning. He hadn't even known he had a daughter, never mind that she was getting married. Her mom still wouldn't talk about it.

Ryudo shook his head. "It was not your father's fault that Tsuke ran amok with his sect of the Order."

Keiko frowned at him. "I thought you didn't like Avatars?"

Ryudo shrugged. "Most Avatars are perfectly polite and actually believe that they are servants of humanity. Only occasionally does one develop a hunger for power as Tsuke did. Avatars are more likely to go in the opposite direction, convinced that they are demon-slayers, and attacking every spirit that is not a part of their order."

Toku's brows lifted. "Demon-slayers?"

"A common trouble in my early days as a guardian." Ryudo poured more wine. "I believe one more cup of sake for each of you. I do not think the guests will appreciate you being unconscious during the ceremony." He lifted the dish to Toku's lips.

Keiko raised her voluminous sleeve and giggled. "These outfits are so heavy, I doubt if we'd even fall over."

Toku slurped enthusiastically and smacked his lips. "The sake was a good idea."

Ryudo lifted a black brow and poured more wine into the emptied dish. "I can see that." He offered the dish to Keiko.

Keiko slurped a bit more loudly.

Toku leaned toward her. "My turn to catch the drips."

Keiko raised her lips to him. "Lick carefully."

Toku's pink tongue lapped at the edges of her mouth, then he leaned back and smiled. "I always lick carefully. After last night, you should know that."

Keiko dropped her veil, suddenly very glad the white pancake make-up was too thick to see a blush through. Toku had very, very carefully driven her completely insane with his tongue.

Toku turned to Ryudo. "Are you sure you don't want to come on the honeymoon cruise with us?"

Ryudo scowled. "I prefer dry land, thank you very much." He lowered his brows. "Try not to sir up any typhoons while you are out there?"

Keiko smiled. "We'll do our best."

A gong sounded.

Ryudo rose to his feet with the sake bottle and dish. "Your ceremony is about to begin, I need to get rid of these." He smiled. "Don't go anywhere!"

Toku snorted. "As if we can move in these clothes?"

Keiko smiled at Toku. "Are you a bit on the tipsy side, dear?"

Toku nodded and smiled right back. "Yep."

Keiko burst into giggles and raised her sleeve. "Me too."

The guests wandered in and seated themselves on the cushions provided, creating a kaleidoscopic display of color in the huge room. Keiko held her head very still, and used only her eyes to look around.

The priest in flowing white robes with extraordinarily large sleeves over midnight green hakima, his little black hat tied very firmly to his head, proceded into the hall with several young acolytes in red and white, and a rather cute young man in yellow playing a bamboo flute following in their wake.

This was it. Keiko was suddenly very glad Ryudo had brought them sake.

The priest came to Toku and Keiko, chanted a blessing over them, then the wedding prayer and then another prayer... A flat dish of wine was passed to Toku. He sipped and passed it to Keiko. She sipped, and passed it back, sipped, and passed it back...

Keiko was unable to keep count of the cup's passing and her sips, but she was pretty sure it was in the vicinity of nine. The wine in the dish wasn't bad, either, but not nearly as good as Ryudo's.

Suddenly it was time for her vow, and the wedding rings. And she couldn't remember a word of what she was supposed to say.

Ryudo appeared directly behind them, kneeling in his customary white robes.

Several indrawn breaths from the audience announced most of Keiko's distant relations. The priest's eyes went very wide. Apparently he could see Ryudo too, but he didn't scream, or pass out.

Keiko was suitably impressed.

Ryudo smiled and coached them both through the vows and the exchange of matching gold bands ornately inlaid with silver chrysanthemums. He then coached Toku through his personal vow. Keiko only had to add her name to the end.

"Almost finished." Ryudo held out his hands and helped them both up off their cushions.

They turned to the altar set up behind them, clutching a blooming peach branch tied with paper zig-zags between them, Toku and Keiko walked to the altar. As they set the branch on the altar, Ryudo set his hand over theirs. All three clapped their hands and bowed.

A gong sounded.

The wedding was done.

The wedding guests proceeded to get very enthusiastic, and very drunk.

Keiko and Toku escaped to the master suite as soon as they were able. The maids and the valets stripped them down for the wedding feast, redressing them in far simpler kimonos, though in pretty much the same colors, then left amid smiles and giggles.

Keiko stared at her brand new husband. *Husband... He was her husband.* For no apparent reason, had to blink back tears.

Toku started. "Keiko?" He took her hands. "Are you all right?"

Keiko smiled up at him. "I'm okay. I'm just happy."

Toku smiled crookedly. "You're sure?"

Ryudo appeared. "Keiko?" He turned to frown at the groom. "Toku, what did you do this time?"

Toku scowled. "Me?"

Keiko reached out to take Ryudo's hand. He had been there through the entire ceremony. He was her *husband* too. "No, really, I'm just happy."

Ryudo rolled his eyes. "I should hope so." He smiled. "Would you like to see your wedding present?"

A present? Keiko blinked. "You mean the big one? The one behind the locked doors?"

Toku nodded and smiled. "It was finished two nights ago."

Keiko nodded rapidly and her head swam just a little. "Oh, too much wine."

Toku frowned. "Are you sure you're okay?"

Keiko smiled. "Just a little muzzy, that's all."

Ryudo lifted his hand. "This way." He led them through the main audience room to the big doors on the far end. The doors Keiko had not been able to open.

Ryudo pressed his palms together, then parted his hands. The doors opened, and sunlight spilled across the floor. "Behold, the heart and soul of the house, the helix."

Keiko stepped outside, into the garden she had seen on the first day she'd stepped foot in the house, only this time, the garden, the fountains, the flowers and the cherry tree in the center, was real. She stared at the blooming cherry tree. It was not nearly as large as the one she remembered, but it was still impressive in size.

Ryudo walked to the center of the garden and pressed his palm to the trunk. "Toku was able to obtain this tree from the same field that my original tree came from." He turned to smile at Keiko. "In China."

Keiko walked over to the tree, placed her palm on the solid living trunk, and looked up at the open sky. "But wasn't all this a room inside the house?"

"Yes, it was. In fact, it was a couple of rooms, but it was a garden first." Toku placed his palm on the tree. "It took quite a bit of skilled engineering, but we were able to recover the entire garden because the rooms were all add-ons. They didn't affect the house's structural integrity."

"Oh." Keiko looked over at Ryudo.

Ryudo was staring at the sky, in his garden, the one that had been destroyed so long ago, the one he missed so much he'd created an illusion to preserve it. He turned to her and smiled. "Do you like your wedding present?"

She leaned against the tree and nodded, and this time she couldn't stop the flow of tears.

Ryudo frowned. "Keiko?"

Toku pointed at Keiko. "I didn't make her cry this time! That was all you."

"Guys, please!" Keiko laughed through her tears. "I'm happy, really, really happy, seriously!"

Both Ryudo and Toku looked doubtful.

Keiko shook her head. "Crying when you're happy is a girl thing."

Both of their brows shot up. They exchanged a glance and a shrug.

Keiko looked around. "The garden is beautiful." She looked at Ryudo. "I am so glad you have it back."

Ryudo's smile disappeared and he turned away. "So am I." He set his palm on the cherry tree. "This is where my...body lies in rest."

Keiko covered her mouth with her hand, stunned.

Toku set both his palms on the tree and stared up at the sky. "Your...remains were still interred under the roots of the original tree." He took a careful breath. "We didn't disturb them when we planted the new tree."

Ryudo smiled. "I know. Thank you."

Toku blinked rapidly. "Damn it, Ryudo." He reached into his sash and pulled out a handkerchief. "Now you have me doing it, too."

Ryudo stared at him. "Me? Doing what?"

Toku dabbed at his eyes. "Nothing."

Keiko wandered over to Toku and leaned against him, looking up at the cherry blooms.

Abruptly a wind came over the wall and rocked the branches of the tree. In a whirl of pink and white, every bloom loosed from the tree, all at once, filling the air with a storm of pink petals.

Keiko laughed and tugged Toku over to where Ryudo stood. Clutching both of her husbands around the waist, she closed her eyes to feel the passing of the petals against her cheeks, erasing the tracks of her tears.

Also by Morgan Hawke

Excerpt from TORRID - A Shounen-Ai/Yaoi Romance

Panting and sweating, Trey leaned against the metal wall of the huge stall and peeled his boots off, scattering crushed and wadded bills everywhere. He smiled. Apparently he was a hit. He didn't bother to count it, just pulled his folded clothes out of his bag and stuffed all the money in as-is. He'd un-wad all of it and count it once he got home.

Barefoot and wearing only his g-string, he padded over to the sinks to try and get some of the sweat and goop off before he climbed back into his clothes.

Unfortunately, the lube proved difficult to get off. A lot of wet paper towels and handfuls of the bathroom's poor excuse for soap later, he finally realized that it was going to take a shower to get the vanilla scent off his skin.

He groaned. He was going to smell like a freaking pudding cake all the way home. He scowled at the wasted paper towels. "Shit."

"Damn, something smells good enough to eat in here." The voice was masculine and very familiar.

At the sink, soapy paper towels in hand, Trey froze. He closed his eyes. *No way... He did* not *follow me in here.* He opened his eyes and turned.-

The guy smiled from the doorway. "You were right; you *are* a damned good dancer."

Oh, shit... Trey smiled weakly. "Um, thanks."

The guy sniffed and frowned. "What in God's name...? Is that vanilla smell, you?"

Trey felt his cheeks heat and looked down at the sink. "I'm sensitive to oils, so I used..." No way, he was going to say lube. "I used something else, and it's vanilla flavored." *What am I saying?* He looked up at the guy in shock. "Scented! Vanilla scented!"

"Is that so?" The guy grinned and approached, his gait slow and easy, a stalking predator. "I don't know. You smell pretty tasty to me."

Watching him closing in, Trey's heart thumped in his mouth. *I think I am in serious trouble here.* He swallowed.

"I think I should check and see." The guy's brows lifted. "Take a taste-test."

A taste test...? Trey sucked in a breath, dropped the paper towels in his hand and backed away. "Uh, let's not, okay?"

The guy's smile sharpened, showing very white and very even teeth. "After that display up on the stage, right in front of God and everybody, now you're shy?"

Trey backed into the wall. "How about—not gay?"

The guy snorted. "Good, me neither." He lunged.

About the Author

"For me, writing is more than a passion, it's an *obsession.*"

Morgan Hawke has been writing erotic fiction since 1998. She has lived in seven states of the US and spent two years in England. She has been an auto mechanic, a security guard, a waitress, a groom in a horse-stable, in the military, a copywriter, a magazine editor, a professional tarot reader, a belly-dancer and a stripper. Her personal area of expertise is the strange and unusual.

Ms. Hawke maintains a close and personal relationship with her computer and her cat.

MORGAN HAWKE
MODERN GOTHIC
EROTIC ROMANCE
DarkErotica.Net

Made in the USA